RISE
to
REBELLION

Best Wishes,

Julie Bates

RISE
to
REBELLION

A Faith Clarke Mystery

Julie Bates

For Bill & Chris

Praise for Rise to Rebellion

"Author Julie Bates's wonderful new novel, *Rise to Rebellion*, brings to life the earliest days of the American Revolution with taut suspense and vibrant characters–including Benjamin Franklin and John Hancock–who leap off the page. A mystery of the American Revolution, to be sure, but also a story about families, courage, treachery, and love in 18th-century Philadelphia. Meticulous research and descriptions conjure a world on the cusp of change and make this a not-to-be-missed story for any fan of early American history or historical fiction."—Mally Becker, Agatha Award-nominated author of *The Turncoat's Widow* and *The Counterfeit Wife*

"Stunning! A well-crafted blend of history, mystery, and suspense that grips the reader on page one and doesn't let go!"—J. C. Eaton, author of The Sophie Kimball Mysteries, The Wine Trail Mysteries, The Charcuterie Shop Mysteries, and The Marcie Rayner Mysteries

Chapter One

June 1776

T he coach jerked sharply as it encountered another pothole. Jeremy Butler grabbed the squabs to keep from falling forward and into another passenger. Like most of the other passengers, he was bruised and weary from riding hours along the bumpy road that comprised the King's highway, which ran from Charleston in the South Carolina Colony all the way north to Boston in the Massachusetts Colony. Butler thanked God that he didn't have to travel the entirety of it. Outside, the steady hiss of rain and slap of mud on the undercarriage added to the cloistered sense of depression within. With the windows covered to prevent rain from coming in, the scents of unwashed bodies and wet fabric permeated the air. Having ridden coaches in the past, Butler had known what to expect. He was fairly certain Faith Clarke had not. He glanced over where she sat on the bench seat opposite from him, her face partially obscured by the dark bonnet she wore.

Faith's face was pale and drawn with exhaustion. Days of bumping along from station to station to change coaches had taken a toll. She had said very little to him or anyone else during the days they had traveled. She had stayed wrapped in her own thoughts. Although escorting her to Philadelphia was secondary to the mission that called him north, he still intended to make sure she was properly cared for. He had been fortunate that her journey provided a cover for his journey as well.

1

The other passengers were a mixture of ages and stations. Butler had assessed people on each leg of the journey. Seven people currently shared the coach with him and Faith. Out of that number, two men had been with them since they had boarded the coach in Williamsburg. A woman with two young children had joined them in Delaware. The little girl held tightly to a rag doll as she stared into space, no doubt daydreaming of a better place. The boy was young, likely not more than four, barely old enough to be in breeches. Riding in the confined coach had been hard on the youngster, who had spent much of his time whining and getting into trouble. Butler had had to remove curious fingers from his pack where he kept his knives, among other things. The stops provided a needed break for him to run about and for the tired passengers to have a break. Currently, the young rapscallion slept with his head in his mother's lap. His mother, who looked young to have two children, was nodding in exhaustion as well. He hoped they would reach their destination soon.

Like him, the two men who remained from Virginia did not sleep. One sipped from a flask regularly. Butler suspected he had refilled it at every tavern stop on their way north. Even though the man sat on the opposite end of the coach, the reek of alcohol and stale sweat could not be avoided. He didn't blame the middle-aged woman sitting next to him for holding a perfumed handkerchief to her nose. Every now and then, a brief hint of lavender drifted over before more earthy scents intruded. The other man worried Butler. He was medium height, with sandy brown hair and nondescript features. Dressed in homespun tans and browns, the only thing that caught the eye was a neckerchief printed in a gay red and yellow pattern. He had barely spoken on the trip, but his dark eyes missed nothing. He was too alert, as if he were waiting for something to occur. He reminded Butler a little too much of himself, although he couldn't be sure if the man was an informant for the British, patriots, or no one at all. He acknowledged that he had no reason to suspect the man, only a feeling. A casual inquiry to the coachman had given him the man's name, but Lovell was a name that meant nothing to him.

Butler pushed his hat partially over his face, feigning sleep as he assessed his options for the coming days. If he had guessed correctly, they were within a day's ride of Philadelphia, where delegates from all the colonies were meeting to discuss their next move in the ongoing rebellion against Great Britain. He could not begin to guess why George Washington, the appointed commander of the army, had written and requested he come meet with him. Butler had carefully burned the note into ash before preparing to leave. The consequences of being discovered by the British were deadly.

Faith Clarke's mission was far more personal and, if Butler were to guess, far more painful. Somewhere, crumpled in her reticule, was a letter from her family, one that, according to Olivia, had reduced her to tears.

Faith's cook and her husband Titus remained primary sources of information on the happenings in Williamsburg. They had worked for him and the Sons of Liberty almost as long as they had worked for Faith at Clarke Tavern. Although Faith was new to the spy network, he found her insight useful, even if she was not the most enthusiastic rebel. Quakers, he sighed mentally. While he respected their beliefs, he had a hard time comprehending the concept of stubborn pacifism in the face of British aggression. He had been young when his family had shipped over from Ireland after his father died protesting the enclosure of land they needed to survive, but the memories of being driven away by British soldiers still peppered his dreams from time to time. In his role as spy for the patriot cause, he couldn't afford to trust anyone easily. Butler relied on those who had proven themselves loyal time and again. In his absence, they and his associate Athena would run the spy network around the colonial capital.

The coach jolted sharply to the right before accelerating sharply, followed by the pound of hoof beats in pursuit. Butler was already pulling at the window coverings when the roar of a gun filled the air, followed by shouts to stop. The coach driver's curses could be heard as the wagon rolled to a stop.

Silence fell over the travelers inside. Butler looked over at Faith. Even in the dim light of the covered windows, he could see her frightened face. She was not alone. Everyone waited to see who had stopped them a few miles short of Philadelphia. A small child whimpered only to be hushed by his mother. Everyone knew travel could be dangerous, whether the threat was from soldiers or militia, disgruntled natives, or brigands looking for valuables. They didn't have to wait long to find out who had accosted them.

The door swung out, letting in the grey misty rain that masked identifying landmarks. Butler had no trouble identifying the uniform of the man who stared at the people grouped in the carriage. "Everybody out, on the orders of the King."

Butler hopped out and turned to help the ladies before being shoved by the soldier. "Get aside."

"The ladies," he protested.

A red-coated officer spoke from behind them. "Let him assist them, Dutton. There is no need to be discourteous to the provincials."

Butler looked at the officer, who met his gaze coolly before gesturing to the open door of the coach. Taking the hint, Butler stepped to the side and helped place a wooden step in place before offering a hand to Faith Clarke and then the woman with two small children, who promptly hid behind their mother's skirts upon reaching the ground. Even they realized danger was afoot. After that, an older woman followed. She eyed the soldiers warily as she moved out of the way. Butler aided an elderly man down and left the last two to manage on their own. He stepped back out of the way as first the dark-eyed man leapt out, followed by the other, still clutching his flask, who soon made it clear he had drunk away his common sense.

"We're Americans, lobster back," As he left the coach, the soldier smacked him in the back of the head with the butt of his musket, causing him to collapse in the dirt. He staggered up, glaring like an angry bull. Before he had gotten halfway to his feet, another soldier smashed his face with a well-placed fist.

The man screamed as he collapsed, blood pouring down his face. "You broke my nose,"

Snickers broke out from the soldiers. "We can break more than that." A boot lashed out, kicking him flat on the muddy ground.

The older man stepped forward on his cane, raising a hand. "Surely such violence is unnecessary," he said. "The British Army stands for justice and

4

is charged with protecting all loyal subjects from India to Africa to these American Colonies. Anyone can see this man is an ignorant drunkard and not worthy of your attention."

The cornet bowed. "Well spoken, sir. You seem to know something of His Majesty's troops."

"I served thirty years in the navy," the man replied. "I live with my daughter and her family in Baltimore. Now I'm on my way to visit my son in Philadelphia." He looked over at the man stumbling to rise.

"Ned, you need to keep your mouth shut so you can make it home. All that liquor has done is get you into trouble."

The other man rose, still moaning as he cradled his bleeding nose. Faith had dug a handkerchief out of her pocket and handed it to him as he joined the other travelers.

They all watched the group of soldiers pointing guns with bayonets attached to the end of their muskets.

The troops swarmed over the coach, pulling out luggage and checking underneath the vehicle. Butler watched as they searched the vehicle before turning to the passengers. The red-coated officer faced them. Underneath the trappings of a cornet, the officer looked young, his fair skin faintly pink from exposure to the sun. Underneath his hat, his hair gleamed red. His glance was cold as he looked the travelers over before he spoke.

"We have received information that someone here has been smuggling goods and information to the enemy. Working against the lawful government of his majesty is treason and subject to punishment by hanging." He looked around at the group of travelers, assessing them. "We will search your persons and your baggage. Anyone possessing items of a questionable nature will be taken into custody."

Faith stiffened. Butler took her hand. "It will be alright," he whispered. "We've nothing to hide."

The driver protested. "All these folks paid their fares to get to Philadelphia. They are farmers, businessmen, and regular folk trying to get to their families. There's no call for this."

Troops pushed them back as a couple of soldiers climbed on top and began pitching bags and parcels to the ground. Butler edged over to the old man who had spoken. "You seem to know what to say to them."

The man shrugged. "I know trouble when I see it. That Cornet, Tarleton has a reputation for brutality. It would be wise to avoid attracting his attention."

Butler eyed the red-haired officer, Noting the expensive uniform, trim figure, and the saber that rested in what appeared to be a well-kept scabbard. He couldn't have been more than twenty-five. To be an officer meant family connections or money. But it didn't tell him how dangerous he was in battle.

The little boy began crying as he clung to his mother's skirts. She shushed him as she picked him up, patting his back. The little girl hid behind her mother, barely visible around her skirt.

The soldiers tossed items onto the wet ground, letting mud seep into both carpet bags and clothing alike. Faith bit her lip as one of her hats fell victim to a soldier's gleeful bayonet. As the men tore through all their luggage and supplies, three of the men approached the travelers. "We need to search all of you."

Butler allowed himself to be taken aside. He said nothing when they found a knife in his boot or as they roughly groped down his body, feeling for anything he might have hidden. They took his money, his knives, and his spare shirt. He had expected as much. These troops were tired and angry. They wanted to be done and back in their base, drinking their allotment of rum.

On the ground, the man with the broken nose moaned as a soldier rolled him over to check his pockets. The man yelped as he was kicked in the ribs. The soldier laughed as he found a few coins in his jacket.

"That's almost worth shaking down your nasty hide." The soldier said as he pocketed the money.

Butler winced in sympathy. Although he didn't care much for the drunk, he didn't like anyone being abused. He had noted that Tarleton had not intervened in the soldier's brutality on the drunken man. The cornet had not reacted, although he had obviously seen what was happening. He cemented Butler's opinion of him when he ordered the ladies to search each other and lay what they found on the ground. The women complied while the soldiers jeered and made suggestions on places to look. Faith's cheeks flushed, but she wisely kept her mouth shut. The mother wiped away a tear as she patted down her own daughter, to the delight of the troops.

Butler hoped they would move on soon, but a feeling of dread gripped him. If they were so determined to find contraband, they would find something, and God help whoever it was they blamed. It was why he destroyed anything that could connect him to the patriot cause.

He breathed in and out slowly, letting his heart slow and consciously relaxing his muscles. All they would find in his pack were tools associated with surveying, which he still did from time to time when he wasn't actively spying.

The breeze picked up, bringing in more rain, soaking them as they stood, waiting for the soldiers to finish. Faith flinched as her bag was torn open, her best dress thrown onto the ground. He knew she didn't have a great deal of money for nice things. He watched the red-haired officer stand stone-faced as the men under his command savaged every possession that had been loaded onto the coach. Butler had seen the brutality of British troops in Ireland; he knew better than to vent his rage against bayonets and guns.

The older woman cried out as a soldier pulled out a necklace. "That was a gift from my late husband," she cried. "You have no right to it."

The cornet raised an eyebrow before walking over to the man and taking it. He dangled it in his gloved hand, watching the pearls catch the light. "A very nice piece," he commented. "What did your husband do to be able to afford such a pretty bauble?"

"He grew indigo and tobacco," she sniffled. "For twenty years, he worked the crops on our farm before a fever took him. Our oldest son took over."

The officer nodded thoughtfully. "A great loss to you, I'm sure. These are treacherous times for those loyal to the king, where everyone has to make sacrifices. I'm sure as a loyal tory you understand these things."

The woman nodded hesitantly. "We've always been loyal to the king."

"Then you will have no objections to donating this to the war effort." He smiled as comprehension dawned on her features. He turned away as tears trickled down her face, tucking the necklace into an interior pocket.

Butler watched as Faith went over to comfort the woman as the soldiers continued to pillage everyone's belongings. He was caught off guard when a soldier came over to them and motioned for them to move out from the scanty shelter of the group of trees.

"You will all be searched again one by one before you are released to continue your journey," the officer announced. "We will start with the men and then on to the ladies."

A hard shove propelled him forward. "Let's start with you, Cotton Top." Butler stumbled forward, barely catching his balance as he was led out into a field. The rain-soaked ground squelched underneath his boots. He doubted he could get much wetter. A musket was leveled at him as another soldier felt up and down his body, squeezing him roughly in tender places. Butler bit back a sharp remark. These men had already shown it took little for them to become vicious, and he would prefer to avoid a beating. They found nothing of interest on his person, so within a few minutes, he was led around to join the rest of the party. Faith eyed him anxiously as he came into view. He caught her gaze and gave a brief nod to let her know he was unharmed. As he took his place next to her, he noticed the dark-eyed man, Lovell, step out from the trees to rejoin the group. Like Butler, he had likely taken a moment to hide something in the trees. His interest sharpened when he saw him slip something to the officer. It was so quick he would have missed it had he not been watching the red-coated cornet. It confirmed his suspicions that the man was likely a spy and made him all the more wary.

The soldiers were eager to move on. They checked the pockets and jackets of all the men and then the two children before turning to the ladies. While they busied themselves with the others, Butler went to the trees to relieve himself, aware of the soldiers watching him. When the man watching him turned away as he unbuttoned his breeches, Butler reached into the crotch of the tree and retrieved his knife before completing his business and returning to the others.

The old woman went first, her head raised in defiance. Her earlier tears had dried. She glanced at the cornet with fire in her eyes. "May God have mercy on your soul," she said as she passed.

He looked amused. "Make sure you search her very carefully," he said. "I would hate to miss anything of importance."

Butler heard her grunt once or twice before she was returned. Her face was flushed, but her back was straight. She spat at Tarleton's boots as she walked by. His face tightened, but he said nothing.

Faith and the young mother were taken together. Faith said nothing, although her anxious gaze revealed her fear. She bit her lip as she passed, keeping her eyes on the ground. There was nothing Butler could do to comfort her.

He waited for her to return, hoping the search didn't turn ugly. As the minutes passed, the rain stopped. A faint gleam of sun parted the clouds. As it hit the canopy of trees, it hit the water drops covering each leaf, causing them to sparkle like diamonds. Then he heard a shriek and the sound of struggling. Butler darted forward toward where the women had gone. He shoved past two of the foot soldiers before he was tackled to the ground.

The shouts of soldiers filled his ears as he struggled to free himself and go to Faith's aid. Light exploded in his head for a split second before blinding pain propelled him into unconsciousness. He was unaware of being picked up under the arms, dragged to the coach, and tossed in like so much baggage.

Chapter Two

P hiladelphia rose tall and stately in the afternoon sun. The coach's wheels splashed noisily as they rolled in puddles left by the rain. Faith looked out the window at the vista, unable to appreciate the gracious parade of fine brick buildings that lined the well-ordered streets. Beside her, Jeremy Butler lay slumped against the corner, held up by the side of the coach. She and the older woman, Mildred Rose, had wrapped his bloody head in her spare petticoat, readily available from her damaged duffle. Two of the men had lifted him off the floor and settled him semi-upright in a corner for the remainder of the trip before tossing the remnants of their belongings back on the coach. No one had spoken as they huddled in the coach, watching the British ride away, leaving them to deal with the damage.

Somehow, she would have to find her older sister, Hannah, in this huge city and beg her for help. Her father's letter had told her she still lived on Walnut Street in the modest house her husband had brought her to after their marriage. That had been after he had told her that her mother lay dying from a sudden attack of apoplexy and was begging to see her. Thinking about her mother and going back left her with an unsettled feeling in her stomach.

Patience Payne had never been an easy person to live with, and Faith had been eager to leave home. Virginia had seemed far enough away that her mother could only reach her with the infrequent letter. Being shunned for marrying outside the Quaker church had been a shock. Although she had expected the church not to be happy, she had not expected reprisals from her family. Faith knew her mother had dictated letters to one of her siblings remaining at home since Patience was only marginally literate. Still, the tone of disappointment that permeated each one rankled.

Her father's note had been brief, but each word reminded her of his soft, even tone as his hands worked on the various jobs that needed doing on their farm. When she had first opened it, Faith could have sworn she recognized the scent of tobacco from his old pipe. His request for her to come home had more impact than a dozen of her mother's notes filled with suggestions on how she could improve herself.

Tears burned her eyes as she thought of seeing him after so much time. Last night, she had dreamed she heard the sound of his flute as she had often heard it as a child, playing long into the night when he couldn't sleep.

Beside her, Jeremy Butler groaned as consciousness returned. His eyes fluttered, then closed against the afternoon sun.

"Rest," Faith said as she leaned close, keeping her voice soft. "We'll be at my sister's shortly." She hoped she was correct. Hannah had wed an affluent man much older than her and moved to Philadelphia three years before Faith had left home. That had been twelve years ago. Hannah's letters had been regular when she had first wed, sharing about her home and life in the city. After her husband's death from a fever, Hannah's writing dwindled down to almost nothing. Faith had been surprised when she sent a note when Faith's husband Jon had passed. She didn't know if Hannah had received her message that she was coming. Given the challenges of travel in the colonies even before the conflict with Britain, there was no knowing if she had received it.

The rising noise outside told Faith they were progressing further into town. She could hear the increased traffic outside the coach. Wagons and horses clattered past them as the dirt road turned into cobbles that indicated the onset of civilization. Inside the vehicle, the children grew restless getting up to peer out, little troubled by the jolting of the coach as it hit a pothole.

Heat from the sun had dried the ground but left steaminess in the air that felt close and stuffy in the coach. She had grown accustomed to the smells of sweat within the coach; now, as they entered town, her nose took in the

11

scent of manure and hair. Her gaze took in a herd of cows that complained from their pen as the coach rumbled past. The buildings grew larger and closer together in heights that reached up toward the heavens. Faith eyed them in wonder. She had always considered Williamsburg large, but the city that lay before her was a huge metropolis of tall brick buildings and wide streets filled with people, animals, and conveyances. She had never seen so many people in one area. It was unnerving to observe the crowds moving about like a colony of disturbed ants. And the noise! The cacophony of voices melded together into a dull roar where no one voice was discernible.

The coach rolled to a stop, creaking as it settled from being in constant motion. She could hear the shouts of the driver as he clambered down and demanded help for his horses. The door swung open with enough force to bang on the side. Butler flinched at the sound and covered his eyes from the sudden glare.

"Everyone out," the coachman barked. "Collect your belongings and be on your way. The station house is in front of you if you plan to continue your journey."

Faith stepped down onto the cobbles with a little assistance from the man she had heard called Lovell. She thanked him before stepping out of the way of the passengers behind her. His dark eyes had swept over her briefly before offering a quick nod and heading off into town. The children hopped out next and ran to the porch of the station, nearly knocking her over in their eagerness to disembark. Behind her, their mother shrieked at them to slow down, to no avail. Freedom had been scented, and they had taken flight.

Faith reached for her duffle and Butler's knapsack. He stepped down from the coach slowly. Although she was relieved he was conscious and mobile, she still thought he looked pale. A nasty bruise was forming on his left cheek.

He walked over to where she had gathered their things. "I can carry my own bag." He reached for the bag, which was remarkably still whole despite being thrown in the mud and cut with a saber.

Faith let him take it. Far be it for her to wound a man's pride, even if she thought the sensible thing to do was accept help. She was done with the foolish pride of men. Her thoughts turned to Will McKay. In the months since he had decided to end their attachment, she had seen him rarely, despite the fact that they were both engaged in the dicey business of gathering information for the patriot cause. He had practically become a ghost, leaving messages with Olivia as she cooked meals for Clarke tavern in the separate kitchen out back and avoiding the main house altogether. She wondered if he still suffered from the effects of the poison that had nearly killed him last summer. Not that it mattered to her. He had made his choice, and she had made hers. Faith didn't need a relationship with any man. She was content with her business and her son, even if a dull ache in her heart protested otherwise.

"Faith," She jumped before turning around to see her sister Hannah standing a few feet away. Her hackles rose at the critical frown on her face. "Hast thou become deaf in the past eleven years? I've been calling thy name." Her sister came closer and took in her torn sleeve and disheveled appearance. Worry crept into her clear blue eyes. "Perhaps it would be best if we talked after thou hast had time to wash up and rest. Come with me. My footman Abner will get your things." Faith eyed the small, wiry footman warily. He looked as if a stiff wind would blow him over.

Faith flushed. Being searched by redcoats had done little for her appearance or emotions. Hannah's greeting had done little to ease her nerves. Was it her imagination, or was Hannah being less than friendly? Five years separated them, five years and three siblings. Never close, Faith suddenly felt a sense of dread of being her guest. Beside her, Jeremy stumbled, barely catching himself.

"You need help," Faith said as she took in his increased pallor.

"I need you two to quit yelling at each other," she growled. He let the footman take his knapsack.

Hannah turned to see who Faith was talking to. Her eyes went up and down Jeremy's form, taking in the dried blood and mark from a fight. "Who is this?" she asked. As she stepped forward, Faith realized the two nearly stood eye to eye. The high roll of Hannah's coffee-colored hair, along with her straw hat, gave her an inch or two, but their eyes were level as each assessed the other.

"This is Master Jeremy Butler, a family friend who escorted me from Williamsburg," Faith answered.

Hannah possessed the clear blue eyes of their mother. Her glance was glacial as she took in Butler. "I thought our brother would return with you."

Faith shook her head. "Seth isn't ready to return to Pennsylvania. He sent a letter, but given how he left, it would cause more trouble if he returned."

Hannah sniffed. "I heard about that." She glanced about the busy street. "Let us get thee and thy friend out of the streets. My phaeton should hold all of us." She strode towards an elegant black vehicle with yellow wheels.

Faith blinked at the brightness, then looked at her sister. Hannah still dressed in the simple style of a Quaker woman, but something was different, whether it was the jaunty straw chip hat or the way she held herself, Hannah seemed less anxious than she remembered. Although as Faith reminded herself, leaving their mother's house could be an easy explanation for that.

The footman stowed their bags behind the driver's seat. After helping Hannah up, he offered a hand to Faith, placing her next to her sister. Butler and he rode in the seat behind them.

Hannah took the reins with practiced ease. It was then Faith noticed the dark leather gloves she wore.

"You don't use a driver?"

Hannah shook her head. "After Amos died, I needed fewer staff. This was his phaeton, which he used to go wherever he pleased. Now it is mine. She clucked at the two bays pulling the conveyance, and off they went into the busy streets of Philadelphia.

Faith grabbed the armrest of the seat to steady herself as the carriage bounced over the cobblestones at an alarming rate of speed. As the horses raced down the road, people in the street leapt to get out of the way. "Is it necessary to go this fast?"

Hannah's eyes remained focused on the busy road, reacting quickly to avoid a slower-moving cart. "I assumed thou would be eager to settle in after all those days in a crowded coach."

"I would prefer to arrive in one piece," Faith retorted.

"Is thou impugning my driving?"

Faith shook her head. Hannah had not changed much. She had always been the strong-willed one. When they were children, it was Hannah who made sure everything ran well when their mother had one of her nervous fits and ran around alternately praying and punishing for offenses real and imagined. Hannah managed their mother in a way Faith could never figure out.

When she had married and moved to Philadelphia, the younger Paynes had coped with their mother with limited success. Faith suspected that Hannah had relished being free from the burden of Patience Payne's moods, being separated by a day's carriage ride.

Faith gritted her teeth and held on for dear life until the phaeton jolted to a stop in front of a two-story brick row house. As she looked down the street, she could see the entire alley was lined with similar homes. Hannah allowed the footman to hand them down. After he stacked their bags on the narrow stoop, he led the horses and carriage away down an adjacent alley.

Seeing Faith's glance, Hannah said, "There's a stable outback that keeps my team and carriage for when I need it. "Let's get thee and thy friend inside." She opened a side door that led immediately up a flight of stairs. "My residence is on the upper floor; my business is on the first. Fortunately, my sister-in-law Lucretia and her son Nathan are managing the store today."

Faith followed her up the stairs, followed more slowly by Jeremy Butler. Once they had reached the second floor, Faith stopped to catch her breath and look around. "How long have you been here?"

"Since a few months after Amos died," Hannah replied grimly. "His children from his first marriage wanted to turn me out, but I had his will, which clearly stated his settlement on his widow and his children. I was willing to surrender the house in exchange for this one, along with my widow's portion." She shrugged. "It worked out well enough. I have the house, and my business keeps food in the larder, and my staff paid." In a softer voice, she added. "And no man orders me about."

Butler had been silent as he had followed them up the stairs. "Where will we be staying?" He was swaying slightly.

Hannah looked at him. "You will be sharing a room with Nathan since you are the only gentlemen in the house. Faith can have the guest room. It's tiny but clean. Right now, we're going where I can check your injuries." A plump grey-striped cat followed them, swiftly ducking in before the door shut. "Jonah," Hannah murmured. "I wondered where thou had been. I'm sure Suzanna has something in the kitchen for you." The cat trotted down the steps with practiced ease. His white feet flashed in the shadows of the twisting stairwell as he went down below.

Faith was surprised Butler didn't protest, but let Hannah lead him to her parlor, where a light-skinned African American woman was dusting the furniture.

"Mary," Hannah said. "I need a basin of water, bandages, and my mullein leaf ointment." She eyed Butler critically. "I think one of my late husband's shirts might fit him; we stored them in the old wooden trunk with the woolens. See if you can find one."

Butler grumbled as she led him into the sitting room and gestured for him to sit. "I can tend my own wounds."

Hannah stared at him. "Really, and where dost thou keep thine herbs and bandages? Or I could always call a physician if thou would prefer one to my skills."

Butler shuddered. "No, thank you." He sighed. "I apologize for my rudeness. It's been a long journey. If you could tend my head, I would appreciate it, as well as the loan of a clean shirt. I have an important meeting to attend as soon as possible."

Abner came up the stairs at that moment, his boots clattering noisily as he carried Faith's duffle under his arm and Butler's knapsack over his shoulder.

Hannah called out to him. "Drop those and assist me with our guest." Abner dropped his load just inside the doorway and stood inside, looking uncomfortable.

"I've no skill with the sick, Mistress," Abner said, shuffling his feet.

Hannah didn't look up. She was busy organizing the tray of items Mary had just brought in, a basin with a pitcher of steaming water, cloth bandages, and a greenish mixture. Hannah's face was flushed; whether from the hot water or the warmth of the June day was hard to determine.

"I just need you to help him remove his shirt and help me bandage him once we treat his injuries," she said.

Butler grunted as the shirt stuck to a wound, and Abner yanked it clear. He sat still as Faith's sister examined his wounds. Faith had retreated to the hall once he had begun to undress.

Hannah didn't seem terribly concerned. Raising a damp cloth, she washed the dried blood off his temple, cleaning the matted hair. "This looks nasty, but it's shallow. Keep it clean, and it should heal fine. How is thy vision—any blurring or spots?"

Butler shook his head and winced as if he regretted the action. "None of that. My head feels like someone is tapping a hammer inside, but I see fine."

Hannah nodded. "I will prepare some willow bark tea for you. It will help with the pain." Her gaze turned to his torso. "It looks like someone kicked thee."

"They did." Butler didn't add he had grabbed the offending leg and thrown the man into the mud, hence the blows to his head by the man's companions.

Hannah touched the darkening bruise gently, stopping as Butler grimaced. "Nothing appears broken, but thou will not feel comfortable for a number of days. Let me bind thine head, and Abner can help thee wash."

Butler nodded, relieved. He wasn't particularly body conscious but he wasn't used to being assessed so frankly by a woman either. As the door closed behind her, he made use of the basin, glad for the feel of clean water on his grubby hide. A young, dusky-skinned woman returned with his willow tea, which Butler downed quickly before thanking her and sending her back with the cup. He dismissed Abner after the man helped him undo his buttons. The rest he could manage. He wouldn't look great for his meeting with Washington, but he would endeavor to look acceptable. Appearances mattered to the General.

Within a few moments, the maid appeared with an ivory shirt and gray breeches, which fit reasonably well. They were plainly made as was common with Quakers, but with good quality cloth. Butler offered a brief prayer of thanks that he wouldn't look like a shabby wreck when meeting his commander. Abner took his boots to clean, and Butler went out in his stocking feet to find Faith and her sister.

He found them down the hall in a modest room that apparently served as a parlor. Both women looked up at his entrance. Although there were some facial similarities, the sisters had some striking differences. While Faith was tall for a woman and a bit rangy in build, Hannah was considerably shorter and more rounded. Both had somewhat round faces with square chins and high cheekbones, but while Faith had gray-blue eyes, Hannah's were the deep clear blue of a mountain lake. Both women had sprinklings of freckles and soft pink lips reminiscent of rose petals.

They quit speaking as soon as they saw him. Faith gestured for him to sit as Hannah poured coffee from a pot on the low table in front of them. Butler crossed the threshold to join them, noting that in the short time he was gone, that a tray full of cakes and dainty sandwiches had arrived. The rich scent of coffee filled his nostrils. His stomach growled at the sight of real food, far better than he had experienced on the trip north from Virginia. Butler sketched a brief bow, rising as his vision started to blur. "How is your mother?"

Faith looked down, biting her lip.

Hannah answered. "She has improved little since the apoplexy struck her down in April. We've been taking turns sitting with her, feeding her and trying to keep her comfortable. It is fortunate that Faith has finally come home."

Faith flushed and said nothing, although her expression indicated she would rather be anywhere else.

"I'm sorry to hear that," Butler replied. He left the settee to the women and chose an upright wooden chair before adding a small lump of sugar to his coffee and accepting the delicate Dresden plate Faith had filled for him. "Thanks," he said, and meant it. Good food was a blessing, and he intended to enjoy it before heading out to discover what the general required of him.

18

Chapter Three

Butler approached the tavern from the busy street. The tall brick building stood solidly in the afternoon sun. His eyes watered in the glare. The scent of roasting meat, along with the rich yeastiness of freshly baked bread, drifted through the open windows, making his mouth water. He had enjoyed the coffee and cakes at Faith's sister's home, but his stomach longed for something solid. Hopefully, this meeting with Washington would include a meal.

He followed a group of well-dressed men up the steps and through the elegantly columned door into the main hall. Passing by the subscription room where the tavern keeper kept newspapers and pamphlets for his guests, Butler headed straight for the bar. A toffee-haired man stood behind the counter, wiping down its dark wooden surface. He glanced up at Butler as he approached. "Can I help you, sir?"

Butler smiled, "I am here to meet an associate. Perhaps you have heard of him—Cincinnatus?"

The bartender's expression did not change. "I can't say as I have. Let me check with my master and see if he can help you." He turned and called to an African-American man who was feeding the fire. "Lawrence, can you mind the bar for a moment?"

Lawrence rose and dusted his hands on the cloth apron around his waist. As the two passed, the first man's eyes flickered at Butler, then back. The other man nodded.

"Can I offer you a drink, sir?" Lawrence's voice was soft and lightly tinged with the cadence of the West Indies. His dark curls were pulled back into a tidy club, fastened with a leather strap. A few curls escaped and hovered over his temples.

Butler accepted a stein of local beer and took pleasure in slaking his thirst. The beer was cold from the cellar and welcome after the warmth outside. He had only gotten a few swallows before the original man returned.

"Follow me, sir. They are waiting for you."

Butler took his tankard and followed him past the coffee room and up the main staircase. At the top, he was surprised to enter into an enormous room filled with long tables. Had the tables been removed, one could have held a ball there. Sunlight streamed through the elegantly draped windows.

"This way," the man said, waiting for Butler to follow. He led him into a smaller adjoining room where three men sat around a table, none of whom was Washington.

After Butler entered, the barman left, shutting the heavy wooden door behind him. The men looked up from the table as he entered. He recognized Samuel Adams immediately. His strong face, with its massive black brows, offered a fierce stare before beckoning him to come closer.

"Jeremy Butler," he bellowed as he rose from the head of the heavy wooden table. "Come sit with us and apprise us of how the rebellion fares in the Virginia Colony. Jefferson tells me nothing. I need the views of an honest man who will not pretty things up to suit his own purposes."

Not much had changed since the days Butler had reported to him and the Sons of Liberty in Boston. Once Washington had been named Commander in Chief, Adams had sent him to the Virginian, who paid him to be a trusted messenger and spy for the patriot cause.

Butler nodded in greeting as he approached the table. The other two men had risen as well. Once his eyes adjusted to the dimmer light in the wood-paneled room, he recognized them as well, although he had not met them formally.

He raised a brow in query at Adams before taking the available seat at the far end of the table. As the others sat back down, a maidservant entered and placed goblets of wine all around. Butler was more than happy to accept another drink. It was a warm day, and his throat was dry.

"Please bring a plate for my friend as well, Molly," Adams said, indicating Butler.

She smiled and nodded at Adams, revealing a small gap in her pearly white teeth. A buxom woman of about thirty, she appeared comfortable at her job. Her lightly muscled arms handled the heavy tray of drinks with ease as she served the men before leaving in short order.

Adams gestured toward the others. "Allow me to introduce my companions. This is John Hancock, president of our Congress, and this," his voice lowered in respect. "is Benjamin Franklin."

Jeremy had heard of both men. Hancock had the shrewd face and dark, intelligent eyes of a successful man of business. Butler knew he was one of the most wealthy and influential men in the colonies. The other man was much older, but had a well-known reputation as well. Benjamin Franklin was famous for his writings, his scientific experiments, and now for his support for the revolt against Great Britain. One would have thought the elderly man almost napping, but Jeremy knew his reputation. That guileless face masked a clever brain; one well-skilled at sending well aimed arrows through the printed word. He glanced around, puzzled. There were no empty chairs, so it appeared no one else was expected. "Where is General Washington?" he asked at last.

Hancock spoke. His cultured voice revealed the quality of his education, as did his elegant clothes. "Ah, yes. Regretfully, our good friend Cincinnatus has important business in New York with the army. He was kind enough to write a letter summoning you to us. He understood that you would be more likely to respond to a request from him rather than from me."

Molly arrived with food at that moment, setting out platters of well-roasted beef and potatoes paired with carrots and green beans. Butler inhaled the air perfumed with food as he looked down at his plate. "I'll be back with bread and more drink," she said as her skirts swished around the door, closing swiftly behind her.

"Gentlemen, let's eat before we discuss business. Master Franklin, will you offer a blessing over our repast?"

Franklin nodded and, bowing his head, offered a brief blessing to the

Almighty. After the echoed amen, he added. "Let us make quick work of this generous repast before it grows cold, gentlemen. In the days ahead, we may not feast this richly for some time."

Adams responded. "Do you fear the British will blockade the entirety of the colonies?"

"Oh, I believe the British will use all means at their disposal to bring us to heel," Franklin said before bringing a generous fork of potato to his mouth. He followed with a sip of wine. Once he brushed his lips with a napkin, he noted, "Wine is proof God loves us."

Butler joined in the meal, eating and drinking carefully. A heavy meal made him sluggish, and he needed his wits about him. He pondered the company who had summoned him. Hancock and Franklin were strangers, although he was acquainted with Franklin's writings. Hancock he regarded with suspicion, although he knew him to be a dedicated patriot, he also recognized him as wealthy and ambitious. Butler recalled he'd had to flee the British when they took Boston last year, although he looked none the worse for wear now. He wore an elegant blue coat with gold facings while a lacy white jabot cascaded down from his throat. Butler soon realized that Hancock's eyes were assessing him as well.

"How was your journey up from Virginia, Master Butler?" Hancock asked.

"Less than satisfactory," Butler said. "My coach encountered a British patrol led by a man called Tarleton."

Hancock winced. "I've heard of him. I take it that's how you acquired your injury?"

Butler nodded and then addressed the man. "Why have I been summoned here?"

Hancock smiled. "Washington said you were direct. He also said you were the best man for the job." He quit toying with his goblet and nailed Butler with a direct stare. "There is a threat to our delegation. You need to find who it is and prevent him from causing any more mischief."

Butler leaned forward. "What kind of threat?"

"Keep your voice down, man," Hancock hissed. "Do you want to incite panic?" He looked at the men around him. "Nothing leaves this room." He looked pointedly at Adams, who flushed.

"I know when to keep my mouth shut. I've played this game far longer than you." He scowled as he took a long draw of wine. Adams pulled at his collar as if it bothered him, but he refrained from further comments.

Franklin said. "Then it's best we say what needs to be said and adjourn before someone takes notice of our presence. Even in our fair city, there are those who would share information with the enemy."

Handcock nodded. "So noted. There have been a handful of disturbing incidents that, taken together, cannot be ignored. Three weeks ago, Thomas Fitzsimons's valet took ill with what was thought to be a summer ague. He died a few days later and was buried. Then we received this." He took out a folded piece of paper. On it was written in neat copperplate, "Who dies next?"

Butler took it and examined it thoughtfully. "Nothing special about the paper. You can buy it at any print shop. He sniffed the sheet. "It smells like your toilet water."

Hancock looked faintly embarrassed. "Now, see here."

Butler quelled him with a glance. "If you expect me to unravel this puzzle, you need to take care not to contaminate any clues." He kept looking. "I can't see anything special about the ink, but there is someone here who knows ink better than me." He looked over at Franklin. "What do you see?"

Franklin took the note from Butler and adjusted his glasses. "As you said, "This is basic laid paper. My shop sells it, but so do many others. But it takes a certain amount of income to afford to send a letter, so whoever is behind this has money. I believe this to be gall ink, also widely used. I agree with Master Butler's nose. The scents of ambergris and vanilla are pronounced. You might consider using less." He set the note down. "Nonetheless, Master Butler, it is a threat and not an idle one."

"What else has happened?" Butler waited for one of the men to answer.

Adams obliged. "The first week we met as a delegation, the chandelier in our meeting room at the state house broke free and fell to the floor. Fortunately, we had taken a break, and no one was underneath it. When a smith came to repair it, the chain was found to be mostly sawn through so that its weight eventually made it break loose. Then there was the incident with Rutledge's carriage."

"Rutledge?"

Hancock answered. "One of the South Carolina delegates. He'd rented a carriage to take him about the city. He had offered Franklin and Jefferson a ride back from one of our local taverns to the State House when something spooked the horses. Luckily, the driver knew his business and brought them to heel before they ended up in the river."

"What else," Butler asked.

"Last night, someone threw a large rock and shattered a window at the State House. Some of our men were cut by the glass, but no serious injuries."

Butler leaned back in his chair. "Do you have any suspects?"

Adams chuckled humorlessly. "This town is full of Tories. It could be any of them. I've no doubt they have their spies throughout the town."

Butler took a drink of wine. It was a far better vintage than he could afford. He sipped slowly, enjoying the feel of it on his tongue. "The horses could have been an accident."

"The chandelier was not," Hancock said grimly. "I had the meeting room inspected before the delegates arrived, and that chain was sound. Someone meant to do us harm."

Franklin interrupted. "Perhaps, or someone had a grudge against an individual. Ever since Peyton Randolph's unfortunate demise last summer, we've all been more aware of our own mortality." He nodded at Hancock. "Perhaps such caution is not without cause. You employ someone to check the food since your last dinner party."

Hancock nodded as he fidgeted with the ruffled cuffs that extended past his jacket sleeves. "I had half a dozen guests take ill after a dinner party earlier this week. All have recovered, but no one has discovered why only those took ill. We all ate the same meal, served by staff I have employed for some time."

"Can you provide me a list of guests, both those who fell ill and those who did not?"

Hancock nodded. "Try not to offend anyone. I do business with many of

24

these people."

Butler's tone was dry. "I imagine they would have a vested interest in discovering who would want to harm them."

Adams snorted. "It's far more likely they will blame him, assuming he was the intended victim. I was up half the night filling the chamber pot, unlike my companions here."

"I take it you were unscathed," Butler asked, looking at the man who had summoned him through Washington.

Hancock nodded. "I had a bad headache that night, so I ate very little past the first course."

"It would appear your moderation kept you from harm," noted Franklin. Light from the windows cast a silvery glow over his spectacles, hiding his eyes. Bushy gray brows rose over the frames, rising and falling with his expression.

Butler mulled over what the men had said. He was pretty certain there were things they were not telling him as well. They watched him, waiting for what he would say next. But then, the past few years had taught all of them to be careful around strangers and wary of friends. No one really knew a man's loyalties until they were tested, and as often as not, a friend could turn when what he valued most was put at risk. He didn't blame them for being frightened; only a fool would not. He was grateful for Washington's trust.

"I will need to talk with people regarding each incident," he said at last. "There are no guarantees, and I cannot guard all the delegates. There are too many of them."

"You don't need to," Hancock said. "Only a few were present at all four incidents."

"Who was there besides you three?" Butler asked bluntly.

Adams answered. "Hancock's servant, Gaius."

Butler leveled a look at Hancock. "Why isn't he here?"

Hancock met Butler's gaze firmly. "Because he has duties at home. I've known Gaius since he was a boy. He would no more harm me than he would attempt to fly off a rooftop. He is not part of this. I would stake my reputation on this."

"But would you stake your life on it?" Butler stared back at Hancock, letting the silence deepen before continuing. "Some of the British have offered freedom to the enslaved. That would be an incredible temptation to a man bound for life. I need to talk to him so I can hear from him directly what he saw."

Hancock nodded. "I will make him available to you. He can accompany me to the state house tomorrow instead of Cato."

Butler looked at the men gathered there at the table. Tiredness and anxiety hung over them. Like all of the representatives gathered for the congress, they knew meetings like this labeled them as traitors to the British. Their lives could well be forfeited for their choices and their families marked. He had nothing but respect for the risks they took. The choices he made in secret, they did in open defiance.

The tinkling of utensils on plates ceased as the meal concluded. A lone maidservant cleared away plates while one of the tavern's freedmen came up with a fresh bottle of wine, showing it to Hancock, who inspected it before nodding his approval. "A fine Madeira,"

He allowed his glass to be filled with the deep red wine. Adams partook as well. Franklin covered his glass with a polite refusal. Butler did likewise. "I'm afraid I lost my taste for Madeira," He said, remembering how it had been used to poison a friend last year. "I need to keep a clear head anyway."

"As do we all," Franklin agreed. The maid poured a clear liquid, which Butler realized, to his surprise, was water. The older man downed it before he rose. "Forgive me; I have some other business to attend before it gets much later."

"As do I," said Butler, who wanted a few moments alone with him. "May I walk out with you?"

Franklin did not object, so Butler followed him to the door, feeling Hancock's eyes boring into his back as he exited.

Despite his age, Franklin moved nimbly down the steps and to the door. "Put my meal on account," he said to the man at the bar, who nodded in acquiescence. Butler told him, "You can put mine on Hancock's tab."

Out in the street, the summer sun beat down, reflected by the cobblestones that lined the street. Franklin turned and headed down Chestnut Street downtown. The wooden heels of his shoes made a solid clop as he walked. The traffic had died down with the rising heat of the afternoon. Butler squinted as he cast his gaze about before falling in step with Franklin.

"Sally will be wondering where I am," Franklin noted wryly. "She worries unnecessarily about her dear papa." He continued east toward the Delaware River. Gulls circled overhead, diving to snatch a meal from unwary carts before wheeling upward with raucous cries. Franklin watched them with a slight smile. "Such efficient creatures, they find a meal where most would see waste."

Butler skirted around the spilled box that excited the birds. The scent of fish was nauseating, although it did not seem to impact his companion. He knew a little of Franklin. He had been fascinated by accounts of his experiments, even if he considered playing with lightning slightly insane. "What do you make of these incidents?' Butler asked as they walked down the street.

Franklin paused before crossing an alley. "Individually, they could be accidental, but taken together," His eyes met Butler's, shedding the guise of a genial old man. "They indicate someone wants to end the revolution before it begins."

Chapter Four

The bottom bruising jolt of the farm wagon had not improved in the years since Faith had last ridden in it. She gripped the edge of the seat as her oldest brother directed the horses toward the farm where she had been born and raised. Caleb didn't talk much. His wife, Elizabeth, whom everyone called Bess, talked enough for the two of them. Faith used the silence to take in her environment. Not much had changed. The road leading out of town hadn't improved. The rough dirt track connected many farms that dotted the countryside. Faith looked across at the rolling fields of wheat and pastures of cattle or sheep. This was why many had come to this colony to farm the rich, fertile land and to enjoy the largess of William Penn's offer of religious freedom. Although Penn had passed, his sons governed, even if they had abandoned their father's faith. Nonetheless, the colony prospered even through the conflicts brought about by people moving in who differed in significant ways from those who had founded the colony.

As the morning haze lifted from the fields, the sun beat down on the straw hat covering her head. Out in the fields thick with grass, cows grazed contentedly. Their brown and black and white spotted coats contrasted with the rich green of the field. A few calves trotted about, never ranging far from their mothers. Off in the distance, she spotted another group gathered under a small grove of trees, taking respite in the shade.

"How are the sheep this year?" She asked.

Caleb's eyes didn't leave the road. Just as Faith was about to repeat her question, he spoke. "Well enough."

Faith let that sink in. She wasn't sure what to expect at the farmhouse. She could not imagine the farm not being run by the nervous energy of Patience Payne. "How is our father?"

"The same."

Faith glanced over at him, irritated. "Can you manage more than two words at a time?"

His eyes flickered over to her before returning to the road. A particularly bad pothole made them both jerk forward. Faith grabbed the side to keep from tumbling out. One of the large draft horses snorted as its tail swatted away flies. "It's been some time since you've been home."

"I run a business," she started before he cut her off with a gesture.

"I'm aware." He softly clucked when the horses slowed down, coaxing them to go just a hair faster. "We'll stop and let them get a drink just up the road. Cadwaller's farm is ahead. He won't mind our horses drinking at his pond."

Silence fell again between them as her brother guided the horses down the road. Her back felt hot from the sun as it rose in the sky behind them. At last, she spotted the faded timbers of a barn ahead. Caleb turned off onto a narrow path made by wheel tracks that led down towards a large stock pond. Geese squawked as they drew close. Faith spotted a mother with her goslings afloat while a gander stood on the bank, giving the evil eye. "I don't think they care much for us," she murmured as they stopped.

Caleb looked over at the partially spread wings of the sharp-eyed goose. "He's protecting his family. Stay on the far side from his flock, and you'll be fine." He helped her down before unhitching the horses and leading them to the water. The gander gave a warning honk before shooting off into the water with his family. The horses paid no attention as they drank thirstily. After securing them in the shade of a poplar, he grabbed a covered basket from beneath the seat. "Here," he said and handed it to her.

They feasted on ham and hard-boiled eggs, along with biscuits and scones studded with strawberries. He passed over a bottle of ale.

Faith sighed. "Bess brews the best ale."

"Aye," Caleb said. "She needs to rest from time to time as her time draws

29

near."

Faith stared at him. "Is Bess carrying a child?"

Caleb nodded. "Our third since you left and the most troublesome. Her back pains her if she does too much."

"When is she due?" Faith asked.

"The midwife thinks it will be in the fall when the last of the apples are being harvested."

Faith nodded, mentally calculating when that would be. "September?"

"If all goes well." He paused. "She lost one last summer."

"I'm sorry," she said. "I didn't know."

He shrugged. "Nothing to say." But the brief flash of pain in his expression said what he did not.

A large bird cast a shadow overhead. It was followed by three companions, moving closer to a field just outside a stand of trees. Large and dark, they drifted down in a large circle before disappearing into the tall grass. Faith's eyes met Caleb's. "Something's dead."

"He nodded grimly. "It must be something big from that number of vultures. Grab the musket and stay near the wagon. I'll go take a look."

"You shouldn't go alone," Faith said, grabbing the gun. "I'm coming with you."

"If it's native unrest, you need to be able to run."

Faith gulped, remembering her father's stories from his time in the military when the native tribes had fought with the French. "There's no outrunning the Mohawk, or so Pa said."

Caleb took out his hunting knife. "If it is natives, it could be any one of a dozen tribes. I've traded with a few, but many have no use for colonists."

"Then we're better off together."

"Stay close," He looked back at her. "And quit talking."

She nodded as she followed him through the long green grass. It slapped against her skirts as she passed, making her nervous as she scanned the nearby trees for signs of life. With the exception of the distant cattle and the birds, they appeared to be alone. She jumped when she heard rustling in the trees but, after a moment, dismissed it as the wind. Nonetheless, Faith kept scanning the tree line, looking for signs of life.

The smell hit her then, the powerful scent of rancid meat, blood, and waste. Caleb's face looked grim, and he turned to face her. "It's Cadwaller. He's been dead for a while. You don't need to look. The vultures have been at him."

Faith's gorge rose. Behind her brother, she could see a leg covered in homespun dark with blood. A bloody mass lay where his head should be. Flies buzzed around it. She nodded, clenching her teeth, and turned back to the wagon. Caleb joined after a period of minutes that felt like hours.

Once he was within speaking range, Faith asked him, "Was it Indians?"

"Not unless they're using rocks. His skull is crushed in. There's a large rock by his head covered in blood and brains." He looked at the house. "We need to tell his family. I think his son still lives there." Gathering back the horses, he hitched them to the wagon before helping her in. Faith kept looking about uneasily, wondering if someone still lurked out of sight. They rode in silence to the wood-framed house. No one came to greet them.

Caleb stopped and stepped down off the wagon, then looped the reins around one of the poles holding up the porch. Faith climbed down to join him. Out back, she could hear the clucking of chickens and the bleating of a goat. She gazed out over the fields visible in front and could see no one.

"Could someone be out back?" She started around when a dark-skinned man emerged from the barn. He was barefoot with homespun tan breeches and a faded blue shirt. A straw hat stained with sweat and use covered his head.

"Hey," Caleb called, waving at the man, who paused as if wondering whether to wait or flee. "Is your mistress about or young master Cadwaller?"

The man eyed him cautiously, but answered courteously. "Master went out into the fields this morning. We'd had reports of wolves from a neighbor, and he's been checking for signs. The mistress has been in the brew house making cider. Young Master Marcus should be back by suppertime. May I ask who wishes to speak with them?"

"Caleb Payne," Her brother took a breath, perhaps to steady his nerves. "Your master lies dead not far from the stock pond. We came across his body when we stopped to water our horses. Your mistress needs to be told."

The man inhaled sharply. "No! That can't be so!"

A woman stuck her head out of the house. Her hair was tied up in a bright yellow cloth. Her skin was like coffee with cream. As she walked out on the porch, Faith could see she was barefoot as well. A pale blue apron covered a dress of striped homespun. "Thomas, why are you hollering, and why have you not invited our guests in? Mistress would want us to bring them in out of the sun. You need to go get her."

"They say Master is dead out by the pond, Eunice," the man gasped.

Eunice looked at them sharply. "What happened?"

"We're not sure," Caleb answered. "He's been dead for a while. We saw the vultures. His head is caved in."

She looked out over the field. "I thought it was a dead animal." Eunice shook her head. "He was worried about wolves. Your daddy stopped by a few days ago saying he'd lost a calf to them." She looked over at them. "Come inside. You tend to their horses, I will tell her. She's been making cider."

Eunice took off for one of the outbuildings, where smoke rose from the chimney along with a sugary sweet smell of very ripe fruit. Sweat ran down Faith's back as she stood on the porch. She didn't want to think of how hot it was inside. Thomas pointed to a fenced area in the shade of a big barn. Caleb followed him, leading the horses and wagon to the barn.

Within minutes, Eunice emerged with a middle-aged woman who walked toward them with a firm, steady gait. Her face was flushed as well as touched by the sun enough to sprinkle freckles across her nose. She was probably about the age of Faith's own mother. Silver strands were mixed with the dark brown hair visible under her cap. She was a handsome woman, well-rounded and full of life. Her eyebrows lifted in inquiry at the sight of unexpected visitors to her domain. The men stopped at her approach. She nodded at Caleb, "Your father visited a few days ago. How fares Patience? We pray for her recovery every day."

Caleb nodded. "We appreciate that." He removed his hat. "Mistress Cadwaller, I regret that I must tell you that as we stopped to water our horses, my sister and I spotted vultures in your field. When we went to investigate, we found your husband dead."

Silence followed, heavy in the air. Faith watched as the other woman heard Caleb's words and then as the meaning took hold. All color faded from her face as a sharp exhale left her body like the moaning of the wind.

"It can't be," she said. "He went to check on the newborn calves in the outer meadow just after breakfast."

Faith took her hand. "I'm so sorry."

"No," Mistress Cadwaller shook her head. "I need to go to him. He's hurt himself, that's all."

Faith didn't want to tell her there was no hope of life. She had seen the crushed mass that had once been his head. She had no idea how her brother had identified him unless it was by his clothes.

Eunice stood before her. "Mistress, you need to come inside. Let the men bring him home."

The new widow's breathing became sharp pants of pain. Eunice took her other hand and looked over to Faith. "Let's get her inside out of the heat."

Faith followed Eunice's lead, helping take the other woman into the house and to the rectangular table near the fire. Mistress Cadwaller sat down in a straight wooden chair with a thump, resting her elbows on the table as she cradled her head.

Outside, Faith heard Caleb talking to the other man. Their voices faded as they went back to the body. No one asked who might have struck the man down and left him lying in his own field.

Faith sat next to Mistress Cadwaller, who shook as if taken by a sudden fever. Despite the open windows, the room was hot. A fly buzzed around her head, dancing insouciantly around her face. She waved an arm to shoo it, but it came back after a moment before zipping out of reach and landing on the table, where Eunice smashed it with a leather-bound book.

"Thanks," Faith said.

Eunice nodded. She poured a small amount of liquor into a glass and handed it to her mistress. "Drink this," she said softly. "You need it to settle your nerves."

Mistress Cadwaller downed the drink in a swallow, coughing a few minutes before settling. "Marcus will be home shortly. He went to town to get some harness mended."

The women sat in silence, each wrapped in their own thoughts. Faith knew only too well the difficulties of losing a husband. Once the shock had passed, the economic realities of being a widow would come, and she would have to deal with them while she mourned. There was no reprieve for the working class.

Faith heard the sound of an approaching horse. Rising to her feet, she went to the door to see a handsome bay horse trot toward the barn.

"That's Master Marcus," Eunice said from behind her.

Faith straightened her shoulders. "I guess I had better tell him about his father." She walked outside. The porch steps creaked beneath her feet as she headed across them. Heat from the sun over the years had shrunk the boards so that narrow gaps appeared between some of them, revealing strands of grass that took advantage of the sun's presence to grow.

The sun beat down on her head and back as she strode across the dusty pathway to the large barn nearby. As she drew closer, the earthy scents of sweat and manure tickled her nose. Rails encircled a grassy meadow next to the building. A colt and its mother stood in the shade of a beech tree, sheltering from the blazing sun. The pastoral beauty of the scene jarred with Faith's vivid memory of the carnage that lay nearby. She attempted to push the image out of her mind as she entered the shadowy barn.

"Hello?" she called out before entering through the open door. Faith paused just inside to give her eyes time to adjust to the dim interior. The horse nickered softly, answered by the man who removed her tack and offered her water from a bucket. He was average height, but muscled, like someone who worked the land.

As the horse drank, the man looked over at Faith. "I'm Marcus Cadwaller, who are you?"

Faith's heart skipped a beat at his rough tone. She stopped several feet away and cleared her throat. "I'm Faith Clarke. I stopped here with my brother, Caleb Payne, to water our horses before heading home." She softened her tone. "We saw vultures in the field up from the pond. When we went to investigate, we found your father dead."

"Dead," The younger Cadwaller stilled. He looked at her without any emotion on his face. "I know the Paynes. You must be the one that went to Virginia. Are you sure he's dead?"

Faith thought about the carnage she had seen. "Quite sure. Thomas and my brother are bringing him to the house."

Outside, a horse snorted, accompanied by the voices of men, one of which was Caleb.

Relief flooded through Faith that she would not have to deal with Marcus Cadwaller alone.

Cadwaller put down the bucket and the cloth he'd been using to wipe down his mount. "Let's put you in the corral with Mamie and her colt," he said, leading the mare out past Faith and into the yard. Faith followed and watched as he unlatched the corral and let the sturdy bay loose in it, joining their two horses inside. She trotted over to join the others in the shade, watching the people in the yard.

The body, wrapped in a blanket, was draped over a horse like a sack of potatoes. Only the booted feet were visible, although as they approached, Faith smelled the sickly scent of blood. A cloud of flies buzzed as they feasted on the swathed corpse. Dark spots from all the blood soaked through the blanket, ruining it for any other purpose.

Marcus Cadwaller walked over to meet them. There was no missing all the blood. He looked over the wrapped parcel as the other two stopped to let him approach. "What happened to him?"

Caleb answered. "His head is bashed in."

Marcus' face revealed no particular emotion. "Let's put him in the shed; no need to putrefy the house with the carcass."

Thomas looked over at him, surprise on his features. "You don't want him in the house?"

Marcus shook his head. "We can lay him on a table in the shed where we smoke meat. It's empty this time of year. If Ma wants to clean him up before we bury him, she can do it there."

Caleb said. "The sheriff should be contacted. We don't know if this was an accident or if someone accosted him when he was out in the field alone."

Marcus answered. "You are making too much of this. He likely fell after taking in too much liquor. He liked his drink more than his family, if the truth is to be told." He nodded to the bundle, "That will only rot in this heat. I will give my mother time to prepare him with help from our slaves, and then he goes in the ground."

"Doesn't the sheriff need to see the body?" Faith said; although she knew he was correct about the heat, the haste troubled her.

"I'm sure he's seen plenty of death," Marcus replied. "In these times, there is little time to investigate what was likely an accident. He has plenty in town to keep him busy. I will lay my father to rest and comfort my mother. She's suffered enough; I will not cause her more pain." He took the reins of the horse and led it to the shed, followed by Thomas and Caleb.

Faith watched as Mistress Cadwaller walked toward her, watching the horse with the body being led away.

"You need to continue your journey home," she said. "Eunice and I will take care of my husband. This is a family matter."

Surprised, Faith turned to look at her. No tears marked her face, although the harsh light of the sun highlighted every crease, making her appear older than she had moments earlier. There was no mistaking the sorrow in her eyes or the determination. She moved forward slowly down toward the bundle that was her husband's body.

Eunice came out of the house with a bucket. "I'll pull water from the pond so we can clean him up."

Mistress Cadwaller nodded. "I'll get some clean rags." She turned to Faith. "Have a safe journey." It was a dismissal. They were no longer welcome.

Once Caleb returned from the barn, they walked back to their own team. He handed her up before hopping onto the wagon himself and taking the reins.

"Is no one going for the sheriff?" Faith asked as they headed out.

"They didn't want him," Caleb answered. "I'm not sure I could get him to come out this far. He doesn't stray far from town these days." He paused.

36

"Neither of them seemed to be overly broken up by the death. Young Cadwaller didn't seem at all surprised. It's almost as if he was expecting it." He clucked at the horses. "Let's get home before anything else happens. I don't favor being out past nightfall. Too many things can happen out on the road."

Faith settled in the hard wooden seat, trying to wrap her mind around the tragedy that a man could die and his family mourned so little.

Chapter Five

J eremy Butler felt his eyelids begin to droop. He shifted his position on the hard chair and stood up. It was his third day listening to the Continental Congress debate, and he would rather be anywhere else. All day long, delegates from all thirteen colonies gathered in the large assembly room, shuttered the windows and met. Some made lofty speeches posed in front of the ornate marble fireplace, while others bickered around one of the tables where differing groups of men sat. It was enough to drive a sane man mad. Butler was beginning to wonder if the delegates were trying to pick each other off. Some of the rhetoric, while couched in polite language, could be construed as a threat. He dismissed the thought. These were businessmen of various sorts. Their goals were to free their livelihoods from the increasingly heavy hand of Great Britain. Although it was early in the day, the sun beat down on the bricks of the building, warming the interior. Franklin sat placidly in the thick of things, his eyes closed either in contemplation or sleep. Butler watched as one of the red-haired delegates from Virginia, Jefferson, walked over to confer with members of the Massachusetts delegation. It could go on like this for hours, with men making speeches while others gathered to whisper in small groups, much like ants working together over a choice crumb.

The hum of voices and lack of action was driving him mad. So far, he had seen nothing that would constitute a threat. He slipped out a door in the back of the assembly room with the intent of getting a breath of fresh air and the excuse of doing some reconnaissance on the building. He had already familiarized himself with the two-story building. Outside in the wide corridor, he watched a bird sail up to the upper floor. If it was fortunate, it would exit out of one of the many open windows above. Downstairs, the windows remained shuttered to hide the men meeting within. Sweat ran down Butler's back as he crossed to the courtroom across the hall. The drone of voices here was almost as bad as delegates from Philadelphia met to discuss their colony's constitution. His head throbbed as he turned to escape the constant clamor.

Once outside, Butler walked out to stand under the shade of a tree grove just past the main door. A few birds blew overhead, their cries barely audible against the bustle of the enormous city. An audacious squirrel approached him before darting towards the steps of the state house, looking for food. To the west, horse hooves could be heard on the cobblestones of Fifth Street as ordinary people continued on their business. He watched both carriages and wagons make their way up and down the street. He wondered how many realized what decisions were being made behind the imposing walls before him.

In the distance, he could hear an auction going on. He hoped it wasn't slaves. Seeing people in chains treated like meat sickened him. He had too much respect for the people of color he knew and worked with to condone the dehumanization of their kindred. Butler carried with him the memories of Athena's heartbreak at the loss of her only daughter to the economics of the slave trade. He doubted they would ever find her, but kept his eyes out for any news of a young enslaved woman with dark auburn hair and green eyes.

The front door cracked open as a man stepped outside. Hancock's servant, Gaius, emerged, resplendent in a bright blue suit. His brass buckles gleamed in the summer sun from their place on his elegant black pumps. Butler slipped back into the shadows of the trees so he could observe him unawares.

Gaius looked about before nimbly trotting down the steps and into the open courtyard. The clock in the tower tolled the hour, informing everyone that midday had arrived. Within another hour or two, the delegates would be heading out for their midday meal. Butler had been intending to interview the servant, but had difficulty finding a moment to corner him. The man had an unnerving ability to disappear whenever Butler went looking for him.

Gaius headed across the green, walking more swiftly the further he got from the state house. Butler suspected Hancock had no idea where his servant was at the moment. As president of the convention, he had his hands full of delegates, all fiercely defending the interests of their own colony.

Butler hurried to catch the man before he reached the busy street. "Gaius," he called out to the other man. "Gaius, stop! I need to speak with you."

Gaius broke into a run, angling for the copse of trees nearest the road. Butler pursued him across the grounds. The only sound he could hear was the huffing of his breath and the pounding of his boots on the cobblestones. Gaius was taller, but hampered by tight-fitting breeches and the slippery soles of his fancy shoes. Butler closed the gap until he was within a few feet of the man.

"I just want to talk," he called. "You're not in any trouble."

Gaius paid no heed, pumping his arms as he sought to escape. His neatly braided que flapped against his back as he pushed himself forward.

Butler's lungs worked like a bellows as he pushed to capture his quarry. Once he was close enough, he could tackle him to the ground. A high-pitched whistle, followed by a sharp burst of wind by his ear, caused him to duck to the ground just as he heard a soft thump. Gaius shrieked and collapsed on the ground.

An arrow stuck out of his back, its shaft quivering as blood spread across the man's back. Gaius lay face down in the dirt just outside the trees. The enslaved man did not move. The sharp, coppery scent of blood filled the air as it spilled on the ground surrounding the body. The air was still and quiet, with not even a breath of wind to disturb the tableau.

Butler remained on the ground himself, looking around for the assassin. His heart beat wildly as he sought the source of the threat. No cover was within easy reach, so he waited flat on the ground to see if another arrow would come whistling from the trees. But the woods were silent, as if the animals sensed the predator and chose to hide within the depths of the trees.

He didn't blame them. He felt naked and exposed. His eyes scanned the area, seeking cover. Gaius didn't move, not even to breathe, as blood pooled underneath his body.

Butler started to rise, then ducked back down as another arrow winged past him to bounce off the cobblestones. He crawled along the ground until he reached the base of a pine. It was faint cover, but preferable to the emptiness of the yard. He listened for the sound of movement and heard nothing at first. A faint scraping of the ground, followed by the crack of a branch, warned him the enemy was further back in the trees. The question was whether he was retreating or advancing. Butler wasn't waiting to find out.

Butler rose off the ground, half crouched in case more arrows came his way. A stray wind moved the trees back and forth, allowing the leaves to whisper to one another. Butler's sharp ears caught the crackling of brush, followed by a faint curse, and took off in pursuit of his quarry. Behind him, he heard cries as more people entered the courtyard in front of the State House, but he had no time for that. Butler took off in the direction from which he had heard the sound. The deep shade of the trees provided excellent cover. He moved carefully, keeping himself behind the trees in case the assassin turned to attack, but there was no sign of another in the forest.

A sudden crackle of limbs warned him seconds before a tree limb came swinging back. He fell to the ground as the limbs swept just over his head. The brush crashed as his quarry fled. Butler scrambled to his feet awkwardly, caught in the briars of a bush. Cursing, he pulled himself free, ignoring the bloody rakes of the wicked thorns. He walked as quickly as he could while looking for traps. His neck, arms, and legs stung from scrapes. Butler wanted to beat the tar out of him, but revenge was to be denied. By the time he found where the assassin had lain, he had escaped into the city. Looking about outside the copse of trees, he saw nothing amiss. A dog trotted across the grass to meet a boy chasing a hoop. A few dark-skinned women walked along the road carrying baskets as they chatted and walked toward the river. Nowhere was anyone who looked suspicious. Butler wiped his forehead with his sleeve. His sleeve was now streaked with dirt and blood. If his sometime partner Athena had been present to see it, she would have scolded him for destroying good clothes while she tended his wounds. He missed the bold freedwoman who had taken care of him after his mother's death many years ago. She was the most valued member of his spy network and performed a valuable service back in Williamsburg. He sighed and wondered if Faith's sister would help bind his wounds. She seemed able enough.

Wandering back into the trees, Butler found a few crushed plants. A partially crushed shrub caught his attention. When he looked down into its branches, he spotted an arrow caught in its limbs. He picked it up for further examination later. A torn piece of scarlet fabric caught his attention as well. The bright pattern told him it had once been a neckerchief. One that looked familiar, although he couldn't for the life of him remember where he had spotted it. He tucked it into his pocket and sighed in frustration. The man had gotten away. Once in the streets of Philadelphia, he would be lost among the thousands who lived within its boundaries. Butler had no idea where the man would be hiding. This wasn't his town, and he was unfamiliar with its streets and neighborhoods.

Back in the courtyard, a crowd had gathered over Gaius' body. Hancock stood nearby, looking furious. "I thought you were here to prevent this," he said. His eyes flashed as he took in the scene. "I have one man dead and panicking delegates ready to flee for home and forget why they were sent here."

Butler held up the arrow. "I didn't realize he would be a target." He looked down at the man. "I only wished to speak to him. Someone felled him before I had the chance."

Hancock's brows rose. "Do you know who is doing this? I'm not paying you to watch my staff die. I expect this person or persons to be caught and dealt with swiftly. Washington assured me you were the man for the job. Are you?"

Butler kept his tone calm. "Perhaps we need to focus on why someone is targeting people involved in this endeavor. Did Gaius have any enemies you know of?"

Hancock's tone was bleak. "I cannot imagine why anyone would kill a slave. He did what he was told efficiently and with a cheerful demeanor. He was a valet, for God's sake. Killing him has no reason to it. Causing panic among the delegates makes more sense. We all know that King George and his parliament would benefit from the loss of this congress."

Butler interrupted. "Unless you know something I don't, King George was not hiding in the trees lobbing arrows. Your assassin is someone closer to home."

Hancock glared at him before dropping his voice. "Come with me. It's better to have this conversation in a more private setting." His eyes shifted over to the door where delegates were spilling out to view the scene for themselves. Voices rose as upset delegates voiced their fears."

"Gentlemen," Hancock called out as he approached the throng. "Let us take a break and regroup later today. My servant, Gaius, has met with an unfortunate accident. We will need time to get him to a physician and clear the area. Go to your favorite tavern; we will reconvene at four."

He waved them off. A few protested before being persuaded to leave by Hancock, Adams, and Jefferson. Handcock returned to Butler, his face flushed with heat and stress. Let's head to my office. I have wine in there. I think we could both use a glass."

Butler followed him back into the building and up the stairway to an elegant room with large windows hung with blue. Above a marble fireplace was a portrait of a man in clothing from a different era.

"William Penn," Hancock said as he saw the direction of Butler's gaze. "He was the founder of this colony. It's a pity his descendants don't share the vision of their illustrious ancestor." He strode restlessly across the richly patterned rug. "We are running out of time to find the villain behind this. I am holding onto this congress by the skin of my teeth. The delegates are frightened, and rightly so. Just by gathering here, we have drawn the notice and ire of the British Empire. These men are brave just to come here. They know it is akin to putting a target on their backs. Have you discovered anything of use?"

Butler shook his head. "Whoever it is knows their way around Philadelphia and is familiar with the comings and goings of the congress. This is not my town. I need someone who is well-connected with this town and knows the people. I need someone who can open doors not just with the gentry but with the everyday people who can tell when something is amiss."

"I believe I can assist with that," Benjamin Franklin stepped into the room from where he had been listening just outside.

Hancock stared at him but said nothing.

"I thought it best to wait until Master Hancock finished speaking rather than interrupt," He continued unperturbed. "As you have noted, it is imperative that this villain be found as quickly as possible. My Junto is filled with like-minded men from all over Philadelphia. I can introduce Master Butler to them and see how they can assist."

"You believe your little group of businessmen can catch this man?" Hancock said incredulously.

"I think a group of determined individuals can do almost anything," Franklin replied. "But my purpose is to supply your man with the information he needs to do his job. We all need this assassin found as quickly as possible. Knowing that a group of skilled and intelligent Philadelphians are aiding the cause might well help calm the frazzled nerves of the congress."

Hancock sighed, "Very well." He looked at Franklin and Butler. "Consult your allies and get every drop of information you can out of them. Use your much-vaunted charm to get them to open up."

Franklin looked pleased. "I will endeavor to impress the gravity of the situation upon them."

Hancock sighed. "Gaius was a good man. I wish you gentlemen well. I need to go tell his wife that he will not be returning home. I fear to think how many more men and women will be sacrificed to the cause of liberty. I bid you both adieus." He brushed past Franklin before walking down the stairs on his way out. His footsteps echoed as he walked down the hallway towards the door that Gaius had used not long ago.

Benjamin Franklin met Butler's gaze. "These are grave times indeed," he said.

Butler held up the arrow for him to see. "Can any of your associates identify where this came from?"

Franklin replied. "I will send word out for us to meet tonight. Where are you staying? I can have a servant come round with a message if I am successful." They walked together down the stairs crossed above the main door before cascading down to the main hall. Butler let the older man lead, watching as Franklin kept a steadying hand on the rail until he reached the marble floor. He paused to adjust his cane before continuing at a steady pace down the road toward home.

Butler's scrapes itched and stung. He longed for a cold drink, a hot bath, and a servant to attend to his needs. He wasn't sure what Hannah White had to offer, but he intended to find out.

The townhouse on Walnut Street was quiet. Within her shop, a few women browsed the offerings of fine china. He walked around to the back so he wouldn't be seen. He went up the stairs, avoiding the public rooms. He spotted Abner on the way up and asked him for a basin of hot water to clean his wounds. Within a few minutes, Abner came in with hot water and clothes. Butler doffed his shirt and began cleaning the scrapes left from his tangle with the briars. Within moments, someone tapped on his door. "Who is it?" he asked. Butler felt relatively safe, but he slipped one of his knives into his hand just in case.

"It is Hannah White. Abner said thou were injured again."

"Give me a moment," Butler hastily pulled his shirt back on, wincing as it dragged over a nasty scratch. She stood just outside holding a small jar. A loose strand of coffee-colored hair had escaped her neat cap and curled gently against her temple. It matched the level brows underneath which her clear blue eyes watched him.

"I thought you might have need of this." She handed the jar over to him. "I also brought vinegar to help counteract any infection. The small jug was tucked under her arm along with a stack of clean clothes.

"It's only a few scratches," he murmured as he took the items from her. "They're a bit uncomfortable, but nothing to worry about."

"I'm not worried," she snapped. "But given how prone you are to injury, I thought it wise to make sure you received proper care."

Butler looked at her. "I thank you for what you have brought, but I am fine." He started to close the door before cracking it back open to catch her expression. "By the way, I am not prone to injury." He heard her snort as he closed the door once again. Her footsteps tapped lightly down the hall and to the steps. Butler took off his shirt and began the process of tending his scrapes, wincing as the steaming water hit an open cut. The nastier ones, he daubed some of Hannah White's ointment on in hopes it would aid healing. He had not had a woman to tend him since his wife's death nearly ten years ago. It depressed him when he realized he couldn't conjure up her face anymore. His mind turned to Hannah White. She was both attractive and intelligent, but he had no business developing an interest. Any woman involved with him was at risk should he be captured by the British.

Once his cuts were dressed, Butler threw his shirt back on and headed back down the stairs. He bypassed the main floor and went down to the kitchen in the basement, lured by the scent of food.

A woman leaned over an iron pot that hung over the fire. A small table behind her held a loaf of bread, a stoneware crock, a salt cellar, and a few apples in a wooden bowl. The woman turned. Her body was blocky but not fat. Her hair, visible around the edges of her cap, was dark but lightly streaked with gray. Her eyes were mahogany brown like her skin, which was dewy from standing over a fire. "Can I help you?' Her voice was low and pleasant, although her expression was wary.

Butler said. "I am a guest of Mistress White, Jeremy Butler. I came in with her sister. I was hoping for something to eat, if you don't mind." He smiled at her to try to show he wasn't a threat. "I assume you are Mistress White's?"

The woman nodded, "I'm Suzanna. I've worked for Mistress White for five years now since I received my manumission. I am a free woman." There was banked fire in her eyes as she told him, warning him that he had misspoken.

He nodded, realizing people probably assumed she was enslaved and treated her accordingly. "I hope one day all people will be free," he said gently. "I didn't mean to imply you were anything other than a cook for this household. I'm sorry if it sounded otherwise."

"Is everything all right, Suzanna?" Hannah stepped into the kitchen and moved to stand beside her cook.

Suzanna looked at the other woman. "Yes, ma'am. He just wanted a bite to eat."

White nodded. "It is about dinner time for all of us. I've closed the shop so we can sup in peace. She looked at Butler as Suzanna set bowls and plates on the table. "There are no slaves in this house. I hire free people, both white and black. My late husband was a fierce opponent of slavery. He purchased both Suzanna and her husband Richard and burned the ownership papers once he manumitted them." Her face saddened for a moment. "I'm just sorry that Richard got to enjoy so little of his freedom before he passed. I had hoped he and Suzanna would have more time together. At least he passed peacefully in his sleep, knowing he was free."

Butler listened as she spoke. He liked the sound of her voice, although he found the thees and thous of Quakers a bit jarring at first. Hannah White's low alto soothed him in ways he did not understand. He also liked the way she met his gaze with none of the shyness or submissiveness of many of the young women in society.

Suzanna paused to set down an earthenware plate containing a pair of yeasty rolls steaming from the fireplace before turning back to tend the fire.

"Do you always eat down here?" Butler asked, taking in the simple setting near the fire. He didn't mind, but he was mildly surprised that Hannah apparently had no formal dining area.

Hannah flushed but returned his gaze evenly. "I run a business out of my home, which means space is limited. We eat down here, as does my staff since the main floor is for our customers."

"I meant no offense," Butler said. "It just seemed unusual."

Hannah nodded. "I gave up many things when my husband passed. I quit worrying about what Philadelphia thought of me when no one spoke up when my husband's family cast me out." She looked about her. "No one will have that power over me again." She took in a deep breath and then took a deep drink of ale, coughing at the end.

Butler didn't say anything, although he understood what she meant. A married woman had no voice of her own and was utterly dependent on her husband. During his own short marriage, he had always allowed Jean to have a voice in their decisions. He looked over at Hannah. He imagined a smile would transform her face. She wasn't classically beautiful, but her face was full of intelligence and vitality, which he found more attractive. Butler brushed the troubling thought aside. What he was offered too much risk to anyone close to him, which was why he kept his distance from his sister, who lived near the frontier.

They focused on eating the meal Suzanna provided. Afterward, Butler rose and thanked her. "I may not be back until late," he said. "I have business to attend in town."

Hannah met his gaze. "Benjamin Franklin is well known here. Be careful of the company thou keeps; everyone's eyes are on the revolutionaries, particularly that group who meet at the state house."

Butler frowned. "Can you think of anyone who might mean them harm?"

Hannah laughed sharply. "You ask that in a town peopled with as many Tories as Patriots?" She paused. "Were it me, I would start with Franklin's son. That relationship has grown as bitter as the colonies with Great Britain."

"Franklin's son?"

Hannah met his gaze. "For a man involved with revolutionaries, you don't seem to know many of them well. Benjamin Franklin has an illegitimate son, William, who is currently the royal governor of the New Jersey Colony. He has a wife in Perth Amboy and was rumored to have a mistress here. He and his father were once close, but that changed when the elder Franklin chose to support the patriot cause."

Butler looked at her. "You know the Franklin family. What can you tell me about them?"

Hannah paused to gather her thoughts. "The question is, what do you want to know?"

Chapter Six

F aith listened to the chickens cluck as they followed her, eating the feed she spread on the ground. She enjoyed the early morning quiet before everyone in the house had stirred. Although she knew her father and older brother were up tending the stock, other family members remained in bed for a few more precious hours. Once everyone rose, people would fill every available space. She had forgotten the feeling of living in a house filled with family, most of whom had questions about her life in Virginia. While she appreciated the welcome, a few moments alone were a blessing. She missed the rhythms of her tavern in Williamsburg, where she made her own choices without real or imagined criticism. She missed Andrew terribly. Leaving her nearly twelve-year-old son had been painful, but necessary. He was only just starting his studies at the College of William and Mary, and she didn't want to interrupt. Ezra's will had paid for his education, and she was not going to waste it. She also saw little benefit in him risking the journey over the rough roads to Pennsylvania. At least in Williamsburg, she knew he was safe. His grandmother would make sure of that.

Her thoughts drifted back home to where Olivia would be feeding Titus and Seth, along with the boys and the other staff that joined them. From there, Seth and Titus would go out to tend the animals while the boys checked the garden for vegetables and helped the women serve breakfast in the tavern.

Here, she felt less certain of herself. Rather than a woman of business, she was another daughter of Isaac Payne, loved but without stature or the ability to make decisions unless her father wanted her to help at the family market stall.

Henry, the large white rooster, chose that moment to crow, letting everyone within hearing distance know that he was master of his domain. Faith snorted, "Conceited animal." Inside, she knew her sister Charity and sister-in-law Bess would be out in the kitchen preparing breakfast for the family. Bess's stomach was queasy some mornings, so Faith volunteered to handle the chickens and gather food from the garden. Charity, her remaining unmarried sister, would take over assisting the cook if Bess felt unwell. They all took turns tending to their mother.

Patience had still been asleep when Faith looked in on her before heading outside. She hadn't recovered from the shock of seeing the shrunken form in the makeshift sick room downstairs. The Patience Payne of her memories had been full of restless energy, never sitting still for long. To see her like this grieved her, although she didn't miss the criticisms that sprang from her mother's mouth without warning. She did miss watching her mother's needle flash as she made and mended clothes or hearing her talk to her chickens as if they were friends. Her mother could be either loving or cruel at a moment's notice, especially with her daughters. Faith had never known what to expect. In the end, her marriage and subsequent move to another colony had been a blessing. She had been content until a letter arrived and pleaded for her return so her mother could make peace before she died. Even now, she wondered at the wisdom of that decision.

Faith had sat with her the previous evening. Patience slept for a time before opening her eyes and staring at her middle child. "I see thou hast returned."

Faith nodded and then spoke since she wasn't sure how well Patience could see her. "I heard you were ill and came for a visit."

"You can rejoin meetings with the family."

"The Meeting disowned me after I married Jon." That had stung, but the elders had strong beliefs about not wedding outside the faith. She had made her peace with it.

Patience's smile was lopsided. "Not any longer. Thou can return home to

50

your kindred."

Faith shook her head. "No. My home is in Williamsburg. I will return there in a few weeks. I have a business to run."

Patience reached out a hand, which Faith took. It was clammy and cold. "Come home. Thee belongs here where thy family can look after thee."

Faith put her hand on top of the coverlet. "My home is in Virginia."

Patience struggled to sit up. Faith fluffed her pillows. "It's late," she crooned. "You need your rest."

Patience grabbed her arm. Her bony hands gripped for a few seconds before she released her and lay back on the bed. "All the children need to be home," she whispered. "Noah, Hannah, Abel, Jacob, Caleb, Faith, Hope, and Charity need to come home."

"Hope, Jacob, and Abel have never left us," Faith said gently. She could barely remember them; she had been quite young when Jacob had drowned swimming in a rain-swollen pond. Hope had passed a few years later of a sudden fever. Faith could remember that her hair had been quite fair. It had gleamed golden in the sun. Abel's life had been brief. Now, they all lay in the cemetery next to older generations of Paynes and Beesons.

"Some left and never returned," her mother said, sniffling as tears leaked down her cheek. Patience wiped the tears away.

"We are here for you now," she said. Turning to the table next to them, Faith picked up a taper and lit it from the small fire that was always kept going to warm the frequently chilled patient. As it glowed to life, the shadows closest to the bed faded, allowing Faith to pick up the leather-bound Bible that rested nearby. "Let me read to you." She shuffled through the pages until she came to the passage she knew her mother loved best. "The Lord is my Shepherd, I shall not want...."

Afterwards, Faith couldn't sleep, tossing and turning until Charity, who was sharing the bed, suggested she get a glass of wine to help settle her mind. But no beverage could settle the restless thoughts coursing through her mind.

Living in the house with Patience Payne had been a series of ups and downs. As a child, she had never known what would greet her when she clambered down from the loft for breakfast. Every day, there were chores. Some days, her mother sang as she stirred the fire and set bowls of steaming corn mush before them, before pouring tea or cider for them to drink. Other days, they hurried through the meal to escape the dark silence that surrounded her, hoping to escape before it erupted in temper or tears.

The rustling of feathers brought her mind back to her task. Faith laughed as she watched the birds chatter as they gathered their food. Some of the ladies were trailed by chicks that scurried to stay under their mother's secure wings. She added water to a pan kept nearby for them to drink from. As the chickens ate, she slipped inside their house to check for eggs. As the weather warmed, the hens were less broody and produced fewer eggs. Her father had built the hen house in order to catch shade from the nearby trees to alleviate some of the summer heat. Even now, in late Jane, it was warm where the nests were but not stifling. Faith felt fortunate that she found close to a dozen before she emerged. She took them to the outdoor kitchen where Charity would be cooking, assisted by Frieda and Albert, the older German couple who had come over as indentured servants and stayed on as paid staff.

Frieda hummed as she fried side meat in an iron skillet over a metal spider on the edge of the fire. Grease popped out of the pan and into the fireplace, flaming briefly before it burned out. Her pale face was flushed rosy pink from being close to the fire. "Guten Morgen, Faith," she called out. "Wie Geht's?"

Faith smiled. "I am well, thank you. How are you?" She set down her basket of eggs. "The hens were generous; I've brought eggs."

"Gutt," Frieda moved the pan off the fire. "I can use those. Come, help me take this inside." She gestured to a pan of biscuits, steam rising off them.

Faith's mouth watered as she watched her pile sausages on a platter, joining the bread. She picked up the pan, just barely resisting the temptation to pop one in her mouth.

Frieda laughed. "Go, child, take this to the table. I will be in with the mush in a moment. Your Da is waiting for his breakfast along with your brothers and sisters."

Faith took the bread and sausages and headed in. Already, she was falling back into the rhythm of her childhood, missing only her mother at the table serving mush from the big pot. As she came in, she spotted her siblings gathered around. She knew her father and brothers had already fed the animals and milked the cows that spent the night in the huge barn.

Charity took charge of serving the mush that Frieda brought in, ladling it into sturdy wooden bowls that her father had carved during one of the many long winters one could count on in Pennsylvania. There was plenty of joking back and forth until her father motioned for silence. Bowing their heads, they offered a brief silent grace before eating.

Faith took the chair Caleb pulled out for her. "How's Bess this morning?" she asked, noting her sister-in-law had not joined them.

"Resting," he replied. "The baby is restless at night, so she sleeps little. I was hoping one of you would look in on Ma this morning."

Charity answered. "She was still resting when I looked in on her. I will take her breakfast and see if the linens need changing."

"I will help," Faith said. She didn't look forward to it, but some tasks needed doing. Her father ate in stoic silence, although Faith knew he had heard every word. The only time he visited his wife was in the evenings when he would come in and play on the old fiddle that he had owned for as long as Faith could remember. Its sweet melody could still move her to tears.

Once breakfast was done, the family scattered to their various responsibilities. She helped clear the table while Charity took a tray to their mother. Although the table was clear and the room tidy, Faith still hesitated. Seeing her mother brought back feelings she didn't want to deal with. Last night, her mother had tossed and turned, muttering under her breath as her dreams tormented her. She could understand why Hannah was taking a reprieve in Philadelphia. She had spent the previous month here.

The sound of voices from the downstairs bedroom warned Faith that her mother was awake. She hurried to lend assistance to her youngest sister. As she approached, she heard her sister's voice softly coaxing. "Try a little of Frieda's good porridge. It will build up your strength."

"Needs more sugar," Patience said. "More sugar." The older woman sat up in bed, feeding herself with a spoon.

Charity replied. "There are three lumps already in it. You always told us two was more than enough for one bowl."

Patience huffed, but continued eating. The left side of her face drooped, causing her to dribble as she ate. Charity wiped her mouth with a cloth napkin she kept at the ready.

Faith was pleasantly surprised to see that her mother was wearing a fresh shift and her hair had been combed and arranged under a clean mob cap.

Charity answered the unspoken question. "Arabella and Rachel took care of her needs a little bit ago. She responds better to them than anyone else."

Faith nodded, unsurprised. The mother-daughter team had helped manage the household for years. They knew how to handle her mother.

"That was good of them. I can sit with her if you would like."

Charity set down the bowl and helped their mother sip some cider from a tankard. Patience coughed before continuing to drink. "I could use the time to sort through fleeces from this spring's shearing," she acknowledged. "I'm behind on my spinning, and there are a large number to sort through since Da sheared a few weeks ago."

"Very well," Faith said. "I can read to her for a bit. If you want, I can help wash wool later today." She looked about for the Bible she had laid down earlier. Although her mother's reading ability was limited, she enjoyed listening to others. Faith, along with her brothers and sisters, had all taken turns reading scriptures, newspapers brought from town, and the occasional copy of Poor Richard's Almanac, which her father enjoyed. Once, he had brought home a copy of plays by a man named Shakespeare. They had enjoyed them thoroughly until Patience overheard a particularly ribald section. After that, Shakespeare was banished to the barn, where they read it in secret.

"What would you enjoy hearing today, Ma?" Faith asked.

Patience looked at her. "Thou came home."

Faith paused. "Yes, I did. I heard you were ill and came to visit for a bit."

Patience settled back on the pillows, closing her eyes. The hair outside her cap was iron gray. Faith remembered when she and Jon had left for Virginia; it had still been mostly dark brown. A lot had changed in nine years.

Patience didn't answer, but instead closed her eyes as she settled back against the pillows.

Not knowing what else to do, Faith began reading from Psalms. "The Lord is my Shepard, I shall not want." Outside, the sky rumbled softly.

Patience interrupted. "Where are the children?"

Faith paused. "Hannah is in Philadelphia, and Seth is helping with my tavern in Williamsburg. Everyone else is here. All your children are well." There was no need to mention the ones who had never left, buried in the churchyard, dying all too young. Faith could barely remember Hope, Jacob, or Abel, who had died shortly after birth. Patience remembered them all and visited them regularly.

A creak of a floorboard alerted Faith that someone was joining them. Bess stuck her head in the door. Shadows underlined her eyes. Her face had rounded along with her belly. Her voice was soft. "Good Morning. I came to see if thou needed anything."

Faith shook her head. "We are fine. Take some rest if thou needs."

Bess shook her head. "I have two other younglings to consider. There is little time for rest."

Faith rose. "Take rest if thou needs. I can watch the little ones for a while. I know that carrying a child takes a great deal of strength."

Bess smiled tiredly. "A child is a blessing always. Rachel took Samuel and Anna berry picking. They should be busy a while." She patted her belly. "This one never sleeps. I will be glad when he or she is born."

Patience said, "Not all children are a blessing. Some are born to cause grief."

Faith and Bess stared at her. The older woman shook her finger at them. "Lizzy should never have been born." She fell back into the bed, shivering as if fevered. Bess and Faith ran to the bed. As they leaned over the elderly woman, Bess whispered.

"Who is Lizzy?"

Chapter Seven

J eremy Butler watched Hannah as she shopped at the market early in the morning. The light touched her rich brown hair, revealing touches of red and gold. A few freckles dotted her nose where the sun had touched her fair skin. She had told him that Franklin's daughter Sally frequented the same market, so there was a chance they would meet. She had been amused when he asked to tag along with her.

"What would you hope to learn?" she asked as she tied on a wide-brimmed straw hat to keep off the sun. "Women go there for the freshest vegetables and fruit. There is fish when the boats have come in. You used to be able to find things from England and France as well. Furniture, fabrics, silver tea sets, one never knows what will be there."

Butler smiled as he carried her large basket down Fourth Street toward High or Market Street. "Why do you do this and not Suzanna?"

Hannah looked over at him. "Her knees pain her if she goes far these days, and I enjoy getting out of the house." She shrugged. "Pa used to take me on market days to run our stall. He said I bargained better than any of my sisters. When the crops come in, I can catch up while getting some of Ma's good cheese, among other things."

As they approached the market, traffic multiplied on the street, with busy wagons going toward the main building along with city residents wheeling carts of bread and meat. Butler watched the growing throng of horses, wagons, and people. He had not known what to expect when he had set out for Philadelphia. Every day, he discovered something new. It was both intriguing and troubling. As huge as the city was, anyone could hide undetected in its many streets and alleys.

"Is it always this busy?" Butler raised his voice, trying to be heard over the crowd. He looked across the street at their destination. He had thought crowds in New York were bad. Philadelphia's streets on market day rivaled anything he'd been a part of. "Crossing is going to be difficult."

"It always is," Hannah said as she stood beside him. "That's why it is best to get here early, before it gets worse." She didn't sound concerned. Her eyes traveled back and forth as she watched the traffic going back and forth over the cobbled streets. A horse reared up, whinnying loudly its objection to a group of children shouting as they darted out in front of it. The driver pulled on the reigns as he called out, calming it before they continued.

"It gets worse?" Butler said, startled.

Hannah grinned at the look on his face. "It can, especially if a fight breaks out." She watched the street intently for a few minutes before stepping out and walking at a fast clip toward the market.

Butler took off after her, jumping to avoid a pile of fresh horse dung steaming in the road. He broke into a run to catch up to Hannah's zigzagging form. A horse narrowly missed the two of them as they darted to the other side.

"Are you mad?" He asked. "You could have been trampled to death."

Hannah shrugged. "There is no easy way to cross High Street on market days; you have to watch and go as fast as you can," she answered. "It's always been this way."

"Will any of your family be here today?" Butler asked. He wondered how Faith was doing. He had had no idea how big her family was until Hannah had explained that there were seven children living and three who had died for various reasons as babes or young children. He found Hannah a useful source of information on the town and on the Franklins, with whom she did some business and had some social connections with Franklin's daughter.

Hannah looked thoughtful. "My oldest brother Noah and his wife often bring eggs and butter in. They live closer than my father. It's too early for wheat. We've all tended the stall at one time or another."

"What about your mother?" He offered a hand to help her over a rough section of the walkway. He was surprised at the muscle under the cotton sleeves of her dress.

"Ma didn't like to leave home," Hannah said, pulling her arm away from his hand. She picked up the pace, making it difficult to converse much. Their shoes crunched on gravel that filled in spaces between the stones that lined the streets downtown. She paused to look over the street. "Welcome to the market."

Butler's eyes surveyed a huge, rough brick structure that covered nearly two blocks. A gabled roof covered the enormous structure, which featured arched brick columns that allowed people to enter inside via stone walkways. He gave a low whistle of appreciation. "Commerce must be thriving."

Hannah smiled. "Indeed it is. You can find most anything inside. I'm going to see what fish is available." Relieving him of the basket, she took off down one aisle, intent on her prey.

"Let's hope so," he murmured as he followed her inside. After the bright morning light, the shadows within the building took a moment to adjust to. Butler was surprised at the enormity of the place. Within the cavernous building were stalls selling just about anything one could want. With the right connections, it could also be a treasure chest of information. Butler hesitated briefly before abandoning Hannah to her shopping and going off to explore the strange new realm he had just entered.

His nose tickled with the scent of spices and cured meat, along with the yeasty aroma of bread. The meat stall held an array of sausages and meats. Flies buzzed around some of the more bloody offerings. His nose wrinkled at the coppery scent of blood and entrails, although he was no stranger to them. Butler hurried past the arrays of fruits and vegetables, the bright colors of squash, beans, and apples arranged to catch the eyes of passersby. He murmured his apologies as he cut through the throng of housewives and ladies' cooks gathered around to bargain. Many had baskets already partially filled with what they had gotten at other stalls. In one corner, he spotted kegs where an enterprising gentleman sold steins of beer. Butler bought one, paying with a few English coins he had. The man smiled when he saw them. "I much prefer these to continentals. One never knows when

the value of colonial money will change, and I still need to feed my family."
Butler nodded. Patriot he was, but colonial money wasn't really worth
much, which was why he traded it away whenever he could.

Back behind the stacked barrels, an informal ring had been set up for
fights. Two men stripped to the waist circled each other while those on
the side shouted and laid bets on the winner. Among the throng of men
was a sprinkling of women shouting and cursing with the rest. However,
some looked like basic working-class women joining their men, and a few
of them were dressed for another profession entirely. He wondered if they
were early risers or spending coin gained from the previous night's work.
Butler knew better than to push deep into the crowd. He could already spot
a few pickpockets slithering in and out, profiting from those fixated on the
spectacle. Instead, he grabbed a pint of ale, went over to a pile of crates, and
hopped on top of one in order to see over the crowd.

The two men circled each other warily. One looked like he participated
frequently. He was big and bald, with a hairy chest covered with muscle.
His nose had clearly been broken and healed crooked. From the tattoos on
his arms and the canvas breeches held up with a piece of rope, Butler made
him for a sailor in between jobs.

The other man was lean and ropy, with a trim beard and dark, coarse
hair tied back. His dark, clever eyes warned that there was more to him
than an idle brawler. Butler recognized him immediately, although it had
been a few years. Clay Maynard had been a guide in the French and Indian
conflict, where a teenage Butler had come along with the man he had owed
an indenture. It had been his first experience in the wilderness, and Maynard
had been one of his few friends.

He frowned. The Maynard he knew avoided this kind of spectacle and
big cities. What had brought him here? Whatever the reason, his attitude
was all business. A cloth tied about his brows kept the sweat out of his eyes
as he watched his opponent. Both were already slick with sweat. The big
man rushed forward, trying to land a punch on Maynard, who danced away
just in time.

"Quit running away, you dirty Indian lover," he snarled as he stopped short of barreling into the crowd.

Maynard grinned, exposing crooked white teeth. "The natives have a reason for what they do, unlike so many of those who have come here. Perhaps your problem, Fletcher, isn't them, but that they won't tolerate your bullying."

The other man grunted as he closed in. Clay got in a quick jab before the other man's ham-sized fist struck a rib, causing him to stagger back. Fletcher raised an arm high toward Maynard's face. As he turned, Maynard ducked under to kidney punch him. The big man fell back.

Both were breathing hard. Their feet stirred up dust from the floorboards of the market, making everyone's eyes sting. Butler swatted at a fly that insisted on bedeviling him and missed seeing a solid blow. He looked up to see the big man start to fold as the air left his lungs. Maynard followed up with a sharp tap to the jaw, and the man plopped on the floor, sitting half-folded over.

Maynard stood back and waited, blood streaming down from his nose. "Are we done now?" he asked. "I came to trade, not fight. My wife and I have prime deer skins that I tanned over the winter for any who will deal with us fairly." He turned to walk out. Maynard paused before staring at the man on the ground. "Treat my wife with respect from now on." He continued walking as the blood ran down into his beard. A roar came from the other man's friends.

"Maybe we're not done with you, backwoodsman," one snarled, leaping forward. "Maybe we will take your skins as payment for all the trouble you and your native friends have been stirring up."

"Maybe you will all go home and sober up before the sheriff decides you are causing too much trouble," Butler said loudly over the din. He had been moving forward and hopped into the ring, a barrel stave in his hand. "This is the city market. We all have business here. What say we go about it peacefully?" He kept his tone light, but everyone saw the stave and knew he meant business. He saw someone pull the loudmouth aside as the crowd parted to let Maynard and him out of the ring.

A man handed Maynard a rag, which he used to mop the blood off his face and added some pressure to his nose.

"You look like you could use a drink," Butler said, handing him a tankard. Maynard drained it before donning his shirt. "The woman I'm staying with is good with injuries."

"Thanks," Maynard said. "I need to get back to Rebecca and our stall. She'll take care of me." His dark eyes slid over to Butler. "It's been a few years since I've seen you, Irishman. I'll be in town trading for a bit if you want to catch up. You can contact me through the Man Full of Troubles Tavern down near the Delaware. They serve an excellent home-brewed beer, if you would like to share a pint."

Butler raised an eyebrow. "Interesting name."

Maynard smiled. "It's an interesting place. Are you in town long?"

"Long enough to complete my business," Butler said as he walked with him out of the belly of the market and toward the outside walls. Maynard made his way with ease, obviously familiar with the huge and crowded space.

He stopped at a stall just inside one of the brick archways. A native woman stood behind the table that displayed furs and hides, all beautifully tanned and preserved. Maynard's face lightened when he saw her. "This is Rebecca, my wife."

She went over to him, exclaiming over his nose as she grabbed a cloth and a bottle of liquid before pulling him to the side.

"She doesn't want me to drip on our stock," Maynard laughed.

Butler nodded. "Shall I keep an eye on things while she tends to you?" He stood by the table where a handful of men examined the skins.

"If you wouldn't mind, I'll be there in a minute." He said over his shoulder as Rebecca continued to fuss as she tended to him. Her native tongue flowed out with the liquid cadence of water flowing down a stream.

Butler smiled. He didn't think Maynard minded the attention. He seemed rather happy. He turned his back to give the couple some privacy and began looking over the wares he was tasked with managing. It had been a few years since he'd trapped hides and tanned them. After fever had taken Jean and the babe away, he had left civilization as if the devil pursued him. He had gone as far away as he could. On the frontier, no one asked too many questions. He could shoot, and his surveying skills made him an excellent choice for creating maps of the lands they traveled. He'd stayed gone for five years. In truth, he probably would never have returned if not for an encounter with Washington on a trip to Virginia to trade his share of the winter's hides and furs. Washington had admired his maps and offered him a job surveying wilderness tracts until the British closed the lands over the mountains.

Washington's respect for Butler's ability to gather information and his understanding of his need to stay moving led to his going north to meet with Samuel Adams and the Sons of Liberty. Greased by the money of affluent patriots like Hancock, Butler became a traveling informant on British movements and investments in the colonies.

Maynard returned to the table, looking far more presentable, although bruises had already started to bloom on his face. Like any true businessman, he checked his table. He looked over at his wife, "Did we sell all the beaver pelts?"

Rebecca nodded. The sun hit her hair, turning it a rich dark brown. Her skin was tanned to the shade of a pecan. Her dark eyes went back and forth between the two men before she spoke to Butler, "You are his friend?"

Butler nodded. "Yes, I knew your husband many years ago, during the great war with the French."

Her eyes got big. She turned and asked Maynard a question in her native tongue. He replied gently before turning back to Butler.

"She wanted to know what you did. Her father's people fought with us. Iroquois," he qualified. "Her father isn't too pleased with the English right now. He sees too many white men coming into their lands. They promised otherwise."

Butler snorted. "I think a good many have learned to beware of the king's promises."

Maynard was quiet for a moment. "That's not a wise sentiment to express in such a public venue, old friend."

Butler dropped his voice. "We live in dangerous times. The British have little tolerance for dissent, which is probably why so many are discussing independence."

Maynard's reply was succinct. "I stay out of government bickering. The poor man is always the one who gets hurt, no matter what side you're on. I'm in town to trade, and then we are heading home to my wife's people."

Butler nodded. "I respect that, but if you could help me learn this town, I would appreciate it. The people I work for would be happy to pay for your time. I'm a stranger here, and it's hard to tell who's a friend and who's an enemy."

Maynard sighed. "Come by tonight and join us for supper. We can talk then." He shook his head. "You haven't learned a thing in fifteen years, have you?"

Butler looked back over at him as he turned to make his way back inside. "I haven't forgotten how to duck."

Chapter Eight

Faith sat outside, stringing green beans. A stack of them rested in her apron, waiting for her attention. A bowl held the ones she had finished on one side, while a pail held the small mound of strings, ends, and spoiled pieces that would go in the feed for the pigs. Her eyes swept the fields, looking for any sign that her father was returning home. Isaac Payne had done an excellent job of avoiding his middle girl ever since she had started trying to ask questions. After a survey of the big barn and the pastures had not revealed his presence, she knew he had gone hunting just as he had when she was younger, and he'd wanted to escape his wife's nagging.

Before she reached adolescence, he had taken her with him from time to time. She remembered fishing in the cold streams and listening to his stories as he carefully checked his snares for the many rabbits who liked to raid Patience's garden. He was the one who had taken her to watch owls flying in the night sky near where he knew they nested. In the past, he could disappear for days at a time. Faith was betting he would not stray far, not with his wife's health in serious decline. As it was, there was plenty to keep her busy, much of it that could be done where she could keep her eyes on the trail her father most often used to head out into the forest.

After spending a few hours mending socks and shirts and other clothing, she had taken the beans to shell. Faith preferred working with fruits and vegetables rather than salting or smoking meat, although she did her share of that. She didn't like the heavy smell of animal, or dealing with the fat and hide.

She fell into an easy rhythm, shelling and trimming the beans. They made a steady tap as they hit the bowl. Out in the corral, a horse stood switching its tail to keep the flies away as it stood in the shade of a tree that overhung the fence. A breeze caused the leaves to flutter and brought the scent of pine from the woods. Faith inhaled deeply, enjoying the scent of the forest. Nearby squirrels chittered in the grove of oaks as they gathered acorns. She'd learned not to go too near to avoid having nuts lobbed at her head. It was the sudden silence that made her look up.

Isaac Payne walked with the ease of a much younger man as he emerged from the darkness of the trees and into the dappled sunlight of the meadow that surrounded his home. His long stride slowed as he approached the house. The brim of his hat cast his face in shadow, making his expression unreadable. He carried a brace of rabbits, their back legs tied with rope that hung from his pack. His long rifle was slung across his back with a strap. He dressed more like a frontiersman than a traditional Quaker farmer. He wore a long homespun shirt with leather leggings over his breeches and boots.

"I see your hunt was successful," Faith said as she continued working on the beans.

He nodded. "I best take these to Frieda." He started around to the kitchen before Faith rose.

"I'll walk with you. I've just finished getting these ready." Faith wrapped her arms around the large wooden bowl and joined him on the dirt path worn in the grass. Her father said nothing as they walked together, pausing briefly to let a black snake get out of their way as it undulated through the tall grass. As they turned the corner of the large farmhouse, Faith looked at the modest-sized kitchen. A faint haze of smoke rose from the chimney of the fireplace where many dishes would be cooking. It took skill to manage the fire to keep food from burning or being underdone, all in a room that was bursting with relentless heat in the summer.

Frieda stepped out to drink a dipper of water from the oak bucket that rested on a bench outside the door. Her eyes rested on the game Isaac Payne had caught. "Those will cook up nicely. Are they dressed?"

Faith's father spoke. "I field dressed them. Give me a moment, and I will cut them up for you. He went to the overhang to the side of the kitchen, where the packed dirt would catch the blood, and he could do his work without disturbing the women cooking.

Faith handed her the bowl. "Is there anything else you need, Frieda?"

The older woman shook her head. "Nein. All is good. I will fry the rabbits in some fat for dinner. They will pair well with a little bread stuffing I've been working on."

Faith nodded and let her talk. Frieda didn't need much encouragement. Soon, Faith was learning about her nieces and nephews, the price of fresh fish, and the baby ducklings in the pond nearby. By the time her father returned, she had learned a great deal about what went on at the Payne farm.

After handing over the fully dressed meat, her father went to the well, pulled up a bucket of water, and used it to rinse the blood off his hands. Once they were clean, he splashed more on his face before cleaning the long knife he always kept with him. Once it was clean, he patted the steel dry before placing it back in its sheath.

Faith waited until he was done. "Mama continues to ask about Lizzy."

Her father's face remained expressionless. He said nothing as he turned to walk away.

Faith caught his arm. "Who is she talking about, Pa?"

Unable to move forward without removing her hand, he spoke. "Your mother's mind wanders these days. "It's hard to say where or what she is thinking about. It has no basis in our lives now."

"She seems like a real person to Ma," Faith looked at him. "Surely it would be a kindness to find this person for Ma so she would quit fretting."

"Lizzy is dead. Don't upset thine mother by bringing up what will only cause grief." He strode off in the direction of the barn. "I have work to do, as do you. There is not time for any of us to waste time with talk."

Faith watched him leave, her brain trying to sort out what he had said. It was a few minutes before she heard Frieda calling her name. She turned to see Frieda looking at her with a concerned expression.

"What is it?"

Frieda paused to wipe her hands on her brightly printed apron. "I heard what you say to him. I know this family a long time. Long ago, I worked as an indentured servant to your mother's family, the Beesons. I knew your mama before she married your father when she was a girl."

Faith nodded. "I'm sure you know many stories about her childhood, but Ma hasn't been a little girl for nearly forty years." She turned to go to the house.

Frieda spoke behind her. "I know who Lizzy is."

Faith spun around so swiftly, it took her skirts a few seconds to catch up. She looked at the troubled gaze of the other woman. Frieda, she realized, probably knew more than anyone about the family. She had always been present through the births of children, deaths, and sickness. In Faith's memory, she had always been at the Payne farm, cooking and caring for them. She'd never stopped to think about where she came from.

Faith sat down on the bench just outside the kitchen and gestured for Frieda to join her. "Tell me about her."

Frieda sat and stared out at the garden where cucumber vines trailed up a trellis to bloom and squash were already putting out fruit. A deep sigh left her body. "Your mother was a very pretty girl. She was the only girl in a family of boys. Her father doted on her. She had long dark curls and those eyes the deep blue of a mountain lake. Lots of boys came around that summer when she was sixteen. I was three years older, so I accompanied her to many places, such as picnics and church suppers. The boys flocked about like bees to honey, and she reveled in it." Her parents planned for her to marry well. The dairy farm was successful, and they thought she could marry someone with connections."

Frieda snorted. "That one was spoiled. When a child has been given her way all her life, she's not going to take orders well. Patience locked herself in her room and refused to come down to meet the man they had chosen, but her father put his foot down. He sent her to Philadelphia to stay with his older sister and her family. They were strict. I went with her, but they put me in the kitchen with the servants. It's where I began as a cook. I learned a lot of things there. It was the first time I could be with young people like myself and not be responsible for another." She smiled wistfully. "There are many Dutch and Germans in Philadelphia. I met my Albert there. He had come over indentured like me, but earlier. He had completed his time and worked odd jobs in town." She paused to take a drink before continuing.

"Your mama was both pretty and used to getting her way. Her aunt and uncle had raised their girls as good Quakers years before. They expected her to follow the rules of the house, but they were older and did not realize until too late that all was not as it should be." She shook her head. "There are too many places to get into trouble in a big city. It is little wonder she came to be with child."

Faith's heart sounded loud in her ears. She could not speak as her carefully constructed picture of her mother fell into dust. "My mother became pregnant before she wed my father."

Frieda nodded. "She was sent home before the knowledge became public. Since I came with her, I was sent home too. I still had a year of indenture left, so I had no choice in the matter."

"What happened?"

Frieda paused. "Albert came here looking for me. He worked for them that year and tried to negotiate with your grandparents to release me. They believed in getting their money's worth. They sent her away. When she came back the following spring, there was no child. Your mother said she was gone."

"She died."

"That is what I assumed. By that time, Albert had come back. He had gone into the wilderness for a few years with a group of men, one of whom was your father. My indenture was complete, so we married and traveled around a bit until your father offered us both a place to work with him on this land."

"My father knew?"

"He didn't care. Your grandparents were delighted and deeded him this farm upon their marriage."

Faith tried to wrap her head around what she had heard. "How did she die?"

"I do not know. I left when I married, and when we joined your father and mother here, Lizzy was gone. I assumed she died. Many children die." Frieda rose. "I must get back to work. That rabbit will not fry itself. You need to leave the past be. Your Ma has lived a gut life. She has many children and grandchildren. Remind her of that."

Faith walked back toward the house. The air was sweet with the scent of lavender from her mother's garden. She wondered who tended it now. Turning aside, she went to the orderly arrangement of shrubs and plants. Rosemary had grown to bush height, its pine-like limbs lightly sprinkled with pale blue flowers. She reached down and rubbed a few leaves between her fingers before bringing her hand to her nose to inhale the fresh evergreen scent. More than any other place, the formal garden bore Patience Payne's imprint. Her father had created it for her when they had come to this place before children came to run through the house and field. Faith remembered her mother pointing out different flowers and herbs and keeping her chubby small hands from pulling the wrong thing.

Weeds were already beginning to encroach on her mother's beloved space. No one had taken time to tend it much, and it stood neglected in the summer sun. Standing amidst the neglect was more than she could bear. Off to one side, not far from the necessary, was a small shed that served as a keeping place for various small tools. Faith walked over and stepped inside. Dust motes danced through the cracks in the boards lit up by the morning sunshine. An old straw hat hung on a peg just inside the door. Neatly arranged down the wall were various tools used in the garden. In the midst of the solidly packed dirt floor was a bench. She remembered her father sitting there to sharpen a blade on a scythe or other tool as needed. Baskets for gathering fruits and vegetables were stacked in a corner, waiting to be put to use. Although she was sure her brothers and sisters had come in here from time to time, there was stillness in the air she was keenly aware of, as if the building was waiting for someone to appear. Someone she knew never would.

Faith took a deep breath to clear her head before grabbing a hoe and slapping the large straw hat on her own head before returning to the garden to work. Within a space of minutes, she was huffing as she strained to eradicate some of the weeds that had grown up in what had been carefully tended beds. She stood up, stretching her aching back to consider the best way to manage the task before her. Taking her hoe, Faith tackled the main pathway, annihilating weeds with all the pent-up rage that could not be released any other way. Weeds fell by the wayside, and she hacked them with abandon. "Die," she snarled as she hacked at a thistle that reared its ugly head at the corner of her mother's lamb's ears. It toppled. Using a corner of her apron, she picked it up to toss it out of the way and gasped as the spines penetrated through the fabric and drew blood from her palm. Flinging the weed far away, she brought her hand up to see if any spines remained. She wiped it on her apron and looked at her work.

"She will appreciate thy effort."

Faith startled and straightened up at the unfamiliar voice. Turning slowly, she squinted in the bright light and looked over to see her Aunt Deborah standing just inside the garden. She nodded. "Ma loved this place. It seems a shame to let it fall apart while she cannot tend it."

Deborah nodded. Her simple brown dress shimmered slightly as sunlight caught the silk threads in the fabric. Married to Faith's oldest uncle, Samuel, she had been a regular presence in Faith's childhood. Her uncle raised many sheep and had done well in the wool trade. It was reflected in their fine house not far from the Schuylkill River and the subtle opulence of their clothes and carriage. Although Faith knew she had to be nearly sixty, her face was relatively unlined underneath her white cap, although her dark hair was now liberally streaked with gray. Her face took on a concerned expression. "Thou art flushed Faith. Perhaps it would behoove thee to come in and join us for refreshment. I will ask for a basin to be brought to thine room."

Faith looked over her mother's garden. She had barely touched the surface of what needed doing.

"Come in, Faith," her aunt said. "I will send one of my servants to tend it tomorrow."

70

Heat shimmered down the rows. The scent of basil and dill perfumed the air. Her father's hives liked to forage in the garden, finding food from the blossoms of various plants.

A faint rumble stirred the air to the west as it stirred a breeze. A storm would arrive before evening, watering the plants and providing a break from the heat.

Faith walked slowly back to the shed, carefully putting the hoe back in place and returning her mother's old straw hat to its peg inside the door. Upstairs in the loft room she shared with Charity, a basin of water and clean clothes waited for her. She stripped down to her shift and used the cloth to wipe the sweat off her face, arms, and chest. Her sister popped her head up a moment later. "Aunt Deborah said thou were here. She suggested I find thee a clean shift and bodice before tea."

Faith met her eyes. "Isn't she full of helpful suggestions?"

Charity bent over her clothes chest. "Some things never change. You can borrow my second oldest shift; it should fit you well enough, and I have a bodice as well we can pin over it. We can let Frieda's daughter take your things down to be washed later, and you can join us for tea."

"Tea?" Faith raised an eyebrow. "We have tea in the house?"

Charity frowned. "No, it causes too much trouble. We dry and brew peppermint, which grows in abundance here. Sometimes Pa or Caleb bring coffee from Philadelphia, but we save that for breakfast."

Faith nodded as she listened to her sister's chatter. Her head was beginning to throb. She let her pin the bodice and followed her down the narrow curving steps to the main floor of the Payne farm. Her aunt sat in a tall, upholstered chair by the teapot. Peppermint permeated the air in a steamy ring that wafted from the pewter tea service that she must have requested Frieda to bring out. An oval pewter plate contained small cakes, cookies, and scones dotted with currants. Despite the attractive spread, Faith felt queasy.

Bess said on a cushioned settee, nibbling on a scone, her apron curved over her rounded belly. Already, the morning heat had caused her porcelain skin to flush. Faith sat next to her and took the cup that her aunt handed to her with murmured thanks. She halfway listened to the talk of ribbons and fashion and needlework while sipping her tea. She nodded at the appropriate places even though she was bored. Her mind drifted to her tavern and what she would normally be doing at this time. She missed the flow of work as well as the discussions regarding the break with England. There was no marking time with idle chat.

Her thoughts went to the subject they all avoided. "Has the doctor said anything about how Ma is doing?"

All chatter ceased as the other women stared at her. Her aunt set down her cup with a faint click on the tray. "Tea is not the place for unpleasant topics. The doctor has not offered any hope for some time. We pray for the grace of God and for his mercy because that is all we can do."

Faith looked at the other women there. "In other words, we're waiting for her to die."

Bess drew in a breath that sounded like a sob. "I keep hoping something will change, but nothing has. No one can get her to eat more than a few spoons, and her mind roams. I pray God will grant her peace."

A fly buzzed into the room, landing on the food that was no longer wanted. Faith set down her cooling tea, unable to swallow for the tightness in her throat. She had known from the moment she received the letter that there was little hope for recovery, but a stubborn part of her soul didn't want to admit it. Her mother had been her adversary, her guide, and a person whose love she had never doubted. She couldn't imagine her being gone, but she was dying day by day. They all knew it. All that was left was keeping her as comfortable as possible until the body ceased to function.

Faith looked over at the silent group. "Has anyone talked to her about Lizzy?"

Her aunt stood up, so suddenly, her chair fell back, crashing into the floor. "That name will not be discussed in this house."

"Why?" Faith countered. "The memories disturb my mother. No matter what choices she made as a young girl, she needs to be comforted. God's love covers all our mistakes. My mother does not need to suffer over events that happened over thirty years ago."

Deborah stared at her. "Thou will disturb her even more by bringing this up. Let it be Faith. I beg thee, do not stir up the past. It will cause more pain than peace."

"Why?"

"I will not discuss this anymore. I will tell Frieda's daughter Nancy that we are done." Deborah walked swiftly out of the room.

Faith caught up with her in front of the immense wooden staircase in the entryway. "We've not finished talking."

Her aunt turned to face her. "There is no point in continuing it." Her voice dropped. "I had heard that you had taken to snooping and prying in Virginia, but you will not do it here."

"Ma asks about Lizzy. She frets about her."

Deborah's face turned grim. "That happened well before thine time. Thou knowest nothing about the circumstances."

"Then tell me." Faith was surprised when Deborah grabbed her by the arm and walked her over to the stairs where the tall hall clock stood.

Deborah bit her lip as she looked up at her niece. "I will speak of this once in hope thou will understand and let it lay for the sake of this family."

Faith waited. They stood close enough to the clock that she could hear the movement of its parts in its case. Her father had brought it home after an excellent harvest when she was small. It had always fascinated her.

Deborah dropped her voice. "That summer, your mother turned fifteen; she blossomed into a beautiful young lady. Patience enjoyed the company of young men. They flocked to her at meetings and whenever they saw her in the street. Your grandmother sent her to stay with Malachi for a time, but neither he nor his wife could control such a willful child.

It was around this time that your grandfather decided to build a house to reflect his wealth. He sent your grandmother to Philadelphia to buy furnishings for it and to take charge of Patience. They stayed with another Quaker family in town that spring until the summer heat sent them back to the healthier air of the country. Not long afterward, she was found to be with child."

Faith struggled to envision this story. It seemed so unlike the person she had grown up with, but explained so many things about her. "Who was the father?"

Deborah shook her head. "That I do not know. There were rumors about her and the Cadwaller boy, but his family denied it. They said he had spent most of the summer buying cattle in the Jersey colony. Your grandparents felt such shame, they kept quiet. They kept her hidden from sight. Samuel was helping with the harvest, so I came, too. We had not been married long, and I was lonely without him. She was lonely too and frightened."

"I imagine she was." Faith remembered the adjustment from being one of many children to being the mistress of her own house. When they had relocated to Williamsburg, she'd had the company of Olivia and Titus, but that had not been the same as having one's family near. Her mother had been alone, ostracized, and hidden from those who had been her friends. Faith felt an overwhelming sadness for the young girl who had suffered for her youthful error.

Within the large farmhouse, sounds of life abounded. Footsteps upstairs as beds were made and chamber pots emptied. Someone sang an old hymn softly, probably to her mother to settle her troubled mind. Downstairs, she knew her sister was busy spinning wool from the recently shorn sheep, preparing yarn for cloth to be woven or yarn for socks and other things. It was a house full of life as it had always been, long before Faith had been born and long after she returned to Williamsburg. The one thing that had nearly driven her mad after Jon's death had been the silence. There had been no guests at the tavern, no family to call, no activities to engage her thoughts as she had come to grips with her new circumstances. Without Olivia, she would have been lost. Her mother had had no one. "What happened to her?" she said at last.

"Patience was sent to stay with your father's sister until the child was born. The little girl was beautiful, but she couldn't keep her. The disgrace would have destroyed her reputation and ruined the family. It could not be allowed."

Faith took in a few deep breaths, trying to take all this information in. Nothing she had ever heard had prepared her for this knowledge. An aching sadness filled her for innocence lost and the pain that must have caused. "What happened next," she said at last.

Deborah nodded. "Her father arranged for the child to go to a couple he knew in Philadelphia. That was the last I heard of her. Patience begged him to tell her where she was, but no one would. It was as if it had never happened."

"They never told her where her child was?" Faith was incredulous. "She carried that child for nine months. Surely, she had a right to know."

Deborah shook her head. "You never knew your grandfather. He died before you were born. His reputation meant everything to him. After that incident, he couldn't forgive your mother. She didn't leave the farm until she married your father."

Outside, Faith could hear the lowing of the cattle in her father's fields as they grazed on the rich green grass. Inside the silence lay as heavy as a woolen blanket, insulating them from the others in the house. The tall clock whirred just before it chimed the hour, startling both women.

Faith stared at her aunt. "I thought the child died."

Deborah nodded grimly. "That's what the family wanted everyone to think."

Chapter Nine

Jeremy Butler paced the floor in the upstairs office Hancock liked to use. If nothing else, the man had taste, if not aplomb. The elegant room was filled with morning light from the high windows lightly draped in deep blue draperies. In one corner was a desk piled with books and papers. A table filled a large section of the room, big enough to seat a dozen men. The portrait of the original colonial governor, William Penn, stared down from its position over the marble-encased fireplace. He wondered what Penn would have thought of the current situation brewing in the colonies. His heirs stood firmly on the side of the king.

One of Hancock's staff had delivered a message that morning summoning him to a meeting. So now he waited for the man to step out of the ongoing congress below and join him upstairs. Butler could think of several things he would prefer doing rather than waiting for an entitled businessman.

A creak on the stairs told him someone was coming. From the sound of things, more than one person approached. Although it was a meeting with allies, Butler moved to the side out of sight until he assured himself no enemy approached.

Hancock entered, accompanied by one of his servants. He looked about, puzzled, before gesturing to his man to set down a tray containing a bottle of wine and two glasses. He walked over to the long table and began fussing with the tray, inspecting the glasses. A dark-skinned man broke the seal before pouring the pale gold wine and setting it in front of his master.

Hancock lifted the goblet and slowly sniffed it before eyeing the liquid in the glass. "This will do nicely, Cicero. I will not need you to attend me for a few hours. Go mail these letters and then see if the tailor has finished my suit." The man nodded and stepped out of the room. The servant bowed and left. The heels of his buckled shoes beat a rapid tattoo as he headed down and out on his master's business.

Butler emerged, deliberately making just enough noise to attract the other man's attention. Hancock jumped before recovering.

"Where did you come from?" He demanded.

Butler shrugged. "You summoned me here. I came."

"I didn't tell you to appear out of nowhere like a wretched cat." Hancock gestured him over to the table. "Come take some wine with me. I have information for you." He picked up the bottle and filled the empty glass.

Butler picked up his wine and sipped it cautiously. It was light and fruity, refreshing for the summer heat. He took a seat where he could see the door and waited for Hancock to explain himself.

"I went through Gaius' things myself, hoping to find answers. You need to see this." He pulled a small piece of much-folded paper out of his pocket and laid it on the table.

Butler unfolded it and laid it flat between them. It was a map featuring a few streets and houses as well as the name Franklin. Neat boxes indicated houses and businesses in town. At the bottom, someone had scrawled a few notes that listed activities such as meets with his cozy group of tradesmen he calls the Junto, goes home for dinner, and writes letters, favors City Tavern. "Someone's been watching Benjamin Franklin closely."

Hancock nodded grimly. "Indeed. Looking back at all the incidents that have occurred, I realized there was one common factor."

Butler answered him. "Franklin."

Hancock's dark eyes met his. "With the exception of Gaius, Franklin has been in the line of fire each time and brushed it off. So either he's aware and ignoring the danger, or he does not care."

Butler stared at the note. The paper was unremarkable. Foolscap could be purchased in any print shop, and there were many in town. He looked at the writing. The neat copperplate hand flowed in neat rows across the page. It spoke of education and learning. "I didn't realize your enslaved people could read and write. That's uncommon."

Hancock flushed. "They don't. It's not necessary for their work." He rose and walked about. "Gaius came to me five years ago as a youth. I know little about him other than he was a quick learner and could be trusted to do things quickly and well." He stood up and paced the floor. "How is it a man can work for me for a length of time, and yet I know so little about him? He never mentioned any family or connections, but then he wouldn't have. The enslaved learn early the dangers of relationships. They have no choices in where they go or what they do." He clenched his right hand into a fist, hitting it into the palm of his left. "We cannot begin to feel what it's like to lose every right, liberty, and privilege that distinguishes a free man from slave."

Hancock passed a hand over his eyes wearily. "I buried the man, but I have no family to contact for him. I don't even know if he had a sweetheart. Then there's this." He gestured to the note. "I would swear on my mother's grave that he did not compose this. My man of affairs taught him the first letter of his name. Making his mark was a laborious task. I have no idea where this came from or why he had it."

"What do you think?" Butler asked. He didn't know Franklin except by reputation. He had found him congenial and well spoken, but reticent regarding his personal feelings unless they were in print.

Hancock went back to the table and sat down. He picked up the note and spread it out flat. "Gaius ran errands for me every day, yet I have no notion of where he got this or who it was intended for. While I'm sure he understood the map, the words would have meant nothing to him." He frowned at the paper. "You need to find out who wrote this and who it was intended for." Hancock sighed. "I cannot lose another man at a convention. When Peyton Randolph died last year of apoplexy, it threw our congress into disarray for a period of days. There is too little time and too much at stake. The future of these colonies rests in our hands." He sat back and closed his eyes. Shadows underneath them indicated a lack of sleep. His shoulders slumped before he became aware and straightened his back. Being President of the Congress exacted a heavy toll. Hancock opened his eyes and fastened his gaze on the other man. "Franklin has been a godsend to this convention. Everyone listens to him. The man has a talent for bringing diverse men together and getting them to find common ground. His presence is needed."

Butler took the note and refolded it. "I need to speak with him. I also need to know Gaius' movements. I assume Franklin's downstairs with the other delegates?"

Hancock nodded. "As he has been every day. He's been working with Jefferson and Adams on a document that will explain our views to King George."

Butler snorted. "I wish him good luck with that. I've heard the arguing in that room. Herding cats would be easier."

A faint smile crossed Hancock's face. "When you put fifty-six men in a room from thirteen different colonies, there is going to be a great deal of debate." He chuckled wryly. "I keep them supplied with liquor, but it doesn't seem to stem the flow of feelings expressed on the floor." He tapped a finger on the table, despite his obvious tiredness, restlessness permeated his body. "My man Cato can tell you about Gaius' schedule. Tell him I sent you, and he will talk."

He looked over at Butler, his dark eyes sharp with speculation. "I know why most of these men are here, what about you? Why do you engage in this dangerous dance with Britain? There is no doubt if any of us are caught, we will hang. In the king's eyes, our demands for equality and just treatment are treason."

"I know," Butler said as he stood up. "And if my life be forfeit to provide freedom for my fellow colonists, so be it. This is my home, my country. I have seen the price ordinary people pay for the King's pleasure." His tone was bitter. "It is always the vulnerable who suffer most under tyrants. They have no protection. They die or rot in prison, and their children are left defenseless in a brutal world." His voice sounded harsh to his own ears as his mind went back to his mother coughing out her life as she tried to protect her two children on the brutal trip across the Atlantic, her husband dead at the hands of British soldiers. His voice faded away.

Hancock said nothing. He poured Butler another drink, which he swallowed quickly, making him cough.

Butler stood and placed the note in his vest pocket. "I have work to do." As he walked down the stairs, the hum of voices from the room where the delegates met could be heard through the closed doors. He had no desire to join them. They would still be at it when he returned.

Out in the sunshine, he paused to take a few breaths. He had said too much. No one needed to know his past. After all these years, he still had dreams about that journey. They were rare now, but vivid when they occurred. Waves pounded on the ship's hull in a stormy sea while he and his sister clung to their mother. Her coughs echoed in the tomb-like hold, which reeked of fish and human waste.

Butler walked out into the courtyard and paused to get his bearings. Gravel crunched beneath his feet in the open area surrounding the state house. He looked over at the grove of trees, alert for signs of an intruder. Squirrels darted about gathering food and chattering as they worked. He watched as a robin swooped down to the grass before pecking at the ground like a small brown and red chicken. A chorus of birds filled the air with their voices calling back and forth as they flitted.

Butler headed downtown toward Franklin's home. Dodging past a wagon loaded with cabbages, he crossed the street, hopping around a steaming pile left by a recent horse. Voices cried out the closer he got to the market, offering flowers, bread, fish, and newspapers. He avoided the market. His business was elsewhere.

Benjamin Franklin's home was an elegant three-story brick building set close enough to the streets to attract business but inset just enough to allow for some privacy. Surrounded by a clipped lawn and a few graceful shade trees, the home reminded Butler of some of the homes just off the main thoroughfare in Williamsburg. The cries of excited children at play caught his attention. Looking over the picket fence that encased a generous yard on one side, he spied two young children being tended by an older girl. One boy laughed joyously as he chased a hoop over the grass. By his size, he had not been long in breeches. The other child toddled close to the girl, minding him, still in the gown of a younger child. Butler realized that they must be Franklin's grandchildren. He wondered how many lived in the palatial home with the older man. Turning around, he went to the front of the house, taking it in for a few moments before he walked up to the door and knocked.

A maid opened the door and stared at him. "Are any members of the family at home?" he inquired politely.

"Dr. Franklin is not here," the girl responded. "Only the mistress."

"I would like to see her," Butler said, doffing his hat as he offered his most disarming smile. The maid looked at him for a moment before closing the door and trotting off. A few moments later, an older man opened the door and gestured Butler in.

"You may join Mistress Bache in the parlor. Follow me." The man turned and walked down a hallway to a modest room. Women's voices drifted down the hall, as did the scent of freshly brewed coffee and baked goods. Butler's stomach growled, reminding him that breakfast had been some hours ago.

He stepped into the room, noting the set of high windows framed by elegant printed draperies from Europe. It was a comfortable room filled with pieces picked up from Franklin's many trips to England. Over the fireplace, a portrait of the man himself gazed down at the two women seated by a table holding a pewter tray of coffee, cakes, and small sandwiches. One of the women was Hannah White.

The servant spoke to a plump, pleasant-faced woman. "This is Master Jeremy Butler, an associate of Master Hancock."

She rose to greet him. "Master Butler, what brings you here? My father is engaged in business at the state house and will not be home until much later."

Butler smiled. Hannah White had not risen but sat drinking her coffee in silence. Her dark blue dress emphasized her eyes and complemented her mahogany hair, just visible underneath her starched cap.

Franklin's daughter gestured to a nearby chair, its frame covered with upholstery. "Please join us. This is Mistress White. We were just discussing the changes in the market in recent years. Would you like some coffee?"

"Thank you, yes. That would be most welcome." Butler sat down on the soft cushion. He wondered if this was Franklin's seat of choice in his own home. He could see how the plush seat would appeal to old bones.

Hannah gazed over at him but said nothing. If anything, she looked somewhat amused at his presence. She grasped the handle of the delicate porcelain cup with the long fingers of her right hand. Her back remained straight even as she leaned over to set her cup down on its saucer.

Franklin's daughter handed Butler a steaming cup of coffee and gestured to the sugar cone on the tray. "Feel free to break off what you wish." Butler had a sweet tooth, but he restrained his impulses. Breaking off a modest lump, he watched it dissolve in the dark liquid before taking a sip. She handed him a plate stacked with small cakes and sandwiches. He thanked her before setting down the cup and enjoying a few bites.

The women waited in silence, sipping their drinks. Butler watched both of them. Sally Bache resembled her father. She shared his mild blue eyes and well-defined brows along with the arrow-straight nose. But while Franklin's face reflected his sharp intellect, Sally's reflected mild curiosity at his presence. Her eyes showed none of the intensity of the perpetually engaged Franklin, but she was no fool either. "What brings you here, Master Butler?" she asked.

"I wanted to ask if you knew of anyone who bore your father ill will," he said as he set aside his cup and plate. "There have been a few incidents he has been close to that have caused concern."

Sally snorted. "You may recall that my father is the man who chose to attract lightning with a kite in a storm. He thrives on incidents. Benjamin Franklin is not a man to sit quietly even at the age of seventy."

"This is different," Butler pulled out the paper. "Do you recognize this?"

Sally looked at it and shook her head. "No, the handwriting looks familiar, but I cannot say where it is from. My father corresponds with many people, so letters come in and out every day." She took it from him and examined it more closely. Hannah leaned in as well, accepting it from Sally's hands. "Why would anyone make notes about my father's schedule? If they wished to meet him, they need only to ask. He's very easy to reach."

Butler took the paperback. "I'm not sure communication is what is desired." Sally stayed quiet as he told her about Gaius' death and the other incidents. "I fear he may be in danger."

Sally shook her head. "He's ruffled many feathers over the years. No one has ever threatened his life. Not even William." She cut herself off sharply.

"What about William?" Butler asked. He knew a little about Franklin's illegitimate son. A clock ticked in the background as silence fell over the room. He waited for her to speak.

Sally looked down at the floor, her face sad. "They are estranged at present."

"Tell me more." Butler leaned forward, focused on the woman seated across from him.

"It is a family matter," she said after an awkward silence. "I have no wish to air grievances to all and sundry."

"I respect that you have no desire to gossip, and I will not spread what is shared in this room. Nor will Mistress White," he said with a pointed stare where she sat. She shot him a look of umbrage. Butler continued, trying to ignore her. "I am charged with keeping him and the other delegates safe. I need to know of any grievances against your father."

"My father is a man of strong opinions, which he loves to share even if it tramples over other's views. If you read any of his publications, you will realize this."

"I've read a few," Butler's tone was dry.

"Then you know that anyone who disagrees with him is likely to be savaged in print. My brother is not the only one to have a grievance, and I doubt he would harm his father regardless of the differences in their beliefs. I do not believe he would cross the Delaware to stir up trouble."

Butler started to speak, but Hannah cut him off. "William Franklin is governor of the New Jersey Colony. He has the resources if he wants to visit his family in Philadelphia."

Sally shook her head. "William has not been here in some time. My father and he disagree about the future of the colonies. William supports King George. His writings have made many patriots angry. My father, as you know, believes these colonies have a far different destiny."

Butler paused to drink his coffee, which had cooled slightly. He looked at the women sharing the room with him. Sally fiddled with her apron, her eyes downcast. Hannah sat upright, her apron and dress neat. Her cap perched on her head just far back enough to reveal her magnificent hair. Her vivid blue eyes met his, and he felt a jolt of connection. Here was a woman who would command her own destiny. Much like her younger sister, she had learned to survive without the help of a husband or father. She was still mad that he had implied she gossiped. He wondered what she would be like with those passions fully roused.

Sally broke the silence. "My brother would never harm his father. It is not in his nature. Besides, he's been under house arrest for some months now. If someone is seeking to do him harm, it would be among his opponents in this city."

Butler leaned forward, catching her gaze. "I need names."

Chapter Ten

Faith sat in the sick room, knitting socks. Her mother dozed in her bed, exhausted by the bath she had received along with a fresh shift and bedclothes. Her damp hair was spread on the pillow, drying in the warm room. Her face was peaceful in repose, although the left side still drooped.

Out in the yard, someone chopped wood. The steady fall of the axe as it struck wood served as a reminder that life continued even as they coped with the ongoing tragedy within the house. Faith closed her eyes briefly. Sleep had been elusive since her arrival. Too many thoughts plagued her mind and seeped into her dreams to wake her during the night.

Last night, she had left Charity slumbering in the bed they shared in the loft and crept downstairs. The house had been wrapped in the velvet stillness of the night, free for once of the ever-present bustling of people. Faith was grateful for the silence. Her dreams had left her shaken and unable to settle. Rather than disturb her sister, she chose to roam.

The front door opened without a sound, a testament to her father's care. A breeze ruffled her hair and caused the hem of her shift to flutter. The smooth boards of the porch were warm on her bare feet as she took in the stillness. Somewhere out in the darkness, an owl hooted as it hunted for prey. Other than that, the steady song of insects filled the night.

Out in the forest, a lone frog croaked his song, hoping to attract a mate. By the end of summer, there would likely be several more engaged in the same task. Faith took a seat on one of the chairs kept for when someone wanted to sit out here in hopes of catching a cool breeze in the summer.

That wasn't the reason she had escaped out in the middle of the night. She longed to go home to her tavern in Williamsburg and a sense of normalcy she craved. She didn't belong here anymore and felt it with every fiber of her being. As her mother lay dying inside, Faith struggled to make peace with all the memories that bubbled up to the surface from the moment she arrived.

Then there was the issue of Lizzy, the half-sister she had never known existed, who may not even still be alive or nearby. Her mother wanted to make peace with her. Faith wasn't sure that was possible, but she felt the burden of needing to do one last thing for her mother that would perhaps please her. A bitter laugh bubbled up inside. She knew better than to think anything pleased Patience Payne. She knew that from experience. Leaving that behind had been a relief, although a part of her still struggled with the concept of being good enough for anyone.

Faith shrugged the troublesome thought aside. She focused on the problem of Lizzy. She would have to go to Philadelphia for answers from her mother's eldest brother. Mordecai Beeson rarely visited. He remained in Philadelphia, running one of the many print shops in town. There was little she could do here except sit with her mother and slowly go mad.

Faith wondered how long she would last. Patience refused to try to rise from the bed except to visit the chamber pot, which she needed assistance to do. She ate only a few morsels at a time, refusing most all food. Her body had shrunken to near skeletal proportions. She could accept her mother's passing. What ravaged her thoughts was her unsettled mind. Patience went from lucid moments where she talked about her grandchildren and her children to periods where she cried and fretted about events long past. In those times, Faith struggled to keep a lid on her own memories of her mother's dark moods. She was no longer a terrified child, but an adult. Her mother's mood swings could no longer touch her except in dreams where she awoke shaking.

Faith took a few breathes and said a soft prayer for peace of mind for both herself and her mother. No matter the feelings that being in this house churned up, there would be no resolution. Even were she to recover,

Patience Payne would never admit to the dark moods that sent her children scrambling to be as far away as possible until they passed. Her heart remained torn between the two different people her mother could be.

In her mind's eye, she could conjure up images of her mother singing hymns as she went about her tasks. She loved her garden and taking her children out to play in the yard as she worked. Faith recalled her mother's gentle hands showing her the difference between weeds and herbs. She was happiest in her still room with the various concoctions she made to keep her family well. They had worked side by side drying fruit and smoking hams. It was from Patience that Faith had learned how to brew cider for the family to drink. For all those things, she was grateful. She clung to those memories when the storms came.

When depression claimed her, Patience couldn't sit still. She paced the floor at turns, angry and bereft. She followed the children around the house, demanding their attention and nothing offered was ever enough. Outrage had consumed her when she realized that Faith was seeing an outsider to their Quaker faith. Only the intervention of Faith's father had stemmed her wrath.

Forsaking the evening air, Faith tiptoed back into the house, intending to head back up to bed. A violin played softly in the night. Only one person in the house played. Memory guided her in the darkness until she came to the door of the sickroom.

Her father stood by the window near the bed where his wife slept. The violin whispered a melancholy tune that crept out into the room and hovered over the bed. Faith watched him play as the sky began to lighten before him, heralding the beginning of a new day. He finished playing the hymn before beginning what she recognized as Greensleeves.

That tune had both embarrassed and pleased her mother. She would blush as she told him that it was not plain.

Her father would smile and say, "Neither are you," before he completed the song. Now she lay asleep, no longer the woman she once was, but still beloved.

Faith's father completed the tune and set his instrument aside before striding to the bedside. He stroked her hair back from her face before bending down to kiss her cheek. Patience did not stir. He straightened and walked past Faith out the door without a word. In the distance, she heard the front door close as he left, seeking solace far beyond the room where his beloved lay dying.

Returning from her memory of the night before, Faith continued knitting the project she had discovered upon her arrival at the farm. She had recognized the sock pattern immediately. Her grandmother had taught it to her years ago. It was a basic pattern used time and again until she could do it from memory. Faith decided to finish them since Patience could not. She had no comfort to offer her father, but she could give him one last gift from his wife. She refused to offer worthless platitudes and kept her prayers silent. Only God heard her inner turmoil. Prayer offered comfort, although no solutions. It offered no criticism either, for which she was grateful. She was well aware of her failings as a daughter. She needed no reminders. She had plenty of family members for that.

The needles in her hands clicked as she completed a round. The feel of the soft wool and the wooden needles helped make sitting with her mother bearable. Despite her name, Patience had never had great tolerance for needlework although she spent her winters working wool alongside her daughter. Grandmother Payne had taught the girls how to spin and knit. It allowed her more time in her precious garden. Faith, along with her sisters, had knitted since they could hold the needles. They had all learned to weave as well, although she had no time for that with her business. Charity, however, could make a loom hum with activity. She had the patience to warp the loom in the basement and weave cloth for their clothes.

Her mother's eyes opened and turned toward Faith. "What time is it?"

"Still early morning," Faith replied, setting her work aside. "Do you feel ready for breakfast?" Rising, she went to the side of the rope bed her father had built years ago and helped her mother to sit up, propping pillows behind her.

Just then, Arabella, who managed most of the house, looked in the door. "Good Morning, Mistress Patience. I'm glad to see you awake. Let's get you ready for the day." Between the two of them, they helped Faith's mother with her personal needs and resettled her in bed.

Faith took a brush and began to gently tame her mother's abundant hair. Arabella went to the large trunk at the foot of the bed and pulled out a fresh cap.

"I will check on breakfast," she said as she walked toward the door.

"Arabella? When will my brother next go to town?" Faith figured that she still kept track of when they had enough produce to take to the market stall in town.

Arabella paused. "Caleb plans to go after the animals are tended here. He and your father loaded up the wagon last night with squash, beans, and melons."

Faith nodded. "If you see him, tell him I wish to accompany him to Philadelphia."

Surprised, the other woman met Faith's gaze. "I'm sure your brother and cousins can manage if you would prefer to remain with your mother."

Faith finished combing her mother's hair and braided it neatly before tying it off and tucking it into her cap. "I have business in town that cannot wait."

"As you wish," Arabella said before she stepped out. Her steady footsteps went down the hall, followed by the sound of the back door shutting behind her.

Patience let her fluff pillows behind her before turning and speaking. "You were in Virginia."

"I still am. I have a business to run. I heard you were ill and came to see you." Faith sat down in the wooden chair nearest the bed and took up her knitting.

Patience watched her work for a moment. "I was unkind to you. I'm sorry."

Faith paused. Her mother rarely apologized. "It was a long time ago." There was no point in bringing up the hurt and abandonment she had felt when her family had cut her off. Only her father had come to see her when they had left for Virginia.

Patience continued. "I need to make amends before I pass."

Faith's hands stilled before she set the yarn aside. "What do you mean?" She wanted to protest that her mother was going to recover and life would return to the way it was, but she knew that short of a miracle, it would not happen. A wave of grief made her eyes sting. She blinked and hoped it went unnoticed.

Patience produced a small, lopsided grin. Her voice was weak and thready, but clear. "You were always the nosy one. You had your hands into everything, no matter how I tried to train you out of it. No one, aside from God, could stop you." Her gaze met her middle child's clearly. "Find Lizzy. Tell her I'm sorry. I had no choice."

The air went out of Faith's lungs. "Are you sure?"

Patience nodded. "Yes. Do this so I can die in peace."

"Where do I find her?"

"Ask my brother; he took her away from me." Patience's face contorted. "I barely got to hold her before they came. It wasn't right." Gasps of breath turned to sobs, which shook her body until she wheezed. Her lips turned bluish as she struggled to breathe.

Faith went over and took her mother into her arms, feeling a jolt of shock at the frailty of her body stunned her. Patience was little more than a bag of bones. She rocked her, humming a tune that her mother had sung to her when she had been hurt or afraid. "I'll find her for you," she promised. "All will be well. Fret no more about it."

Arabella stepped in with a tray. She looked over at them with concern. "Is Mistress Patience all right?" She set the tray down on a nearby table and came over.

Faith nodded. "She will be." Giving her mother a gentle hug, she released her and stood up. "Can you feed her breakfast? I need to speak to my brother before he leaves. I have an errand in town."

Arabella started to protest. "Surely your place is here."

Patience looked up. Her eyes were red, and she snuffled before speaking. "Go, Faith, do what I ask."

Faith swallowed hard. She had no idea if she would succeed. "I will try my best." She moved toward the door as Arabella took her place.

"Faith," her mother called softly.

"Yes?"

"I love thee, child."

Her voice wobbled in response. "I love you too, Mama."

Chapter Eleven

A breeze blew off the Delaware River, smelling of fish and rotting plants. Jeremy Butler watched as the bow of the boat he rode cut cleanly through the brownish-green water as it headed across to Camden, New Jersey. Gulls cried out overhead, seeking food. They were over a hundred miles from the Atlantic, but he had seen them further inland. Who knew what drove them to fly this far? Near the shore, a lone heron dove down into the water, rising back moments later with a fish in its bill. It disappeared into the tall grass that lined the bank to enjoy its hard-earned meal.

He kept an eye on the boatman. They had haggled over the price before the man agreed to take less as long as it was British or French coins. Butler kept a small amount for emergencies, such as when he couldn't argue someone into accepting the continental money with which he was paid. He didn't care much for colonial currency, either. Its value fluctuated wildly, which made it unreliable.

On the approaching shore, Butler made out the outline of Camden, the colony where William Franklin governed. Hancock had arranged for him to have a horse in order to expedite the journey to Perth Amboy, where he resided. He hoped the younger Franklin could provide some answers. Benjamin Franklin provided none. Butler huffed in annoyance. Even when presented with evidence of a credible threat, the old man refused to put any credence in it.

Butler spent the previous evening sipping wine and talking with Franklin Senior in the parlor of his comfortable home. Although the summer still lit the early evening sky, shadows darkened the room. Candles illumined the room, filling it with the scent of beeswax.

The flickering light highlighted the lines on Franklin's face, making him look old. "You believe someone wishes me vanquished from this earth," he stated, as his eyes focused on the amber liquid in his glass.

"It's a distinct possibility," Butler said. "You've been present or close by to all the attacks, and the note we found documents your comings and goings." He gave the other man a moment to absorb the information. "The question is, who would want to harm you? Do you have any enemies or anyone with whom you have had a dispute recently?"

Franklin looked pensive. "I have debated the future of these colonies with many." He looked at his wrinkled hands before stating, "When you live as long as I have, you develop a reputation for opinions, some of which are lauded, others are decried." He smiled wryly.

"I have tried to convince others that independence is the only reasonable choice for those of us who live in the American Colonies," Franklin added dryly. "Not everyone agrees."

"How does your son feel about that?"

Franklin's jaw tightened. "William will not acknowledge that these colonies are destined to separate from England. He refuses to consider the most reasonable of arguments. Rather than being my son, he has decided he a king's man."

Butler pressed. "He is the royal governor of the New Jersey Colony. Should these colonies succeed in becoming an independent country, he would lose that position and all that comes with it. I imagine a man in his position would do almost anything to retain that power."

Franklin shook his head. "William would not harm me. Decry my view in person and print, yes, he can and has. But he abides by the rule of law, of that I am sure."

Butler put no faith in family assurances, which was why he was now crossing the Delaware into New Jersey. Experience had taught him that the bonds of blood frequently meant nothing when issues of pride, passion, or power arose. Whoever wanted the elder Franklin dead was motivated by one of these things, which made speaking to the younger Franklin necessary. The oars splashed as the boatman pulled against the river's current. Neither spoke after they had conducted their business the night before after he had left Franklin's comfortable home. Maynard had known where to find someone who would take a passenger on a moment's notice without asking questions. Once again, Butler was grateful to have one ally in this vast city.

Boats and ships lined the shore. Men worked on the docks, preparing to go out onto the water. It was impossible to know what side, if any, they were on. He had watched the activity warily as they had slipped out in the dusky light of early dawn.

He disliked leaving Philadelphia. He had persuaded Hancock to employ Maynard to watch over Franklin. He'd wanted some militia to guard over the delegates, but Hancock had demurred. "Secrecy is our greatest strength. Militia would draw attention to our gathering. We cannot afford the British and their allies to know what we plan. It would destroy us before we've begun." Instead, Maynard had found some of his wife's kin to watch the state house out of sight and report to him any suspicious activities.

Cries from the looming shore informed him his ride was soon to end. Once the boat had landed, he paid the boatman and hopped ashore to the stable, where a mount waited for him. It was a two-day ride to Perth Amboy over a road patrolled by bands of British soldiers and militias on either side. The New Jersey colony was unfamiliar to him. Relying on the word of others was always dicey, but he had no choice.

Butler kept off the main roads and kept a wary eye out. He had no desire to be stopped by anyone. He kept moving, stopping only to rest his horse and grab a quick meal in a tavern while he listened to the local gossip. New Jersey differed little from Pennsylvania in that the feelings of the people varied from place to place. Some felt the British should rescue the younger Franklin; others thought every royal governor should be imprisoned. Butler sipped ale in silence, listening to a group of men murmuring at a table. He cocked an eyebrow at the barkeep. "Was Franklin really all that bad?" He said. "I'm not from these parts. I was trying to figure out what the man had done to be made prisoner in his own home."

The barkeep leaned over. "You'd best keep your mouth shut, stranger. Everyone has an opinion on that." He sighed as he wiped down the oak countertop. "I've lived here nigh on twenty years. He seemed a fair man for a Tory." He shook his head. "There's no telling what will happen to any of us in these times. There are too many armed groups of men roaming the country: Tories, patriots, and just plain thugs. Be careful on the road. It's no time to be traveling alone."

Butler nodded. He was aware of the danger, which was why he stayed off the main roads whenever he could. He also kept his mother's old rosary in his pack. He couldn't remember any Latin, but he felt sure God understood him anyway.

Fortune favored him. The one time he was stopped, he produced a letter he had found in Hannah White's desk from her husband's aunt in New York. Hannah had apparently been writing her and offering encouragement. The old woman apparently didn't know that her nephew had died, which made the letter invaluable since she asked for him to come see her soon.

The militia man had taken the letter and glanced at it. "So you are going to see your Aunt Mary in the New York Colony."

Butler nodded. "She has no children of her own, so I thought it best to check on her. These are challenging times for us all."

"You're a dedicated family man," He handed back the letter. "Have a safe journey, Master White."

Butler tipped his hat and continued his journey after carefully tucking the missive back into his pocket. He let out a deep breath as he watched the half dozen men ride off, thankful that they weren't really interested in him. One never knew the temper of these bands of pseudo-military.

No further incidents plagued him on his journey north. A light mist started falling just as the governor's residence came into sight. Proprietary House was a tall white building that rose above the rest of the town like a beacon. The city lay on a peninsula surrounded by rivers that fed into the nearby Atlantic. Across this lay the busy New York Colony, a stronghold of British power in the colonies.

Butler rode down the street at a leisurely pace, taking in the building and all that surrounded it. Although he would rather see William Franklin immediately and be done with it, he knew better than to rush into a strange place unprepared. This was a royal governor, and he had no letter or connections to get inside. He clucked his mare gently. She was as tired as he was. A few streets down, he spotted a tavern. It looked clean and cared for, so he dismounted, looking for a place for his horse.

"There's a stable behind the building," A dark-skinned man not much taller than him called out. "They don't charge much, and David takes good care of the animals."

"My thanks," Butler said. "Maisie and I have had a long journey. Is there lodging available?"

The other man hopped off the porch. "Aye, I think there's space inside. It's been pretty quiet since that group of Patriots left over a week ago. I'm David, by the way. I tend the animals and help out where needed inside."

Butler nodded and listened as he took his mare's reigns and led her around to the stable. David walked next to him, chatting. From him, he learned what ships had docked and how close British Warships heading in and out of New York had come. He handed off his horse with a few extra coins for oats and a rub down for her and left her in the hostler's capable hands.

He headed toward the entrance, anticipating a hot meal, when David said, "Everyone's still talking about how they took the governor away."

Butler whirled about. "Who took the governor away?"

"Soldiers, I reckon they were Washington's men. They rode right up to Proprietary House and marched him out. Governor Franklin was real angry, too. I hear he went yelling and uttering threats about what the British would do for their kidnapping a Royal governor." He shook his head. "It didn't do any good. They put him in a wagon, and off they went to God knows where." He looked at Butler. "Why are you so mad? I had nothing to do with it." He backed away.

Butler endeavored to calm himself. He wanted to strangle Hancock for sending him on a fool's errand. "Of course not. This is shocking news. A royal governor has been taken from his home. Does anyone know where they took him?"

David shook his head, still keeping his distance from Butler. "Not that I've heard. I hope they told his wife. She's still there, although she hasn't gone out much since it happened."

Butler nodded and walked inside. It took a moment for his eyes to adjust to the dimmer light inside. A man tended the bar. His eyes took in Butler. "Could I offer you a drink?"

"Some ale would be most welcome, as would a room for the night." Butler took a seat at a nearby table and took a cautious sip. One never knew what the local brew would be like. He was pleased that whoever they got their ale from knew his craft.

"We have space. I can arrange for a bath as well for you." The man's face was expressionless as he made the offer.

Butler grimaced. He probably smelled like a horse or worse. "That would be most welcome," he said. His plans had changed with the unwelcome news of William Franklin's removal from his residence. However, it made it unlikely he was behind the attacks on the delegates in Philadelphia or his father. Nonetheless, since he was here, he was going to speak to his wife. Perhaps she knew something useful.

The meal and the bath put him in a better frame of mind, as did relief from spending hours in the saddle. The tavern had few guests, so Butler did not have to share a room. The space was small, tucked up against the angle of the roof. Little more fit into it than the bed and a short table that filled the space between the bedpost and the door. In some spots, the ceiling slanted low enough Butler had to duck down, but it was worth the aggravation for a private space.

Pulling off his boots was a luxury. He padded barefoot to the room down the hall where his bath awaited. A bath and a hot meal did much to soothe his temper, although he intended to have a talk with Hancock upon his return. Surely, the man knew that Washington intended to take custody of New Jersey's governor. If not, he was deeply concerned about communication among the patriots.

Early the next morning, Butler presented himself to Proprietary House. His hair was neatly combed and braided. He had paid a woman to press his jacket so he looked presentable. The servant who opened the door looked at him warily when he asked to speak to the governor's wife.

"She's not receiving visitors at this time," He said before attempting to close the door.

Butler pushed forward through the door. He hadn't come all this way to be turned away. "Tell her I've come from Philadelphia to speak with her." He stood in the entry room, stubbornly ignoring the open door behind him.

The butler huffed angrily. "I said she is not receiving visitors. If you will leave your card, I will let her know that someone from Philadelphia came by." He banged a stick on the floor. It echoed in the room and down the hall.

"Let him in, Benton," A dark-haired woman stood just inside the interior door. "I will see him in the drawing room. Come this way." She walked swiftly, the skirts of her elegant dress swinging back and forth as she went.

A pair of comfortable chairs sat in front of an ornate marble fireplace. Light from a tall window lit the room. She gestured for him to sit while she took the other. Dark eyes studied him. Her skin was like the finest porcelain, with only the faintest of lines to show age. Butler thought age would only make her more attractive. Her tone, while civil, was lethally direct.

"Maria will bring us tea. We still have that." She met Butler's gaze. "My husband has already been taken prisoner, so what do you want?"

"I wanted to speak to your husband," Butler admitted.

Elizabeth Franklin's laugh was sharp as glass. "You are a few weeks late. The provincial legislature took him into custody. Apparently, you patriots do not communicate well. She gestured to a table where ink and a pen lay. "I was writing yet another letter to William's father. He has answered none of my queries about his son. I doubt he will answer this one. Perhaps you will do me the courtesy of delivering it when you go, so at least I cannot fault the post." Her eyes were bright with anger. "He acts as if William were already dead. His only living son."

Butler nodded as she spoke. "Has there been any contact between them?"

She snorted. "Not for months. Once William made it clear he would not abandon the king, Benjamin cut off all contact." She drew in a ragged breath.

"We have no one to turn to in our time of need."

"Your husband was taken into custody a few weeks ago. Did the officers say why?"

"They said he had broken the terms of the house arrest they had placed him under." She stirred restlessly when a maid brought in a tray and set it down on a low table nearby. Elizabeth Franklin poured two cups and handed him one. "I'm afraid I have no sugar at present."

"It's fine," he said and drank real English tea for the first time in months. Butler pondered his next move. His best suspect was in prison, although that didn't mean he was helpless. A man as powerful as a royal governor very likely had ways to connect with the outside world. He looked at the woman across from him. Elizabeth Franklin was both beautiful and intelligent. Her entire world had been torn apart by this conflict, symbolized by the break between father and son.

"I imagine this split between your husband and his father has been difficult."

"They both hold strongly to their ideals. William hopes his father will see his own foolishness one day. These colonies will fall into anarchy without the leadership of Parliament. They have no organization, no way to establish order. They run about like petulant children, and we who try to maintain justice and keep the peace, we bear the cost." Elizabeth Franklin's voice stopped as she struggled to control her emotions. Shadows under her eyes bore testimony to her exhaustion and stress. As she rubbed her forehead, Butler noticed her hands. Her nails were chewed down to the quick.

"I imagine William was very angry with his father's position."

"He was very disappointed in the turn of his loyalties. William pointed out that he could hang for treason once this rebellion is put down."

Butler leaned forward. "Having a treasonous father would not reflect well on a royal governor seeking to advance his career."

Elizabeth set down her cup. It rocked before settling into the saucer at an awkward angle. "What are you implying?"

"Someone has been trying to kill Benjamin Franklin. There have been several attempts."

Her face was incredulous. "You believe William is capable of patricide? That is obscene. William has ever been the loyal son, helping him with his experiments, traveling with him to London, and working as his secretary. He never left his side before he became governor. Now, Benjamin wants him to throw all he has worked for aside for this foolish revolution. And you provincials," She spat out the term. "Come up here to accuse him of attempting to harm his father while he is unlawfully imprisoned. I think it's past time you left and returned to that poisonous hole you call Philadelphia." She rose swiftly. "Get out."

Butler rose as well. "I meant no insult, Lady Franklin. I came up here to seek answers from your husband."

"He's not here." She hissed. "Go talk to that woman he kept in the city. The one he would find excuses to meet. I read the letters she sent him and told him to make his choice. I watched while he burned them in this fire and swore he was done. She came up here to see him soon after, but he had already been taken away."

"What woman?" Butler paused at the doorway, waiting for an answer.

"Lisette Fournier," She hissed. "I'm surprised you haven't heard of her. She's the toast of Philadelphia. I doubt there's a man she doesn't know throughout the colony." Her sarcasm wasn't lost on Butler. He stepped outside the door to the stoop. The door slammed behind him.

Weariness settled between his shoulders. He had a long ride back and none of the answers he had hoped for, only the name of a mysterious woman he knew nothing about.

Chapter Twelve

After bumping about in the wagon with the dawn and spending half the day selling vegetables, Faith had a few hours to herself. She wiped dust from her hands onto her apron and asked for directions to Hannah's house. Caleb had pointed its direction on the ride in, and she memorized the location. After helping a woman with a brightly patterned head scarf select cucumbers, he lifted another crate of produce onto the table. Caleb shook his head. "This will only cause trouble."

Faith bit her lip in order to prevent the tears stinging her eyes from falling. She knew her mother had little time left. She couldn't continue sitting while Patience suffered. Every day after sitting with her, Faith escaped the room, wanting to scream. She had begged God to ease her mother's suffering and gotten no response. Continuing to sit and do nothing was driving her mad. "She needs to know what happened. She begged me to find Lizzy. I cannot ignore her request."

Caleb passed her his handkerchief, plain and white and smelling faintly of the dried rosemary Bess put in the clothing chest. "Do what you must. I don't know how you will find her."

Faith sniffled. "Pray I find answers." She left him at the market, calmly selling vegetables to cooks from all over Philadelphia.

Faith dodged a wagon full of barrels as she darted across the street to where her sister lived. Somewhere in this vast city lay the answers she sought. She needed Hannah's help to locate her mother's oldest brother. Her uncle knew what had happened all those years ago. It was long past time he shared what he knew. Only God knew how much time they had. She passed a church on the left. Somewhere nearby, there would be a graveyard where their dead rested. For all she knew, Lizzy lay on the ground, felled by some long-ago fever or mischance. The thought sobered her and compelled her to walk a little faster.

The assault came without warning. A sharp hiss at her back made Faith whirl about to face the enemy, whoever it might be. The strike hit across her leg. A long snake-like neck undulated as an enraged gander attacked with a series of throaty cries. Her skirt bore the brunt of the assault as she backed away, trying to escape. It charged and caught her apron in its beak. Wings opened wide like ship sails as the goose cursed her roundly for encroaching on its territory. Behind the beast, his harem of geese cheered their champion with honks and fluttering wings. Faith turned and ran.

The stab of stays in her ribs compelled her to stop a short distance away. Wheezing, she turned to see the gander flap back to the wide expanse of grass near the pond where his kindred congregated. He honked his victory cry as he settled back. Lungs heaving, she watched her enemy warily until she was certain he would not return for another round. "Wretched animal," she muttered as she continued on her journey. Her heart pounded as she sought to regain her composure. As she hurried by, she fantasized about roasting and eating her nemesis, although the hours involved in such a task made it completely unfeasible.

Hannah's tidy brick residence, surrounded by others virtually identical to it, came into view. She wondered if her sister was responsible for the colorful red shutters and door or if she had kept it as it was when she had moved in. Either way, the bold color made identifying Hannah's residence simple. She walked in on the heels of a mahogany-skinned woman who wore braids wrapped around her head like a crown. Faith admired her regal bearing as she walked beside a well-dressed middle-aged woman, either her owner or employer. She hoped it was the latter.

Hannah's voice carried across the room as she extolled the virtues of the china she carried. Her voice broke off when she saw Faith before she recovered and continued her spiel. A white-haired woman examined a plate in her hands. Faith waited inside the entryway until Hannah had completed her transaction. As her customer left, she locked eyes with Faith. "What are you doing here?"

Faith noticed that when conducting business, Hannah dropped most of her Quaker mannerisms. "A lovely good morning to you too, sister," she said. "It's been a bumpy journey from our parents' home. Perhaps you could offer me some refreshment while I share news regarding our mother's health?"

Hannah flushed. "Some of us have work to do. Fortunately, Lucretia and Nathan are here. I will see if they can manage without me." She walked over to her sister-in-law, who stood near her son, who rested on a stool. A cane leaned against the wall next to him. The two women walked away as they discussed business, leaving Faith with Nathan White.

He couldn't be much older than Faith or Hannah, but his hair was already streaked with gray. A simple peg took the place of one leg. He caught her looking and smiled. "I'm afraid I won't be asking you to dance."

"I have little opportunity for that these days anyway," Faith replied. "Have you worked with my sister long?"

"Two years now, since farming is no longer an option. Hannah was kind enough to invite me to help her. My mother decided to come as well." Despite his courteous tone, his eyes roamed the shop.

"I'm sorry," Faith said.

He shook his head. "You didn't run over me with a wagon." He studied the shop. "I do well enough. I earn my bread and have a place to lay my head. It's better than many have." A faint sheen of sweat beaded his forehead despite the cool morning breeze circulating through the room from the open windows. Faith wondered if he was in pain. Nathan's clothes fit somewhat loosely, as if he had lost weight.

Hannah left Lucretia and rejoined them. "Please excuse my sister Nathan. We have family matters to discuss." Taking Faith by the arm, she maneuvered her out of the main room and towards the narrow stairwell. "Go on up. I will see if Suzanna has coffee ready and bring it up with me."

Faith nodded and headed up as her sister went down below where the kitchen lay. Within moments, she returned with a small tray with a pot, two cups, and a small plate of baked goods with an enticing scent.

"Thou art fortunate. Suzanna decided to make ginger cookies. She has tremendous talent for baking. I am blessed to have her here." Hannah poured coffee and offered the plate to Faith. Hannah gave her a moment to sip coffee and take a few bites of the thick, chewy confection.

"These are delightful," she said once she had finished one. "Would she share the recipe?"

"Perhaps. Suzanna can be very generous to those she likes." Hannah set down her own cup with a decided clink. "Why are you here? I thought you would be staying to help nurse our mother."

"She's not getting any better," There were no words she could add to soften the facts. Neither sister spoke for a moment.

"I'm aware," Hannah said gently. "That is why I wrote, so thou had a chance to see her one last time. Our God teaches us that death brings rest to the weary and release from pain."

Faith nodded. Tears welled up that she wiped away. "She's not at peace, which is why I'm here. There is a matter that must be addressed. Did you know we have a half-sister, born before our parents wed?"

"That's not possible." Hannah looked shocked. "You shouldn't say such things, especially not now. Whatever you heard cannot be more than malicious gossip."

"Listen to me," Faith said. "This is what I know." She started with Patience's ramblings about Lizzy, followed by what their aunt had shared. Hannah said nothing. Her eyes never left Faith's as the narrative continued. When she finished, both sisters sat silent.

Outside the open window, birds and insects continued the bright noise of mid-morning. A distant cloud rumbled, suggesting it might bring rain later that day, while bells from a nearby church announced the hour. Out in the street, a boy hawked newspapers, his cries penetrating the thick silence within.

"What dost thou plan to do?" Hannah asked. "There is no way to know if any of this is true. Even if it is, you cannot expect to find one woman in a city of several thousand." She adjusted the tray on the table before moving on to smoothing her apron over her skirt. Downstairs, the front door opened

104

and closed,

Faith shook her head. "This must be the truth. There's no reason for Frieda or Deborah to lie, especially not with our mother so ill. I had to press them to speak about it at all." Her voice gained strength as she made a decision. "I need to speak to Uncle Mordecai and Aunt Ruth. They know the truth. If anyone can locate Lizzy, they can." Her words sounded brave. Faith felt anything but. Her childhood memories were faint, but enough to remember her mother's eldest brother's dour demeanor scared her. She dreaded renewing the acquaintance.

Hannah stared at her. "Thou art going to visit our Uncle, an elder in one of the largest Quaker meeting houses in Philadelphia, and asking him about an illegitimate child his sister had more than thirty years ago. What makes thou believe he will answer?"

"I'm not leaving until he does," Faith answered. "Our mother needs to know the fate of the child she gave up." Her voice grew rough with emotions she could not hold in check. "She asked me to find her. I have no intention of failing her."

Hannah met her gaze. "Then we will do this together. Uncle Mordecai owes more than a few explanations for decisions he has made regarding our family. He's been a virtual ghost since my husband passed. It's past time he discussed his reasons."

Faith wasn't sure what else Hannah wanted to discuss, but she knew there was no dissuading her. Her older sister had a stubborn streak.

"We have a few hours. He spends mornings attending his business, but he comes home afternoons for dinner and to work on his correspondence. Our Uncle does not support the rebellion growing in these colonies. If you want to learn about our mother's past, do not tell him about your patriotic leanings."

"I am neutral," Faith protested, but hushed when Hannah shot her a cynical look.

"The man who came with you is not neutral. I have seen him going in and out of the State House, where representatives of the colonies have been meeting. He keeps company with Benjamin Franklin and other well-known rebels. Associating with such people is not neutrality."

"Jeremy Butler is a friend of the family." Faith blustered. "I have no say in his comings and goings." She was tempted to add that he came and went like a bad summer storm but thought it wiser not to.

"We have a few hours before he will be home. While you're here, you can help out," Hannah said. "There's always more than enough work to be done."

Faith said nothing, but let her sister lead to a pile of mending next to a comfortable chair set where the window's light would shine on it. "You expect me to darn socks?"

Her sister indicated the basket with needle and thread. "Cloth is an expensive commodity, as you no doubt know. The conflict with England impacts us all, whether we wish to be involved or not. I have learned to make do with less than I once did. I would appreciate your help while you're here. As I recall, you always had a fine hand with needle and thread."

Faith sat down. "I will help out, but I intend to see Mordecai today."

"We will go when I can arrange a time to call." She eyed Faith critically. "Thou cannot go dressed like that anyway." Hannah reached over and picked a feather off of her skirt. "You look like you spent time in a barnyard. What is this from, a chicken?"

Faith snorted. "A territorial gander. I'm lucky to have escaped alive."

Hannah chuckled. "I know the one. I've learned to walk on the other side of the street. I suspect one day, I will discover that someone has had enough of his bullying and will make a meal of him. The Barnwells own him and that pond he patrols. She says he's a better guard than their dog."

"I'm sure he is." Faith leaned over to look through the basket of clothes. "When do you plan for us to go to Mordecai?"

"I will send Abner with a note for Aunt Ruth. I will let you know as soon as he returns." Hannah walked to the door and out. Her footsteps echoed as she went downstairs to tend to her business.

Faith picked up a man's shirt with a ripped sleeve. Despite the laundress' best efforts, a faint stain still spotted the white fabric. Taking a needle, she began mending the tear. The shirt was well made, its full sleeves neatly gathered at the shoulder and cuff. As she closed the hole, she realized it must belong to Jeremy Butler. The damage had come from his altercation with the British on their journey up. If his shirt was here, she wondered whose clothes he had been wearing. Then Faith remembered that Hannah had pulled items from her late husband's trunk when they had arrived. She wondered why she still kept them and how she felt seeing them on another man.

Amos White had died a few years before Jon Clarke. The only things Faith had kept were items she thought their son Andrew might appreciate one day. She wondered what motivated her to keep so many of his belongings. But then, from the sound of things, it sounded like his older children were unwilling to let her have much of anything.

Faith had not inquired why Butler was in Philadelphia. He would not have told her. When he had volunteered to accompany her north, she had been surprised. Even though they spoke little on the trip, she had been grateful for his close presence. One evening, when a man had attempted to get friendly, a meaningful look from Butler had sent him off, much to her relief. Nothing could be done about the incursion with the British soldiers. Butler was fortunate they hadn't caved his head in as a parting gesture.

Faith shivered. It had not occurred to her that British Soldiers would be so brutal. It was a lesson she would never forget. Her mind skittered briefly to Captain Stephen Grant. He had been charming, yet he had chosen to marry a woman with affluent family ties rather than pursue the attraction he and she had shared. She would not forget his heartlessness for some time.

Then there was Will McKay. Her anger burned at the thought of his bony face and graceful ink-stained hands. Even though he was bound in servitude for a few more years, she had been willing to wait for him, but he had spurned her. Fearful that the effects of the severe poisoning he had endured would leave him an invalid, he had broken off their relationship. She hadn't seen him in weeks. Any information he gathered for the Sons of Liberty he sent through Titus. She considered him a coward and had told him so the last time she had seen him, when she had discovered him in her barn, wiping down one of the horses, Ezra kept for the information ring he had run until his death.

Downstairs, indistinct voices murmured as Hannah conducted her business. Who would have thought one could make money selling china? But Hannah seemed to be doing well enough. In many ways, their lives were similar. They had lost their husbands at an early age and found ways to survive in a world that had little expectation for women other than to marry and bear children. Hannah had no children despite having been married for a number of years. Faith felt fortunate to have Andrew. Having him kept her focused on the future.

Faith completed the tear in Butler's shirt and checked it for other holes. Despite their association, she knew little about him. Did he have a wife hidden away somewhere? She doubted it. He seemed a loner with the exception of his sometime ally, Athena, who had remained in Williamsburg. Faith shook herself. She preferred not to think about her much, although she had come to appreciate her ability to ferret information out of the virtual air.

Faith set her project down. What would Athena do if she had to find Lizzy? She would probably forge a connection with the staff of her uncle's house and see what they knew. Faith wasn't sure she could do that, but perhaps she could reach out to her Aunt Ruth. Her main memories of her aunt were of her trying to cope with the large number of children she had. Mordecai and Ruth had five children still living; she wasn't sure how many had not survived infancy or childhood. It was a brutal world in which so many children died young of disease. Faith shuddered and sent a prayer up for Andrew's continued health. She couldn't imagine losing a child.

Faith picked up her needle again. By the time Hannah returned upstairs, she had made a small dent in the pile. Her sister nodded at Faith's work. "My thanks. You have gotten over half of it done. Put that down for now. We need to find you something decent to wear."

Faith laid her work aside and rose to follow her older sister to her room. A stack of clothes lay across the bed. Hannah closed the door before speaking, "Aunt Ruth has invited us to tea later today. It doesn't give us a great deal of time, but this is family, not society so I believe we can make do."

"What's the matter with what I'm wearing? I'm sure they know I run a tavern. I doubt the scandal has died down."

Hannah shot her a look. "I'm not sure which caused more excitement, marrying outside the faith or running a tavern in the Virginia Colony. You would have been welcomed home after thy husband died." She began sorting through bodices and skirts.

"His name was Jon," Faith said. "I preferred to manage my own affairs in Virginia rather than return to the farm. I should think you would understand that."

Hannah nodded. "I do, although our elders were somewhat shocked." She picked up a bodice in a medium indigo shade. "Remove thy apron; we won't be going to the kitchen to peel potatoes." She eyed Faith's skirt, which was medium gray, with a lighter gray feather pattern. "That's pretty and reasonably plain. I may have a jacket that will pair with it."

Faith started to protest until she looked down and spotted more goose down on her front. "Someone should roast that gander."

Hannah chuckled. "Many have threatened to. But he does a good job protecting his ladies. He's not heading to the table anytime soon." She picked up a dark blue jacket. "Try this one. I will help you with your pins."

Finally, Hannah was satisfied with Faith's appearance. "You're a fine-looking woman when you make the effort." She offered Faith a white cap with a white silk ribbon that she used to tie it atop her head.

"Let's go." Hannah went down the narrow stairs with the ease of practice. Faith took her time, not trusting the twisting, uneven surface. By the time she reached the main floor, Hannah was tying on a jaunty straw hat encircled with a navy ribbon. "They live north of us in a more affluent section of town."

Hannah walked with the sure sense of someone familiar with her location. Faith followed her, barely keeping pace despite being the taller sister. Hannah slipped through the busy streets with practiced ease. "Not everyone is as familiar with Philadelphia as you," she huffed as they paused at a corner.

Hannah glanced over at her sister. "Perhaps you do too much sitting at your tavern." She gestured to a tree-lined street. "It's not much further. Let us hope that they are amenable to talking about this."

They stopped in front of a three-story brick house that shared a wall with the house next to it. Rows of tall windows lined each floor. A road cut through on the other side, whilst a tree rose in the tiny front yard of the Trinity House, pointing its slender branches toward the sky. Faith stared up as Hannah knocked on the door.

"Don't gawk. Thou looks like thou has never seen a house before."

"It is an elegant building," she answered. "Our aunt and uncle appear to be doing well."

"They keep a comfortable standard, though I do not like some of the means used to attain it."

"What do you mean?"

They were interrupted by the opening of the door. A young African-American woman stood in the doorway. Hannah met her gaze. "I'm Hannah White, and this is my sister Faith Clarke. We've come to see our aunt, Ruth Beeson. She is expecting us."

The girl nodded. "I will check with my mistress." She closed the door. Her unhurried footsteps faded away.

Hannah's voice dropped. "They own and trade slaves. That poor child is property to them."

Faith looked over at her. "Surely the meeting condemns this."

Her sister's voice was tight. "Not every Quaker believes in the abolition of slavery. Last year a group of us formed The Society for the Relief of Free Negroes Unlawfully Held in Bondage. The tide is rising, but not everyone feels the movement of the spirit to free the oppressed. I pray for their eyes to be opened. We are all equal in the eyes of the Lord."

The door opened. This time, a middle-aged man greeted them. As they entered, he spoke; his deep voice hinted at exotic origins. "Mistress Ruth waits for you in the parlor. This way, please." They followed him down a narrow hallway with doors that opened on either side. Instead of going into one of these, he led them up the narrow stairs at the end of the hall. Faith let Hannah go ahead of her up to the parlor.

They entered a graceful room with polished wood floors and tall windows covered with sheer draperies that allowed light in while still shielding the privacy of those inside. Their aunt sat at a round table before the fireplace. Her upright carriage helped her appear taller than she was. She smiled at the sisters.

"Please join me. Adelaide will be up shortly with tea and shortbread. Mordecai has managed to keep a supply of English tea for special occasions."

Faith and Hannah allowed the butler to seat them, carefully maneuvering their skirts around the long linen tablecloth. Faith admired the simple elegance of the room. A tall clock stood in the corner, its ticking a soft undertone. The cream-colored walls were clean of pictures other than a landscape over the fireplace.

After tea was served, their aunt looked at them. "What brings thee here? It's been some time since I've seen either of you."

Faith wasted no time. "Our mother, as you know, is not well. We seek information to set her mind at rest. She had a child before she married our father. She frets about the fate of this child."

Ruth said nothing, although the pleasant expression she'd worn had vanished. Skin stretched tightly over her face as if what it contained was too much for it to hold. Glancing down, she centered her delicate porcelain cup on its saucer. "I don't know what thou speaks of."

Faith didn't believe her. The pastiness of her aunt's face belied her words. "I believe you do. All I wish is to give my mother peace of mind before she passes from this world. This is not a time to judge what happened long ago. Tell us what we need to know."

"There is nothing thou needs to know regarding this matter," Their Uncle Mordecai stood in the doorway. His long bony frame filled the space. "No matter what thou has been told, the matter died many years ago. Nothing can be gained by digging into the past." He looked over at his wife. Ruth appeared to shrink in her chair. Mordecai walked over to the table. His cold gaze warned them not to inquire further.

Hannah's voice was cool. "Thou hast led this family for some time. Whatever our grandparents did regarding this matter, I am sure thou knows. Surely, after all these years, the scandal matters little in these times. We have no wish to stir the pot, only to reassure our mother regarding the fate of this child."

"She was called Lizzy," Faith said.

Mordecai moved to stand behind his wife. "Thou knows nothing about what happened thirty-five years ago. Nor is there any need for it to be discussed. Patience wanders within her mind. Whether she lives or dies is to be determined by our heavenly father. Nothing thou does will change that. Go and do not discuss this matter further."

Faith stood with Hannah, frustrated at his obstinacy. "Why won't you help us?"

Mordecai motioned for the butler to herd them out. "The matter is closed. Go back to your mother. We will continue to pray for her." He walked behind them all the way down the stairs and to the front door. It shut firmly behind them.

Out in the street, Hannah looked annoyed. "That was a wasted journey."

"Maybe not," Faith said, pulling her around the corner to the solid brick side of the house out of sight. "Let's wait and see." She had learned a few things since she began gathering information for the patriot cause. One of them was patience. Sure enough, after a brief span of minutes, Mortdecai Beeson emerged from the house and headed down the street toward town at a brisk pace. Faith waited until he had gone nearly a block before she began following him.

Hannah joined her, catching on quickly to using trees and other objects to keep from being in plain sight. Mordecai didn't look back. His long stride indicated a man focused on his task. Rather than head into the market, he turned down a street lined with neat row houses, their brick edifices rising up toward the sky. He went up the steps to the doorway of one and knocked on the door. Within minutes, he was admitted.

"Now, what do we do?" Hannah asked.

"Whose house is that?" Faith asked in between breaths. Keeping up with her uncle in the busy city streets had taken effort. It was not midmorning, and the summer heat reflected off the buildings and street.

"Let me find out," Hannah said. Leaving Faith, she walked around the house to a door on the side of the building. Standing on the narrow stoop, she knocked. After a few moments, the door opened. Hannah conversed with the woman at the door for a few minutes before bowing and taking her leave. Hannah's pace was unhurried as she rejoined her sister under the wide branches of the poplar tree. Faith noticed her satisfied expression.

"Well, what did you discover?"

Hannah shot her an amused glance. "It's a good thing our mother didn't name thee after herself. That would have never worked." She gestured for her sister to join her as they walked down the side of the street away from the traffic of horses and carriages. "I inquired if they had come by my shop looking for fine blue and white table china. I let them know I had just received a shipment via Holland."

Faith shot her an aggravated look. "You were hawking wares on the doorstep?"

"It's not like I'm standing on the street corner shouting my price," Hannah snapped. "Many fine people make inquiries about particular items. It pays to keep them informed when something special comes in. That is a very nice residence for an attorney. I'm sure his wife makes sure that their furnishings are good quality in order to impress his clients."

Faith stopped and grasped her sister by the arm. Hannah looked over, her eyebrows raised in query. "How do you know that house belongs to an attorney?"

"Their housekeeper told me that, among other things." Hannah's expression became smug. "That house belongs to James Cranford and his wife Elizabeth."

Chapter Thirteen

J eremy Butler sat across from Benjamin Franklin in a local tavern. Each
had a tankard of ale before him. He had come in once or twice before,
once he had discovered that whoever brewed it was a master of his
craft. The summer heat beat down outside. It was a good time to seek shelter
and wet one's throat. It was just past the dinner hour, and a handful of men
were finishing their meals. Franklin had recommended the shepherd's pie,
which Butler had enjoyed thoroughly. The older man enjoyed socializing
and had spent a good hour chatting with individuals who recognized him
and came up to ask him about his experiments with electricity. Once the
last one went back to his table, Butler asked him. "What do you know about
your son's activities?"

Franklin looked pensive. "I had not realized that William's letters had
led to his imprisonment. He had been under house arrest because of his
intolerant views." He shook his head. "I have tried to reason with him many
times, but his loyalties lie with the king, not his father or his country."

"When was the last time you saw him?" Butler gave him a moment.

Franklin chewed his lip before answering. "Last year. I went to see him
at his residence in Perth Amboy. It's a long trip for an old man." He smiled
ruefully. "Age changes one's perception of time and effort. I find I must
choose my errands more carefully. These bones remember rough journeys
long afterward."

"What did he have to say to you?" Butler signaled for more ale. The
barkeep obliged, walking over to refill their cups before returning to his
place at the bar.

Franklin paused to drink. "Nothing he hasn't said before. He is a king's man. He said I would live to regret my choices. He was quite angry."

"Angry enough to do you harm?"

Franklin shook his head. "I raised him better than that. He has written me many times over the past months. Were his sword as sharp as his pen, I would be awash in blood. But physical violence has never been his chosen weapon. He and his wife Elizabeth refuse to accept that they have chosen the wrong side in this fight." He sighed. "By the time they face the consequences of their decisions, the wound will be too deep to ever heal cleanly."

Butler took time to choose his next words carefully. "Has your son ever mentioned a woman called Lisette Fournier?"

Franklin's face became slightly more guarded. If Butler had not been paying attention, he might not have noticed. "Madame Fournier is the toast of Philadelphia. Since she and her husband relocated here from the French West Indies, they have become prominent members of society."

Butler pressed. "Did William have any connection to her?"

Franklin sipped his ale slowly. "The Fourniers are invested in keeping trade open. They play the game with whomever they deem will help them: the British, Prominent Quakers in town, and the few of us with Patriotic leanings that might have some influence." His tone was dry. "Anyone who plays friends with both sides will eventually be stabbed in the back by one while engaging with the other."

He raised a hand to silence Butler. "I know what you ask. Madame Fournier loves to play the coquette with men, even me," he chuckled. "I have no doubt she enjoyed flirting with someone as prestigious as the Governor of New Jersey, but I never saw evidence of anything else." He raised an eyebrow. "You may want to talk to Master Hancock about her. He has taken supper at their home a few times since his arrival in Philadelphia."

They sat in silence, each nursing their drink. Butler scanned the room. Near a window, a man read a newspaper. He spread it over the table and used a finger to follow the words in each column until he came to the end, then repeated the process in the next column. Surrounded by his mustache and scrawny beard, the man's lips moved silently as he read to himself. A few tables over, three men engaged in a game of dice. They rattled as they struck the tabletop, before the next man scooped them up. Nothing looked amiss, but the hair on the back of Butler's neck rose, tingling a warning that someone, somewhere, was watching. It disturbed him that his eyes picked up nothing untoward. His instincts knew better.

At the bar, the owner wiped down the wooden bar in between pouring drinks. He said little beyond what he needed to accomplish his task. It occurred to Butler that such a man would be a useful source of information about happenings in town. He decided it would be worth dropping by this particular tavern more often to see if he could discover whether the owner favored patriots or Tories.

Franklin set aside his drink and, using a cane, rose to his feet. "It's time I returned to work. Jefferson has been busy writing a document to express our views to the world." He chuckled softly. "I've been invited to take a look and add a little wisdom. John Adams, that clever lawyer from the Massachusetts colony, has been working with it. It has been an interesting experience."

Butler walked with him outside. Franklin paused before turning onto Dock Street. The tall white spire of the state house rose above the other building between them and it. The older man's stick tapped the cobbles as they walked toward the imposing building. A youth hawked newspapers on the corner, his cries rising above the sounds of wagons going down Walnut Street behind them as they headed into the heart of the city.

A hammer rang out from a nearby blacksmith shop. The scent of hot iron touched Butler's nose. A throaty neigh told him a horse was in the process of receiving new shoes. The fire flared from the forge as an apprentice manned the bellows. It smelled of sweat and hot metal as they passed by. Butler took note of the fine sabers and swords lining the wall. When he had a moment, he was returning to replace the knives he had lost to the British on the journey to Philadelphia.

Nearby, a group of African-American men worked in a small yard assembling barrels. One man held the iron bands while another pounded in the staves to make it tight. Another man trimmed staves with a side axe in order to shape them so that they fit correctly. Still another man planed wood. They sang as they worked, harmonizing with an ease that spoke of long practice.

All around, people went about their jobs, except two men idling outside a coffee shop. One looked familiar. It was Lovell. Butler moved to have a word with him, but the man slipped into an alley, disappearing with the ease of a rat in a sewer. He paused, considering his options, and then chose to stay with Franklin. He would find Lovell later.

His eyes returned to the other man, who had not moved. He made no effort to enter the coffee shop or the tailor's next to it. A wide-brimmed brown felt hat concealed his eyes and threw his face into shadow. The afternoon sun was low enough that surrounding buildings shaded most of the ground, including where the stranger stood. Both hands were in his pockets as he leaned against the outside wall of the shop.

Franklin's voice droned on; Butler heard him mention Adams's name but paid no real attention. Experience had taught him there was a reason for everything. There was no reason for a healthy man to be idling in the street. He wasn't drunk, and he wasn't delivering something. He waited for something or someone.

Then he straightened and stepped away from the wall he had been leaning against. One hand left his pocket. It drummed restlessly against his leg. The other hand, his right, remained concealed between his jacket and shirt. His head moved to follow Butler and Franklin as they continued down the street.

As they came closer, he stepped off the porch of the coffee shop and began walking in their direction. His unhurried pace belied the way he would look across the road at them, before turning away to watch the faint traffic in the street. Butler moved to where his body blocked access to Franklin.

Franklin's voice dropped. "Is something wrong?" He stopped. The light reflected off his spectacles as he gazed about like a curious owl.

"I hope not. Keep walking." Butler adjusted his tricorn. He had bought it to replace the one that had been destroyed by the British on the journey to Philadelphia. He really didn't want it damaged the day he had gotten it.

The stranger picked up his pace. One hand remained tucked into his jacket, out of sight. Butler swore softly and reached for the sheath strapped to his wrist. Not fast enough, the man pulled a dagger. The sun gilded the edges of the blade as the man ran toward them; his footfalls the only thing Butler heard as he prepared himself for the conflict.

Butler held his own blade in his right. He grabbed a barrel stave that had been discarded by the cooper and raised it in time to deflect the first blow. The man panted as he twisted to get another strike.

"What do you want?" Butler followed the man's moves, using the stave to ward off strikes as he protected Franklin, who was trying to edge away.

Beads of sweat gathered on the stranger's upper lip, glittering among sparse strands of hair that a razor had missed. He said nothing, feinting left as he attempted to get around Butler. As he sidestepped, Butler kicked his shin, causing him to stumble. He struck quickly, slashing through the fabric to the flesh beneath.

The man hissed in pain. He looked at Butler, his flat brown eyes assessing his enemy. "Get out of the way; I've no business with you." Blood seeped from the cut he had received, turning his shirt red where it touched.

Butler shook his head. "You're not getting through. Who hired you?"

The man feinted, narrowly missing Butler's ribs.

Butler danced out of reach. His opponent was nearly six inches taller, with the reach to match. But he was used to fighting larger opponents. Darting in quickly, he nicked the other man's ribs before ducking away. Not fast enough; the flash of the blade nicked the side of his wrist, stinging as a few drops of blood splattered on the ground.

The afternoon sun beat down on both of them. The man turned to catch Franklin as he moved further away, Butler tripped him. As the man stumbled, he grabbed Butler's ankle, pulling him down with him.

Butler's knife fell to the ground as he instinctively tried to catch himself. A kick to his stomach stole his wind, and he dropped wheezing on the cobbles. He turned to watch the man run to Franklin, who raised his cane. Just as the man approached, Franklin unsheathed a hidden sword in the stick and lunged, stabbing him in the thigh.

118

The man cried out as he staggered back, staring at the older man. His eyes darted about the street, seeking an escape. Blood soaked the leg of his breeches and stained his stocking. His ragged breathing filled the small space just outside the alley where all three men stood.

"Who hired you?" Butler repeated as he moved closer. His ribs made breathing painful, and he was still short of breath. He bent to retrieve his knife. As he did, the man rushed forward, away from Franklin and Butler, toward the open street. Butler sprang to tackle him, getting a sharp kick in the shoulder for his trouble.

The man fled into the street, pursued by Butler. A team of horses pulled a wagon coming down that street at a rapid pace. Butler jumped back to avoid being trampled. After they passed, he looked about, but their attacker had vanished. He walked back to Franklin, who stood in a classic fencing pose as he waited. "Are you alright?"

Franklin looked at him. "I'm in far better condition than you." He wiped his sword on a nearby stretch of grass. After inspecting the blade, he reinserted it into the base of his cane. He handed Butler a handkerchief from his vest pocket.

Butler eyed the cane as he bandaged his wrist with the linen cloth, which stung. He would get it tended later. "Nice piece, that."

Franklin shrugged. "Not my invention. It was a gift from a friend on my last trip to London."

"I doubt you will be returning there anytime soon," Butler said dryly.

Franklin shook his head. "I have too many enemies there, now." His smile was sad. "I had a good many friends there too."

Butler tapped his arm. "Let's get you to a safer place."

Franklin's face turned grim as they continued down the road. "I doubt there is one in these colonies anymore."

Chapter Fourteen

Hannah listened to the hum of voices as a small group of women compared china patterns on the shelf where she had them displayed. She wished they wouldn't pick them up. All it took was one small slip, and another piece of her precious stock would be in shards on the floor. Not that the women cared. They were the pampered darlings of Philadelphia with no worries about how to afford food and shelter.

That life had vanished with Amos' death five years ago. His adult children had descended on their home like wolves and sent her packing. Carefully, she rolled her shoulders back and unclenched her fists. Anger was a poison she needed to release. She was fortunate that her late husband had left a detailed will in the hands of a lawyer unwilling to be bullied by the cries of Amos' sons and daughter. Bitterness poisoned her smile. She had never been anything but kind to them, but they had never forgiven their father for wedding a woman so close to them in age. She was fortunate that Lucretia and Nathan had not felt that way. They had helped her reinvent herself without having to crawl home to the farm she loathed.

Her front door opened and closed with the jingle of the bells Nathan had hung there when they had started the business four years ago. Hannah brushed her skirt and looked to see who had come to peruse her stock.

She recognized the servant first, although she had to rack her brain to remember where she had met the woman. Her dress, with its vertically striped panels of bright blue, had stuck in Hannah's memory, as had her delicate heart-shaped face surrounded by dark springy curls. They had spoken on the day she and Faith had followed Uncle Mordecai, which meant the well-dressed woman with her could only be one person.

The maid approached Hannah with her employer in tow. "Mistress, this is the lady who spoke to me about the china." She moved back.

Hannah pushed unpleasant memories out of her mind and moved forward. "Greetings, I am Hannah White. Welcome to my business."

The other woman smiled. "Good morning, I'm Elizabeth Cranford. I've come to see your china." A wide-brim hat of straw covered in white fabric covered her head. Hannah took a second to admire the contrasting deep blue around the brim and crown, before letting her eyes drift to her face. Her features were pleasant but not extraordinary: a faintly round face with mild blue eyes and dark brown hair. Hannah wondered if their mother had looked like this in her younger years.

Hannah led her to the wall where she had set up a series of prettily patterned plates on display. "We just got these in from Holland. My nephew has been busy unpacking our shipment. We have services from England, France and Italy, among others. We have selections of the best china on the Continent."

Mistress Cranford nodded. "I'm hoping to find something to enliven our table for when we entertain. My husband is a respected attorney in this colony."

Hannah nodded. She had never heard of him before her uncle had led them there, but there were circles of society she had never touched the edges of, nor was she likely to. She watched the other woman peruse the various designs in reds, blues, and greens. It was all a bit garish for Hannah, but she had been raised plain. She pursed her lips as she examined a design of bold red flowers; the expression reminded Hannah of her mother when Patience would check to see if they had executed a chore correctly. She had hated the constant criticism and having to redo things until her mother was pleased, which was rare.

Elizabeth Cranford maintained a pleasant expression even when examining every plate for flaws. As she glanced downward, Hannah realized she had a faint double chin like their mother had before her illness. Despite her stays, it was plain to see that Mistress Cranford was slightly plump in a well-rounded way that softened her features and added to her curves.

"Did you say you just had a shipment arrive?"

Hannah nodded. "Yes, my sister and my nephew have been busy unpacking it and taking inventory. With the blockade, we are grateful when we receive anything. Apparently, this captain was wilier than most."

"I want to see your new items that have not been put out on display yet."

Hannah's eyebrows rose. "Those are still packed in barrels of straw. I assure you that these patterns are from this season and among the best to be had."

Elizabeth Cranford tapped her foot, revealing elaborate pewter buckles. "Nonetheless, I would like to be taken where I can see what has arrived." She smiled, softening her determined glance. "I would gladly pay for something unique that my peers in society have not had an opportunity to purchase."

"Very well," Hannah could see that Elizabeth Cranford was not used to being told no, and she was not of a mind to turn away business. She led her to the room where she had put Nathan and Faith to work earlier that morning. Their shoes clacked as they went down the pie-shaped steps that twisted into the tight spiral staircase. Just as they reached the basement, Faith sneezed; the sound echoed through the small rooms.

A few strands of straw lay on the floor of the room just off the kitchen, where Suzanna was busy at work. "Hello," Hannah said to warn them. "I have a guest who wishes to look at the stock we just received."

As they entered, Faith stared at Elizabeth Cranford. A sharp glance from Hannah warned her she was being obvious. Chastened, she returned to the list she was using to check in stock, quill in hand.

Nathan looked up from the barrel he had just opened. A lock of hair flopped over his long forehead, making him look like a spaniel. He shook it back as he looked up at the women who had just entered. "There's quite a lot. We've only gotten to the second barrel. If you can return tomorrow, we should have far more checked in for you to examine." He shot an appeal at Hannah as Elizabeth Cranford stooped to look inside the barrel resting between his knees.

Elizabeth Cranford picked up a plate, holding it toward the window, ignoring the dust motes dancing in the rays of the sun coming in. She walked closer, her feet narrowly missing a stack of cups on the floor.

Nathan sighed as she missed stepping on them in her journey toward the window.

Elizabeth Cranford paid no attention as she studied the plate in the light. It was pure white with a pattern of blues and greens. "I wonder what they're using in London these days," she murmured.

Hannah moved inside the door, looking a bit worried as she watched the other woman move about the cluttered room. "I assure you. We deal only with the best sources of china on the continent. Madame Fournier was in here just yesterday surveying the latest arrivals. I believe she settled on this pattern." She lifted up a plate with a pattern of deep blue with red flowers and touches of gold. "It is English, by way of Holland. We are fortunate to be able to acquire it during these times."

"Really," Elizabeth Cranford drifted back from the window, setting the plate down on the table. It wobbled before Nathan grabbed it and put it back with its kindred. "I am surprised you do business with such notorious British Sympathizers.

Faith's eyes met his. "Nice catch," she mouthed. He nodded before wiping his brow. They waited to see what would happen next.

Hannah smiled. "We Quakers stay out of political conflicts. Let me tell you about this pattern," she held out a plate for the woman to see. Elizabeth nodded as she touched the gilding. "Perhaps you would like to see the pieces we have already put on display in my shop. The lighting is so much better in there."

Elizabeth Cranford pursed her lips. "This may suit Madame Fournier, but it's a trifle bold for me. Perhaps you could show me more of that pattern from Italy, the Majolica?"

"Certainly," Hannah purred. "I have a small amount of that left. It's quite exclusive and difficult to get."

The other woman nodded. "Let's see what you have. My husband and I would prefer to have the best quality for when we entertain."

"Certainly," Hannah said as she guided her prey across the hall. "Sometimes we are fortunate enough to inherit fine things from our mothers; other times we must invest in quality items as our circumstances change."

Hannah stepped carefully over one of the mounds of straw that littered her cellar. Their guest sneezed and backed away, her eyes watering.

Nathan's tone was apologetic. "The dust and straw get to us all sometime."

Hannah said, "Perhaps it would be better to come back after the unpacking is complete."

Elizabeth nodded as she sniffled. She pulled a handkerchief edged in lace from her pocket. "Can you send a messenger when it is complete? I would like to see what you have before it goes on display. I can pay for an exclusive set."

Hannah nodded. "I'm sure that can be arranged." She guided her guest out of the room. "Why don't we have some tea, and you can tell me what you are looking for."

Their heels clacked on the steps. Hannah said. "Do you have family in town? I can offer discounts to families who come in."

Faith listened as the sound of their voices faded away. She wished she could have spoken to Elizabeth longer. She had stared at the woman from the corner of her eye, trying to determine if there was any resemblance to her mother. Faith wasn't sure. She dipped the quill into the ink pot beside her and tapped off the excess. Looking over the list on the table before her, she asked. "How much do we have left?"

Nate looked about the room, "Five barrels in here and four more in the barn. We will be busy for some time. We're fortunate we're still able to get products from Holland and France. I don't know what we will do if that stops."

"Perhaps this conflict will come to an end," Faith said

Nate shot her a look. "Do you truly believe either side is willing to concede to the other?"

"No," she admitted. "I don't know when this will be over, but it cannot be too soon for me."

Nate held up a plate, admiring the bright red and blue flowers decorating

124

the wide rim. "Apparently there is still money enough to afford such things." He set the plate down on top of a stack in its pattern. "Hannah sold a tea service yesterday, and the lady paid in British coin. She was ecstatic; normally, we're awash in colonial currency from surrounding states. We had a few from Georgia the other day." He shook his head.

Faith's mind went to Williamsburg. She missed Andrew terribly. She wondered how his studies were going. She longed to be back in her tavern, back home, where she knew where she stood and managed her own affairs. She jumped when Nathan whistled.

He stared at her. "I tried speaking to you, but your mind was far away."

Faith picked up her quill and checked the tip. It was still quite sharp. Questioning her sister would have to come later. Hannah would have a lot of questions to answer before the night was over.

Chapter Fifteen

I t was late in the day before Franklin had finished his work with Adams and Jefferson. Outside the second-floor assembly chamber, there was little noise beyond the murmur of voices and the scratching of pens. Butler had not interfered but stayed nearby as the men talked. He already knew that Jefferson did not care much for criticism. It showed in his wounded expression whenever one of the other men pointed to a section on the document they all pored over. Franklin had already told him that Jefferson would work on editing it again in his rooms on Seventh Street.

The windows that lined the long gallery allowed Butler a clear view of the grounds outside. Butler saw nothing to cause concern. Philadelphia's streets remained busy with horse and wagon traffic. A few carriages trotted by, taking their occupants from Society Hill to the marketplace, their wheels blowing up fine dust from the road. Were it not for the attack on Franklin, he would have felt useless. He paced the length of the gallery as he replayed the attack on Franklin over in his mind. The man had been waiting for him. He had known Franklin's routine and planned accordingly.

"I prefer to meet here when possible," Franklin admitted as they entered the state house. "I've grown old enough to appreciate shorter walks whenever possible."

He had left them upstairs once he had satisfied himself that no dangers lurked within. He had insisted the curtains remain drawn to ensure no more arrows found their mark. It irritated him that his quarry had disappeared, as had the man with the dagger. Although it had occurred to him that they could be one and the same. But there were no clues as to who they were, which troubled Butler. He suspected someone had hired them, which would make finding the true culprit even harder. Franklin had wounded one man so he would not be moving swiftly for a while. Butler could only hope he worked alone.

Downstairs, delegates from all the colonies met, negotiating what form their union would take. Behind the closed doors, all he could hear were voices humming like an enormous collective of bees. He walked passed, headed outside to clear his head and look about. As he reached for the door handle, footsteps echoed behind him. Butler whirled as someone cleared their throat. A dagger was already in his hand before he realized Hancock was walking toward him.

"Peace, man," Hancock raised a hand in mock supplication, although it took a moment for him to wipe the startled look off his face. "I give my word that I plan no assault on your person." His fancy-heeled shoes clacked on the polished floor as he drew close to Butler. "I only wished to inquire if you have discovered anything."

"Not really," Butler acknowledged. He didn't like admitting that he knew little more than when he had begun. A fly buzzed by his ear; he waved it away, his hand coming into brief contact. It was an enormous horsefly. It made a wide circle around the two of them before speeding away to find tastier prey.

"Join me upstairs for a brandy, and tell me where your inquiries have led."

Butler shrugged and followed Hancock back up the stairs to what had been the governor's chambers. Franklin and his cohorts met in the Committee of the Assembly Chamber. It was quiet on the upper hall. Windows at either end of the long gallery were wide open in the hope of catching a stray breeze. The heat was oppressive. Butler pulled at his collar. He refused to wear a heavy jacket on such a day. He didn't know how Hancock managed in his suit. He had never seen him in his shirt sleeves or without his wig. If that was the price one paid to be in the upper echelons of society, Butler was happy not to be part of it.

Hancock gestured for him to sit at the table as he placed two glasses down and poured them each a drink. It was warm on his tongue. Butler thought it tasted faintly like caramel with a lighter feel than some whiskeys he had imbibed. He took a few moments to enjoy his drink before getting to business. "What do you know of Benjamin Franklin's son?"

Hancock looked surprised. "William Franklin was the Royal Governor of the New Jersey Colony until his activities made it necessary for him to be taken into custody. I doubt he could be involved in this considering that."

Butler shrugged. "There are ways to get messages out even when under watch." He had done it himself once or twice. "Franklin senior will not discuss the matter, but it's obvious the two had a falling out."

Hancock nodded, his face sober. "I'm aware. They have chosen different sides in this conflict, and it has torn their relationship apart." He sighed. "It's only been a few short years since Benjamin conducted scientific experiments with William's help. They seemed as close as two peas in a pod. Now, they couldn't be further apart. It's a tragedy being played out throughout these colonies. I cannot help but hope that when this conflict ends that common ground can be found so that we all can be at peace."

"Until that day comes, I have to look at everyone who bears grievance to Dr. Franklin, including his son and his allies. I presume he has some."

Hancock stared down at his glass, swirling it gently. "He does. Most every Tory in this town would consider William one. He kept some business contacts related to trade. He and Frances Fournier were involved in the rum trade not long ago."

Butler leaned forward. "Who is Frances Fournier?"

Hancock looked surprised. "He is one of the major forces in the sugar trade. He came here from the West Indies a few years ago with his wife, Lisette. He has entertained the Penns, the Shippens, the Drinkers, as well as the Franklins, father and son." Hancock tapped a restless finger on the table.

Surprise quickened Butler's blood. "Both Franklins have been to the Fournier's home."

Hancock barked a short laugh. "Most every influential family has. I've been there a few times. It's business, man. Fournier dominates the sugar trade. Because of his connections with the British, his ships get through the blockade."

Butler stared at him. "You still do business with loyalists?"

Hancock stared at him. "Someone has to fund this conflict. Money is made through trade, not through idealistic speeches. I will continue business as long as I can." He offered a self-deprecating smile. "Presenting myself to the British would be hazardous at this time, but there are plenty enough middlemen who do business with me as well as my foes. At some point, the British will realize I continue to trade and move to cut off my contacts, but until then, I will make what money I can." He shrugged. "It's quite possible I will lose all I have worked for, but it is a risk that must be taken. Fournier does business with everyone. His ships make regular runs across the Atlantic."

Butler paused to sip his brandy as he collected his thoughts. He wanted to disagree with Hancock about doing business with the enemy. But he saw the logic in his choices. He had faced the problems of too little money himself. There were times he had to supplement his meager pay with various jobs. He looked over at Hancock in his expensive suit. He doubted the man had ever gone hungry or slept in the rain, yet here he was, risking it all for the sake of independence.

Hancock finished his drink. "I've been invited to supper at their home later this week. Why don't you join me?"

Butler looked at him and down at his own clothes. He was still wearing items borrowed from Hannah White's late husband.

A look of understanding came over Hancock's face. "I have a line of credit at one of the local tailors. I will have Cicero take you there. You need the proper clothes for the occasion. I have heard your things were pillaged by the British."

"That's one way of putting it," Butler said. His ribs were still sore from his encounter with the British officer, Tarleton.

Moments later, Butler found himself negotiating the streets of Philadelphia with Hancock's servant Cicero. The well-dressed Black man said little as they walked together down the street. The enslaved man negotiated the busy streets with ease. He moved at a swift pace down the street, adroitly avoiding piles left by animals and debris from the many tradespeople moving back and forth. Butler stayed on his heels, shadowing his movements as they wove in and out of groups of people also traveling by foot in the city.

They stopped in front of a small, brick-fronted shop featuring large windows that showed selections of gloves, waistcoats, and neckcloths. A wooden sign over the door said, L. Cabot, tailor. Butler followed Cicero inside. A wooden counter ran the length of the room. Behind it, rolls of fabric lay stacked in a series of shelves. On one side, a young man sat at a work table, stitching what looked like a pair of breeches. His hands worked swiftly, drawing the needle back and forth through the fabric. His eyes focused on his work, ignoring the activity in the shop around him. On the opposite wall, a series of wooden pegs were set into the wall. These held various types of finished clothing; jackets, waistcoats, breeches, and jackets.

A man's voice hailed them. "Greetings, Cicero. I'm sorry to tell you, but Master Hancock's new waistcoat is not finished. My journeyman, James, should have the work done in plenty of time for him to attend the ball later this week."

Cicero nodded. "I'm sure he will appreciate knowing that. My master has sent me here on other business." He turned to Butler. "This is Master Butler, a friend of Master Hancock. He requires a suit for a formal dinner later this week. Can you help him?" He added delicately. "You may add it to my master's account."

The man looked at Butler, his eyes shrewdly taking in his size. "I will need to take measurements, but I'm sure we can accommodate him."

"Who are you?" Butler asked as he was led back behind the curtain that separated front from back. This room contained a mirror and a bench and little more other than a huge cushion filled with pins and a tape measure.

The man looked at Butler. "Lorenzo Cabot, at your service." He sketched a bow. "I will need you to remove your vest and breeches so I can measure you." He eyed Butler's clothing. "Those were made for another man."

Butler nodded and tried to stem the flush he felt rising up his neck. "Regrettably, much of my clothing was damaged on my journey here."

Cabot nodded. "I'm sorry to hear that." He pulled a plain strip of fabric from a drawer. "Let me mark your measurements on this tape. I will keep it for whenever you need to order clothes so that we can craft patterns for whatever you need." Butler allowed himself to be poked, prodded, and measured as he stood on a low stool following the soft-voiced directions of the tailor. On the other side of the curtain, he listened to the voices of men as they entered the shop, attended to by one of the other men working there.

Cabot paused after every measurement to snip into the tape so that it was notched in a distinctive manner. After he was done, he allowed Butler to redress and come out to select material for his suit. His eyes took in the bolts of fabrics lining the shelves. Cabot pulled down one of fine white.

"Linen does well in the summer for shirts," he suggested. "I also have a quantity of lightweight wool that can be made up into a suit that would work well for dining in society."

Butler nodded, allowing the tailor to guide his choices. He had no idea how much money he was spending, but since it was Hancock's idea and purse, Butler decided not to worry about it.

He fingered the deep blue of the wool. The rich color reminded him of the nighttime sea. He tried to keep the tailor from adding too many ruffles. He had no desire to look like a peacock. But agreed that being too plain would stand out when he was seeking to blend in. They wrangled about trim until they found something that pleased Cabot without offending Butler. He nodded when the tailor suggested adding buff breeches and another waistcoat to add to his wardrobe. If Hancock wished him to look fit for society, then he could pay for it.

He was finishing up when the door opened, and two men entered speaking French. Butler could recognize the language but not much more. He turned his head to see who had entered. Cabot looked pleased.

"My dear Master Fournier, how good of you to visit. What can I help you with today?"

The newcomer switched to English. "Cabot, my friend. Lisette sends me out for a new coat. She insists I must do my part to look like a gentleman, so here I am to beg your assistance." He smiled, revealing faintly crooked teeth that took nothing away from his rugged attractiveness. His silver-streaked hair was tied back into a neat queue although a few curls had escaped and adorned his temples. His lively, dark eyes went from Cabot to Butler. "I see I have caught you with another client. Perhaps I should return later?"

"No need," Butler said. "Master Cabot and I were just concluding our business."

Fournier offered his hand. "We have not met; I am Frances Fournier, originally from the West Indies, but for the past five years, a dweller in this fine city." He met Butler's gaze easily, standing only a few inches taller.

Butler took his hand in return. Fournier's handshake was firm and dry. Up close, he could see the deep creases along his eyes and the sides of his face. His skin had the leathery look of someone who had spent long periods under the hot sun, indicating he was no pampered dandy, whatever his current circumstances.

Fournier appeared amused by the scrutiny. "Perhaps you would like to join me for a drink once our business is concluded? City Tavern is nearby. They serve an excellent meal along with their drinks." He winked. "I should know. I keep their cellar supplied." His deep, throaty laugh took some of the other customers by surprise.

Butler found himself nodding. He was quite amenable to food and drink while learning more about Fournier. A breeze lightened the air as they walked the short distance to the tall brick building. A whiff of spirits tickled his nose as they drew closer.

Fournier smiled at his expression. "They have a brewery across the street. The beer isn't bad. I prefer the cognac." He smiled, showing a deep dimple. "I know where it comes from."

City Tavern hummed with activity. The coffee rooms were full of men. The hum of their voices filled the space. Butler followed his host through both rooms and to the elegant wooden staircase that Butler had been up before. A servant met them at the base of the stairs.

He nodded at Fournier. "Would you like a table in your usual space?"

"Oui, mon ami," Fournier replied. "In the Cincinnatus room, please." He followed the man up the stairs. The pewter buckles on his shoes shone as he passed through a beam of sunlight from a nearby window. His stockings shimmered, revealing the silk in their threads, all indicative of the man's enjoyment of finer things.

Butler noted that the other man's shoes had heels that added a couple of inches to his height. He suspected that without shoes, they would be on eye level. They clacked as he ascended the steps. They were led into an elegant room of square tables and tall backed chairs. The walls were painted a medium blue. Candles glowed on the cloth-covered tables. This room had few inhabitants. Butler recognized a few men from the congress but chose to ignore them, letting his glance skim past them around the room.

They were seated not far from one of the tall windows, where the draperies were tied back to let in light as well as air. Fournier allowed the server to seat him before requesting a bottle of wine and fried oysters. "You must try them," Fournier exclaimed. "They are the best in the city."

Butler had never cared much for oysters, but allowed himself to be swayed by his host.

To his surprise, they were quite tasty, with a crispy coating on the outside and tender oysters inside. They sat eating for a while, interrupted only by a few men dropping by to offer greetings to Fournier.

"You have many friends in the city," Butler observed.

Fournier chuckled. "I do a great deal of business in the city. The patriots have decided I am of some use to them, so I am tolerated, if only for my ships." Light from the candle highlighted the lines on his face. Deep creases fanned from the outer corner of his eyes and from the corners of his nose to the edges of his mouth. He glanced at Butler. "You stare, Monsieur. Have I spilled wine on my neckcloth?"

"Not at all," Butler said. "I was thinking you had the look of a man who had spent some part of his life outdoors."

Fournier raised an eyebrow. "Indeed, you are correct. " He leaned forward. "For many years, I sailed with my cargoes, spending many months away from home. My first wife called herself a widow of the sea." He looked sad for a moment. "I was at sea when yellow fever swept through our plantation, taking her and our infant son."

Butler nodded, letting him talk while they ate. "You are alone?"

Fournier shook his head. "No. You have not met my Lisette. She keeps me young. I moved here for her as much as for my business. She is a fair flower that all the bees hover around." He leaned forward. "But she is mine. She has not yet provided me with a son, but we have our Emily. She will make an advantageous match one day. I am sure." Leaning back, he bit into an oyster, chewing thoughtfully before speaking again. "You must come for supper one night and see how my lady entertains."

"It would be my pleasure." Through the open windows, a fiddler's tune wafted in, soft and sweet, as the musician used his instrument to cajole passersby to drop a few coins. Butler's eyes roamed the room, curious about who else was there. He recognized a few faces from the delegation at the state house. Buckles gleamed on knee britches and shiny leather pumps. Most wore well-cut jackets with buttons and other embellishments. There was little doubt he was among the elite of Philadelphia. From the stares he received, Butler recognized that he was not considered among them. Hopefully, Hancock's generosity would help him overcome that.

Fournier glanced over at him. Butler was glad he had taken the tailor's offer of a new waistcoat. He was beginning to see that clothes mattered in this affluent city. "What business brings you here, mon ami?"

"I had some personal matters to attend to," Butler answered.

Fournier nodded. "Those are the trickiest. It can be very easy to be led astray by those issues closest to the heart. N'est pa?"

Butler nodded. "It can be." He wondered how much the other man knew of the rumors regarding his wife and William Franklin. Looking at Fournier's shrewd dark eyes, he doubted he was easily led astray. He pushed back from the table with regret. It had been a wonderful meal with interesting company. In another time and place, he suspected he would enjoy Fournier's company. But that was a luxury he couldn't afford in these times. His job required he wear a different face for different people, and he could confide in no one, less he end up at the end of a noose. He stepped out onto the street full of belly and empty of soul. As he walked back to the state house, Butler spotted a boy rolling a hoop across an expanse of green. A man joined him rolling it back to him. His heart panged at the simple joy of it, but he knew a wife and family was never to be his fate. He had made the revolution his mistress, and there was room for no other, no matter how lonely it was.

Chapter Sixteen

Hannah looked over at her sister, picking at her food. Faith had been quiet since their brother Caleb had dropped by. Their investigation had turned up little so far. Every day in the Pennsylvania Colony was another day her sister spent away from her son. Hannah had heard her pacing the floor in the night and could figure out the cause. There was nothing easy about the circumstances that had brought them together. While death happened to everyone eventually, it was difficult to accept when it impacted one that had impacted their lives so thoroughly. Their mother's illness had dragged on for nearly two months with no sign of recovery. It hurt Hannah every time she saw her to see how she had weakened. She took a quick swallow of cider to quell the rising lump in her throat.

Hannah struggled with her brother's news as well. She had spent the first month after her collapse at her side before having to return to the city because she had to support herself. Now, their mother was refusing food and would only drink tea. Her mind did not accept that tea had become exceedingly difficult to get. It had left the family scrambling. Hannah had dug into her stores for what little English tea she had hoarded away and sent it with him. But that was not the answer to what was plaguing her sister.

Faith had come back to Pennsylvania to say goodbye to their mother, and Hannah suspected she had not been able to do that. She had no doubt returning in itself had been a shock after all these years, much less in such tragic circumstances. Like her, Faith would have to return to her home soon. Neither could afford to stay away long. Hannah only prayed Faith could make her peace before their mother died. She didn't want her little sister haunted by the ghosts of a troubled relationship.

Faith picked up a napkin and wiped her eyes. Her face reminded Hannah of when she was little and troubled. She had gone to her older sister rather than their mother. Hannah would deal with the situation without histrionics.

Hannah's voice was soft. "You need to go back."

"And do what?" Faith asked. "Watch her suffer while I do nothing? She needs to be at peace. She wants to see Lizzy, not me. I have to find her."

"She longed to see you as well. She told me so. You need to make peace with her," Hannah said. "It's not easy to forgive someone who made your childhood a difficult place. We all bear the scars. I honestly don't see how Charity has managed to stay there all these years."

Faith sniffed. "Charity spends her time in the wool barn, spinning and combing fleece. She spends more time on the loom than with our mother."

They both knew that Patience had little interest in working with fiber. When their grandmother had been alive, she had commanded the loom, and her daughter-in-law had avoided her, choosing to take charge of the garden and preserving the harvest for winter. Patience Payne hated sheep. It was little wonder all her daughters had found their way to the wool barn and the room where the loom lived. It was a place of relative peace for them all.

Hannah had been relieved to leave when she had wed Amos White. He had been far older than her, but he had been a calm and steadying influence. She had run his house, and he had given her the freedom to explore her interests. While she might have missed some of the more intimate parts of marriage, she had felt that she had found a refuge until his heart failed him, and her world had fallen apart in a space of days. Hannah had survived, and she would never let anyone have the power to hurt her again.

Upstairs, the clock toned the hour. Soon, it would be time to reopen the shop for afternoon customers, and there would be no time to talk. Caleb had refused to join them for breakfast, saying he needed to get back to the market. Hannah missed his solid presence. He reminded her of their father, quiet but not to be pushed about. In their childhood years, he had been the protector, the one who could soothe Patience when her anxieties ran rampant.

Faith said nothing, but pain radiated from her bones. Hannah looked at her with concern. She had worried when Faith had been widowed suddenly so far from home. None of the family had gone to help her. Hannah had been too poor to afford the trip but had let loose her fury that their mother had not. In her opinion, a lack of compassion was a far worse sin than marrying outside the faith.

Faith paused, "I'm not sure I would do her any good."

Hannah heard the hesitation and the pain of a child who had never felt good enough. She understood all too well. Patience had adored her sons, but had little appreciation for her girls. The blatant unfairness had left its share of scars. Were it not for Amos' kindness, Hannah would still feel the rejection. But in many ways, he had set her free, and she would be forever grateful for that. She broke the silence. "Go home. Not for her but for thine own piece of mind. She will never change, but she is our mother. Forgive her so you can go on with your life without the bitterness."

"You make it sound easy," Faith's voice turned husky. She took a slow slip of cider, shuddering as it went down her throat.

'It's not," Hannah answered. "It took me many years to overlook her pettiness. I still wake up in the night expecting monsters, thanks to her nervous imagination, but I can remember good things, too. She taught us how to do many things, and she always made holidays seem special." She paused, "I think she loved us as much as she was able. She always feared what could happen to us girls. It made her desperate to have us all safely wed."

Faith snorted. "To an appropriate Quaker."

Hannah nodded. "She wanted us cared for more than she was." They had always known the bitterness Patience held toward her family; they just hadn't known why until recently.

Faith met Hannah's eyes. "I wish I could go home to Virginia to my son and my people." She looked around at Hannah's parlor with its simple blue drapes and painted walls. "Pennsylvania is not home anymore." She paused.

"I keep having dreams about her calling for me, but for some reason, I don't hear her until it's too late, and I've fallen short again."

"Oh, Faith," Hannah said in surprise. "You've never fallen short. She didn't want you to move so far away, but she didn't blame you. After you left, she would walk across the fields to where your farm had once been and stare into the fields as if she could conjure you back. She missed you terribly."

"She never wrote," Faith said. "I wrote her many letters, and not one came back, not until she was struck with apoplexy. Then the letters came from you, from Papa, from Charity, Caleb's wife." She sniffled. "I'm here now for all the good it does. I've accomplished nothing."

"I disagree. You've come home. Now go make peace while you can." Hannah rose from the table, brushing nonexistent crumbs from her apron. "Caleb will not have left the market yet. I will send word that you wish to return. He will come for you."

Hannah watched her younger sister head upstairs to pack. The steps creaked mournfully under her feet. She knew this was hard. It had been hard when she had gone back herself when Patience had first collapsed. She had spent weeks by her bedside expecting her to die, watching over the woman who had given her life and caused her an equal mixture of joy and pain.

Returning to the city had been difficult, but she had to earn her bread. It would not be given to her. Just as she knew Faith would have to return to Virginia before long. Although their mother was failing, no one really knew how long she would last. Hannah swallowed the knot that rose in her throat. Seeing her mother confined to bed had been painful. Thinking of the woman she knew as opinionated and active laid low troubled her still. Patience had never been still. Her voice and her hands had always been busy throughout the house. So much so that Hannah had marveled at the quiet of her late husband's home. Amos had been a merchant dealing in imported spices and fabrics from Europe. Their life had been comfortable. That he was old enough to be her father had not troubled her, nor had the frailties of age that limited their activities. He had given her the freedom to read what she wanted, visit whom she pleased, and pursue her interests. They had been friends, and his death had been a painful shock. His son's desire to take everything had given her something to do besides grieve. Anger had propelled her to seek the help of an attorney who had ensured she received her widow's portion even if he could not save her house. Hannah rolled her shoulders as she made her own way up the steps to her shop. This was her place now, and although not affluent, she was free to make her own choices. It was enough.

The hours passed swiftly. The affluent of Philadelphia society came in and out the doors, looking for ways to show their wealth in exotic dinnerware choices. Hannah helped them, showing them plates and cups that had come in from Europe. When Caleb came in to collect their sister, she left Nathan in charge so that she could spend a few moments with them.

The sturdy farm wagon carried a fine layer of dust. Inside were empty boxes that had held produce that he had brought to market before dawn that morning. Caleb took Faith's bag and put in it behind the seat. Faith tied her straw hat over her cap. An expression of dread was on her face.

Hannah hugged her. "I will be down in a week, if all goes well," she said. "I will send word if I discover anything."

Faith nodded before letting Caleb help her into the wagon. The seat creaked under her weight. Caleb climbed in next to her. Lifting the reigns from the seat, he clucked to the sturdy farm horses to tell them it was time to head out. Hannah watched them proceed down the street, joining the afternoon traffic of people heading back home to the countryside.

As she turned to go back inside, she spotted her guest, Jeremy Butler, walking towards her. He was accompanied by an older man and someone who was clearly a servant by his garb. The servant was carrying a medium size bag. Hannah folded her arms and waited, wondering what her guest had in mind. Bemused, she listened to him tell the servant to take the older man to her parlor and wait for him. Once they entered the building, he turned toward her.

"I need a favor of you."

"I imagine you do," She said dryly. "Dr. Franklin has lived in Philadelphia far longer than I have. I assume there is a reason you have brought him to

140

my house."

Butler put a hand to her back gently. "Let's talk inside."

Hannah let him propel her back into her own home and to the small room to the side that she used as an office. She watched him close the door behind them. Her desk was in front of the window. She could make use of the light and enjoy brief glimpses of the squirrels that inhabited the sturdy oak outside. A tall, backed chair was pushed into it, waiting for when she had a few moments to tend her accounts. She chose to stand while she waited to hear what he had to say.

"Dr. Franklin needs a safe place to stay for a few days until I can determine who is threatening him. His daughter and her small children are at his home. He does not want them to be placed in danger."

"I didn't realize Dr. Franklin was being threatened." She was somewhat aggravated that her guest had brought another guest without consulting her.

His voice was soft. A faint lilt threaded the edges of his speech from time to time, indicating he had come to the colonies from elsewhere. She didn't want to admit it, but she found him attractive even though she suspected his activities might get her into trouble.

"Where is Faith?"

"She's returning to care for our mother. She left a few hours ago." Hannah felt sorry for Faith. Their mother could be challenging to deal with, but it was their duty to tend to her. Of her mother's love, she had no doubt, but it was a critical, neurotic affection that left one feeling damaged over time. She had spent nearly a month on the farm, and she knew that at some point, she would have to return. It was not a trip she looked forward to taking.

"Then her room is available for Dr. Franklin," Butler said. He placed a placating hand on her arm. "He would be grateful for your help, and I'm sure he will pay for room and board."

Hannah sighed. "I haven't had time to tidy it or change the linens, Master Butler. And I must point out that he is used to far finer accommodations than I can offer him."

"No one will look for him here," Butler pointed out. His foot tapped restlessly as he looked about. His voice softened. "I didn't know where else to go. I've pledged to protect him, and he refused to place his family in danger."

Hannah felt herself weakening. He was desperate, and as most of her family knew, she couldn't turn so much as a stray cat away. But she refused to be bowled over. "Thou will be responsible for him, Master Butler. And I expect fair recompense for lodging and food."

His smile took her breath away. "My thanks are yours, Mistress White." He leaned over and captured her hand, placing a kiss on the palm. Her skin tingled all the way up, raising hairs on her arms. "I'll tidy the room so you can go about your business. We will be no trouble to you whatsoever." He trotted up the stairs, calling out to the maid for coffee as he went upstairs.

Hannah walked more slowly out into the foyer and towards the rooms that housed her shop. She already knew from the way her heart was pounding that she was in trouble, far deeper than boarding a known patriot.

Chapter Seventeen

Jeremy Butler stared into the steel mirror attached to the door of the room he shared with Nathan White. His suit had arrived that morning, just in time for his dinner engagement with the Fourniers. His new pumps shone with polish and sported elegant pewter buckles. He doubted he had ever been so well dressed in his life. Hancock had been quite generous, and Butler was grateful, although a little voice in his head wondered what was expected in return for such largesse.

He appreciated the talent of the tailor in not making him roast or itch. The lightweight wool was as soft as butter. Butler eased his shirt cuffs out from underneath the jacket, relieved that Cabot had not gone overboard on the ruffles. It would be easy to slide out the knife sheathed to his wrist if necessary. His buff breeches fit like a glove, as did the embroidered waistcoat. He just needed to tend his hair, and he would be ready in plenty of time for the carriage Hancock was sending to pick up Franklin and him.

A soft tap echoed on the door. "Come in," he said, expecting Nathan. His roommate was a quiet man except when dreams of the accident that crippled him disturbed him. He found the young man likable and would have liked to have forged a friendship, but his position meant he could confide in no one. To his surprise, Hannah White stood outside the door. Her eyes widened as she took in his appearance.

"Thou hast an engagement tonight."

He nodded. "Hancock has asked me to accompany him to the Fournier's tonight."

She nodded. "They ride high in the social circles in Philadelphia. There

143

will be many important people there." Her face was faintly wistful. "The music will be lovely and the dancing will go on all night."

He shot her a surprised look. "You've been?"

Hannah flushed, then recovered. "Not to the Fourniers. They arrived in Philadelphia after my husband died. But before my circumstances changed, Amos and I attended some functions with friends. Those I believed were friends," she amended. Her tone became somewhat mocking. "It's only been in recent years that I learned some relationships require money and social standing to endure."

"I'm sorry," Butler said.

Hannah shrugged. "I'm not. 'Tis far better to know what people really think of you than be deceived by polite smiles. I have far more freedom than I did as a wife, and my choices are my own." She stepped into the room. "You can't wear your hair like that to a ball. It will send the wrong message. It's better to look polished and make them wonder whether or not they should cultivate your acquaintance. She gestured to a nearby chair. "Sit, I will braid it for you."

Surprised by the offer, he complied. Hannah picked up a brush from a nearby table and ran it through his hair. Her touch was firm as the brush ran from crown to nape. Butler was surprised at how soothing her steady strokes were. If she were to continue long, he would be in danger of falling into a complete stupor, but soon, she stopped and ran his hair through her fingers, separating the locks into three. He felt the regular tugs of hair being braided.

Hannah worked swiftly until she reached the end. "What does thee plan to tie it with?" She asked.

"I have a piece of leather." He gestured to the table.

She picked it up and wrapped it about the end of his queue. Hannah stared at the thin strand. "Many Quakers would leave it like that, but I do have some ribbon if thou wants it fancier."

Butler shook his head. "I'll leave the ribbons for the ladies." He looked over at her. "I appreciate the offer."

She smiled. "I imagine you will cut a well enough figure amongst the

144

ladies anyway."

"If you say so." He stood and brushed imaginary wrinkles from his breeches. Looking about, he spotted his new tricorn on the bed. "I'd best get downstairs. Hancock is picking me up in his carriage. He doesn't strike me as the patient sort."

Hannah followed him out. Downstairs, they could hear Nathan whistle as he continued to open barrels of china. Butler had heard the tune Yankee Doodle a few times before, so he knew the words. Although it wasn't a song he would have chosen, he wasn't going to interrupt Nathan's cheer with any criticism.

The front door slammed. Butler was halfway down the steps to the main floor. He had to go almost all the way to the bottom before the curve allowed him to see Hancock's footman in the entryway. He had seen the dark-skinned man before. His deep blue livery was trimmed in gold braid with ivory facings on his jacket.

The man nodded. "Master Hancock is waiting in the carriage. Is Master Franklin ready as well?"

Butler had forgotten about the guest he had brought home hours earlier. He turned to go back up when he heard a voice float down the stairwell.

"You can tell Master Hancock I am prepared to sup and socialize with the finest of Philadelphia society, regardless of their rumored Tory leanings." His cane tapped as he came down the twisting staircase, placing each foot carefully before moving the other. He wore a beautifully cut black jacket with matching knee britches and ivory stockings that Butler suspected might be silk from the sheen. Given Franklin's many trips to England, he had probably visited a tailor or two when abroad. His tricorn featured a jaunty gold braid around the edges, whereas Butler's was plain black.

Butler allowed the footman to proceed before gesturing for Franklin to wait. Once outside, he scanned the street. Although there was still plenty of light, the angle of the sun caused deep shadows to form in front of buildings to the west. The streets had quietened in the intervening hours since he had last stepped out. An older man on a horse trotted by, likely heading home for the day. Down the street, he heard the steady chopping of wood from a nearby yard. He could smell food from nearby kitchens as well: succulent beef and yeasty bread. His stomach grumbled. It had been a while since he'd eaten with Franklin at the tavern.

The footman opened the door. Inside, he spotted Hancock resplendent in a burgundy suit with ornate trim. Pure white lace spilled in abundance from his cuffs and collar. His wig looked as if it had been freshly curled and powdered. Butler's nose itched in confirmation of the latter.

Hancock examined Butler's appearance. "I knew he could accommodate you. I hope I can persuade him to move to Boston when all this is over. He does excellent work."

Butler did not know how to answer, so he settled for a nod. Like Franklin, he settled back into the cushions as the footman shut the door before stepping up to the footplate on the back just as the driver clucked to the horses to move. Once they got underway, he cut a look at Franklin, "What makes you think the Fourniers are Tories?"

Hancock made a choked sound, but Franklin ignored it.

His mild blue eyes met Butlers. "In this city, it pays to know who one associates with and what societies one supports. Fournier is very discreet, but he has been seen with men who speak in favor of remaining part of the British Empire, Galloway, and Allen, among others. He and his wife are also good friends with Jacob Duché, the rector of Christ Church.

Hancock interrupted, "Duché served as chaplain to our first congress."

Franklin nodded. "I remember, but as we have moved toward open rebellion, he seems less eager to support the cause." He shrugged. "Perhaps I have become overly suspicious in my old age."

Butler didn't believe that at all. Franklin might be old, but he was no fool.

It took very little time to arrive at the Fournier's home. Carriages were already lined up at the entrance, the horses snorting as they waited to be led away from the crowd. As they got out, Hancock called to the driver. "You can come back for us before ten. Make sure they get a drink and a good rub down." The man nodded before heading back out into the street. As the other men took a moment to straighten their jackets, Butler gazed up at the sky, glittering with stars and lit by a luminous moon that had almost waxed full. In his eyes, it was far more beautiful than any opulent ball society could muster. Hancock interrupted his thoughts. "Shall we go, gentlemen?" Together, they strode toward the entrance to the mansion where the Fourniers lived.

Once inside, they joined the crowd, entering the grand house. Their hosts waited just inside, greeting their guests. Fournier looked resplendent in a pale blue patterned suit with pearl buttons at the sleeves and jacket. The lace on his cuffs was nearly four inches long. More lace frothed in a deep wave from his collar. His elaborate wig towered over him. Butler wondered how he managed to keep it attached to his head.

He bowed to his host and the woman he assumed to be his wife. Lisette Fournier was young enough to be his daughter, with silvery blond hair styled high on top her head and enormous deep blue eyes that gazed deeply into his. He noted that a few long curls tumbled artfully down her shoulders. One brushed forward to rest on the rise of her bosom as she leaned over to extend her hand. A lofty white feather graced the side of her head.

"Master Butler," she said. An enormous sapphire set with diamonds graced one hand. Butler could not even begin to imagine what such a gem had cost her husband.

He took her hand and bowed over it. The faint scent of lilies floated off her flawless skin. He looked up into her deep blue eyes, noting the beauty mark just to the left of the same eye. Butler was not expert but he suspected her lovely face had been highlighted by the careful use of cosmetics. He smiled as he released her hand, noting how the candlelight caused the silk of her gown to shimmer.

Lizette Fournier turned her attention to Hancock. She purred as he took her hand and touched his lips to it. "Master Hancock, I am delighted you could attend. I have heard there is much activity at the statehouse. I have also heard you are a magnificent leader of men."

Hancock smiled at her. "I assure you that most of it is true, and only a small portion is the embellishment of the newspapers."

A small dimple decorated one cheek as she chuckled. "I will keep that in mind." She turned to the next person entering the ballroom, pausing half a second before extending her hand. "Dr. Franklin, welcome. Are you staying long in Philadelphia?"

Franklin smiled in return. "Not the Franklin you are used to seeing, I'm sure." He looked about the enormous room, taking in the silver candelabras winking throughout the space as they illuminated the room. "You have a magnificent home. I am sure you and your husband take a great deal of pleasure in entertaining a variety of personages."

Lisette Fournier's voice lost some of its warmth as she gazed back at the elder Franklin, who gazed back at her. "I see that your reputation is well deserved."

"Reputations, like respect, are earned, my lady. I can assure you that whatever has been said behind my back is probably minor to that which has been said to my face." He smiled serenely as he walked past her, his cane tapping across the wooden floor.

She turned to the next guest in line and greeted them with a smile. In a corner, a man began a melody on the nearby harpsichord, and couples took to the floor to dance.

Butler skirted the edges of the room, taking in who was there with whom. His ears noted when the harpsichord was joined by a collection of strings. It wasn't often he got to enjoy orchestral music, and he appreciated the opportunity, even if he had no intention of joining the dancers. As with most formal affairs, groups of well-dressed young ladies with hawk-eyed mamas surveyed the crowds.

Butler avoided them as he circled the room. Hancock was already engaged in conversation with an older man off to one side. Franklin found a comfortable seat where he was soon encircled by a mixed crowd as he exerted his charm. Given that he was surrounded by paramount families of Philadelphia, Butler felt certain the old man was quite safe. He scanned the room, looking for familiar faces. A light touch on his arm caught him by surprise.

Lizette Fournier smiled up at him with a guileless expression. "Forgive me, Master Butler, but I appear to be without a partner for this dance. Would you do me the honor?"

Bemused, he allowed her to take his arm, and they entered the dance floor. Butler hoped he didn't make a fool of himself and forget the steps. It had been quite some time since he'd been called to do so. When he had served with Washington as a youth in the French and Indian War, the then colonel had seen fit to teach him dancing. The colonel, now general, was both an excellent dancer and teacher. Butler felt a debt of gratitude to him as he led Mistress Fournier into a well-known country dance.

Lizette Fournier was light on her feet. Her delicate blue gown, with its deep, frothy lace, reminded him of seafoam as it moved back and forth as they danced. Her eyes watched him as he turned and swayed along with her.

"You are a fine dancer, Master Butler," she called as they drew closer. "I wonder that I have not seen you at some of our other gatherings."

Butler waited until they were close again. "Regrettably, I have had little time for entertainment since I entered this fair city."

"Really, I wonder what sort of business would keep an attractive man such as yourself away from the very gatherings that allow men to make connections valuable in conducting a successful business."

Butler nodded as they turned. "I have seen many of Philadelphia's finest families represented here tonight, but not all business is conducted at a ball. The ladies expect better of us than to take time away from the festivities."

"It would be a shame," she agreed. "That's why so many of our fine men slip away to the card tables so that they can drink and gossip with impunity."

Butler laughed. "Is that how it is done? I will keep that in mind, Mistress Fournier." He bowed before her as the dance ended. "Perhaps I had best excuse myself and move to that room." He moved swiftly before she could compel him to another dance. Fortunately, he had spotted the adjacent room set up for cards as they had moved across the dance floor.

Candelabras surrounded the group of square tables set up in an elegant room papered in blue and white toile print. Dark blue draperies partially drawn across the windows gave the room an intimate look. The windows were open to allow breezes inside and allow smoke from cigars and pipes to drift out into the night.

Butler recognized some faces from the congress. Jefferson's red hair was easy to spot as the young man sat with a goblet on one side and a stack of cards on the other. A basket holding cards sat in the center of the four men, one on each side. After a moment, Butler recognized they were playing Papillion with a French card deck.

Another table was engaged in playing Whist. As his eyes swept the room, Samuel Adams met his gaze, gave a brief nod of acknowledgment, and returned to his game. Butler watched as men played cards as they drank, talked, and smoked. He saw nothing of interest, and the rank smell of the cigars was making him queasy. He turned to leave the men to their games.

As he passed by the settee where Franklin was ensconced, he heard a girlish giggle. He had been joined by a pretty young girl in a pale pink dress covered in bows. Had she been a few inches closer, she would have been in the older man's lap. Butler watched as Franklin leaned over to kiss her cheek and chuckle heartily.

Butler briefly wondered if he had been entrusted with the defense of an old lecher, but he saw nothing further of concern from either Franklin or the girl as they sat talking animatedly. He moved to stand behind a chair next to where they were.

Franklin basked in the attention of the young lady, her mama, and a few others as he shared a story about one of his experiments regarding electricity. "We soon discovered that lightning would strike the highest point in the vicinity in order to reach the ground, and," he leaned over to whisper conspiratorially, "whatever it struck would explode as if shot from a cannon." He leaned back and saw Butler. "Master Butler, could you find me some refreshment? Regrettably, my throat has gotten quite dry with the sharing of my scientific work."

Butler bowed before shooting Franklin a look. "It would be my pleasure."

"Thank you, my good man." He turned to the girl. "Now, my sweet Felicity, where were we?"

"You were about to tell us about attaching a key to your kite," she replied. Chestnut brown curls were piled artfully on top her head while two or three large sausage-shaped ones drifted over her bare shoulder. She couldn't have been more than sixteen.

Butler shook his head as he went in search of the punch bowl. Franklin knew how to charm, that was evident. He had seen some partiers sipping syllabub earlier. Following a faint trail of glasses, he soon located their source. Because he was a gentleman, he brought a glass for the young lady with Franklin as well.

They had moved on to another of Franklin's experiments by the time he arrived. Butler handed him a frothy goblet and passed the other to the girl. Franklin drank deeply, draining the glass before setting it on a nearby table. Felicity sipped delicately, holding the stem with practiced grace.

Butler smiled over at Franklin. "I believe I read that your son assisted you in many of your experiments. I imagine having another pair of hands must have been useful."

Franklin nodded. "William helped a great deal. He served as my assistant and recorder. He could be very useful when he chose."

Felicity asked. "Where is your son now, Dr. Franklin?"

Franklin remained silent for several moments, his expression unreadable, then he said. "William is far away from me now."

One of the other ladies started talking about the chances for rain in the coming days, and the moment passed. Butler left to get a drink for himself, pondering how two men once so close could grow so far apart.

Avoiding the syllabub, which he found disgusting, Butler acquired a glass of wine and settled along a wall to watch the spectacle. Before long, he was joined by Frances Fournier, also with a glass of wine.

"It is a fine party, is it not mon ami?" Fournier's glass was almost buried by the enormous cascade of ruffles flowing out from the cuffs of his jacket. The pale ivory of his waistcoat stood out in contrast to the blue of his suit. All were covered with embroidered roses that must have taken some poor tailor hours to produce. Fournier gazed with pride at the crowd filling his home. "My wife does an excellent job with these things."

Butler nodded. "She seems very talented. You must be pleased to have such a beautiful and skilled lady at your side."

Fournier nodded sagely. "She is a remarkable woman, my Lisette, and tolerant of my eccentricities." He smiled expansively. "She will pretend not to notice if I slip away for a few hours with a like-minded friend."

Butler wondered what Fournier was alluding to. There was very little a wealthy man could not discreetly do. "It is good she is an understanding woman," he said at last.

"I have not seen you with the ladies, with the exception of my charming wife; perhaps you too prefer the company of men?"

The question was posed delicately, but Fournier was watching for a reaction.

Butler realized what he was asking. He smiled to show he meant no judgment against his host. "I'm flattered you would ask, but that is not my interest. I lost my wife years ago and have no interest in forming an attachment with anyone." He stepped back from the wall. "Now, I think it best if I check on my companions before they take in too much of your well-stocked cellars. I wish you a most pleasant evening." He walked slowly into the crush, aware of the older man's eyes on his back. Butler had no intention of commenting on his interests, although he suspected it was known in society. His mission was to protect Franklin, not judge other men's choices.

Butler walked outside to the garden to clear his head. The constant press of people made his head throb. He longed for a few moments of peace and quiet. Couples strolled the well-ordered pathways, seeking a few brief moments of privacy. He didn't blame them. Courting while being watched would be challenging for the heartiest of souls. Strains of music drifted out into the shadowed garden, lit by a few scattered torches. A tall tree beckoned from a corner. Its canopy provided a large dark space where one could shelter and not be disturbed. Butler stood beneath it, taking in the night air. An owl hooted in the distance, hunting for prey.

In the garden, whispers drifted across the grounds, providing Butler with information, some useful, some not. Young swains sputtered their affections to their young ladies. A few men discussed an upcoming horse race on the edges of town the next day. One apparently was short of funds. Butler paid attention to that. A man desperate for money might be willing to share

152

information for some coins.

A flutter of skirts caught his eye. A pair of women walked together outside. Their furtive glances caught his interest. Butler decided to follow. He recognized his hostess as well as one of Hannah's customers, Elizabeth Cranford. Intrigued, he followed at a discreet distance in order to see what they were up to. Gravel crunched under their feet as they walked swiftly away from the revealing light of torches that had been placed just outside the house. Butler kept to the shadows surrounding the fruit trees on the edge of the formal beds.

Within the raised beds, pale blossoms of flowers glowed in the shadowed garden. The waxing moon provided ample light to see the path. Butler listened to the hoot of an owl in the distance, warning smaller creatures that it was on the hunt. He watched as the women made for the pergola at the end of the main path. Painted white, it stood out in the darkness.

One of the women stopped as her skirt became caught in the boxwood edging one of the flower beds. As she bent to free it, Lisette Fournier whispered. "Hurry, it won't be long before we are missed."

Mistress Cranford rose. "I'm not tearing my skirt. The dressmaker delivered this yesterday." They continued their journey, stepping inside the pergola.

Butler lingered outside, concealed by trees and shrubs.

Fournier spoke first. "Has your husband revealed anything about where he stands in this conflict?"

Cranford's voice sounded exasperated. "We are Quaker. He says we are neutral, but he meets with men like Franklin and George Clymer. He is angry at the threats the British have made. They imply that if he doesn't support the King, he is a patriot even if he does nothing." Fabric rustled as skirts brushed by the narrow walls of the enclosure.

Fournier nodded. "The British are of like mind. They have no use for pacifists." She raised her head, looking at the sky. Her face was a pale oval, unreadable in the shadowed structure. "The British will come," She said. "We need to prepare. Our husbands may choose to blindly ignore the danger, but we cannot. Our children depend on us to provide a future for them."

The other woman didn't reply but stood gripping her own hands.

"Elizabeth," Lisette grasped her hand. "I realize this is difficult, but you can do this. Talk to your husband and listen when he brings his associates home to dinner. Let me know what you hear; that is all you need to do."

The other woman shook her head. "James won't like it if I pry in his business. It would be unseemly. His family was disappointed he did not marry into a more affluent family. It has been better since Simeon was born. His father dotes on him and his sisters."

"It is for your children you should do this. When the British come, they will take this town and punish anyone they believe sympathetic to the revolution. It is up to us women to discover their plans." Her voice deepened. "Men pay no attention to us, but we are necessary to their comfort and wellbeing. Therein lays your power. Be the perfect hostess and entertain your husband's associates with loving kindness. They will speak and never realize you are present. We can use that information to protect our families from ruin."

Elizabeth Cranford drew in a breath. "This is a patriot stronghold. Do you really believe the British will come?"

"I'm sure of it. British Troops are gathering in New York, waiting for the right moment. Frances' contacts have told him that a massive fleet has landed there, intent on retaking the colonies. It's a matter of time before they march south."

"But Washington," Elizabeth began.

Lisette shook her head. "He works with militias: men of very little training and short commitment. My friends tell me they are not prepared to meet a professional army."

Butler couldn't argue with her logic. Great British had the most powerful army in the world, but he still believed a miracle could happen. He couldn't let himself contemplate otherwise. He wondered who the lovely Lisette shared her information with. It would be very useful to discover.

"It's time for us to return to the ball. Our men will miss us," Lisette murmured. "Sleep on it. I will call on you tomorrow, and you can let me know if James has expressed any opinions to his clients. I have heard that Master Hancock has met with him."

Elizabeth nodded. "They have discussed business contracts. Master Hancock wants to expand where his ships go and find a way to avoid the British navy."

Lisette snorted. "Good luck with that. We're all trying to avoid them, as well as the privateers that seek fat ships to loot." She looked about before stepping out onto the pearly pale gravel that lined the garden's walkways. Both women walked swiftly back toward the house, where the strains of a minuet drifted from the open windows. Butler watched them go, pondering what he had heard. Lisette Fournier was far more than a pretty woman. In the right hands, she could influence the course of the conflict here in Philadelphia. The question was, whose side was she really on? It might be possible to sway her to share intelligence in order to garner favor with the prevailing side. Butler recognized she could be a source of tremendous intelligence, but if he wasn't careful, she could also be his doom.

Chapter Eighteen

I t was close to midnight when Hannah heard her front door open. Although she was fairly certain it was Jeremy Butler returning from his evening out, she still came out to the landing to make sure Suzanna's son Micah hadn't inadvertently let in a burglar. She needn't have worried. The tapping of Franklin's cane could be heard across the floor of the entryway, followed by the soft sound of leather shoes crossing the hardwood floor. Hannah looked down to see both men at the base of the curving stair.

Butler looked surprised. "My apologies, Mistress White. We had no intention of waking you."

Hannah leaned back, tossing her hair back over her shoulders. "I was already awake. Did you enjoy the ball?" She felt awkward standing out in her shift. It would have been more prudent to have grabbed a shawl before dashing out. She backed into her doorway as the men came up, wrapping her arms around herself. She wasn't quite sure whether to duck back into the security of her room or wait.

Her decision was made for her, given the speed with which Butler ascended the stairs. Franklin moved slowly using his cane with the hand not resting on the stair rail. In the shadowed light provided by the moon outside, he looked his age, although his smile was as charming as always. He nodded amicably as he stepped onto the landing. Without pausing, Franklin went to his own door, turning the nob. He turned before stepping inside. "Good Night, Mistress White. It is long past the time I normally retire."

The door shut firmly behind him. Hannah heard him moving about, grunting with effort. The cane clattered against the floor as it tumbled from wherever it leaned. The mattress whooshed as a weight settled on it. After a series of creaks, soft snores came through the door.

Butler had not moved from the landing. He appeared lost in thought. Moonlight caught his fair hair, highlighting it in the dim space. His eyes met hers. "It was a most intriguing evening. I wish you could have been there."

Hannah flushed. She was no longer part of that society and was unlikely to ever be again. "I have no need of fancy balls."

"No one does," Butler replied. "But I think you would have enjoyed the music, and I would have enjoyed the conversation of an intelligent and attractive woman."

Hannah wondered how much he had had to drink. He didn't seem the worse for wear. He cut a handsome figure in his well-cut suit with its silvery embroidery. She was glad he chose not to be ostentatious as some she had seen. She had little use for excessive frippery. He looked like a man of means, attractive and confident and far from the station in life she now occupied. Hair straggled across her shoulders in a tangled web as she stood before him barefoot in her well-worn shift.

Butler met her gaze steadily. "Fancy gowns and jewels aren't necessary to make a woman attractive, Hannah."

She stared at him for a moment before acknowledging the compliment with a nod. No one else stirred in the darkened house. Silence closed around them like a heavy blanket on a cold winter's night. A smile curved his lips.

"It's time I turned in as well. Good night, I pray your sleep will not be further troubled by latecomers or ill dreams." With that, he stepped into the room he shared with Nathan, leaving her to stare after him, wondering what thoughts went on in his head.

Morning came soon thereafter. Hannah felt the sun appeared far too soon after her head hit the pillow. Its pale beam lit her room in shades of gray as it worked up its courage to emerge from the horizon. She could sympathize. Her bed was warm underneath its nest of coverlets, and she would have much preferred to stay underneath, but she had responsibilities to tend.

Beneath her feet, the floor felt cool. A breeze from the open window goose-pimpled her flesh as she changed her shift after washing her face with water from the pitcher at the table nearby. It took a moment to find one of the garters she used to keep her stockings up. Once her shoes were on, she could attend to her stays.

She smiled as she tied on her pockets. Plain she might be, but her pockets, unseen by the world, were colorful, made of fabric gotten cheaply as it was off the end of a bolt. The rich red pattern pleased her every time she saw it. Hidden underneath inner and outer petticoats as well as her apron, no one need know her secret. The slits in her skirt allowed her to access them when needed with no one the wiser. Once she had secured her jacket and tied her cap, she was ready to head down to breakfast.

No sound came from the other room other than the muted rumble of Franklin's snores. Hannah wasn't surprised. After such a late night, no one with a choice would be up early. Although she knew Nathan would be down before long. He never spoke of it, but the constant shadows under his eyes told her he rarely slept well.

As she descended the stairs, Suzanna's voice rose from the kitchen. Her vibrant soprano filled the room with joyful sound. Hannah paused to listen, enjoying the music. Somewhere in her past, Suzanna had learned a large repertoire of music in many languages. Today, her choice was Italian.

"O del mio dolce ardor," Suzanna sang as she cut biscuits from dough on the sturdy wooden work table. She stopped when she saw Hannah in the entry to the kitchen.

"You don't need to stop," Hannah said as she walked into the room. "You have a beautiful voice."

Suzanna smiled. "Thank you, Mistress Hannah, but I don't want to disturb anyone." She placed the cut bread in an iron Dutch oven. Once the lid was in place, it went into the fireplace. Using long tongs, she placed hot coals on top to ensure even cooking.

Soon, bacon was frying in a pan on top of a spider as coffee boiled in the pot. Jeremy Butler came down with Toby, the cat. He looked wistfully at the coffee pot before helping set the table. Hannah placed a jar of maple syrup from the market on the table, along with butter and salt. Before long, she heard the tap of Nathan's peg on the steps, followed by Lucretia's heavy steps from her room in the attic. Fresh eggs gathered just after dawn finished their meal.

After a brief grace, they dug into the meal with relish, breaking their fast before the day sent them in different directions. Butler helped clear the dishes and took them out back for one of the staff to clean. He spotted Nathan with an axe chopping more wood for Suzanna's cooking. Spotting another axe in a block nearby, he picked it up and joined him, their axes falling into an easy rhythm as they added to the pile.

Nathan looked over at him. "We normally don't ask guests to pitch in."

Butler replied. "There's always a need for more wood. I see no reason not to lend a hand to what needs doing."

"Don't say that to Hannah; she'll tell you to go shovel out stalls."

Butler snorted. "I'm sure she would."

Inside her shop, Hannah dusted her already shining china supplies. The moments before opening gave her a few precious moments of peace where she could collect her thoughts. She had never considered she would end up running a business to make ends meet. Her dreams had been of working alongside a loving husband and tending to children, but that dream had been cut short. Most days, she didn't mind the aloneness; nights were tougher and left her wondering what her purpose in life was. She was grateful when she could fall in bed, too exhausted to dream.

Her musings were cut short by the sound of her front door opening. Micah escorted a slender woman inside. Her petticoats rustled as they brushed against the door frame. She was followed by a taller woman that Hannah recognized instantly as Elizabeth Cranford. Both women had maids, likely enslaved women, with them. Although they entered at the same time, they immediately parted and went to different areas of the shop. Mistress Cranford stood engrossed in a teapot, while the other woman approached Hannah and held out a gloved hand. "Bonjour, I'm Madame Lisette Fournier. Your shop was recommended by an acquaintance. I need to select China for an upcoming event at my home. Can you assist me?"

A boy was the last to come in a few moments later. He looked about eight years old, dressed in the formal garb of a footman. Madame Fournier spoke. "Timothy, you may wait in the entry. When I have packages ready, I will call you to take them to the carriage. His eyes looked sad as he took his position, removing the tricorn he had worn inside and holding it in his hands.

Hannah was grateful she had decided to put on her newest gown, a deep blue that accented her eyes. "Welcome to my shop. How can I assist thee?"

Lisette Fournier smiled as she assessed Hannah. "I plan to host an intimate supper party to follow up the splendid ball last night. We thought you might have something special to brighten up the table."

"I would be happy to show you what I have. Here is what we have recently received from Holland." Hannah led them over to the display she had carefully set up to highlight all the colorful patterns. Some edged in gold. Out of the corner of her eye, she spotted Nathan speaking to Mistress Cranford. Grateful for his presence, she focused on her client.

Fournier stood in the center of the room, her eyes seeking out every corner. Her eyes skipped over the other woman before going back to the entryway, near which the enslaved boy waited, his eyes on his neatly buckled shoes. She looked up the staircase before her gaze returned to Hannah.

"Are you looking for something in particular?" Hannah asked. Lisette Fournier walked over to a collection of plates in bright blues and red, fingering the gilt edges. Nathan's gentle baritone extolled a pale pink pattern on an ivory background that had come recently from Holland.

The door opened again, letting in an elderly woman Hannah knew well. Mistress Boggs bought cups and saucers regularly for her gatherings. She greeted her with a smile. "I believe we have your order ready. Shall I have it delivered to your home or would you me to direct your driver to where it can be picked up?"

Lucretia stuck her head inside the doorway. She held a silver tray with a coffee pot and two cups, along with a plate of food. She caught Hannah's eyes. "I'm taking this up to Dr. Franklin. His joints are a trifle stiff this morning."

Before Hannah could answer, a loud crash sounded through the room, followed by the tinkle of broken china. She whirled around to see a shard of broken china rolling across the floor. Elizabeth Cranford stood in the shop, wearing a horrified expression.

"I'm so sorry. My reticule must have hit something." She backed up, her face pale.

"You're bleeding," Nathan said, setting down an ivory cup before moving toward her.

Cranford looked down at the blood dripping down her fingers from a cut on her hand. All remaining color drained from her face as she went limp. Nathan dove forward to catch her, losing his balance so that they both went crashing to the floor. Elizabeth Cranford lay across his lap, supported by his arms.

Nathan looked up at the people around him. "I can't lift her on my own." As he shifted his weight, he drew in his breath sharply. "I think I landed on something sharp."

Hannah grabbed a broom she kept hidden behind a cabinet. "Stay still. I will clear a path, and we will get you both up." She glanced over at Micah, who stared in equal parts horror and fascination. "Micah, go to the apothecary and get the doctor. Run!" She urged.

He jumped at her sharp tone before barreling out the door. The thud of feet on the stairs told her Jeremy Butler had heard the clamor and was responding as well. She was relieved when he entered the room. He squatted by Nathan, taking in the scene. He was accompanied by a backwoodsman Hannah had never seen before.

"Maynard and I will carry Mistress Cranford," He said. "We can take her to your office. There's a settee in there we can lay her on."

Hannah nodded. The two men lifted the limp woman and walked carefully out of the room and into her office. She went before them and made sure the settee was clear. They lay the woman down gently.

"That's a nasty cut," Butler noted, taking out a handkerchief and wrapping the bloody hand firmly.

Hannah was about to agree when Lucretia looked inside, still carrying the tray. "Go ahead and take Dr. Franklin his breakfast," she said. "There's nothing else to be done besides clean up and wait for the doctor." She spotted

Lisette Fournier in the entry. "Can you sit with Mistress Cranford until the physician arrives?"

Fournier looked shaken as she joined them. She pulled an upright chair close to Elizabeth Cranford, who was beginning to stir. She looked up at Hannah. "Do you have some spirits? It would help restore her."

Hannah nodded. "I will check on that." She walked out of the room and into her shop to check on Nathan.

The man Butler called Maynard had an arm underneath Nathan's, taking some of his weight as he recovered his balance. A dark streak on his breeches affirmed he had been injured by a piece of the sharp porcelain.

Suzanna had come upstairs and was busy sweeping up the mess. Hannah's eyes took in all the blood on the floor. For a moment, her vision swam.

Butler grabbed her arm and led her to a chair. "There have been enough injuries today. Sit down and put your head on your lap. It will help."

Hannah complied and felt better after a few moments. "I was going to get some whisky from the cellar," she said, sitting up to relieve the pressure from her stays.

Maynard handed Nathan off to Butler before he took the broom from Suzanna. "I can finish this if you can get the liquor. I'm sure you can find it far quicker than me."

Butler led Nathan over to a chair. "Looks like you got stabbed in the ass,"

Nathan grinned shakily. "Just my luck. It feels like something is still in there.

Butler glanced over at Hannah. "You may want to step out for a few minutes."

Taking the hint, she shut the door to her shop behind her. Since Hannah was the only one in the entryway, she opened the door to let in the physician and his apprentice. "We have two injured, one in each room. She explained the injuries to the pair. The doctor nodded before going in, where Elizabeth Cranford rested while the apprentice split off to tend to Nathan.

Upstairs, a woman screamed as something crashed to the floor. Fear washed through Hannah as she ran up the stairs to confront what other disaster had struck.

Lucretia stood shrieking at the edge of the parlor. Benjamin Franklin sat frozen in his seat, a spilled cup of coffee spreading from the table and onto the deep blue rug that a happy client had gifted her with last Christmas.

On the rug, the cat that Suzanna kept to quell rodents convulsed on the rug. It's back arched in agony as it made choking sounds. Coffee and cream streaked the floor, pooling much like the blood downstairs.

Butler ran in behind Hannah. "What in hell is going on up here?" A nasty-looking knife gleamed in his hand as his eyes swept the room. His glance danced off Franklin and then to the two women before he saw the cat twitching on the floor.

Franklin's voice was shaky. "I poured coffee onto the saucer to cool it. The cat jumped up and drank before I could stop him. Within seconds, he started acting like that." His voice trailed off as he looked at the animal who had quit moving.

Butler grabbed the cup. "Did you drink any?"

Franklin shook his head. All color had washed from his face.

Butler looked at the liquid remaining in the cup. He sniffed it but only picked up the faint scent of coffee. As he swirled it about, a small amount spilled on his hand, making it tingle. He wiped it on his breeches, but the tingling remained. "Don't drink it." He opened the pot and peered inside. "Who made this?"

"Suzanna," Hannah answered. "She makes coffee every morning for all of us. I had a cup myself just before I came upstairs. So did Nathan and Lucretia. You drank some, too."

Butler picked up a spoon and fished around in the pot. A wilted plant with bluish-purple blooms dangled from the utensil. "Does she put plants in it? What is this?"

Hannah frowned. "Suzanna doesn't put anything in the pot besides coffee. I watched her make it as she stirred the mush."

Butler squinted as he eyed the plant, searching his memory back when Athena had insisted he learn all the plants in her garden, both culinary and medicinal. "It's Wolfsbane. Some people use it as a rub for achy joints but ingested its deadly poison." His thoughts turned briefly to the powerful

African-American woman who had raised him. Athena would be proud he remembered some of what she had taught him. It came in handy at moments like this and probably had helped keep him alive more than once. He thought of the important work Athena was engaged in back in Williamsburg. He knew his fledgling spy network in Virginia was in good hands while he was away.

Hannah looked startled. "I've never heard of it. I certainly don't use it."

Butler looked about him. "Then we need to discover who brought it here and how it got in Dr. Franklin's coffee."

Micah looked over at the cat, who had quit twitching. His face was angry. "He deserves a decent burial." He glared at Butler. "Get who did this. Toby was my friend." He rolled the animal in the rug and took it away, leaving the adults to stare after him.

Hannah drew in a shaky breath. "Could this day get any worse?"

Butler replied, "I don't know. Let's go downstairs and find out."

She followed him down to where the doctor was packing up his bag. "How's Nathan?"

The doctor offered her a brief smile. "He won't be sitting comfortably for a few days, but otherwise he is fine. My apprentice cleaned and bandaged it. It was a relatively shallow wound."

Elizabeth Cranford sipped whisky, and her color improved. Lisette Fournier sat nearby, watching her as one of the maids fanned the air with an edition of yesterday's newspaper. The other patted her mistress' forehead with a damp cloth.

Butler looked at the tableau for a few minutes before interrupting, "Where's the boy?"

Hannah looked at him, puzzled. "Micah went to bury his cat."

"Not him," Butler interrupted. "A young boy came in with these ladies. He was small, dressed like a footman."

She looked about the room. Hannah remembered the sad-eyed boy in the stiff uniform. There was no sign of him.

Butler went into the room where the women sat. "Where's your footman?"

"How would we know?" Lisette Fournier's voice was brusque. "I assume if he's not still in the shop, he went out to the carriage. Go check with Horatio, my driver. He should be coming around to take us away from this wretched place."

Butler went out front. He didn't see the boy, although the carriage, along with its driver, was just outside the door. "Where's the boy?" He asked the driver.

"He went in with the ladies. I haven't seen him since," the driver answered before looking at a man who was busy wiping down the other carriage. "Aaron, did you see Timothy come by?" The man standing by the open carriage door shook his head. His face was turned away from Butler. "Nope. I haven't seen him for a while. He probably went around to the woods to take a leak. That boy's not going far. His mom's inside with the mistress."

Neither man seemed terribly concerned. Nor did they seem worried about their mistress inside, although he was sure they had been informed. Butler found the situation odd. He walked down the street for a block or two, hoping to see him before returning to Hannah's home. Butler intended to keep an eye out for him.

He paused before reentering the shop. He had a feeling that the little footman had either seen or done something. He needed to know what. Once again, the enemy had struck, barely missing the mark. If he wanted to keep Franklin alive, he had to find the enemy before he succeeded.

Chapter Nineteen

Hannah spent the rest of the morning cleaning her shop and hoping the morning's drama would not scare off her clients. She didn't like to admit it, but the ongoing dispute with Britain had made staying solvent challenging. Getting goods through the British blockades took skill and connections in the right places. She was fortunate that one of her clients had put her into contact with John Hancock. His ships were not cheap, but his captains were skilled at making it into port.

A small felt mouse rolled out from a corner. A lump rose from Hannah's throat. She missed Micah's cat. In addition to clearing out vermin, he had been her constant companion since she had started her business. Although claimed by Micah, Toby had been in the house when she moved in, and she had had no heart to move him after her own experience with upheaval. He deserved better.

She put the broom down. It fell against the wall with a thump. Micah looked at her. He had cleaned the floor and helped put the shop back together. The shop had remained quiet as if word had gotten out that danger lurked inside. Hannah jumped as a fly buzzed by her ear.

"Take a walk," Lucretia said. "I can manage the shop."

Hannah looked out at the deep blue sky dotted with thin strands of clouds. In the distance, a man called out headlines as he sold newspapers. Horses clopped up and down the street carrying their passengers in and out of town. Everyone was moving but her. She looked over at the older woman. "Are you sure?"

Lucretia nodded. "Go. It will do you good. I can manage whoever comes in." Just then, the door opened, letting in an older couple. She nodded as they walked into the shop. She gestured for Hannah to leave.

"I suppose I could go see what's in the garden. Taking a wide straw hat, she tied it over her cap and slipped out the back to the garden hidden behind the house. A group of chickens scattered from the path as she approached, settling not far away to continue their search for bugs. Hannah admired their speckled feathers as they busied themselves. Suzanna loved her Dominiques and swore they provided better eggs than any other variety. She accepted her cook's authority in such matters and appreciated their productivity. That she found them beautiful, no one needed to know.

They clucked busily as she came close. A few approached, their eyes alert to see if she had brought food. Hannah laughed softly. "No, it's not dinner time. Go back to your work." A few bolder ones stayed about her skirts as she walked about the beds. The apple trees that formed a border with her neighbor were full of green apples. A few had started to blush with color. Before long, they would be ready to pick.

She walked the pathway, paved with shells that served to gravel the path. Micah and Suzanna had already picked vegetables for that night's dinner, so there was little for her to do besides appreciate the well-tended beds. A sprinkling of tiny blue flowers decorated the rosemary bush. It had shot up as the weather warmed, benefiting from its position near the south side of the house, which kept it from freezing when winter struck. A butterfly settled on a blossom before floating off to explore other blossoms that had opened in the sprawling garden. The feverfew she had started earlier that spring to help Lucretia's bad headaches was thriving.

It had grown large and was covered in white blooms. Later tonight, she would harvest some to dry in the attic to keep a steady supply on hand.

She paused to wipe sweat from her brow. The humidity was rising as the clouds gathered overhead. Hannah suspected that evening they would be graced by a rain storm. She just hoped nothing worse than that occurred. Wild weather caused too much damage.

The maid came out behind her and into the yard to shake out a rug. Hannah recognized it as the small one from the room her guest occupied.

It was a good time to clean while he was out. Butler had taken Franklin to his meeting not long after the attempted poisoning. She didn't expect them back any time soon.

Hannah was puzzled. She had never heard of the herb Butler had so easily identified. She didn't grow it and knew of no one that did. How did it end up in the coffee pot? Those distinctive blue blossoms did look somewhat familiar. Could someone be selling it at the market? It was possible. Most anything could be found there, whether it came from the many outlying farms or was brought in by ship. Hannah pondered who would carry such a thing. Memory of gossip overheard at her shop fueled her footsteps as she stepped outside the gate and walked swiftly to the market.

Not as many folk were about this time of day. Many of the ladies or their cooks came early to get the choicest items. She stepped into the huge building and paused for a few moments, waiting for her eyes to adjust. Light from the afternoon sun streamed in from the windows, alleviating some of the darkness.

Hannah glanced about, taking in the many tables and their wares. The rustle of bird wings overhead told her that some had made nests in the rafters. She had little doubt they found plenty to eat in spilled grain on the ground.

She paused before turning down one of the wide aisles formed by the tables. A dog sniffed at her skirts before continuing on its journey. Hannah could smell the blood from the butcher's stall as well and endeavored to avoid it, although the buzzing of flies warned her it wasn't far away.

The stall she sought was in the back, far from the more productive spots. Bundles of herbs hung from twine tied between two poles, their ends secured in crates weighted by stone. Hannah's nose picked up the scent of lavender and basil, among others that tickled her nose but were not readily recognized.

An older woman managed the stall. Strands of snow-white hair had escaped from her cap and curled wispily around her face. A dark ribbon encircled her cap. In the light, Hannah could not tell if it was black or dark blue. The woman did not speak but waited for Hannah to begin.

168

"Good day," she began awkwardly.

"Good day, Mistress White," the woman responded. Her light-colored eyes seemed to bore through whoever she looked at. They looked almost white in the dim light of the market. Her fair skin was faintly wrinkled with a few spots of age. Her hands were bare as they arranged herbs into bundles that hung around the table. One hand showed clear signs of having been scalded at one point in time. The long sleeves of her jacket came down to the wrist so that Hannah could not see how far it went.

Hannah inhaled nervously. "I'm looking for wolfsbane. Do you carry that?"

The woman stilled before she lifted her head to meet Hannah's eyes. "That's an unusual request, mistress. Not many people grow it here." Her voice was high and thin like a child's, but her eyes assessed Hannah with a look that wasn't childlike at all. "Why do you ask?"

She was beginning to understand why this woman had the reputation of being a witch. There was an unworldly air about her with her pale skin and odd eyes. Her dark clothes only made her seem paler.

"I was wondering if you had sold any to someone else recently, mistress," Hannah said. "I have heard mention of it and was curious about its properties."

"I am called Mistress Reede," the other woman replied. "It has been many years since there was a Master Reede. She gestured around her space. "I make my bread, selling my herbs here at the market. My mother and my grandmother before her knew a great deal about plants, how to grow them, when to harvest them. I learned what was helpful and what was best left alone. Wolfsbane can be a beneficial rub for achy joints; it can also be a lethal poison if swallowed." She paused thoughtfully. "I find it best to leave it alone. It's far too easy to be blamed for other's poor judgment. I learned that in the Massachusetts colony." She looked around at her simple stand with its racks of lavender and rosemary perfuming the air. "I keep nothing that is harmful to man, not in my garden and not here."

Hannah frowned. It wasn't the answer she was expecting. "Do you know anyone who does sell it? I'm trying to figure out where some came from." She looked about the market, where people gathered at various tables, haggling for goods. Across from where they stood, a group of men stood about engaged in a game of dice, far from the bustle closer to the entrance.

The woman shook her head. "You need to be careful, my lady. Anyone who deals with it means harm. She took a bundle of silvery leaves down from her stand. "Take these. Sage protects from evil." She grinned. "It's also very good for flavoring fowl. Use it as you see fit." Her face turned serious. "I will pray for your safety, Mistress White."

Hannah took the herbs with her thanks and walked slowly out of the market. It wasn't until she was halfway down the street that she realized that Mistress Reede had called her by name. "Now, how did she know that?" She wondered.

The sun had reached its zenith and was starting to descend when Hannah arrived back home. Her stomach growled as she entered the gate. She could hear voices from the open windows of her house. Apparently, her business was doing fine without her. Nathan's tenor replied to a question. Laughter ensued.

Her nephew could be quite the charmer when he wished. She hoped he would find a young woman who could overlook the leg and see the noble soul inside. Nathan deserved to be loved.

Outside, she was surprised to find Jeremy Butler stripped to the waist, chopping wood. By the stack next to him, he had been busy. She paused to watch him work, not sure what to think. As he worked, she walked down to the cellar where they kept their drinks cool and poured a large cup of cider from the keg they kept just inside the door. When he saw her approach, he paused and put down the axe, taking the cup and downing the cider.

"My thanks," he said, handing the mug back.

"The thanks are mine," she said, gesturing at the pile of wood. "Suzanna and I are grateful for all thy hard work."

He smiled. "Suzanna said there would be chicken pie for dinner and possibly cherry slump. How could I let such a hard-working woman run out of fuel for her fire? It would be a tragedy for all concerned."

Hannah laughed. "I see Suzanna has discovered the key to your cooperation."

He looked over at her. "You should smile more often. It transforms you." Seeing her startled expression, he responded to her comment. "I've been in places where good food was rare, much less someone willing and able to cook. I'm grateful."

Her eyes took him in. He was lean but in good shape, shorter than most men, but she had never considered height a method of measuring character. She blushed when she realized he had noticed her observation of him. Hannah looked about. "Where is Dr. Franklin? I thought thy primary task was keeping him from harm."

He nodded. "That is so. Apparently, his business at the State House was short. He came here to rest before dinner, and then we will return."

Hannah nodded. She turned to give him privacy as he wiped himself down with a cloth before donning his shirt.

Suzanna called out to them from the narrow window in the basement. "Dinner's ready."

"We're coming," Hannah replied. She heard the front door shut as Nathan ushered their customers out before closing for mealtime. She watched as someone upstairs raised the window as high as it would go. The figure paused, standing in front of the window bare as when he had been born. It was Franklin. His pale skin glowed in the bright afternoon sun as he took in the view outside his window, hiding nothing nature had provided him.

Hannah's jaw dropped. She whirled to face Butler. "He's naked."

"I can see that." Butler squinted against the sun's reflection on the glass. Dr. Franklin stood upright, facing outside, his legs spread as he leaned against the frame.

Hannah hissed. "What is he doing?"

They watched as Franklin turned, raising his arms, and presented all possible views to the world below. His round bottom almost hung outside the glass as he paused to bend over. On his next turn, he spotted them and offered a cheery hello as he continued his activities.

Butler's face was a study as he watched Dr. Franklin expose himself with no concern whatsoever to being seen.

"He's gone mad," Hannah whispered.

"I don't think so," Butler said thoughtfully. "He's written about the benefits of fresh air on the body. I believe he is acting on his own advice."

"Here? In my house?" Hannah's tone was incredulous. "Thou needs to speak to him immediately. This madness must end."

Butler looked over at her, "Me? Why must I speak to him? He's doing no harm."

"Doing no harm," Hannah sputtered. "I run a business here, in this house. Ladies of society come here every day to purchase items to decorate their homes. I can't have a naked man running about."

Butler sighed. "I hear you, but I must point out that he's doing this in his own room, not in the middle of your shop."

"It doesn't matter," She said. "What if word gets out of this? It would be ruinous."

"At least his window doesn't face the street," Butler said in a tone meant to be soothing.

Hannah wanted to strangle him. Oblivious to the excitement he was causing, Franklin continued his vast display of flesh.

Hannah moaned. "I cannot believe I let you bring him into my home."

"He needed a safe place to stay," Butler pointed out. "Someone is trying to harm him."

"If he does that everywhere he goes, I don't blame them. Your assassin is probably some genteel member of society who made the mistake of hosting him only to discover his presence is more revealing than one would ever imagine."

"I don't believe Dr. Franklin has left anything to the imagination," Butler noted dryly. "Let's hope he dresses for dinner."

Hannah's eyes goggled. "Surely, he wouldn't."

Butler shrugged. "Who knows? He's a man of many ideas. He has experimented with electricity, among other things. Perhaps this is another experiment." He backed away when he caught Hannah's expression. "I will speak with him.'" He jogged into the house and was halfway up the stairs before Hannah entered.

Thankfully, when the men joined them, Franklin was once again dressed like a dignified gentleman. His expression looked innocent, as if he had spent his time napping or reading a respectable tome. His tone was gentle as he heaped praise on the food and the house.

Suzanna was not immune to the charm offensive. Her smile was wide as she set down a platter with her chicken pie. Golden crust covered the plate from end to end. As she cut it, a cloud of steam arose from the inside, revealing the rich filling of chicken, carrots, peas, and cut-up potatoes. Gravy pooled in each plate.

Hannah poured cider for everyone before sitting down herself. She cast an eye on Micah, reminding him silently to wait until the blessing was offered. Not even Dr. Franklin protested as they offered thanks for the meal before them.

Hannah felt grateful for the prolific garden out back as she watched her family eat. Amos had never given her children, but she had these wonderful people around her, and they were more precious than gold.

Franklin said little as he ate, choosing instead to focus on filling his stomach. The others followed suit. Hannah had no desire to reveal the doctor's insanity, so she remained silent as well.

Lucretia led the conversation after the first course. "Mistress Cranford sent word that she is resting at home. She apologized for the incident and sent money to pay for the broken plate."

"She did," Hannah said. "How generous of her."

Lucretia nodded. "Mistress Fournier wants to buy a complete set of the rose pattern if we have it in stock. She asked if Master Butler could deliver it to her home tomorrow."

Hannah paused, taking a sip of cider. "Master Butler does not work for me. He is a guest in this house. We must offer our apologies."

"I will do it," Butler interrupted. "Loan me your carriage, and I will take it."

Hannah looked over at him, puzzled. "Are you sure? What of Dr. Franklin?"

Butler studied his plate before placing his cutlery neatly on top. "I have an old friend who can help me with that. He's been trying to track down that boy."

"The footman," Hannah said. "Why are you concerned about him? If he has run away, surely you do not want to return him to a life of bondage."

Butler shot her a warning look, "We will discuss it later."

Nathan interjected. "He's not the first slave to make a break for freedom. It happens quite often. Enslavement is not a happy situation for anyone. I'm glad we do not support it in this house."

Hannah nodded. "No one should be made to feel like a horse or cow. Man was made in God's own image. My father used to say that no man should own another."

"A noble sentiment," Franklin agreed, "But difficult indeed to persuade those who profit from it. Mark my words, one day, mankind will pay a heavy price for this evil practice."

Hannah nodded. On the day when slaves were sold, she avoided the market, unable to face the incredible misery before her. Freeing Suzanna and her husband had been difficult but worthwhile. It was one of Amos's lasting gifts that he had declared there would be no slaves in their home.

After the meal, Hannah followed Nathan and Butler out back, where they were busy helping wash dishes. Micah brought ashes and vinegar from the kitchen that he poured into a tub. Nathan rolled his sleeves to the elbow and began scraping off food before rinsing it off and handing it to Jeremy.

"The pigs will eat well tonight on all those scraps," he noted.

Butler looked surprised. "I didn't realize you kept any pigs."

The water splashed a bit as Nathan worked on a pot. "We have one out back. Lucy had piglets not long ago, so we've been making sure she and the little ones are well-fed. I can introduce you later if you like."

"That's not necessary," Butler said quickly. "I worked with pigs when I was a boy. They can be nasty sometimes."

Nathan protested. "Lucy is as gentle as a lamb unless you frighten one of the piglets, then you're in trouble."

Butler shuddered. "I will stay away from her area. I promise."

Hannah interrupted. "Why are you looking for that boy?"

Butler stood up and set aside the pot he had just finished. He wiped his hands clean of the brick dust he had just used before setting it down to be wiped and dried. Micah and Nathan continued the work as Butler took Hannah by the arm and walked her out of hearing of the others.

"He very likely poisoned your cat, although I'm certain his target was Franklin."

Hannah shook her head. "I don't believe that. He was a child, an enslaved child, dragged to a place I'm sure he did not want to be. He had no reason to do such a thing."

Butler stared at her in disbelief. "You cannot be so naïve." He tipped up her chin so that they were eye to eye. "Each and every one of us has a price, including that child. Either he was offered enough money to make escape feasible, or someone dangled the offer of manumission over his head. All he had to do was make sure the poison made it into Franklin's food or drink. With the uproar, he had the perfect opportunity."

Hannah shook his head. She kept thinking of the boy's huge, sad eyes. "He didn't look like a killer to me. He looked like a child."

Butler sighed. "He may not have known what he was doing, but he was the only one no one paid any attention to. The fact your sister-in-law brought that tray up where he was made it even easier."

Hannah looked at him. "Lucretia was helping out." Her stomach felt queasy, remembering what had happened earlier. It still felt unreal.

Butler nodded. "I know. She was being kind to a guest. But that coffee pot provided an opportunity, and someone took it when no one was looking."

"That's because Mistress Cranford fainted." Hannah paused as the thought took hold. Her glance met Butler's. "It wasn't an accident." She shook her head. "That makes no sense. Her husband is an admirer of Franklin. There are some that believe he may come out in favor of the revolution."

He smiled without humor. "I'm sure it was planned. I don't think Mistress Fournier's appearance was by chance either, although I don't know what connects them." His fingers tapped against his leg before he said. "But I intend to find out."

"That's why you're delivering the china," Hannah said. She shot him a narrowed gaze.

"It is indeed," he said. He smiled at her, revealing a faint dimple in one cheek.

"She finds you attractive," Hannah said. She didn't like admitting the idea made her uncomfortable. Jeremy Butler could be charming when he chose, and she suspected he made good use of the ability.

He shrugged. "I believe she does, and that may incline her to talk more than she normally would."

Hannah's tone dropped. "Be careful. Lisette Fournier has a reputation for toying with men. Only her husband's influence keeps her out of trouble, but this town teems with stories of her exploits."

"Duly noted," Butler said. "I have no intentions of developing an intimate relationship with the woman. I only wish to find out what she knows."

"What if she refuses to share that information with you?" Hannah said.

The air grew silent as she waited for his reply. A hawk's cry echoed across the sky as it claimed its prey.

Butler's smile turned predatory. "There is more than one way to get the information one desires." With that, he strode back to where the others continued washing dishes, leaving Hannah to watch his retreating back.

One thing was certain: she would not want to be in the way of something Jeremy Butler wanted. She had the feeling whoever did would pay a dreadful price.

Chapter Twenty

Butler clucked to the horse, encouraging it into a brisk trot as they took off down the street toward the neighborhood where the Fourniers lived. In the back were four barrels of china and other accouterments, well packed with straw that he had helped load first thing that morning. In spite of the fact he was playing the role of delivery man, he had taken the time to dress nicely. Lisette Fournier struck him as a woman who appreciated appearances. He had no intention of disappointing her. He had high hopes that the lovely socialite could prove a valuable source of information for his cause. His knives were on his person as well, strapped to his wrists and inside his boot, just in case this was a less-than-friendly visit. One never knew in these times.

Maynard had installed himself inside Hannah's house as a safeguard against any threats. Suzanna had brewed a fresh pot of coffee and made fresh corn cakes with honey. The backwoodsman had been happy to down another breakfast after he had explored the grounds for threats. Butler suspected he was somewhere he could observe all the comings and goings in Hannah's business without being seen himself. She had said little about the arrangement, but she had watched them load the wagon. He suspected the little Quaker had watched him go down the road to his appointment. Butler had no doubt she would be full of questions upon his return. In her own way, Hannah was just as nosy as her sister. "Women," he muttered, knowing full well Athena would have cuffed him for saying it. Truth be told, he admired them. They had made a success of their lives in a world dominated by men. To do that took courage and tenacity. They were in no way the weaker sex, no matter what society said.

Hannah's horse was in a fine mood. The big bay stepped briskly down the road, ears twitching as he took in the activity in the street. They both seemed to be enjoying the outing. The horse clopped along steadily, his broad shoulders carrying the weight of the wagon with ease. A light breeze tousled his dark mane and tail. Butler let him have his head. He was in no hurry. He talked to the steed Hannah called Samuel as they went down the road. "You are fine animal," he said, "too beautiful to be shut in a barn all day. When we get home, I will put you out in the pasture, where you can enjoy the breeze and get a cool drink from the trough. I will draw the water from the well myself in thanks for your hard work."

Butler also intended to sneak a carrot or apple from Suzanna's kitchen if possible, but he didn't want to promise what he wasn't sure he could deliver. He was fond of the cook and had no interest in arousing her ire. Angering the house's cook carried long-term consequences.

Once he turned the corner, taking him off the main road, the horse picked up the pace, enjoying getting off the hard cobbles and onto the packed earth road that led to the edges of town. The pristine white pickets of the Fournier home came into view just a short jaunt head. Wisteria vines wove themselves through the top pickets, forming a basket weave of vines interspersed with the heady scent emitted by large clusters of purple blossoms.

A stable boy ran out to greet him as he pulled up just outside the gate. He ran up and took the reins Butler handed off to him. He eyed the animal with dark, shining eyes.

"Treat him kindly," Butler admonished. "I should be back within a few hours." He strode off to the house as the boy was joined by a group of men who together led the horse and wagon to the back where they could unload and give the animal a much-deserved drink.

The door opened before Butler had a chance to knock. An enslaved man in a light blue jacket bowed as he let him in. "Mistress Fournier waits for you in the parlor, sir."

Butler nodded as he wiped his feet before stepping onto the highly polished floor of the entryway. Going down the center passage, the doorman knocked on a door on the left, just before the doorway that opened into the large room that had housed the previous night's ball. As he entered, Butler noted the elaborate rug decorated with a pattern of ocean blue and red medallions. It was set off by simple walls painted cream and draperies also in blue.

"Welcome to my home," Lisette Fournier said. She stood before an unlit marble fireplace, a vision of loveliness in a pale blue gown festooned with rosettes of ivory and blue at the neckline and sleeves. Delicate pearls hung from her ears, highlighting the perfect oval of her face. She showed no tiredness from the previous evening or from the previous morning's debacle. She looked as cool and composed as a rose and probably just as complex.

Lisette offered him a quick smile. "Master Butler, it is delightful to see you again. You are looking well this afternoon."

He smiled and bowed. "Thank you, milady. You look lovely. I hope your companion, Mistress Cranford, is recovering?"

Her smile faltered slightly. "I know Mistress Cranford slightly; our husbands have differing views regarding these colonies. I believe she is resting at home. It really was such a small injury to cause such a fuss. I imagine she has already recovered." She gestured to an upholstered chair on long, skinny legs. She sat across from him in a matching one. A low table sat between them. A servant came in, leaving a tea tray with cucumber sandwiches and small cakes. "I thought you might enjoy a drink and some refreshment after your journey."

"How kind of you." Butler waited while she poured a cup for each of them, watching intently as she did. Before she could hand him a cup, he rose and selected one for himself. "Allow me to assist," He sat back down and waited for her response.

Her eyes narrowed slightly before she recovered her smile. "Would you care for a sandwich? I have an excellent cook. Her skills in the kitchen are akin to magic."

"I'm sure they are," he said after he took a careful sip, following her lead. It was rare he got to drink real English tea. It was challenging to acquire. Nothing tasted untoward, even if he normally didn't drink it black. "Unfortunately, I ate not long ago. Send regards to your cook. I'm sure she is quite skilled."

"Guilia will be quite disappointed. She greatly enjoys making refreshments when company calls. Are you sure?"

He eyed the greenery dangling outside the edges of the bread, covering the cucumber. It was most likely parsley, but he had no desire to tempt fate. "Quite, but don't let me stop you. It would be a shame to disappoint Guilia."

Lisette took a small square of cake and put it on her plate after nibbling an edge. "I do like her ginger cakes. She knows how to use just the right amount of spice to do its job but no more."

"That is a notable talent." Butler sipped his tea before setting down the delicate cup. "This china is beautiful," he indicated the translucent cup on the table. "I'm surprised you need more."

Lisette shrugged. "Fine china breaks easily. In the wrong hands, beautiful things can be destroyed. One has to be very careful in handling many things. One would hope the gentlemen meeting in our fair city realize this." She watched him from under her lustrous lashes. "It's a rare few that know to care for things properly."

He nodded. "I imagine it must be difficult living in these colonies during such a conflicted time. For men like your husband, conducting business must be challenging. Not everything receives the attention it needs."

Lisette's eyes looked down. "Conflict arises no matter where one lives. That there is so much discord with our government is unfortunate. In order to survive, we all must learn what we need to do. But I imagine you know that. Butler is an Irish name, is it not?"

Surprised, he met her gaze, noticing again the deep blue of her wideset eyes. A man could become lost in such a gaze. "It is," he admitted. "I came to these colonies as a child. I consider myself American now."

She nodded. "You are among those who favor independence." Her tone was matter-of-fact. But then, given her husband's business interests, she had probably been witness to many conversations regarding the future of the colonies. "One must be careful who to support in these times. The British army is a powerful force to be reckoned with. n'est ce pas?"

Butler offered her a smile. "Ah, but David did slay Goliath, did he not?

180

Perhaps the wisest move would be not to put all one's eggs in the same basket." He took a sip of tea.

Lisette Fournier gazed at him unblinking. "That could be said for you as well, Monsieur Butler."

Butler nodded. "I don't deny it. As you said, I was born Irish. I've witnessed the brutality of the British Army. I believe it is in the best interest of these colonies. Great Britain has shown little interest in listening to our concerns. Parliament continues to treat us like a fiefdom, our people serfs to be ordered about."

Lisette Fournier offered a small smile. "There are many places that would enjoy free trade with these colonies. They have much to offer."

"Such as islands in the Caribbean?" Butler suggested dryly. His sources had told him that Fournier was heavily into the rum trade and owned a large plantation on one of the islands.

She nodded. "The West Indies has traded many commodities over the years. But countries such as France and Spain would also come to these ports if the blockade were lifted."

Butler understood. "Your husband does a great deal of business with other countries, doesn't he?"

"Yes, that was the purpose of our move. Frances thought there would be more opportunities for trade here. We had not considered that the colonies might turn rebellious. It seems such a foolish idea to break away from such a prosperous nation.

Then there was the matter of our daughter. We desired to keep Emily safe from the fevers that run through the islands. We also wanted her to have more opportunities to move in society that could not be found in Jamaica." She pinpointed her gaze on Butler. "My husband has no wish to choose sides in a war. But he favors an arrangement where his ships can come into port without interruption. He has done this under British rule for years. He would like to continue regardless of what government rules these colonies."

Butler nodded. "It's all about business." He paused to gather his thoughts. "What if your husband could be promised access to ports and preferential trade agreements once the colonies solidify their independence?"

A cat-like smile spread over her face. Her faint French accent purred. "You seem quite certain of victory, Monsieur Butler." Lisette quit toying with her cake and set it down alongside her barely touched tea. "And what person would be capable of making such promises?"

Butler paused. He wasn't sure what he could offer without revealing too much. But Washington had known he would become infamous once he assumed command of the Continental Army. "General Washington commands the army. He also wields tremendous influence in the continental congress."

Lisette's restless fingers stilled. "Your congress meets in the state house now, does it not?" She leaned forward, close enough to reveal her décolleté through the tissue-thin lace surrounding the wide neckline of her dress. "What could be of such import to gather such men together?"

Butler glanced at her. "Trade between the colonies has always been a contentious affair. "Perhaps that is what they discuss." He was sure she was aware of what she was doing. Everything from the musk of her perfume to the light touches of cosmetics on her face told him that she had set out to snare him.

Lisette rose and moved to Butler's chair. He rose to meet her. Her petite frame placed the top of her head just below his nose. Her heady scent filled his nostrils, almost intoxicating in its power. Once again, he was aware that she was a remarkably beautiful woman.

She gazed up at him, her eyes faintly wide, soft pink lips faintly parted, and he felt the temptation to move closer. Her chin raised in anticipation of a kiss. "I ordered my staff not to disturb us," she whispered as her hand reached out to stroke his.

Butler inhaled deeply. He avoided entanglements with women. It only led to trouble. He knew that. Yet this woman was not only remarkably beautiful but had access to information his cause could use. For a heartbeat, he considered seducing her. That she was willing was clear as her pale fingers stroked his arm, sending shivers of delight up and down his skin. He wondered if this was how she had snared Franklin's son.

Butler stepped back. "I could not be such a cad as to compromise another man's wife," he said softly. "You have been kind to welcome me into your home and offer me refreshment. It would be wrong to take advantage of a lady."

Lisette blinked before regaining her composure. "How noble of you." Her tone was flat. "It is rare to find a true gentlemen in these times." She returned to her side of the tea table. Her skirt brushed against the edge, dislodging a cup. It rocked briefly before crashing to the floor, splashing its contents on her gown and on the rug below before rolling to a stop underneath the table itself. She stared at it and down at the stain on her gown, anger tightening her skin and making her look older than Butler would have guessed.

He handed her his handkerchief. "Here."

Lisette Fournier daubed a few seconds before giving up and tossing the handkerchief on the floor. "This is hopeless."

Butler tsked. "Never assume a situation is hopeless. Your maid may know a way to lift the stain."

Lisette snorted. "My maid has all the intelligence of a chicken. But she is remarkably good with hair, which is why I keep her. She also knows how to keep her mouth shut."

"Perhaps you had best have her tend to you before the stain sets."

Lisette looked at him. "You're not bound to that little Quaker in the china shop, are you?"

"Hannah?" Butler said, surprised. "No, she has provided me a place to stay in town." He looked at her. "Are you still involved with William Franklin?"

Lisette paused. "The royal governor of New Jersey is a prisoner of the rebels. I doubt he has a relationship with any woman right now, including his wife." She turned to the doorway, "Maud! I need you!"

Butler continued. "But that has only been true for a few months. I imagine he was in Philadelphia often to visit his father."

Lisette shrugged. "It was over months ago. William feared discovery from his sanctimonious father as well as his proper little wife." Her lips thinned. "I went up to Perth Amboy before his arrest. "We met in a lovely house I rented. Then he said goodbye one evening and never returned. I have no use for cowards." She looked at him. "Let me know what your general says.

I am sure we could benefit each other." Her eyes flicked up and down his frame. "You can send word to me if you change your mind."

Butler shook his head. "I will not. But if you would like to discuss an exchange of information, you can reach me at Mistress White's house." He exited and made a beeline for the door, which the butler opened for him. As he mounted the waiting wagon, he wondered what kind of benefits Lisette Fournier had in mind.

Chapter Twenty-One

H annah checked the basket on the table. It held some of her best homemade jam and dried peppermint for tea. She was normally hesitant about social calls, but Elizabeth Cranford had been injured in her shop, and she could very well be her half-sister. It was worth the effort to try. She brushed her hands down her apron, which she had just changed. She knew she was being ridiculous, but her nerves got the better of her. Hannah was well aware that appearances mattered. She didn't want to be brushed aside by her own sister. It brought back too many memories of her fall from society once Amos had died and his children decided to oust her from the family despite having once been fairly close. Hannah swallowed. It was better to push the memories aside and move forward just as she always had.

Suzanna watched what she was doing as she busily peeled peaches for pie. Wiping off her hands, she pointed to where she had set out the loaves of bread she had baked earlier. "There's a small loaf of my bread you can take if you like, Mistress."

Hannah looked over at her. "I thank thee," she said as she added the small golden loaf to her basket. "Thou does not need to call me Mistress, Suzanna. We are all equal in the eyes of God."

Suzanna shook her head. "I work for you. It would not be respectful."

Hannah looked at her. "Yes, you do, and I could not manage without your help. But you are a free woman. No one has ownership over thee."

Suzanna stilled as her dark eyes considered Hannah. "You really believe that." Her normally genial expression turned bleak. "Listen to me. We are not equals. Your husband was highly regarded here, and even as a woman in trade, you are still held in some regard for sharing his name. I will always be viewed through the lens of color. You know this. You have seen how my people are treated in the markets and streets in this town. We cannot even sit together in the worship of God."

Hannah bit her lip as Suzanna's words struck home. There was no denying what she had said. She would never know what life was like for a woman like Suzanna. She disliked acknowledging the bigotry that resided throughout the colonies. "I refuse to give it reign in my house," she said at last.

Suzanna sighed. "You treat me and my family well, Miss Hannah. We are grateful for that. I haven't forgotten that you bought my grandson and set him free. We're proud that he attends school here in Philadelphia."

Hannah looked down at the basket she had filled. Her mind turned to the enslaved boy who had entered her shop to poison Benjamin Franklin. "But it's not enough, is it?"

Suzanna's voice was soft. "There aren't enough people like you in this town."

She turned away to stir the big iron pot that bubbled over the fire. Silence fell between the two of them as each became immersed in their own thoughts.

Hannah left her working in her kitchen. Lucretia and Nathan were busy in the shop. She paused to let Nathan know where she was headed before tying on her hat and stepping out. He nodded his acknowledgment from the stool where he sat from time to time to ease the discomfort of the peg against his stump.

The sun brightened the sky to a clear, cerulean blue. She could feel its warmth on her back and arms. Her wide straw brim protected her eyes from its brilliance. Down the length of Walnut Street, people were about their business. A wagon passed by, its wheels bumping noisily as the huge gray horses harnessed to it pulled it down toward the market. Dappled pools of shade from nearby trees provided intermittent reprieves from the afternoon glare. It was beautiful weather for walking. Her wooden heels clopped against the street cobbles as she walked into town. In the fifteen years she had lived here, Hannah had never ceased to marvel at the size of Philadelphia. No matter the hour, it brimmed with activity from the docks alongside the river to the edges where small farms lay scattered about, growing food and stock for the many lives sheltering inside the town.

Amos had been amused by her never-ending fascination with city life. Before his health failed, they had explored many areas of town except for those he had said were too dangerous for a lady to venture into. As age and illness had set in, he had provided her with a carriage and footman for her adventures. After a life on a modest-sized farm, Hannah had thoroughly enjoyed the opportunities afforded by an enormous and affluent city. She refused to contemplate returning to her childhood home, even when fate had turned her life upside down.

Engrossed in her thoughts, it took a few minutes for her to realize that a small crowd was gathered outside an alleyway. Many of the people she saw were people of color, but that didn't really surprise her. A large number of freed people resided in various sections of Philadelphia. Hannah wondered what had caused so many to gather. The air filled with sobs of the heartbroken. Curiosity led her to cross over to see what was going on.

The man Butler had introduced as Maynard stepped out to block her way. "You don't need to go there," he said. His darkly tanned face looked grim. His long shirt had rusty stains on the sleeves. "Let these people grieve in peace."

Hannah's nose caught the rusty metallic scent of blood. Muted sobs filtered through the crowd, warning her of tragedy. "What has happened?" she asked.

Maynard's face was bleak. "Someone murdered a child," he said. "That boy Butler set me to find was garroted and left in the alley like a piece of trash." His large hands clenched open and shut. "I hope they find the bastard. I'll help string him up."

Hannah heard grief in the roughness of his voice. "Garroted?" She asked, unfamiliar with the harsh-sounding word.

His eyes were the pale amber of a coyote and just as cold. "Someone used a wire to strangle him, ma'am. It's an incredibly brutal way to die." He looked at his callused hands. "I tried to remove it, but it was embedded too deep in his neck. It takes the devil's own to do that to a child." He spat on the ground.

Hannah felt sick as her mind drew a picture she never wished to see. Around them, more people gathered, curious about the hue and cry. Merchants, farmers, apprentices, people stopped their businesses to come gather and see what was wrong. She watched as a group of men with grim faces cleared the way, pushing aside crates and barrels that lined the narrow alley. Some bore the imprint of Boston, which surprised her given the British blockade of that town following the incident with tea. She stepped back into the street, stumbling over a loose stone. Maynard grasped her elbow to steady her. He blocked her view of the alley, although nothing could block the wails of grief. Bitter sobs echoed into the street as if nothing could contain the grief.

Hannah looked up at him. His wide felt hat blocked the afternoon sun that was peaking just over the rooves of the houses nearby. "Butler asked you to look for the enslaved child that disappeared from my house. Why did he want to speak to him?"

Maynard's tone was blunt. "Ask Butler. I'm not going to stand here talking about a dead boy while his mother grieves nearby. Go home, Mistress White, to your nice house in the better side of town and leave these poor wretches alone."

Hannah stared at his retreating back. She barely knew him, but she knew men like him. Leathery-skinned frontiersmen who braved the frontier facing hardships she could not begin to imagine. The harshness of his tone told her that the child's death struck a nerve. She shivered, trying not to think of the small figure struggling as someone choked the life out of him.

A large, dark-skinned man carried the body out wrapped in a blanket. Two small feet shod in black leather shoes dangled out one end. He was followed by a woman Hannah recognized as one of the maids who had come to her shop with Lisette Fournier and Elizabeth Cranford. Her face was covered in tears as she sobbed. "My boy, my boy. What did they do to you?"

There was no decent answer to such a question. It ripped at the heart, causing a knot to rise in Hannah's throat. She stepped back out of the way, bowing her head in respect for the grieving. The mother was surrounded by a group of other men and women from the community. A few shot angry glances at Hannah as they passed. She felt grateful that Maynard stood nearby. He was right. This was not a place to be. This was a community in pain. Hannah didn't blame them for their anger. People of color suffered, whether they were free or not, treated like less than they were. A brutal crime cut deeply into the fabric of their community and worsened the wound. A wave of helpless anger swept over her that innocence could be taken away with such swift brutality.

Chastened, Hannah continued her journey to Mistress Cranford's home. In her mind's eye, she saw the small figure with the sad, dark eyes, forever robbed of the chance to grow to manhood. He had run away from the house, from his mother, and the people who had enslaved them both. She prayed for the little soul, freed from all who had endeavored to hunt him down.

Hannah intended to have a conversation with Jeremy Butler as soon as she saw him again. Sheltering Franklin was becoming dangerous. It was past time to tell her who he was and what he was involved in. He slipped in and out of her house at odd hours, which made her suspect he was up to no good. He needed to tell her more than he had been willing to share. While she was willing to help her sister's friends, she refused to support stirring up trouble with either the British or the rebels. It was far too risky for a woman in her position.

Within a few minutes, she stood in the tree-lined street outside the Crawford's three-story home. She watched as the traffic of horses and carriages went down the street. They weren't far from Market Street, but this was a far different neighborhood. Only people of affluence could afford these homes. Their stately doors were for their friends and associates. Servants and people in trade had to use a door in the back where they could come and go unobserved. Not so many years ago, she would have gone to the front door with impunity as the wife of a well-to-do Quaker. Now, she would be expected to go around to the back entrance. Hannah White was a woman in trade who lived by her own hard work. She had undoubtedly lost a great deal of respect for doing so, but it kept her from starving. Regardless, she was here to check on the woman of the house, not sell china.

She watched as a wagon bumped around the house on a side street, undoubtedly making a delivery. The man next to the driver held a musket across his lap. A stray breeze pulled back the canvas covering the load. Hannah stared at the small kegs next to large wooden crates. To her surprise, the wagon stopped. Cursing, the man with the gun set it down and jumped out, running to the back to secure the cover before jumping back on board to continue their journey. She shook her head at the oddity. Everyone knew the militia was gathering munitions any way they could. Why bother to hide it?

Taking a deep breath, she smoothed her skirts and went to the front, knocking firmly on the door. She waited a few minutes, then knocked again. She was beginning to wonder if she had picked a poor time to call upon the mistress of the house when she heard footsteps coming to the door. A maid answered and looked at her inquiringly. Hannah smiled. "I've come to call on Mistress Cranford. She fell ill at my home yesterday."

The maid stared at Hannah, her expression making it clear that she did not belong. They looked at each other, neither giving any ground until a voice from within the house said, "Let her in, Nettie. I know Mistress White, and I would appreciate having someone to talk to."

Elizabeth Cranford stood in the main hall. Other than the bandage wrapped about her hand, there were no signs of yesterday's upset. Her light brown hair was pulled up with a few delicate curls trailing down her back. Her outer gown was the pale pink of apple blossoms. The split skirt allowed the ivory, ruffled underskirt to be seen. The bodice featured delicate embroidery in cherry, sage green, and white. Although the neck was cut middling low, a light fichu kept her bosom from being revealed. A small cap decorated with cherry ribbon completed her outfit.

As Hannah came closer, she noticed dark circles under the other woman's eyes along with a wax-like pallor of her skin. "I came to see how you were doing," she said. "I brought some of my cook's bread and some strawberry jam for you." She offered the basket. Elizabeth Cranford took it and glanced at it briefly before handing it off to a maid who whisked it away, presumably to the kitchen downstairs.

Elizabeth Cranford eyed her for a brief moment. "The last time you were here, you came in the servant's entrance. I normally do not allow tradespeople in through my front door. Nonetheless, I could use some company. My husband busies himself in meetings with those men who have come into town from all the colonies. I have had no one to speak with all day. It is quite tiresome. Come we can sit in the morning room, and you can tell me the news you have heard." She turned and walked down the hallway, the skirts of her dress swishing as she walked. Elizabeth Cranford paused in the doorway, her skirts wider than the frame. After a few brief tugs, the hoops popped loose, allowing her entry into her own parlor. Hannah hid her smile as she crossed the threshold with ease since she dressed for practicality and could move far more freely.

Hannah didn't care for the welcome, but she followed the other woman into an elegant room whose walls were covered in ivory wallpaper festooned with vines of pale pink roses in full bloom. It was a woman's room, with rosy pink draperies tied back from windows that nearly went to the floor and a plush rug also in ivory and rose that covered a length of the wooden floor. It was a light-filled place with padded chairs covered in striped and floral damask. An ivory marble fireplace graced one wall; its fire was unlit in the summer heat. A series of botanical prints graced one wall. A large portrait stood over the mantel, its gilded frame gleaming. Hannah studied it briefly. It featured a woman with three children of different ages. The woman was obviously Elizabeth Cranford, holding an infant in a gown and cap. The children were somewhere between two and three, which made it difficult to detect gender. The woman in the painting was younger, which made Hannah wonder how many little Crawford's there were.

Her hostess caught her glance. "My husband commissioned that when a well-known portraitist came into town from England eight years ago. That is my oldest, Edward, and his sister Sarah. Our baby Jasper developed a croup and passed that winter. He's buried with his sister Mary and my husband's first wife in the Quaker cemetery on Arch Street."

Hannah's voice softened. "To lose a child must be a tremendous grief. I regret thy loss." She looked about the room with its elegant furnishings and expensive décor. No toys lay on the floor. No voices echoed from the back. She wondered where the children were.

Elizabeth Cranford sat down in one of the striped chairs. "I have had three children since. Fortunately, they have been well. One never knows with children." She smiled faintly. "It takes both a nursemaid and a governess to care for them. They have gone out for a walk and should not return for a while."

"Family is very important," Hannah said as she looked at the other woman, wondering if they bore any resemblance to each other. "My mother lost a child once. She never forgot her even though it happened before I was born."

Cranford's face showed no interest. Perhaps she didn't know, or given the passage of years, she might not care. An open decanter sat on the low table between them. Rather than wait for a servant, she poured into two goblets sitting on a tray by the bottle. One glass looked like it had already held liquid.

Although surprised to be offered wine rather than coffee or tea, Hannah accepted it without comment, although she wondered how many drinks her hostess had already imbibed.

The white wine tickled her tongue as she sipped. It was light and fruity, with a flavor reminiscent of strawberries. She sat it down carefully on the table between them. "It is amazing how so many things are still available despite the blockades. Your family must have excellent connections, Mistress Cranford."

Elizabeth Cranford watched her. "My husband considers himself a connoisseur of fine wines. He goes and bids on shipments when he receives word they have come into port. I believe he got this off of one of Master Hancock's vessels. It is good, is it not?" She considered her glass. "My husband listens to men like Hancock and Dr. Franklin. He sees what a stranglehold the king places on our economy. You are a woman in business. I am sure you have seen this as well."

Hannah hesitated. She had been very careful not to take a side. Her business relied on people on both sides of the conflict. "I'm sure that there are many people who would prefer to avoid conflict and conduct their business without stirring up either side." She paused to sip her wine. "How is your hand?"

Elizabeth frowned and eyed the snug bandage. "It is healing well enough. It was clumsy of me. I know how to manage my skirts by now. I should not have disturbed your display."

Hannah paused to consider her next words. "You seem well situated in Philadelphia, as busy as this city is. Have you lived here long? I wondered if your family was from around here. So many people have come from different places, near and far, and then married. Who knows? We two might even be related."

In the back, men's voices murmured. Hannah could not make out the words, although she was certain they were speaking French. She pretended not to notice as the voices rose, then faded away as the back door slammed shut.

Elizabeth glanced at her; the only indication of surprise was a faint widening of her eyes. "That's an interesting question, Mistress White. My maiden name was Biddle, and we have been here a very long time." She leaned forward, setting down her empty glass. "You're Amos White's widow, the second Mistress White, that is. The first Mistress White was a Wister. She died in childbirth. He waited over thirty years to remarry, and then he chose you. No one in town ever understood why. As I recall, your family lives out in the country on a farm. How could we possibly be connected?"

Hannah flushed. She knew the snobbery of the old Philadelphia families. She had felt it when she had first wed and foolishly had thought it had faded away until Amos died. When his adult children had turned on her, most of her friends faded away. "My family has farmed animals, fruits, and vegetables to feed both the high and low of Philadelphia. Honey from my father's bees has sweetened tea at many tables. I have always been grateful that they raised me not to judge others by their name but by their character. As to whether we share blood, that depends on your origins. There is a story that my mother's first child, a daughter, was given to a family in Philadelphia to raise as their own. I would very much like to find my sister before my mother dies. It would mean a great deal to her."

Cranford sniffed. "That is most certainly not me." She eyed Hannah up and down with pursed lips. "We have nothing in common. You have none of the features of a Biddle." Disgust colored her tone. "My mother would never let another woman's bastard pollute her home. I and my brothers sprang from the same stock, people who have helped Philadelphia prosper with the investments we have made."

Her arrogance appalled Hannah. She paused, catching her breath before her emotions got the better of her. "On my way over here, I saw a crowd gathered in one of the freed neighborhoods. Someone found your footman dead in the alley, strangled."

Elizabeth Cranford turned pale. "That is unfortunate. His mother works for Mistress Fournier sometimes. She sold him to me earlier this year since he was of an age to train. He was coming along nicely. It will be difficult to find a replacement." She fiddled with her glass before setting it down by Hannah's. Her eyes gazed out at the room, focusing on nothing as the silence fell between them.

A flash of anger ignited in Hannah. "He was a child, an innocent in this world, not a piece of property to be traded back and forth. It seems strange that he met with such a terrible end only a day after your accident, which was followed by an attempt to poison my guest, Dr. Franklin."

The other woman's eyes rose to meet hers. "What are you implying?" Her tone took on a frigid note. "You cannot prove anything. We came to your business to see what you had. No one sets a better table than I, especially not that woman from the West Indies." Elizabeth Cranford sneered. "She actually believes we're better off as chattels of King George. It was her idea to sell him. I merely completed the transaction and provided him with a comfortable home and the chance to better himself."

Outrage coursed through her bones. Hannah was tired of self-entitlement. "No one who traffics in humanity can claim clean hands. I do not care whether you are a Tory or a Patriot. Many of the voices crying for freedom and fair treatment ignore what transpires in their own homes. Have you never wondered if those who serve you so dutifully might long to be free? The business you do impacts the lives of many here."

Elizabeth Cranford took a moment to respond. "A just cause requires sacrifices, Mistress White. We can't all pretend to be nonpartisan while the choices of others place our homes and families at risk. Choices must be made in order to benefit the well-being of those who will one day manage these colonies. I hope you will come to accept that fate decrees sacrifices must be made. I have always enjoyed your shop. I regret what needs to be done."

Her host wasn't making sense. Hannah rose, smoothing her skirt. "I bid you good day. I have other business to attend." Her legs felt unsteady as she walked toward the parlor door. Tears rose in her eyes as she hurried to leave. She didn't want to break down in front of this insufferable woman. She drew in a deep breath to still her shaking. As greyness filled her vision, Hannah realized she wasn't going to make it home. She could feel herself falling before everything went dark.

Elizabeth Cranford stood as well. She walked to stand over the other woman's unconscious body. "Someone should have taught you to hold your tongue." Walking to the doorway, she called her maid. "Get Jethro and Tom to harness the wagon. I need you to help me roll up this rug. I will tell them where it needs to go."

The young enslaved woman's eyes widened as she looked down at the floor.

"Keep your silence, and I will let your child stay here with you," Elizabeth whispered. "You will always be together."

The other woman swallowed and nodded before bending down to roll the rug around the still body on the floor.

Chapter Twenty-Two

J eremy Butler arrived home to a quiet house. He had expected to be
confronted by Hannah once he arrived, but he saw no sign of her
presence. Shrugging, he went about his business. Mistress White was
a busy woman. She was very likely at the market or checking on the status
of a shipment. In the shop, Lucretia and Nathan spoke to the well-to-do
matrons of Philadelphia who had come to select china. He walked softly up
the steps to avoid interrupting them. He knew they depended on sales to
keep food on the table.

Upstairs, Franklin worked with quill and paper at a table. One leg
was propped up on a stool. Butler's presence did not disturb the steady
scratching of his pen on the parchment. Once he had finished, he set down
his quill and blew gently on the page before setting it aside to dry. "I trust
your journey was fruitful?" Franklin's gentle inquiry was guileless, but
Butler knew better than to believe his expression.

"Madame Fournier knows how to say what she wants."

Franklin raised an eyebrow, but Butler did not elaborate.

"What's the matter with your leg?" Now that Butler had gotten closer, he
could see it was swollen, stretching out the stocking like a balloon.

"Gout, the punishment of the elderly," Franklin groaned. "Mistress White
promised to treat it when she returned from her errand, but she is not here.
Can you at least inquire if dear Suzanna has any more of that fine cider she
brought with my breakfast?"

"I can do that," Butler paused. "It that the document you have been working
on with Jefferson and Adams?"

Franklin shook his head. "No, it is merely a letter to the man I once called son." Sadness filled his expression, followed by bitter anger. "His own stubbornness and pride have placed him in his current predicament. Had he been willing to listen to reason, he could have been given the rank of general in our continental army. But my son prefers to continue to lap at the breast of our imperial rulers. It is a waste of the opportunities I have provided him throughout his life. He refuses to see reason, so I have no recourse but to wash my hands of the matter."

Butler paused. "He is your only son. Is he not?'

A sigh escaped the older man. "Alas. It has been many years since Franky passed from the pox. He was a joy to all who knew him." Franklin paused to collect himself. "William is the only son left among the living even though he is as good as dead to me now. At least there is his son Temple and my Sally's children. "

Butler kept his face neutral. He had no children, having lost a wife and infant son to fever, so he could not relate to Franklin's dilemma. The whole conversation made him uncomfortable. "How goes the work of the congress? Are you ready to announce your intentions to the world?"

Franklin's tone was wry. "While I have published many a statement in my day, the bulk of the work has fallen to one of more tender years. Jefferson has been selected to write our declaration. On it, he works for hours alone in his rooms. It is my job to temper his remarks and make suggestions to his work."

He abruptly changed topics. "Be careful around Madame Fournier. She's a beautiful woman, but I've noticed her favor tends to fall with men who support the king."

Butler nodded. "I've heard that." He looked over at the sheets of paper drying on the desk. "Are you hoping to turn William to our side?"

Franklin shook his head. "William has made his position clear. He continues to support the crown and will stubbornly do so until it kills him." He tapped the pages. "I am telling him that ending me serves no good purpose. This revolution will continue long after I am in the ground."

Butler glanced at him before pulling up a stool to sit near the older man. "Do you really believe William could be involved? He's being held by members of the patriot cause. It would be difficult to plot an assassination."

Franklin's face turned grim. "Don't underestimate my son. No matter how well he's being watched, he will find a way to accomplish his goals. Of that, I have no doubt."

Butler paused. "Have you spoken to him about your feelings regarding the future of these colonies?"

"Many times." Sorrow crossed his face. "It would be far better for him to join the ranks of the enlightened before this war destroys him. A man with his background could easily become a general. In time, he could become a governor again for a free and independent country, but he refuses to listen." Franklin shook his head. "He has made his choice. Governor Trumbull has charge of him, and he can keep him. I have washed my hands of the matter."

His reaction surprised Butler. The parting of father and son must have been bitter indeed. And now Franklin seemed unfazed by the notion that his only living son could be plotting his end. "Perhaps it would be better to discuss this in person. Letters do not always reveal what one is really thinking."

Franklin shook his head. "I'm too old to be running off at a moment's notice. My responsibilities lie here. If you wish to speak to my son, I will write you a letter to allow you to see him."

Butler shook his head. "I don't have time to travel up to Connecticut. I'm needed here."

Franklin smiled grimly. "Everyone thinks William is there under Trumbull's care, but I tell you, he hasn't been transferred there yet. He's over the river being held near Camden until he can be safely transported north. Not even his wife knows lest she betray his location to any would-be rescuers."

Butler considered the information. It would not take long for him to go downriver. "Write the letter. I will arrange for your protection while I'm gone. It's long past time I spoke to your son."

Franklin groaned as he shifted his leg. "Ask Suzanna if she can fix me a poultice for my leg. I cannot wait for her mistress." He reached over for his quill, checking the sharpness of the tip before dipping it in ink to begin his next missive.

Butler trotted down to the basement, where Suzanna was already busy preparing for dinner. A wave of steamy heat washed over him as he entered her workspace. He didn't know how she stood it. The cook chopped vegetables on a sturdy wooden table just a few feet away from the hearth. He watched her knife fly through a stack of carrots that she neatly slid into a bowl before pouring them into a large pot that hung over the fire.

A bright yellow cloth covered her hair, keeping it out of her way as she worked. She looked over at him as he stood in the doorway. "Can I help you, sir?" Her voice had a slight nasal sound like those who had been born and bred in the northern colonies.

Butler smiled. "I hate to disturb you, but Dr. Franklin's leg is causing him great pain. Is there anything you can recommend to help him?"

Suzanna paused, her brow wrinkled in thought. "He ate a good portion of my beef stew last night, along with some pork and dumplings. He also downed some port before turning in. That's a lot of rich food for an older man." She walked over and pulled a roll of wooly cloth out. "We will keep his leg warm with wool and wax, and I will start an infusion of tansy for him to sip." She placed a small black pot on the iron spider at the inside of the huge fireplace and dropped a stubby candle inside.

She stepped to the narrow door that led outside and called, "Micah!"

"I'm here, Grandma." The boy's head popped in along with the rest of his lanky frame.

"Fetch me a handful of tansy from the garden. It's over by the cucumbers. It's a tall plant with bright yellow flowers."

"Is that the one the bees are all over?" Micah's tone turned wary.

Suzanna snorted. "Sometimes they like it. I didn't say to dig the whole patch up. Just get me three to four heads, and that will be plenty. The bees want flowers, not you. Don't' smack at them, just blow on the blossom and they'll move."

"Yes, ma'am," her grandson sounded resigned.

Jeremy smiled in spite of his worries. Micah reminded him of himself at that age, going in and out of Athena's kitchen. It had been a long time since he had been that young.

"No use you waiting around," Suzanna said, eyeing Butler. "I'll send it up when it's ready, and Micah won't let anyone tamper with it either." She huffed as she went back to preparing the meal. "I need to finish chopping these vegetables if we're going to have dinner."

Jeremy left her to it and headed back upstairs. On the main floor, Nathan held a delicate cup up to the light to showcase its eggshell-like translucence. The light caught the gold edges as he slowly turned it to the oohs and aahs of the couple watching him. He brought the cup down with a flourish and offered them a winning smile. "With such a setting as this, you could serve the finest families in the colony."

The woman asked about another pattern while her spouse inquired about cost. Given that his suit was cut from the finest broadcloth and his wife wore silk to go shopping, money was not a problem. As Nathan tallied their order, Jeremy offered him a nod of respect. Nathan ignored him, but a small smile indicated his pleasure.

Once the couple had gone over to arrange the shipment of their purchase, Nathan walked over to where Jeremy stood. "So, how is Dr. Franklin today?"

Jeremy shook his head. "Not too well. Suzanna is making something to ease his gout. I do not think he will be walking over to the state house today." The shop had quieted. Lucretia was in one corner showing pewter spoons to a woman, but otherwise, they were alone. He looked about the room. "Where is Hannah? I would have thought she would be here too."

Nathan shrugged. "She went out a few hours ago to make a call. She's probably drinking coffee and listening to some matron drone on about the cost of ribbons for hats."

Jeremy grinned. "I really cannot see a Quaker woman having much sympathy for that."

Nathan offered a wry grin. "You're right about that. We're not much for embellishment. But she'll listen and then find a way to comment on china."

"She goes to homes to hawk her wares?"

Nathan shook his head. "Nothing so indelicate. Hannah got into this because she has a good eye for detail. She can tell you where a cup or plate came from and when the pattern was popular. She can also spot flaws in design and structure and inform the owner. She won't buy poorly made stuff. It's won her a loyal following. People here know she will not sell them inferior goods."

Butler didn't hide his surprise. "I had no idea it was such a complicated business."

"It can be," Nathan continued, packing the cups and plates in straw before placing them into a barrel already partially filled. "Did you need anything?"

Butler nodded. "I may be out of town for a few days. My friend Maynard will keep an eye on the doctor in my absence. Can I trust you to keep watch as well?"

Nathan shot him a look. "What do you expect me to do if something does happen?" He didn't look down, but Butler knew he was referring to his leg.

"Do whatever you deem necessary," Jeremy responded. "Maynard will be close by if you need help. You are in the best position to see if any strangers try to go upstairs."

Nathan shrugged. "There is that." He limped over to a nearby stool and sat. "I thought the Dreyers would never settle on a pattern. Thank God that is done. Where are you off to?"

"Downriver to Camden," Butler said. "There's someone I need to speak to. The sooner the better."

By dinner time, Jeremy Butler had made his way to the river, passing a coal yard as well as the business of ship joiners, wood sawyers, and grocers. The scent of yeast drifted out of the door of a bakery, making his stomach grumble. Butler paused to purchase a loaf and some cheese to assuage his hunger. It would not replace the fine meals he had come to enjoy at Hannah White's house, but it would fill his belly for now. The closer he drew to the water, the stronger the scent of fish became. Men hauled their catches ashore, sorting them into barrels. Others brought in oysters, emptying their traps on the wharf into bins that men and women looked at as they shopped for their businesses and households. Overhead, gulls circled as they sought an easy meal. Their raucous cries filled the air as they awaited an opportune moment to dive in and snatch away a succulent morsel. On a day like this, they were thick as flies. A stray feather floated down to earth, joining others on the wooden boards of the dock that jutted out into the water.

Before long, he stood on the Vine Street Public Landing waiting for the ferry. In his pocket was a sealed letter from Franklin to his son. It surprised him the number of businesses that had grown up along the waterfront. Among the shipwrights and wood sawyers, he spotted a small tavern, a boarding house, another grocer, and a shoemaker. Given the amount of traffic on the Delaware, there was likely plenty of coin to be made.

Before long, the ferry loaded its cargo and left. Two men rowed at the bow while another manned the helm guiding the large flat-bottomed vessel into the main channel. He shared his ride with a peddler who held a donkey laden with his goods as well as a family consisting of a well-dressed gentleman and a lady wearing a large feathered hat. She held a little girl by the hand. They stood near a carriage with a pair of handsome grays harnessed to it. The little girl gazed in awe as they left the shore and moved onto the river. He smiled at her, silently enjoying her wonder. There was little he could do until he reached the other side. Franklin had sent him to a tavern near the waterfront to meet a man who knew where the younger Franklin was being held. They had met in a murky corner where the window was covered with sailcloth, making it difficult to see the man's features, although his voice marked him as being German or Dutch at one time in his life.

By the time they had reached their destination, he was tired and grumpy. The longer he was away from Philadelphia, the more time an assassin had to make another attempt. Maynard was good, but his area of expertise was the wilderness, not a large city. Butler took time to help the family disembark. As the man helped his lady down, Butler caught the little girl as she raced to the end of the platform and lifted her down before she jumped. She laughed as he spun her around and returned her to her mother, who watched with an anxious face.

"Be careful, little one," He admonished. "I would hate for you to get muddy river water on such a pretty dress."

She hid her face in her mother's skirts as he spoke. Her father offered his hand. "My thanks. She's excited about visiting her grandparents."

CHAPTER TWENTY-TWO

Butler nodded. "I wish you a safe journey, then."

"You too, sir." With that, he strode off to hand his wife and child into the waiting carriage while the horses waited patiently. With a cluck of the tongue and a flick of the reins, they were on their way into town.

Butler unloaded his own mount, a dappled gray borrowed from Hannah White's stable. He wondered where she was and what she was doing. He had been disappointed not to see her before he had left, but he realized her life was far different from his. He respected her hard work and determination to succeed in a world dominated by men.

Following the Dutchman's directions, he went into town, stopping at a local stable to inquire after a man named Edward. Edward was a man even shorter than he, who was joined by a man who grinned at Butler with a broken-toothed smile. That was the last he saw before a feedbag went over his head, and he was knocked to the ground.

Butler tried to fight, but there were too many. They dragged him to his steed and tied a rope around his arms, leading him like an animal. His hands were bound in front of him with rope that scratched his wrists. "What are you doing?" He demanded between breaths. The bag was stuffy and smelled of oats.

"Taking you to see the governor," Edward said. "The former governor, that is. We'll remove the sack once you're there. We don't need anyone telling the Lobster backs where his hoity-toity ness is at present. He'll be going to a better place in a matter of days. We weren't expecting callers, so you will have to accept our rules." A horse nickered nearby. "Put your foot in the stirrup, buttercup."

Butler complied, allowing himself to be hoisted back into the saddle of his own horse. He wobbled in the saddle before he was able to grab his saddled horn. It was a bumpy, uncomfortable ride. Although Butler could feel the sun, he could see nothing through the coarsely woven bag. The scratchy fabric irritated his face and neck, and he feared he was going to suffocate. He took slow, steady breaths and prayed the ride would not last long. Disoriented as he was, it felt like hours before the hood was lifted, and he beheld a large farmhouse built of fieldstone surrounded by trees. "Where am I?"

Edward stared at him. "You don't give up, do you?" He gestured to the other men who had come out from the stable. "Get him down and take him over to see the Gov."

Butler wobbled before he steadied himself. Fresh air filled his lungs, and he was grateful to breathe freely, even if the scent of farm animals was everywhere. In the distance, he heard the cries of gulls, which told him the river was not too far away. He waited while his captors removed the ropes. He rubbed his arms and wrists as he stood in the yard waiting.

Edward stared up at him with a hard glance. "They say Washington speaks highly of you."

Butler nodded. "The General is an honorable man."

"That may be, but I don't know you. You get one hour with Franklin, and then you will be returned. If you try to come back, we will shoot you and leave your body where no one will find it but the crows. Understand?"

Butler nodded. He had no doubt Edward and his cohorts meant it. These were dangerous times, and holding a royal governor captive was a hanging offense. He didn't blame them for their caution, even if he resented being trussed up like a turkey. "We are on the same side of this matter," he replied. "Once Franklin answers my questions, I will be happy to go back to my own business and leave you to yours."

Edward nodded and went into the house, leaving Butler in the company of two other men. Neither looked like the type to be trifled with. They led him past the wide porch of the farmhouse to a smaller building alongside. Were he to guess, Butler would say that this was the original building and the larger one had been added as the owner prospered. Whatever its age, the house was well cared for. The railings had been painted recently, as had the shutters, all in a rusty red that contrasted sharply with the cool gray of the stone.

One of the steps squeaked as he went up. His heart jumped before he continued up to the narrow porch. The only sign that this was other than another part of the farm was the guard outside. Although he was dressed plainly in breeches and tunic, a musket stood nearby with a bayonet attached to its barrel. The light of the sun glinted off its edge, making it gleam in the shadows of the porch.

The sentry glanced at Butler. "That him?"

The other man nodded, then gestured to the door, which was shut. "He's inside. We'll wait out here. If we hear anything off, we'll deal with it whether the problem is him or you."

Butler nodded. "I will keep that in mind."

He opened the door and went in, not sure of what to expect. The room was spacious, with a broad, unlit fireplace and a couple of comfortable chairs on either side. A wooden table sat near one window where light streamed in. A man sat in a plain wooden chair in front of it, writing swiftly. The scratching of the quill was the only noise in the room. Engaged in his thoughts, the man completed his missive before setting down his quill and blowing gently on the letter to dry the ink.

When he looked up, Butler could see the resemblance between the governor and his father in the heavy-lidded gray-blue eyes and thick brows. They both had pale, rounded faces with high foreheads accented by the hair pulled back behind the head. Franklin looked thin and tired. He studied Butler for a few minutes before rising. "I presume you have come to see me," he said in a courteous tone.

"Yes," Butler replied. "I need to know if you are behind the attempts to kill your father."

William Franklin froze. "My father." He caught his breath. "I believe the real question is whether or not I can help you discover who is."

Chapter Twenty-Three

Hannah woke to a throbbing head and queasy stomach. She slowly opened her eyes, widening them as she realized the room was completely unfamiliar. Heart pounding, she sat up, slowly conscious of her spinning head. The bed she lay on was in a corner of the room. Overhead, a small window offered grayish light so that she was not in total darkness. She soon became aware of a rocking sensation and the cries of gulls. She was on a boat, moored only God knew where, but likely somewhere on the Delaware. Hannah rose and went to the door and tried the handle. It held fast. She was locked in. Rattling the handle and pounding on the door did little good. She yelled and pounded for a few moments. All she heard was the echo of her own voice and the slap of waves on the hull. Either no one was listening, or she had been abandoned on this vessel. It was hard to say what frightened her more.

Hannah resumed exploring her prison, intent on finding a weapon or a means to open the obstinate door. She took stock of the objects around her. In addition to the bed was a cabinet of sorts with drawers and shelves. Over it, rolls of paper rested on angled wooden stakes that formed shelves. She unrolled one to realize it was a map of the coast of the middle colonies. In fact, all the rolls were maps of some kind. Hannah rerolled one and took another, trying to get a sense of what this boat was used for. As with the other map, it contained a detailed drawing of water channels around the rivers and coast. It could be used for a multitude of things, from honest trade to smuggling.

Footsteps approached. Hannah moved back to the bed, feigning unconsciousness. The door rattled from a key in the lock before it swung open. From underneath her lashes, Hannah barely cracked an eye open enough to see the figure of a man step in and look.

"She's still out. They must have given her a hell of a dose," He muttered before turning and going out into the hall. He spoke to another person. "I won't be held responsible if you've killed her."

A woman's voice answered. "She's not dead. It would be easier if she were, then we could just dispose of the body. When my associate arrives, we will decide Mistress White's fate. It's unfortunate she chose to visit at such an importune time." The door slammed shut, muting out any further conversation.

Hannah recognized Elizabeth Cranford's voice. She didn't know why she was here, but she was not waiting for them to return. There had to be a way out. She listened to make sure no one was lurking outside the door before rolling out of bed to search for an escape route. The door was heavy with a metal knob and keyhole. It didn't move when Hannah threw her weight against it. She kicked it in frustration, with her heel wincing at the resulting throb. Rattling the knob told her the key might still be in the lock, but her chances of knocking it out and under the door were slim.

Hannah went to the window next high up on the wall. The bottom of the sill was just above her chin. Unfortunately, it was small, offering only a smidgen of light to the occupier of the room. She might be able to squeeze through it if she removed all her petticoats. Unfortunately, someone had nailed it shut. She was as neatly boxed as one of her china shipments. Hannah checked the walls, hoping for something helpful. She found a coil of rope hanging on a hook that was firmly secured to the wall. The bed frame had drawers built into the base. These contained a man's shirt and belt as well as a few fishing weights and hooks, which she pocketed. A ragged pair of breeches yielded a small knife which she also slid into her pocket. It was the only weapon she had, and it was pitifully small. "Lord, get me out of this," she whispered into the shadows. No answer returned. All she heard was the panicked pounding of her heart.

Desperation caused her to break out in a cold sweat. Whatever threat she posed, Elizabeth Cranford could not afford to have her tell the tale of her capture. It would ruin her standing in town. She had been brought here to be disposed of. Her captors intended to kill her sooner or later. The idea terrified her. She continued to whisper pleas for help from the Almighty as she searched for a means to escape.

Footsteps warned her that she would soon not be alone. Rather than feign unconsciousness, Hannah chose to sit in the room's one chair and face her enemies. If she could discover why they had taken her, there might be a way to bargain for her freedom. Hannah could only hope.

The door rattled as it swung open. Hannah got a brief glimpse of a large metal key in the door. The ring contained a few other keys that jangled against one another as the door swung wide. Elizabeth Cranford stared down at her. "I see you are awake now."

Hannah stared back at her. "Why am I here?"

Cranford looked at her. "You ask too many questions. And now your own foolishness has gotten you into trouble. God only knows what I'm to do with you." She swept into the room. Elizabeth Cranford had changed into a riding habit of deep blue with gold trim. Her wide triangular hat fit neatly over her hair. She looked like a lady out for a ride in the local park, not someone who plotted mayhem and discord. She smiled at Hannah's stare. "It would have been far better for both of us if you had stayed home and managed your business rather than interrupt mine, but here we are. No one was supposed to see me receive a shipment, that's why I sent most everyone away. One slip of the tongue would undo all of us, and I can't have that. You may as well sit down and have a drink. We can't do anything until our latest shipment arrives from New York."

Hannah regarded her thoughtfully. "The British hold New York, and your husband supports the revolution. In order to be receiving goods, you have to know someone with powerful connections. I would not have guessed you were a smuggler."

Elizabeth Cranford smiled. "My husband doesn't ask what I do with my time as long as I entertain his associates. He remains enraptured in his cause." Her expression changed. "Those who survive this war are the ones who know how to conduct business with either side. Powder and munitions are commodities of power. Supporters of either side will eagerly pay for them."

Hannah gazed at the other woman. "You would betray your own husband."

Cranford's gaze hardened. "I would make sure my family survives." She rose, brushing imaginary creases out of her skirt. "While wealthy men like Washington and Jefferson pontificate, those of us not born to privilege must ensure our survival." She lifted a hand gloved in fine kidskin. "This is about economics. Those of us with connections and the ability to provide what is needed will be valued by either side." She stared at her prisoner. "Anyone who gets in the way will be eliminated."

Hannah heard her own heart pounding as she listened. Underneath the patina of middle-class respectability was someone else altogether. It made her sick to realize that this was very likely her half-sister. "Why did you kill the boy?"

Elizabeth Cranford looked puzzled. "What boy?"

Hannah hissed. "I'm talking about the little boy in livery who accompanied you to my shop the other day. Or did you not realize he had been garroted in an alley far away from your palatial home."

Her face cleared. "You are referring to my footman." Her tone was dismissive. "He ran away. I hadn't had time to place a notice for his return. He's dead, you say." She sighed. "Now I will have to train another. If these people would quit running away, they might not come to such gruesome ends."

"Maybe he preferred freedom,"

Cranford shot her a bewildered look. "Why would he want that? He had a good home, a warm bed, and regular meals. There was no reason for him to go. He had everything he needed."

Hannah stared at her as if she were an idiot. "He had everything but the right to make his own choices. He wasn't a horse or a dog. He was a human being, made in the image of God with the same ability to move and breathe and dream as you or I."

Elizabeth Cranford sniffed. "You're one of those, aren't you? I've heard of those who believe in freeing all slaves. It's a ridiculous notion. The Africans were brought here to work. The economy of these colonies depends on the labor they provide. They are the means by which crops such as indigo, cotton, and tobacco are produced. No one could afford to pay for such labor. It makes as much sense as paying the horse or the cow for what they provide."

"I don't know whether you speak from ignorance or lack of heart, but never have I heard such evil spew from someone's mouth. A mindset such as yours is nothing but evil and begets its own dark end." Hannah walked up to her nemesis. "I will not stay and listen to this any longer. I have more pressing matters to attend." She went to pass the other woman who stood to block her. Hannah shoved her aside. The other woman staggered before regaining her balance and grabbing her by the arm. Hannah swung about and slugged her in the chest.

The bones from Elizabeth Cranford's stays bruised her knuckles but caused the other woman to gasp as it knocked the air out of her. She collapsed against the chest before dropping to the floor. Seizing her opportunity, Hannah ran to the door. It swung open with a wave of air redolent of fish and freedom. She caught a faint glimpse of the sky before her path was blocked

by a large man in the canvas pants and shirt of a sailor. Mousy brown hair was captured in a straggly braid tied with a rag. He smiled showing broken teeth. She took a step back.

"What have we here? A pretty woman all set to show me a good time." He stepped into the room, casting a glance at Cranford. "What say you, Mistress? She looks like she would put up a pretty good fight before I and my men finished with her."

Hannah balled her fists up in her skirt. She would fight and claw with every ounce of her being, but she knew she would not win. She looked back and forth between her captors, trying to find a means to escape.

A satisfied expression came over Elizabeth Cranford's face as she watched Hannah. "Not yet. We may still have some use for her. Keep her in here until I return, and then we can discuss what to do." She walked up to Hannah.

"You should keep your hands to yourself." Raising a gloved hand, she struck her across the face, the sound echoing in the tiny room. Cranford exited, followed by the sailor, leaving their prisoner alone.

Hannah sank down to the floor. Her face stung from the blow. She reached, shaking fingers to touch where she had been struck. It burned as if she had been branded. Her breath came in short gasps as reality sank in. Bitter sobs shook her body as she wondered if anyone would discover her fate. Worse, would anyone care enough to find out?

Chapter Twenty-Four

William Franklin ran a nervous hand through his thinning hair, which was shot with gray. Agitation laced his tone as he paced back and forth in the main room of the place where he remained incarcerated. "I have always been a good son, no matter what my father believes," he said. "This rebellion will cause nothing but irreparable damage to the name of Franklin." He shook his head. "I have never laid a hand on my father, nor would I encourage anyone to harm him, no matter his seditious beliefs."

Prison had not been kind to the former royal governor. His clothes hung on his body as he had thinned down to skeletal proportions. Although Butler knew he had to be in his forties, the lines etched on his face made him look far older. Once he had read his father's letter, Franklin had been unable to sit still as agitation sent him to his feet and pacing frenetically across the space of the room.

"I cannot believe he believes that I could be part of such a thing. Surely he knows me better than this." He raised his hands to stare at them as if they belonged to someone else. "I could not raise a finger to him even now when I know he works to destroy everything we built together." A sob tore through him. "I have always been loyal to my father and to my country. All my life, I have endeavored to live as an honorable and upright man, and here I am betrayed by all I once held dear. It is beyond comprehension."

Butler watched Franklin in silence, letting him wind down on his own. His grief and outrage seemed genuine enough even though Butler knew the man's own actions had landed him in prison rather than the comfortable house arrest the patriots had placed him in at the governor's residence in Perth Amboy.

Eventually, Franklin turned to him. "My father." The silence lengthened to a few moments. "Is he well?"

"Well enough. His gout was troubling him when I saw him before beginning this journey." Butler remained seated. He would have preferred to stand, but he didn't want the younger Franklin to realize his agitation was affecting him.

William Franklin returned to his seat and sighed. "My father's writings have led to this, I am sure. He has aggrieved the wrong person, and whoever it is means to silence him permanently."

"You don't believe the British are behind this?"

Franklin shook his head. "No, there are men that pose far more of a threat than my father. His writings may anger Lord Howe and his brother, but not to the degree that they would send an assassin. They are gentlemen."

Butler chose not to comment on the civilized qualities of British gentlemen. He had known a few whose actions he would not describe as being rational, much less civilized. He interrupted Franklin's musings with a question. "And what of the women you have dallied with? Could a man you've cuckolded be exacting revenge? Lisette Fournier is a beautiful woman. I doubt her husband was pleased to discover your affair."

Franklin paled. "Lisette doesn't need a man to exact vengeance for her. I would warn any man to keep their distance from that woman, less they come to grief."

Butler leaned in. "What do you mean?"

"I mean, she is dangerous." Franklin's eyes met his. "I was taken in by her beauty. Lisette has tremendous charm and wit, enough to ensnare any man." He ran nervous fingers through his hair. "All was well until I tried to end it, then she became hysterical, almost deranged. She followed me to my rooms and created a scene." He shuddered. "For the next few weeks, I could not get rid of her. She had my rooms watched and would interrupt my meetings with her presence. She could not accept that our liaison had run its course." He sighed. "She became an embarrassment. I left Philadelphia. She sent letters which I burned. She came to Perth Amboy with her husband under the pretext of business." He shook his head. "I could have made a great deal of money with Frances Fournier, but I could not risk having her near. I feared what she might do next."

Butler looked at him. "Is she capable of murder?"

Franklin shook his head. "I do not know. She sent me a dead bird once with a necklace I had given her wrapped about its neck." He sighed again. "She is beautiful, is she not? I greatly enjoyed dancing with her at a ball hosted by the Shippens. But underneath that lovely façade is someone else entirely." He paused to take a sip of coffee, grimacing at the taste. "We had much in common, you know. Both of us were bastards, hungry for recognition and success." He looked at the other man. "It leaves a scar, you know. No one lets you forget the ignominy of your birth, so you spend your whole life proving your worth to an unforgiving world. Very few people in society appreciate your work when they know your origins are mired in sin."

Butler didn't comment. Although not a bastard, he knew the sting of being judged by one's birth. To many of the landed gentry, being poor and Irish was nigh on a criminal offense.

"Did she tell you this?" Butler wondered what else she had shared.

Franklin nodded. "Intimacy lends to sharing other things as well. I think she hoped I could help her find her birth parents. She knew they were around here somewhere. Her foster family had told her that much."

"I thought she came from the West Indies."

Franklin shook his head. "I thought so too, but the people who adopted her moved there when she was a child. It's where she learned French. As to how she became Fournier's wife . . ." he shrugged. "When she sets her mind on something, she will not let go." He got up once more and moved to stand in front of the dead fireplace. "She sent my wife letters detailing our involvement. She hoped to drive a wedge between us." He shook his head. "I hurt my Elizabeth terribly, yet she chose to forgive me. I have only myself to blame for the offense. After Lisette did that, I was finished with her. I told her in no uncertain terms that our liaison was over." His expression grew distant as he remembered. "She cried copious tears, then raged and shouted at me. She could not believe I would reject her. Then she came at me with her claws." He rubbed his cheeks. "She left quite a mark. I left Philadelphia as soon as I could mount a horse."

"And you never returned?" Butler watched the other man. The story was incredible, but he believed the man. It made him wonder what else Lisette Fournier might do if thwarted.

Franklin shook his head. "There was no point. My father had rejected me, as well as the rule of law. I had no desire to encounter Lisette ever again. It was far better to shake the dust of that town off my boots forever. There is nothing good left there for me. I went home to my wife in Perth Amboy and devoted myself to the people of the New Jersey colony. I still received letters from her, mad, half-hysterical notes that were equal parts entreaty and threat. I burned every single one." His tone turned bitter. "Now I have to rely on the mercy of my jailors in order to send and receive letters even from my beloved wife."

Butler heard the whirring of the clock on the mantel, its movements showing the passage of time. He needed to return to Philadelphia as quickly as he could. Franklin, for all his faults, was no killer. His own sense of honor had separated him from his father and placed him in prison. God only knew whether he would survive the war or not.

He left as the sun was beginning its journey down the sky. Butler worried about what he would find when he returned. Meeting Benjamin Franklin's son had left him with more questions than answers and an uneasy feeling that things were about to get worse.

His captors chose not to bind or place the noxious bag over his head. Edward mounted his horse from the stable block and led the way, followed by another man in a straw hat.

Butler said nothing as they went in a southwestern direction across rolling farmland. They rode single file on a dirt track until they came to a road where they could ride abreast.

Edward looked at him. "Our boss speaks well of you."

"Who's your boss?"

Edward shook his head. "He said you would ask. He said to remind you of words you once told him: the fewer names exchanged, the safer everyone will be."

Butler glanced over at him. "He didn't say that when you trussed me up to bring me here?"

"Keeping Franklin Junior's location secret was most important. That doesn't matter now."

"Why?" Butler was curious.

Edward chuckled. "Because he won't be here come morning. William Franklin will be in the custody of the colony of Connecticut. We don't even know where they're putting him."

Butler considered the information. "It's too dangerous to keep him in the colony he so recently governed. There are enough loyalists who might contemplate mounting a rescue if they knew where to find him."

The other man nodded. "I knew you were smart. William Franklin is dangerous. No matter how we contain him, he has gotten messages out to the enemy." Anger darkened his face. "His troublemaking has cost us some good men."

"I'm sorry to hear that," Butler said. The horses slowed as they spoke. "I need to get back to Philadelphia. There is pressing business I must attend to before someone gets hurt." He urged his horse to a trot, eager to end this journey. As they crested a hill, a long, snaking ribbon of the river became visible, loaded with barges and ships heading up to Philadelphia, men poling their way out into the channel before raising sails to combat the current.

Edward stopped; his companion did likewise on either side of Butler. "Here's where we part company. Down there's the Delaware. You should be able to catch a ferry back to where you came from and get back to your business. We need to return to ours." With that, he clucked to his horse, turned, and went back down the hill to the road back from whence they had come.

Butler's horse's ears twitched, hearing things beyond the range of his rider's abilities. "Come on, horse. Let's get back to Philly." The horse nickered before heading down the hill toward the river. As they drew closer, he kicked his ride into a gallop, heading toward the landing where a barge stood. Who knew what awaited his arrival across the wide expanse of the Delaware?

Chapter Twenty-Five

There had to be a way out. Hannah searched the cabin once more, desperate for an opening. The window was too narrow and high up. Even if she stripped down to her shift, she wouldn't fit through the frame. The door was heavy and fit tightly in its frame. She had tried shaking it to no avail. She was running out of options. There was no way Elizabeth Cranford would let her walk out of here alive. Soon, she would tire of the game and order her death. Hannah had no intention of being here when that happened.

The door creaked as someone inserted the key into the lock. Once again, she faced the sailor with the broken teeth. He slapped a pan that contained bread and beans along with a demijohn of some liquid. "Mistress said to feed you, so here it is." He caught her expression. "While you're here, you can eat like the rest of us."

Hannah sniffed. "I wouldn't dream of it." She kept her distance from the man, which made him grin.

"There's no use putting on airs, my lady. You'd best make use of the time you have. You're a handsome woman. We could have some good times before you go." He winked as he ran his eyes up and down her body.

Hannah glared at him before turning her gaze to the plate. The beans were an unappetizing lump of a purplish hue. A glaze of fat hung over them, provided by the sliver of some mysterious meat-like substance that poked out of the mound. The bread was a thick slice from a crusty loaf. A faint cloud of steam rose from it, telling her it had just come from an oven.

"Don't worry, mistress. We won't poison you. The ladies have other plans where you are concerned." He laughed as he turned to go

"Wait," Hannah looked at him. "What ship is this?"

He cocked an eyebrow considering. "You're on *The Grey Goose*, mistress, for all the good it will do you." The door slammed shut. The force of it echoed in the room, causing the glass in the window to shiver. Unfortunately, it did not break.

Her stomach growled. By her estimate, she had already spent several hours in this prison. There was no way for her to tell how many. Even if Nathan and Lucretia raised the alarm, no one would be searching ships for her. There would be no reason to since her business rarely took her to the docks. She would have to rescue herself. Hannah stared down at the plate. Faith probably served better fare at her tavern. The thought produced a faint grin. Little sister had never excelled at standing over a fire for hours. Her attention had always been elsewhere. If her tavern was a success, it was because someone far more disciplined was running the kitchen.

Her smile faded. If she wished to see her family again, she needed to find a way out of her current circumstance. She sat down at the table and dipped into the food. Eating meant keeping up her strength. Chewing slowly, she considered her situation. Her jail was too sturdy for her to escape. There were no loose boards, and the heavy door fit snugly into the frame. Someone had nailed the window shut, which she considered ironic, considering it was too small for anyone but a child to crawl through. Her heart constricted at that thought. She didn't want to end up like the boy in the alley, cast aside like trash when his purpose had been completed. Besides the small knife she had found, she had only her wits to use. Hannah would have to find a reason for them to keep her until escape was possible.

Tears stung her eyes, causing her to drop her spoon in the pan. The noisy clang caused her to jump. "I have to get out of here," she said. Hearing the panic in her own voice horrified her. "God help me," she prayed. There was nothing she could do inside this room. Abandoning all thought of eating, she paced, trying to come up with a plan.

She nearly fell when the boat moved, causing her balance to shift. The faint sound of voices penetrated her prison. Something had changed.

They were heading out into the water. Hannah listened for the sound of footsteps. When none came, she went to the window and positioned the chair underneath it so she could get a look outside.

Dirt formed a film over the glass, making it difficult to see outside. Hannah looked until she found a section she could see out onto the deck. Men moved about performing their various jobs. The faint sound of shouts, likely orders from the captain, penetrated but not enough that she could hear his words. Hannah pounded on the glass, but no one appeared to notice. She remained trapped like a bird in a cage.

Hannah wasn't sure how much time had passed before the door to her prison rattled as the door was unlocked. Once again, the sailor entered. He tsked when he saw how little she had eaten. "Come now. Was our food not to your liking? It's a shame to waste it. I've been on many a voyage where we would have fought for such a feast. You've never had to deal with weevils in your bread or rats."

"Thank God." Hannah despised vermin of all sorts. She eyed the sailor as if he were one of them. He smelled of tar and stale sweat. Her nose wrinkled in spite of her attempts to remain unmoved by her captors.

He grinned. "It's time you met our captain. He's not sure what to do with you. We have a delivery to make to Camden, so you had to come along for the ride." He took her arm and led her to the door.

Hannah shook him off. "I can manage." She shook her arm, hoping he did not have lice. She walked ahead of him, taking in all she saw and storing the information for later. It took a few moments for her to adapt to the feeling of continual motion under her feet. She had rarely used the ferry since her arrival in Philadelphia. The boat was an experience she might have enjoyed in other circumstances.

The Delaware River was brownish green in the light of day. It was peppered with fishing boats and ferries along with ships like the one she was aboard. Water splashed along the sides of the boat as sailors worked to get the boat deeper into the channel. The sails lay in wait for the right moment to be unfurled to catch the wind that would enable them to gain speed as they headed downriver toward the sea.

Hannah prayed they were not going there. The sailor urged her to continue until they reached the door to the captain's quarters. Her guard opened it and gestured for her to enter. He did not follow but shut the door firmly behind her. There was no way for her to go but forward.

She paused to take in her surroundings. It was far more luxurious than she had expected. Light streamed in from a row of windows that overlooked the bow. White-painted walls were framed with dark wood trim, while long ropes ran down the ceiling before being tied off near the center.

Someone sat at the head of the large mahogany table, a dark hat covering the head. A woman's voice beckoned. "Come sit with me, Mistress White. We have much to discuss." The voice was cultured with a faint French accent. Hannah had heard the rich contralto before. By the time she had placed a hand on one of the elaborately carved chairs, she knew who sat before her.

"Mistress Fournier," Hannah said. "What an unexpected surprise."

She laughed, a tinkling sound like a clapper striking a bell. "I imagine so. You were expecting our captain. He elected to take a turn on the deck. He prefers not to know too much about what we do. Working for a woman is unusual, but I have made it worth his while to accept my authority." Her lips twisted into a smile. "I ask so little of him, really. Elizabeth and I prefer to keep our liaison quiet. Our business works better if run discreetly."

Hannah raised an eyebrow, but didn't comment. Obeying the gesture from the other woman's gloved hand, she pulled out a chair and sat down across from her. She looked at the hard blue eyes staring at her. "One of you acts like a Tory, the other a Patriot; no one would ever dream you were working together. It's quite a clever scheme, although I don't know why you thought it necessary to kill Benjamin Franklin."

Lisette Fournier nodded. "I knew you would figure it out. All that snooping, either you or your paramour asking questions and going places where you do not belong. Now I have to get rid of both of you. It's most inconvenient."

"My paramour?"

A deep chuckle rose out of Fournier's throat. "Come now, ma petite. It's far too late to play the innocent. Neither you nor I have had that luxury for some time. I have seen the way Monsieur Butler looks at you and you at him. It is plain there is passion between you. You live in the same house. How easy would it be to visit each other's beds, No?" She shook her head at the look on Hannah's face. "That's a shame. That's a man who knows women. I imagine he would be quite enjoyable."

"Is that why you brought me here?" Hannah could feel her face flushing. There was no way she was going to admit to this woman that she had felt a buzz of connection with Jeremy Butler. There was no point in acting on it. He was in bed with the revolution, and she had no intention of becoming another man's property, even if a part of her still dreamed of having a family of her own.

The smile faded from Lisette Fournier's face. "No, I want to know about your sister."

"Why?" The women stared at each other from across the expanse of the table. Hannah felt her breath go in and out with every moment. Now that her fears had been confirmed, her head was clear. She didn't know if she would survive the day or not, but she would not go meekly. She would fight to her last breath to be free.

Lisette Fournier broke the silence. "My friend Elizabeth told me an interesting story. She said you were looking for a lost sister, one that your mother had abandoned before you were born. Tell me about her."

Hannah stared at this elegant woman who hobnobbed with society and lived a life of luxury and wondered. Lisette used cosmetics to highlight her blue eyes, but they were the same deep blue as Hannah's own or her mother's. They both had pale skin with a faint dusting of freckles. Her hair was silver blonde, like one of Hannah's aunts. Her breath quickened as realization hit. "You're not originally from the French West Indies, are you?"

Lisette shook her head. "No, I am not. The people who adopted me moved there when I was a child. My father managed a plantation over there for many years. I shared a governess for many years with the owner's daughter until she died of yellow fever along with his wife. We grieved together, first as friends, then as lovers. It was then my father revealed that I was not his true child, but a bastard he had been paid to take in." Her face turned cold. "He died from a fall from his horse. The girth strap broke, then so did his neck." She shrugged. "My mama told me my mother lived outside of Philadelphia, although she didn't know her name, just the name of the man who arranged it, Mordecai Beeson."

It was a shock to hear her uncle's name uttered by Lisette Fournier. Hannah looked over at her beautiful half-sister and realized she was consumed by hate. "You live a privileged life. Your husband is affluent, and you have a daughter. What more could you want?" As soon as she uttered it, she realized it was the wrong thing to say.

Lisette said nothing as a variety of expressions crossed her face. Outside, the shouts of the sailors and cries of birds were faint against the pounding silence. The boat creaked as it moved through the water, taking them further away from Philadelphia. "Do you know what my father said? The man who sired me, then abandoned me, and the woman he got with child?"

Hannah shook her head. She had no idea who had gotten Patience pregnant so many years ago.

"He said he was well rid of me. Furthermore, he told me a bastard, especially a girl, was of no use to him." The last was said almost in a whisper, barely heard across the table.

"I'm so sorry," Hannah said. "No child should hear such ugliness." Although childless herself, she knew she would never abandon her child, or any child for that matter. A wave of regret washed over her that she had never had a chance to have children. Amos had been unable to beget a child. Now, she realized she would likely never know how it felt to hold a child of her own.

Lisette glanced over at her. "He thought he could abandon me and go on with his life. He should not have said those things. Monsieur Cadwaller deserved his fate."

Hannah felt dizziness wash over her. Her brother had mentioned the death of their neighbor. She had not heard the details. "You killed him?"

Lisette shook her head. "No. I merely finished what the hand of God started. He fell and hit his head on a rock. It was little effort to lift it and drop it on his skull. It cracked like an egg." She wiped her hands together. "The angels avenged me that day, and he went to face judgment for his crimes."

Hannah looked at her, wondering how she could use the almighty to justify her actions. She was not innocent, but this was beyond belief. "So, do you believe God will hold you accountable for the people you have killed?"

"The end justifies the means." Lisette pushed back from the table. Hannah rose with her, watching to see what she would do next. She smiled over at her. "I am glad we talked, Hannah. I never had a sister to talk to growing up. I think had we met as children, we would have been close. I regret that we will never have the opportunity to develop a relationship, but it's far too late for that." She walked toward the vast expanse of windows that lit the room. Hannah joined her as they took in the broad expanse of river. The bow cut through the waves, leaving a narrow wake of foam through the brownish water. She could barely see the shoreline on either side as they passed.

Lisette sighed as she watched. "I spent many days as a child sailing back and forth among the islands. My father handled trade for many of the plantation owners. He took sugar cane, rum, timber, and bat dung back and forth among the islands."

"Slaves?" Hannah asked.

Lisette shook her head. "It takes a bigger ship to cross over the ocean to Africa and back. My family had nothing so large. I did not board a large ship until my husband relocated us to these colonies."

"Is that what your husband does? Trade to the highest bidder?

Lisette grimaced. "You do not know when to stop. You are too naïve to realize everything has a price: rum, land, people, and information. There is always someone willing to pay. Enough, I grow weary of your questions. I have one for you. What is your mother's name? I wish to meet the woman who gave me life."

Hannah shook her head. "I don't think that is wise. She has been very ill. I'm sure you wouldn't want to disturb her."

"Why not?" Lisette's eyes glittered as she whirled to stare directly into Hannah's eyes. "She abandoned me years ago. I believe I am entitled to a few moments of our mother's time. We need to become acquainted."

Hannah shook her head harder. "No. I won't do it." The other woman's behavior unsettled her. She was beginning to wonder if Lisette Fournier's interest in her origins had become an obsession.

Lisette reached out her hands and grasped her about the shoulders. "You will. You have no other choice if you wish to exit this ship alive."

Hannah shook her head. No good would come of having this woman go to see their mother even if Patience Payne were cognizant enough to recognize her. Lisette wanted more than recognition, she wanted revenge.

"I can go to the market and see who it is you have visited so frequently." She smiled tightly. "It is hard not to connect with family when they are so close, is it not?"

Hannah froze, not trusting herself to speak.

Lisette chuckled. "I thought so. Who is that young man who drives a wagon into town every day? A cousin, a brother?" She watched Hannah's expression. "He's your brother, Master Caleb Payne. Isn't he? Once I deal with you, it will be easy enough to track him down."

The door opened behind them. It was the sailor. "Mistress, we will be hitting main channel of the river before long. Do you still want to disembark at Camden?"

Lisette nodded. "I have business to attend there." She gestured to Hannah. "Take our guest back to her room. You can deal with her once you get further downriver."

Hannah said nothing as he led her away. She had already made her plans. As they crossed the deck to head down, she watched the sailors working to ready the sails for when they would be needed. No one paid much attention to her. She was cargo, to be stowed away until the time came to unload her.

As they moved toward the back of the ship, she once again saw where the rail dropped away low along the sides. Her captor moved swiftly at her side, eager to be rid of her and back to more pleasant duties. As they walked, he called out to a few of the others, bantering back and forth as he commented on their work. One offered a particularly colorful reply to the sailor's comments. As he paused to gather his thoughts, Hannah took off, racing to the side.

She heard the shout behind her as she ran, grateful she had left her extra petticoats behind in her prison below. Hannah took no time to reconsider. Taking a flying leap, she left the ship, the wide expanse of the river spreading out before her, grateful that her father had taught her to swim. The waves seemed to reach out and gather her in, the deep blue water embracing her as she plummeted into the depths.

Chapter Twenty-Six

Butler remained on deck watching the restless water. He took care to stay out of the way of the busy sailors. The captain, a slim, swarthy man, kept an eye on the entire operation, ensuring his vessel made good time and stayed out of the way of others using the river.

On either side of the river lay canopies of thickly leaved trees and rising hills. In some places, trees had fallen over from the bank, their branches snaking out into the water, reaching out to snare an unwary boat. Small towns peppered the banks, breaking through the forest to stake a claim to the bank. As they drew closer to Philadelphia, the waterway grew busier as boats, ferries, and sailing vessels made their way into the vast expanse of the Delaware, either going to Cambridge or heading downriver to Wilmington or Cape May before going out onto the wide expanse that was the Atlantic.

Restless, he paced the length of the ferry, avoiding the men moving the boat forward with their poles as well as the team of draft horses with their attached wagon. Two men with poles plied them into the water, keeping watch for shifting bars. Butler watched as one used his pole to push a log away. It drifted past before spinning as the strong current caught it and carried it downriver.

The opposite shore was lined with buildings and docks teeming with people. He longed to be among them, where he could move at his will down the streets and back to the house where he was staying. William Franklin's warnings about Madame Fournier had unnerved him. She was a beautiful and intelligent woman. If the younger Franklin were to be believed, she was also obsessive and determined to get what she wanted. With the power and influence of her husband, she would be formidable. But was she vengeful enough to try to kill her former lover's father? Someone was. As soon as he landed in Philadelphia, Butler planned to post Maynard to keep watch on her home while he ensured Franklin was safe. He needed to be taken out of the city where he would not be easily found. Then, it was time to confront her and see what the lovely Lisette had to say.

He watched the ferry's captain as he scanned the river to ensure his vessel avoided the other ships or debris that floated by. He spoke to the men using the poles about a sand bar that had been shifting with the recent rains. Butler kept his hat pulled down low, letting the brim shelter his eyes from the bright sun overhead. Despite the precaution, reflections from the water caused Butler to squint as he watched the fast-flowing current.

Suddenly, the captain came to alert. "What the devil," he exclaimed as he lifted his spyglass to get a better look. "What the hell is happening on that schooner?"

Butler joined and cast his eyes where the captain was looking. A ship cut through the waves, headed across to Camden. On its deck, figures could be seen running across the deck while faint shouts could be heard over the water. "Let me borrow your eyepiece," Butler requested. Fitting it to his eye, he swung it around to the deck of the approaching vessel. Watching the racing figures, he wondered what motivated such a commotion. He tracked the figure with his eyepiece until he could focus on it. It was a woman. Her skirts flowed behind her as she fled. Her hair flew loose in the wind as she ran down toward the stern. As she turned, Butler drew in a sharp breath in recognition. "Hannah."

He watched helplessly as she ran where the ship's rail stood low. His heart pounded as he realized her intention. "No, don't do it."

She couldn't hear him as she leapt off the side and into the unforgiving water. The river was treacherous. There was no telling how many people had drowned beneath the waves, never to return. Its dark waves rose to swallow her. He searched the river frantically until he spotted her head breaking through the waves. She was trying to swim, but her skirts impeded her progress. "Quickly," he called. "We have to get her out."

The captain called out to the men steering the ferry, "Hard to port, men, we've someone to fish out of the water." The men complied, leaning on their polls as they fought the current. "I take it you know the lady."

Butler nodded. "I do." He watched the schooner to see what it would do. The ferry was no match for a vessel of that size. It turned in the water slowly because of its size. No rope was tossed to the woman in the water, nor did they deploy a smaller boat for rescue. They left her to drown in the wide expanse of the Delaware. Men watched from the side, seeing if she would drown.

"Hurry," Butler called. He could see her head just above the waves. The river was full of boats. He feared few would see her bobbing about, and she would be run down, never to emerge again. She fought to stay afloat, her face small and pale in the dark, heaving water. He swore as he pulled his boots off and shed his coat and vest. Hannah wasn't going to last long out in the water. The current was too strong.

The captain watched him strip down. "If you bring her aboard, I expect her fare to be paid." He stared out at the current. "No sane man would jump into that water."

Butler stared at him.

The other man sighed before handing him a length of rope. "Tie this around you so we can haul you in. I hope she's worth it."

Butler knotted it about his waist. "I'll let you decide for yourself." He scanned the waves, looking for her. When he couldn't spot her among the waves, panic raced through his veins as he feared the worst.

"There!" One of the boatmen shouted, pointing.

Butler spotted a white hand rising from the dark water for a few seconds before it disappeared. He dove in, gasping as the force of the water hit like a blow. A wave slapped Butler's face as he surfaced, causing him to cough as he fought for air. Kicking off from the ferry, he cut through the water looking for Hannah. When her head popped out of the water, he silently thanked God.

"Hannah!" His shout was snatched by the wind. She treaded the treacherous water, her skirts floating up around her. Hannah didn't respond to his cries; the roar of the water blotted out all other noise. She was startled when he grabbed her. Her shocked gaze met his.

"I've got you."

"I can swim." She said as he drew her in. Hair covered her face like seaweed. Her eyes were wide between strands of hair.

"I can see that. Let me get you to the ferry before we drown." He drew her against his chest and made for the boat. Her legs kicked beside his as they worked to get through the powerful current.

"Quit struggling," He shouted in her ear. Thankfully, she complied. Tension on the rope tied to him tightened as the crew worked to bring them in. Something flashed by as they cut through the water. Butler looked up to see another harpoon coming from the front of the schooner bearing down on them. It loomed like a giant beast intent on their demise. If it continued, it would crush them and the ferry.

A loud bang sounded behind him, along with the smell of powder. His shoulder bumped against the side of the ferry as it drew alongside him. Waves pushed Butler and Hannah back from the craft as the men used their poles to steady the craft. Water slammed him against the side, making him grunt in pain. Arms reached into the water, hauling both of them onto the craft. Butler lay next to Hannah, gasping for breath, grateful to be alive. He looked up to see the captain holding a long rifle in his arms, faint wisps of smoke drifting from the barrel.

"Damn fools," he said, looking across the water at the larger boat. "This river is no place to play around. The current is too swift, and there's too much traffic." He watched the ship from which Hannah had come drift close before passing by and heading away.

"My thanks," Butler said, his voice raspy from the water he had inadvertently swallowed. He coughed, spitting over the side into the dark water that had almost taken him. Despite the warm summer day, he shivered. He looked over at Hannah. He could see breath moving in and out of her body, but she made no sound as she lay on the platform.

A blanket smelling of horse dropped over him. Butler wrapped it over his shoulders, grateful for having something dry. A woman leaned over

Hannah, helping her with another blanket. It was the teamster's wife. He glanced over to her husband, who stood by his horses, holding their harness. "I'm grateful for your help." The man nodded in acknowledgment.

Hannah looked back across the water with fear in her gaze. The schooner was already almost out of sight.

The ferry captain stared after. "I've never seen a crew act like that."

"Whose boat is that?" Butler asked.

"Lawrence Turner captains the *Gray Goose*, but as to the owner, I'm not sure."

"Lisette Fournier," Hannah said hoarsely. She coughed up water through her mouth and nose as she leaned over the side. She straightened and wiped her mouth. "She planned to kill me."

Butler stared at her. "Why?" He looked at Hannah's frightened face and wondered what she had been through. Anger shot through him. She had no part in this business. They should have left her alone.

"Elizabeth Cranford and Lisette Fournier are partners," Hannah said. "Together, they smuggle and sell goods to the highest bidder on either side of the conflict." She shook her head and coughed. Her voice was raspy. "I saw a wagon making a delivery. I didn't realize it at the time, but it must have been going to the Cranfords. I saw the kegs of powder. I assume there were muskets as well."

Butler stared at her. "That's a dangerous thing to do. If they get caught, either side will be merciless in the reprisal." He shook his head. Selling to both sides is madness."

Hannah kept shivering. Butler shot her a worried glance. "We need to get you out of those wet clothes and in a safe place." He wanted a hot bath for himself as well.

She looked up at him. "She told them to end me and hide my body where it wouldn't be found." She struggled to stand, accepting a hand from Butler. Her arms hugged the blanket around her body. Her hair hung in long, drippy strands over her shoulders. "They have to be stopped."

Butler nodded. With her wide blue eyes and long mass of hair, she looked like a mermaid.

"I need a pistol," she said. "That woman is not invading my home."

Tough mermaid. He hid a smile. "Do you know how to use one?"

"My father taught me." Hannah sniffed and pushed hair off of her face. The air was beginning to dry a few strands that kept blowing on her face. A man offered a flask.

"Have some brandy. You both could use a shot."

Butler sniffed the open flask before taking a swallow. It was indeed brandy and good quality stuff. "I appreciate it," He said before handing it to Hannah.

She took it from Butler and took a cautious sip. She coughed as it hit her throat and handed it back, shaking her head when offered more.

By the time they arrived at the dock, Butler had decided where to go. Taking Hannah home was too dangerous. The Fourniers and the Cranfords had many friends. While the Fourniers were accepted as Tory sympathizers, their trade connections made them valuable, and as long as Frances Fournier acted like he might consider changing sides, no one would antagonize him by arresting his wife. The Cranfords were close associates of the elite of Philadelphia. Reaching them was going to be nearly impossible.

Butler paid the ferryman before he took Hannah by the hand and led her to the dock. He paused, thinking about where they could go. They both needed dry clothes and a bath. A woman eyed them before approaching. He recognized her as one of the proprietors of the tavern Maynard favored. "My husband operates a tavern nearby. We can provide you and your wife with a room and dry clothes for a fair price."

"Throw in a hot bath, and you have a deal." Hannah shot him a look but said nothing. Butler spent a few minutes haggling over a price before they came to an agreement. They followed the woman to a two-and-a-half-story brick building. A narrow balcony was visible on one side. Butler caught the sign out front. Hannah saw it as well and snickered.

The placard showed a man and a woman together. A monkey rode on the man's shoulder. Underneath, the couple read "A Man Full of Trouble." The woman led them around to a side door for which Butler was relieved. Even though it was past dinner time, he could hear the raucous sound of sailors in the main room of the tavern enjoying their rum. While he was used to the company of sailors, he doubted Hannah was, and in her current state, they might get the wrong idea about her. He placed a hand on her shoulder. "It's going to be okay."

She shot him a look. "I still want a pistol."

The woman shot them an odd look as she led them upstairs to a middling-sized room with one bed in it. "The sheets are clean," The woman said. "I keep this one for my couples. The single men go to my large rooms upstairs." She smiled at Hannah. "It's a shame you fell in the river."

Butler offered the woman a coin and smiled. "I would appreciate it if one of your staff could start bringing up hot water for my lady's bath. It's been a long day." He handed her an extra coin. "Discretion is always appreciated." She nodded as she took the coins.

The woman examined the coin before dropping it into her pocket with a smile. "I'll send up my men with the tub and hot water shortly." She eyed Hannah's soaked clothes, muddy from the river. "I'm sure I have a dress that would fit her as well."

Butler smiled and gave her another coin. "That would be most gracious of you, mistress." She left with an extra swish to her skirts. The door shut behind her with a rattle of the knob. That was the last of his French silver. He hoped she appreciated it.

Hannah stood with the blanket swaddled close around her. "Why did you let her think we were wed?"

"I figured you wouldn't want to share a room with a dozen drunken sailors." He walked over to the window. It went nearly to the floor. Afternoon sunlight trickled into the room. "I will protect you." He looked at the room. "This tavern is for stevedores and sailors, none of your social circle. Maynard trusts these people. He says the owner knows to keep his mouth shut. No one likes a gossip."

Someone tapped on the door before opening it. Two large young men came in carrying a large wooden tub and sat it down on the floor. One of them grinned at Hannah before he saw Butler's expression and exited swiftly behind the other man.

They returned soon after carrying buckets of steaming water. Butler pulled the curtains closed. "Do you need help getting out of your clothes?"

Hannah shot him a glance. "I'll manage." Her tone was withering.

He raised his hands in surrender. "I wasn't volunteering. I was going to see if the tavern keeper's wife or one of the bar maids could help you."

Mollified, she sniffed. "You could help me best by stepping outside the room."

"As you wish," he went out the door and leaned against the outside wall. He watched as the tavern's mistress came up the stairs holding a gown on her arm and a bar of soap in her hand. She eyed him as she reached the landing. "I take it your mistress is not pleased with you."

"Why would you think that?"

Her eyes were sympathetic. "A fine-looking man like you should be comforting your wife, like Adam did Eve after Abel's death. She's probably shaken up from being in the river."

Butler smiled. "It's been a trying day."

"I'll make her a hot toddy to help with the shock." She looked at him again. "No one's in the room next door. I'll have the boys bring up another tub for you. There's spare breeches and shirts a plenty. You'd be amazed what some of these sailors leave behind."

She went into the room, shutting the door behind her. Butler heard the women talking to each other. From the splashes, he knew Hannah had made it into the tub. He had worried when he pulled her from the water, but her resilience impressed him. She had survived despite the odds.

Within minutes, he was enjoying a bath of his own. Steam rose off his skin as he indulged in lathering his limbs. Once he had finished scrubbing, Butler poured water from a bucket over his hair to rinse off the soap. He sighed as the heat of the water soothed his sore muscles. All he needed was a hot meal and some ale, and life would be perfect for a few blessed moments.

The tavern keeper's wife was as good as her word. She had found him canvas breeches, a shirt, and vest. She sent one of the boys to bring them to him. "Mistress says to tell you dinner will be come to you and your missus in an hour."

Butler sighed and reached for a drying cloth. Now came the hard part:

figuring out how to deal with people so powerful that they expected to get away with murder.

Chapter Twenty-Seven

Hannah tossed and turned in the strange bed. No matter how exhausted her body felt, her mind would not still. Too much had happened, and there were too many questions unanswered. Jeremy Butler slept on a pallet on the floor. He had insisted she take the bed. No matter how odd it seemed to share a room with him, she was grateful for his presence.

An owl hooted outside. Its voice echoed through the open window. Seeing the night sky outside comforted her. She didn't want to think about being shut in that room on the boat, waiting for her captors to end her.

Jeremy's breathing reminded her she wasn't alone. Hannah would have never believed she would find comfort in a man's snore. Amos had been loud enough to penetrate the wall between their rooms. He had been older than her father but kind. Theirs had been a marriage of convenience for both of them. It gave her the freedom she longed for and provided him with a discreet caregiver who would never reveal the truth of their relationship. Her only regret was that she had never had the chance to have a child. Sometimes, she wondered what it would be like to bear life and hold a tiny piece of oneself and watch it develop into a person with thoughts and feelings independent from hers. She was over thirty, well past her prime for the marriage market, not that she cared. Hannah had no desire to be anyone's property. Yet she still felt a sense of incompleteness.

Outside, light flashed in the distance, followed by a low rumble of thunder. When a breeze came through the window, she rose and went to enjoy a brief respite of coolness from the warm summer night. After the dunk in the river, she had thought she would never feel warm again, but the hot bath and the rum toddy their hostess provided had warmed her enough to feel the summer heat in their upstairs room. The wind whipped up blowing hair from her face and pressing her shift against her body. She lifted her head, enjoying the cooling breeze along with the scent of incoming rain.

At this hour, no one stirred. Hannah drew in a few deep breaths trying to ease her mind into sleep. Tomorrow, she would return home, although she would never feel safe again. Hannah didn't know how she would run her business when she would be searching every shadow for danger. Her breath became quick and shallow as she thought about how easily she had been taken away.

"Bad Dreams?" Jeremy's baritone whispered behind her.

Hannah looked over at him. His pale hair tumbled over his shoulders. The wind played with a few strands, lifting them to touch his cheek. She reached to brush them away, feeling the warmth of his cheek beneath her fingers. She didn't want to admit to being a coward.

He caught her hand, gently stroking the tender inside of her wrist before releasing it. "Anyone who threatens you will have to go through me."

Hannah nodded. She swallowed hard. "You can't stay by my side forever. Sooner or later, you will have to return to wherever it is you came from, whereas I will remain here."

Jeremy Butler did not respond at first. His gaze went out to where the wind picked up, causing the branches of the trees to wave about frantically. "You don't have to stay here," he said at last. "If need be, you could join your sister in Williamsburg. I'm sure Faith would be glad for another pair of hands."

"You want me to flee to Virginia. My life is here." She stepped back from the window, wrapping her arms around herself. "This is my home." Hannah hated how pitiful that sounded. "I can take care of myself. I have for some time now."

"Not from this sort," He grasped her shoulders gently, although his voice was hard. "But for the grace of God, you would be dead now-don't you realize that?" He drew in a deep breath. "Seeing you jump off that ship

237

terrified me. I didn't think I would be able to reach you in time.

Hannah put her hand on his chest. Like her, he wore a long shirt, thin as a whisper, but enough to cover one's essential parts. "My father taught all of his children to swim." Never had she been so grateful for all those summer evenings at a nearby lake, splashing and paddling the steamy heat away. Her mother had been scandalized, but her father had insisted his daughters, as well as his sons, know how to handle themselves in water. She had not realized what a gift that skill would become until she had been impelled to jump ship in order to save her own life.

"That river is full of deep currents and shoals. It takes lives. It nearly took yours," He took a deep breath.

Hannah felt a deep shudder that went through him. "I'm alright," she whispered. Her arms went around his neck. She felt his arms wrap around her waist, drawing her close. Hannah rested her head on his chest as she listened to the steady beat of his heart. All the pent-up tension and fear left her body as he held her close. Together, they breathed, glad to be alive.

After a few minutes, he released her and stepped back. She knew why. The thin material of their clothes kept no secrets. Her eyes met his. "You don't have to go."

A smile creased his cheek. "It would be wiser if I did." He moved away. "I can bunk outside the door."

Hannah followed him. "Don't be ridiculous. Drunken sailors will be falling over you all night long. Stay with me."

He stopped, so suddenly she ran into him. They both stumbled. Hannah fell back. Jeremy looked at her half-sprawled on the bed. There was no more beautiful sight. "Hannah," his voice turned husky. "I watched you nearly drown. There is nothing I want more than to prove to myself that you live."

"I would like that too." Hannah looked at Jeremy. He stared at her as a variety of expressions ran across his face. Rising, she went to him. "I have spent the majority of my life caring for others, doing what others want, following society's rules. Just for once, I want to know a man's love, feel treasured for who I am, and not for what I can do." She met his gaze. "There are people who will do anything to end us, and they may succeed. I'm afraid." She held out a hand to silence him. "Not of them, not right now. I'm afraid I may die without really ever knowing what it means to live."

Jeremy took her hand and stroked the callused fingers as if they were silk. "Are you sure this is what you want?"

They were virtually the same height. It was easy to lean across and kiss him. Hannah felt his quick intake of breath just before he pulled her to him.

Reaching down, he pulled her shift over her head, causing goose bumps to rise on her flesh. His shirt joined it on the floor. He backed her over to the bed. As he pushed her down, she hooked an arm around his waist and tugged. Jeremy fell over her with an oomph.

"Is that how it's going to be?" he said with a laugh.

She smiled at him a little nervously. Hannah wasn't used to dealing with someone who wasn't frail and needy. Jeremy was unlike anyone she had ever known.

"Change your mind?" He asked softly, watching her expression.

Hannah shook her head. "I'm not sure what you like."

He grinned. "Why don't we focus on you? Jeremy stroked her hair, letting his finger drift down the side of her face and the sensitive skin of her neck. He followed with his lips nibbling lightly on her ear.

The bed creaked with his shifting weight. She giggled as he moved his weight on one elbow, making the mattress groan. "This has to be the noisiest bed I've ever heard."

"Be glad it's a bed. Hammocks are trickier." Just then, the wind picked up outside, followed by the roar of an incoming storm. They both looked at the open window where the driving rain poured in.

Leaping up, Jeremy went to shut it. The swollen pane stuck, refusing to close as the water rain pelted him. As he cursed, Hannah slipped around to help. As they pulled, their combined weight caused the window to slam shut as they fell on the floor. Rainwater made their skin stick together. As they peeled apart, Jeremy's eyes met hers.

"Dawn will be here soon." He offered her a hand.

She allowed him to help her up to where she stood a few inches from him.

She reached to touch his chest, curling her fingers around a few strands of golden brown hair. He watched her silently. His hands flexed at his sides, waiting for what she would do next.

Jeremy's hair shone like silver in the shadowing room. She reached up to run her hands through the silky mass. He smelled of the soap they had both used. Hannah pushed him back toward the bed. He grabbed her waist, taking her with him. The bed groaned mightily beneath them. She giggled until he rolled her beneath him and began kissing her thoroughly.

Rain pounded outside, insulating them from the world. The earth below received the bounty of water, absorbing it as much-needed nourishment to its flesh. The darkness enveloped them as need met need, and the longings of two lonely souls found rest at last.

Chapter Twenty-Eight

Butler watched Hannah sleeping, her hair spread out over the pillow in waves of rich, earthy brown. She was beautiful in a way that needed no embellishment. A faint sprinkle of freckles danced over cheeks and nose as her mouth curved in a smile. She needed to smile more often. He got out of the bed carefully so as not to disturb her.

He drew on a shirt and breeches as he pondered what to do about this lovely, complicated woman. Butler knew what honor demanded. He also knew that he had little to offer any woman. Were he to be discovered by the British, he would hang. The risks he took for the Patriot cause had not troubled him before now. After the death of his wife and child, his life had lost all meaning and purpose until a chance meeting with Washington had set him on this course. He had purposely avoided relationships and the baggage they carried. Now, Butler rested his eyes on the sleeping woman. He had been drawn to Hannah from the beginning and fought being drawn in, and then he had seen her in the water and realized what he might lose. Now that morning had come and his sanity with it, he realized he may well have gotten her pregnant. The thought terrified him.

"Where are you going?" Her voice was soft and sleepy, but her eyes were alert as she watched him pull on his boots. She sat up, sweeping a curtain of dark hair from her face.

"I need to check on Franklin and discover what those two witches are doing."

"Witches? Oh." She scooted to the side of the bed. "Madame Fournier had business in Camden." She wrinkled her nose in thought. "She may have mentioned something about Trenton. I'm not sure."

"There's a barracks in Trenton occupied by the British. If she's spying for them, someone could be coming down to meet her." He frowned. "It would be useful to know who her contact is." He considered his options, but the pragmatic side already knew he had little chance of catching up with her.

Hannah watched him in silence before sliding off the bed to gather her clothes. The innkeeper's wife had been true to her word and had discreetly left dry clothes for them as they had bathed. Stockings, belts, and stays had been returned to them clean and mostly dry. He appreciated all she had done.

"Where are you going?" He watched Hannah pull on stockings and step into her shoes, which squeaked from their recent dip in the Delaware.

"I have a business to manage." She moved to the basin on the dresser and poured water from the pitcher into it before splashing it on her face and wiping it with one of the cloths stacked on the dresser. She scanned the room. "Is there a comb available?"

He offered her his own wordlessly. She took it and began to work her way through her mass of wavy dark hair. Her breath drew in sharply as she hit a tangle. "Let me do it." He reached out a hand for the comb.

"I wasn't aware that you had experience dressing women's hair." She paused in her task to stare at him.

He laughed. "I had the task of combing and braiding my sister's hair from an early age. I'm good at braiding." Jeremy ran his fingers gently through her hair, stopping when he hit a tangle. Using his fingers, he teased the knots loose before running a comb through the bottom and gradually moving up to her crown. He could feel the tension leave her shoulders as the comb ran smoothly through the waves. His tone was gentle as he spoke. "We're going to have some decisions to make."

Hannah said nothing, although her back straightened. She took the comb from him as she stood. "I can manage now, thank you." With the ease of practice, she twisted her hair into a knot and walked over to the dresser to grab hairpins to hold it into place. She eyed the damp pocket that separated from her skirt before setting it aside and going on to the petticoat and dress

242

their benefactor had provided. She looked down at the dark red and gold flowers that covered the ivory fabric. "It's not very plain."

"It's lovely," Jeremy said as he took in her appearance head to toe. Her face flushed at the remark. "There's nothing wrong with the way you look. God created beautiful things for people to appreciate his creation."

"You're not Quaker," she muttered as she tucked in her neckerchief and placed her cap on her head.

"No, I'm not." He admitted. "Is that important?"

Hannah stopped and considered. "Not really. Do you believe in God?"

He nodded. "Yes, I do." Jeremy didn't think it was time to tell her he kept his mother's rosary, along with a few other personal items stored at his sister's farm in Maryland.

Hannah nodded. "Well then, that's something we agree upon." She went toward the door. She stared at Jeremy as he blocked her path. "You need to move."

He shook his head. "Not until we talk for a moment. You nearly died yesterday. The persons behind that are still out there. ."

Hannah put hands on her hips. "At home, I have friends and family around me. I refuse to spend my time hiding in an inn of dubious reputation."

Jeremy put his hands on her shoulders. "Give me a few hours to discover the lay of the land. I need to apprise people of the situation and make sure you are protected. No one will look for you here. I swear I will return and escort you home myself once I know what we are facing."

He reached over and cupped her face in her hands. "I can't do what I need to do if you are in danger. I need you to be safe." Tipping her chin up, he brushed his lips with hers. Her eyes looked troubled. "Wait here for me. I will have the innkeeper bring you breakfast. I will return as soon as I can." Leaving her there, he stepped out and trotted down the stairs, eager to discover what the enemy was doing.

Once he had made arrangements for Hannah, Butler went to find Hancock. As expected, he was overseeing the convention of delegates who continued to discuss the wording of their declaration that would be sent to the English king. As president of the convention, Hancock sat at the front of the room on a raised platform, watching the delegates buzzing about the room. Butler wondered how he kept that benevolent expression on his face all day.

He rose when he spotted Butler and made his way through the crowd. "Let's go upstairs, Jefferson has read a draft. Now it will be discussed." He grimaced. "It will take hours for them to work their way through it."

"Is the document that long?" Butler was mildly curious.

Hancock shook his head. "No, but everyone has an opinion to share. I imagine it's a painful experience for Jefferson. I doubt his life in Virginia prepared him for such a vocal lot. It's a good thing Adams is there to keep order."

"Isn't Franklin part of that team?" Butler had spotted him in the room, sitting back with his eyes closed as if in deep thought.

Hancock nodded. "Yes, but all this head-butting exhausts him. He's taken to napping during the debates. He gets away with it because of his age and the enormous amount of respect the others have for him."

As they passed through the large hallway back toward the stairs, Butler spotted Maynard standing just inside the front door. Their eyes met briefly before he continued back toward the office Hancock had temporarily taken over.

Hancock gestured for him to proceed into the room before following. The morning light highlighted the lines of weariness that had worn into his face. Managing the congress had taken a toll as the weeks rolled on. After looking out the window to the busy street below, he turned and looked over at Butler. "What do you have to tell me?"

Butler laid out the facts compounded with his suspicions. Hancock said nothing as the other man spoke. His expression darkened when Butler mentioned Hannah's escape. Silence fell over the two men for a long stretch of moments.

"What possible reason could they have to assassinate Benjamin Franklin? He's no more involved than the rest of us."

Butler shook his head. "I'm guessing that was personal. At one time, Lisette Fournier was involved with his son. She wasn't happy when he ended the relationship."

Hancock looked at the other man sharply. "Be careful what you say. Madame Fournier is a lady with many friends in this town. Calling her an adulteress and a murderer will cause discord among people we cannot afford to offend."

"A lovely face can hide a boatload of secrets," Butler snapped. "I believe Hannah. She didn't jump into the Delaware River for her health. Lisette Fournier wanted her dead."

The line between Hancock's brows deepened. "Very well. I will speak to one of our Pennsylvania delegates. I also need to warn Adams. Once our declaration becomes public, there is no turning back. Our signatures may well become our death warrants."

Butler nodded. He had accepted the risks when he had agreed to gather intelligence for the Sons of Liberty and then Washington. He knew discovery would only lead to a noose and an unmarked grave. His mind turned to Hannah. They had to settle things before Washington sent him off on another mission. If she could not have his protection, she could at least have the respect of his name. It was all he had to offer.

Hancock's voice was quiet. "I've done quite a bit of business with Fournier. I would not have reckoned him to be a spy. His interests have always seemed to center on making a profit."

"I don't know that he is involved," Butler pointed out. "He may be unaware of his wife's activities. The same may be true of Cranford."

Hancock shook his head. "There are only so many things the fair ladies can do in this society. I cannot believe they acted entirely on their own. Their husbands have some degree of culpability, even if it was turning a blind eye. Regardless, we cannot allow spies to infiltrate our cause. Too many lives could be lost."

Butler was tempted to point out that lives had already been lost. His thoughts were interrupted by Hancock going back toward the door. "We have no time to lose. Once word of our Declaration spreads, the British will react. "

Hancock moved swiftly down the stairs. Slipping inside, Hancock moved to whisper into a few choice ears. Samuel Adams came out of the room, followed by another man Butler did not recognize.

Adams stared at the other man. "You have a pair of snakes held to the bosom of this fair city. You'd best cut them off at the head before they strike."

The other man paled. "You are talking about important members of our society. We can't go around arresting people based on the word of this person." He glared at Butler. "I know nothing of this man's family or his reputation, whereas I have done business with both Cranford and Fournier for some time. They are respected members of our community."

Adams glared at him. "Ignoring such a threat is the height of stupidity. The British are everywhere, and there are those who have no desire to part from their lap. You know this unless you are blind."

The man's face flushed. Hancock broke in before he spoke. "Surely we can send representatives to speak with them. They may be able to offer information that could prove enlightening to all." He met the other man's gaze. "If what Butler says is true, then all our lives are at risk."

The man chewed his lip for a minute before absently scratching his head. His wig slid to one side only to be yanked back by an impatient hand. "I can send people to check on Cranford and Fournier. We will see what they report."

Adams let out an exasperated sigh. "Have you not realized this is war? The British Army could come marching down from New York at any time and capture us all if they don't shoot us on sight. You don't need to speak to them. You need to arrest them."

"On what charge?" The other man shot back. "You have proof of nothing."

Butler interrupted. "We have the testimony of a woman Madame Fournier held prisoner on one of her husband's ships. She, too, is a longtime resident of Philadelphia."

The man sputtered before replying. "We will see what our men report."

Butler left them as they continued to argue. He refused to wait for whatever decision they might come to. He had neither forgotten nor forgiven what had happened to Hannah, and he was worried about her. No one knew where she was, but that was no guarantee of safety. He sprinted across the street before pausing to consider his next move.

The Man of All Troubles was quieted as he reentered the main room. An old sailor sat near one of the windows, nursing a stein. His chair was positioned where he could see the door. Butler nodded to him as he headed toward the stairs.

"She left," the man said as he drew close.

"What?" Butler turned to face him.

Despite his ragged clothes, the old sailor's hair was neatly combed, his beard trimmed. He raised his mug cheerfully. "She bought me a drink, your missus, and a fine breakfast as well. She's a pretty little thing, but there's fire in those eyes." He chuckled. "I bet she keeps you warm nights."

Butler shot him a look. "Did she say where she was going?"

The other man chuckled. "Home. She said to tell you she was going home."

Butler swore. "How long has she been gone?"

The man waved to a dark corner, "Ask him."

Whirling around, Butler spotted the man in the corner. A dark-eyed man looked up at him. "Do I know you?"

"Cyrus Lovell, at your service." He gestured to the seat across from him. "Have a seat. We need to talk."

Butler waved the woman serving drinks aside. "You rode the stage with me here." He stared at Lovell. "I think you work for the British."

The other man neither denied nor admitted it. "The British hold dominion over these colonies. Within a few years, this little uprising will be nothing but an unpleasant memory. A man with your skills would be well rewarded for his work by the British empire."

Butler shook his head. "I don't think so." He cocked his head, studying Lovell. "Have you been trying to kill Franklin?"

Lovell sighed. "Like you, I'm only as good as the intelligence I'm given. I regret that sometimes my sources see fit to spread intelligence based on vengeance rather than fact." He fiddled with his stein. "The old man need not fear assassination from anyone I know." He cocked a look at Butler. "Once this conflict is over, there will be penalties enough for those who dared rebel against the king."

"I'll take my chances," Butler said, rising. "Now, do you know where my lady went?"

"She left not long after you did. She went right out that door and up the street. She also asked me where a lady could buy a pistol." He grinned. "I hope for your sake she's not angry with you. I gave her the name of a man I know."

Butler turned to leave.

"One more thing she said to tell you." He paused expectantly.

Butler stared at him. The sailor looked wistfully at the empty stein before him. Rolling his eyes, Butler signaled for the tavern keeper to refill it.

He took a hefty swallow. "The *Grey Goose* is back at the docks."

Butler's blood chilled. There was no time to lose. He hurried up the street, dodging fellow pedestrians in his effort to get to Hannah's home. He shot in the door and looked about frantically. "Where's Hannah?" he bellowed.

She stuck her head out into the entryway. "I'm right here. You need to keep your voice down. You will frighten my clients."

He wanted to shake her. "What are you doing here?" He went to where mere inches separated them. She wore an elbow-length blue jacket over a tan skirt. An ivory fichu was tucked into her neckline. Her gaze challenged him to continue.

"I left you safely hidden where no one would look for you," Butler's teeth ground in frustration. "I can't protect you if I don't know where you are."

Hannah looked over her shoulder. "Lucretia, mind the shop for a moment, please?"

Her sister-in-law voiced her agreement. She stepped out into the entryway. "As you can see, I am fine. I have Lucretia and Nathan here with me." She crossed her arms. "I'm not letting those women rule my life, nor will I allow you. You are neither my husband nor my father."

Butler looked at her. His voice dropped. "You can't slay dragons on your own no matter how brave you are."

She took one breath, then another. "All I want is the freedom to make my own choices, to live my life as I see fit without being ordered about like a foolish child." Tears glittered in her eyes before she blinked them away. "I've learned it's far better not to depend on anyone for my survival. That only leads to disaster."

Butler gave her a moment to compose herself. "I would never do that. But I would keep you safe to live your life. There are no guarantees either of us will survive the coming war." He put up a hand to silence her. "Please listen." He struggled for the right words. "What happened last night could have consequences. We have to plan for that. I don't know where I may be called to serve next in this war. All I can offer you is my name and the promise I will return if at all possible."

"You're proposing marriage," Hannah said at last. "In case I'm carrying your child. I was married nearly ten years, and that never happened."

He shot her a glance. "We both know why."

She flushed and looked away.

"There is no shame in choosing to care for someone you love, even if they cannot be all you might wish." He took her hand, stroking the sturdy palms that tapered into long, skinny fingers. "You loved your husband and allowed him to finish his days with dignity."

"I didn't think anyone would understand."

Butler kissed her palm before releasing it. "Once my work is complete, I will look for a priest for the ceremony."

"A priest?" Hannah blinked in surprise. "You're Catholic?"

He nodded. "For the most part." It had been ages since he'd been to mass, and he'd given up confession after he became a spy. He wasn't sure what that made him.

"I'm not,"

They stared at each other for a few moments. "Perhaps we can find a church that we can agree on." Butler had no idea what that could be, but he already knew he would make a poor Quaker.

The door banged shut, making them both jump. Maynard came in, followed by Franklin, who moved slowly. "I believe I will take a nap before dinner," he said before slowly going up the steps.

"I had to hire a chaise to get him here," Maynard said softly. "They plan to read their declaration tomorrow. I'm not sure how much more of this the old man can handle."

Butler watched Franklin pause on the steps. "I'm quite capable of carrying this through to the end."

"I meant no disrespect," Maynard said to his back. Franklin continued up the stairs, one hand on the rail, the other holding his cane. Maynard turned toward Butler. "Hancock's man came back from the Cranford's house. It looks like they've fled. Hancock thinks they're probably headed to New York."

Butler grunted. "That makes sense. The British army controls the colony. No one could touch them there. What of the Fournier's?"

Maynard answered slowly. "That's the one that puzzles me. I saw their maid leaving the Market when I went to get food. I carried her basket for her as I escorted her home. She admitted her Master and Mistress were not at home, but they're not headed to New York. She said Madame Fournier needed to see her mother before she fled."

Hannah gasped. Both men turned to her. She looked at them with wide eyes. "She's my half-sister. She's going after my mother."

Chapter Twenty-Nine

Faith paused to roll her shoulders. She had brought the large spinning wheel out to the porch earlier. She had been walking back and forth to spin wool for most of the morning trying to clear her head. The large oak tree cast a deep shadow on the porch keeping it cool from the sun. Out in the nearby woods she could hear the buzz of cicadas as they sang their never-ending song, hoping to find love. "Good Luck with that," she thought sardonically. Faith had tired of relationships with men that did not last. She had decided to focus on her business and her son. That was more than enough, or so she kept telling herself.

When Patience had asked about Jon last night, Faith said he was fine. Her husband had been dead two years now, but in her mother's troubled mind he still lived. She didn't have the heart to correct her. She had loved him deeply, but he was gone. Sometimes she couldn't remember his face although his laugh still echoed in her memory from time to time. He lived on in their son's curls and dark brows, in the deep widow's peak on his high forehead. Time would only tell if he was more Jon or her as he grew. Right now he was a gangly twelve-year-old with an appetite that was challenging to meet.

Faith's voice was hoarse from reading to her mother most of the night. It helped calm her when she woke from sleep agitated and afraid. She wasn't sure how much longer Patience Payne would last. She had started refusing food a few days ago. Faith had managed to coax her to take a few swallows of cider. Patience had choked after a few minutes, so she had set it aside.

Inside, she heard the steady rasp of her father's knife as he whittled another piece of wood. After the cows had been milked and the stock fed, he had returned to the house. Her brothers and brother-in-law had gone out to check on the wheat and hay crops. He hummed a hymn as he worked, keeping his hands busy to ease his mind.

Faith wondered how much sleep he was getting, if any. Every time she rose, he was in the sick room, either reading scripture or holding her hand. He said nothing as the other family came and went, tending to Patience and whispering prayers.

A plume of dust in the distance warned her that someone was coming. She went to the edge of the porch, squinting. She had sent Caleb to fetch Hannah from town. It was time for the family to come home.

She frowned as the vehicle drew closer. It wasn't a farm cart or wagon like their neighbors drove when going to market. In fact, she had never seen such an elegant vehicle this far out in the country. It traveled at breakneck speed, bouncing as it struck a hole in the dirt road. There was no need to urge a fine set of horses like that in this heat unless it was a life-or-death issue.

Concerned, she set down the rolag she had been spinning and came down the steps. Perhaps someone was hurt? Faith wracked her brain to think who this could be and what assistance might be required. Her mother had taught her what herbs to use for medicine, and she could set simple breaks, otherwise, she preferred to defer to a surgeon. If the driver needed more than that, they should be driving hard to Philadelphia, not here.

The driver snapped a whip off the side of the animals as they galloped up. They stopped in front of the house. The horses' sides heaved. The driver hopped down and opened the door. A footman ran over to the horses, stroking their noses and speaking softly.

Faith walked up to them. Speaking to the boy, she gestured toward the main barn. "My brother is in the barn. He will help you water and rub them down."

"We have little time for that," A woman's voice spoke as she was handed down by the driver.

"You need to make time if you want them to be able to take you back from whence you came," Faith shot back. Nothing angered her more than abuse of an animal. She nodded at the boy who stood waiting, a faint plea on his face. She had little doubt he was enslaved, separated from his family to do another's bidding all the days of his life. Some of her outrage must have leached out.

The woman waved a hand covered in kid leather to the boy. "Very well, ma petite homme, go tend the animals." She turned to Faith. "My husband would scold me for not caring for his beloved steeds. Forgive my thoughtlessness." She smiled, revealing a small dimple below a tiny heart-shaped mole on her cheek. "Would you be so kind as to invite me inside? This sun, it is very bright, is it not?"

Faith nodded, wondering who this was. She was dressed far too fine for the country. "Come inside. I can offer you some peppermint tea." The woman followed her inside, taking a seat in the room Patience reserved for guests. Feeling awkward, Faith asked Charity to see about tea and refreshments for their guest.

Charity stared into the parlor. "Who is that woman? Why is she here?"

"I have no idea," Faith whispered back. "But it's rude to be unhospitable. I'll try to find out her business while you get tea."

Charity sniffed. "Who made you lady of the house?" She walked down the hallway toward the outdoor kitchen, head held high.

Faith rolled her eyes. Dealing with a younger sibling on a daily basis was not something she had missed. Charity hadn't given her time to invite her to join them. Shrugging, Faith returned to their mysterious guest.

To her surprise, the woman no longer sat in the best chair, but was gazing at the collection of silhouettes on the wall, one for every child. Patience had insisted on having a memory for each of her children. Faith had been gratified to realize hers was still there after the drama of her marrying a non-Quaker. All the upheaval had been long ago, although she acknowledged some of the hurt still remained. After Jon's death, it was as if the storm of argument and being cut off from the family had never existed.

Faith put a smile on her face as she went over to stand beside the woman. "Forgive me. I did not introduce myself. I'm Faith Clarke."

The woman turned to look at her. Despite her elaborately dressed ash blonde hair, something about her heart-shaped face and deep blue eyes reminded her of Hannah. "I am Lisette Fournier." She extended a gloved hand, which Faith took. The touch was brief before the woman slipped it away. She walked to the middle of the room, taking the layout of the space. "Your name is Clarke; I had thought this was the Payne Farm."

"It is," Faith responded. "My father is Isaac Payne. He has farmed this land for many years." She caught Madame Fournier's gaze. "Do you have business with him?"

Charity came in bearing a tray with a kettle along with a plate of small cakes and tiny sandwiches. The rich scent of ginger and molasses filled the room, making Faith's mouth water. "Frieda has been baking this morning, so these are fresh from the oven," She sat down the tray and looked over at her sister.

Faith mouthed her thanks before turning to pour tea for all three of them. She was gratified that Charity had placed a sugar cone on the tray for them to use. She handed a cup to their guest before serving her sister and herself.

Madame Fournier took a large lump of sugar and dropped it in her cup before taking a sip. Her nose wrinkled slightly. "I imagine it is difficult to get English tea this far out in the country."

Faith's tone was dry. "The British navy makes it challenging to get many things in these colonies." She nibbled on a small piece of ginger cake. "What brings you to our home today, Mistress Fournier?"

The other woman smiled over the rim of her cup before taking a delicate sip and setting it down. "For the past few years, I have done a fair amount of business with your sister in Philadelphia. Dear Hannah has talked about her family here in the country. I decided I must pay a call to the people who produced such an intriguing and successful woman. I had hoped to meet her mother, for surely it is her influence that has made all of you what you are."

Faith shot her a startled look. That didn't sound like Hannah at all. Something was going on that she was unaware of unless somehow her sister had found their half-sister. Her heart beat a little faster. "I'm afraid my mother has been very unwell. Is there a personal matter you would like to discuss?"

Fournier shot her an assessing look. "You could call it that. I would like only a few moments of her time. It is indeed a pressing family matter. I understand that sickrooms are not places to entertain guests, but I need to see her."

Faith and Charity exchanged glances. Once again, Faith looked at her. Lisette Fournier had their mother's eyes, deep blue as the sea. "Are we related?" She held her breath, waiting for the answer.

Lisette Fournier nodded. "You know, then." Her face turned sad. A few crystal tears shimmered in her eyes. "All my life, I have wondered who she was, the woman who gave me away. It would mean a great deal if I could tell my daughter who her grandmother is."

Faith and Charity rose as one. Faith extended a hand. "Very well, sister, let me take you to meet our mother." Faith walked in front of the petite woman as they went to the sick room. Their father sat in the chair by the bed, whittling. He looked surprised as they entered.

Faith looked at him and then at their visitor. "This is Lizzy."

Chapter Thirty

J eremy urged his horse forward, keeping a steady pace that would not exhaust the animal. Hannah and Caleb followed close behind in the wagon. They planned to leave it at a nearby tavern to retrieve later and get fresh horses while they were there. Butler worried they might already be too late, but he didn't share his concern with Hannah. She was upset enough.

The tavern rose up in the distance, a sturdy wooden framed building of at least two stories surrounded by stone and rail fences. A huge tree shaded the front of the building. Grass had been worn away by the frequent traffic of coaches. A wooden sign hung from a post set beside the road leading to the building. Wayfarer's Tavern, it proclaimed. Underneath the title was an image of a man on a horse.

Caleb pointed to the barn. "I know the hostler. I'll go see him about the wagon and fresh horses." He handed Hannah down before continuing to the stable.

Jeremy dismounted and joined her. He looked at Hannah's drawn face. "Are you all right?"

She shrugged. "I'll be fine. I'll be better once we get back to my parent's home."

He touched a finger under her chin. He'd noticed she didn't refer to the place of her birth as home. But then, her independent streak was one of the things he found attractive about her. "I will do everything in my power to protect your family."

She blinked and swallowed hard. "I know, but that woman is mad, and she has a head start."

They walked toward the entrance. Jeremy intended to see if anyone had seen Lisette Fournier. A beautiful woman like that would be hard to miss. About a dozen waited inside for the next coach. They all had the worn-down look acquired by a lengthy period of traveling on a rough road in a crowded vehicle. He repressed a shudder when he recalled he would have to take another such ride to return to Virginia with Faith. He preferred a good horse any day.

Leaving Hannah at a table near the window, he went to find the innkeeper, who would know who had stopped by. He stopped mid-stride at the sound of a man's voice singing softly in French. It was a voice he knew. Whirling around, Jeremy sought the source. In a corner by the empty fireplace, Frances Fournier sat nursing a ceramic mug as he sang to a little girl. He walked over to stand in front of him

Fournier finished his song and gestured to the girl. "Monsieur Butler, I do not believe you have met my daughter. Emily Rose, this is Monsieur Butler, an acquaintance from Philadelphia."

The girl rose and curtsied gracefully before returning to her seat. She looked at her father curiously.

"Continue your meal, my child. We will leave as soon as your Mama completes her errand."

The girl pushed her plate away. "I am finished, Papa. May I go out and play?"

"You may go with your nurse," he said. "Martine, please take Emily outside for a walk. Do not go far." A middle-aged woman rose from a nearby table and took the girl by the hand, leading her to the door.

Butler waited until it shut behind them. "Where has your wife gone, Fournier?"

Fournier fell silent. He took a few sips of his drink, frowning over it. "Alas, cider is all they have to offer here. I would give a great deal for whisky right now." He turned to look at Butler. "Don't fall in love with a young, ambitious woman, mon amie. They will warm your bed, and they will break your heart." He stared down before offering a hard stare.

"I did not know she was gathering information with the British, I swear." He shook his head. "My goal is to stay out of this conflict. I only wish to conduct my business in peace."

"Did you know she was killing people?"

Fournier looked shocked. "She would not do that. She had been indiscreet in sharing her favors, but murder. No, you must be mistaken."

Butler pitied him. Despite his denials, he could see the realization in the older man's face. "Where is she? I need to know so I can stop her from striking again."

Fournier sighed. "She set out about an hour ago for some Godforsaken farm. I think the family name was Payne. I told her we needed to leave. The patriots will come for both of us once word reaches them of her activities."

"They know," Butler said with pity. "Hancock has informed the militia. It won't take long to track you here. They will check all the stage stops. You need to go now."

"Lisette," he said and stopped. "I've already lost her, haven't I?"

Butler nodded. "You have a child. She will need at least one parent alive. You have a limited amount of time to make it to New York."

Fournier sighed. "She took our coach with her. She said she had to see her mother one last time, so I let her go." He rose. "Thank you for your counsel, mon amie. Maybe we will meet again under better circumstances."

Butler watched his retreating back. "I hope so." Within a matter of moments, Jeremy, Caleb, and Hannah were mounted on fresh horses, hurrying down the road that led to the farm where the Paynes lived. Hannah rode well. There had been no side saddles available, but she seemed comfortable riding astride, ignoring that her skirts rode up to expose her stockings.

Caleb called to them. "We can shave off some time if we take this path through the woods. He turned and rode ahead without waiting for them to answer. Hannah followed quickly, followed by Jeremy, who hoped they knew what they were doing.

Single file, they rode the well-trod path. Hannah turned to look back at him. "It's a shortcut my father taught us. It leads to one of his favorite fishing spots. It will also take us close to the barns."

Jeremy didn't mind being out of the sun. He wore a wide-brimmed hat to keep it off. He'd long since learned that sunburn was a singularly unpleasant experience. The gnats were another matter. The irritating beasts nibbled at him every step of the way. Holding the reigns with one hand, he slapped with the other.

Hannah looked over at him sympathetically. "My mother has a salve that will keep them off. I will get it for you when we arrive."

He nodded to her. "Let's get there first." Butler worried about what he would find. He couldn't imagine why anyone would kill a dying woman, but Lisette Fournier's motives seemed unfathomable. She should have been fleeing the colony, not heading to a place where she must know people would look for her.

They entered a clearing. Caleb Payne pointed to the buildings ahead. "I see my brother outside the barn." Putting his heels to the horse, he shot ahead, followed by the other two.

Butler's heart chilled when he saw the carriage sitting outside. Two horses stood in an open corral, watched by a footman. They grazed contentedly, their tails switching to keep away flies.

Butler bellowed at the boy. "Where is she—your mistress?"

The boy pointed to the farmhouse.

Butler dismounted, followed by Hannah. They bumped into each other in the hurry to get inside. Faith looked up at them as they entered. "It must be the day for visitors," she said.

"Where is she?" Hannah asked between deep gasps of air.

Faith straightened up at the urgency in her tone. "You are referring to Lizzy? She asked for a few minutes alone with our mother."

Hannah didn't reply but ran to the sick room, followed by Butler and Faith. The door didn't open. She twisted the handle, but it refused to turn. Butler pushed her aside and put a shoulder to it. The sturdy wood refused to yield. Hannah muttered a few words not commonly heard from Quakers as she shook the knob violently. "Open the door," she shouted.

No reply came from the room. The door remained shut to them. "Let me see it," Faith said, pushing the other two aside. She held a large hairpin in her hands. "This door likes to shut itself when there's the slightest amount of wind. I've had to deal with it before." She put the long pin in and felt the lock move inside the mechanism. It kept refusing to turn. She felt the weight of the other two beside her as panic caused her heart to race. Taking a deep breath, she focused on the task before her. The lock snickered as it released and allowed the door to open. They fell through it together, catching themselves midstride.

Lisette Fournier stood by the bed holding a pillow over Patience Payne's face. She turned to stare at them, displaying an angelic smile over crazed eyes. "She sleeps."

Butler lunged, pulling her away from the bed. He staggered as Lisette resisted by elbowing, then raking him with her claws.

Hannah jerked the pillow away from her, falling against the bed. She turned to see her sister leaning over their mother. "Faith," she called urgently.

Her sister turned. "I can't tell if she's breathing."

Hannah joined her as Lisette Fournier let out a cackle. "Now she knows WHO I AM!"

Lisette grabbed up a knife left by Isaac Payne when he sat by his wife and whittled. She slashed the air in front of Butler. He grabbed the pillow as she stabbed at him, sending a flurry of feathers into the air. He coughed as he accidentally inhaled down. His forearm stung as his adversary took advantage to strike before she, too, began to cough.

Lisette Fournier shoved a chair in front of him as she fled the room. She made it to the main room before she was stopped by Isaac Payne. The older man blocked the door, an iron poker in his hand. His steely glance warned her that he planned to use it.

Butler stood in the door she had just come from. Her glance went down the hallway. The back door slammed shut as Caleb Payne entered. His eyes went from Butler to his father to Lisette Fournier. He said nothing but braced himself as he waited to see what would happen next.

Lisette's eyes roamed the room like a wild animal seeking escape. The knife blade was streaked red from Butler's blood. She held it to maim anyone who approached.

No one moved for a few moments. Butler spoke. "You can't escape, Lisette. You need to surrender and face up to your crimes."

"Crimes," she cried. "Crimes! What about me.?" She abandoned me, left me in the care of strangers."

"And what about Hannah? Why did you want to kill her? Or your partner's footman, who was a child?" Butler tried to move in closer. He picked up a piece of kindling to fend off the wicked knife. She raised her weapon, warning him she would strike if he got too close.

Lisette's face contorted. "What of them? Your Hannah should not have meddled where she had no business. That is on her. As for the slave, Elizabeth hired someone to be rid of him. She was both sloppy and a fool."

Isaac Payne spoke from the doorway. "What grudge doe thou bear my family? My poor wife did what she could to ensure thou had a home when she could not care for thee. Patience was a victim of an act of violence when she was little more than a child herself."

Lisette eyes flickered to him. "That crime has been avenged."

Payne's eyes met hers. "So thou hast put thine self in the place of God to decide who should live and who should die?"

She laughed. "Why not? He's done little enough for me."

Isaac shook his head. "Child, your soul is in peril. Hate and pain will consume you if you let them. Do not listen to them. Make your peace with God. He is waiting."

Lisette looked at the men surrounding her. "Why let him wait any longer?" Taking the knife, she plunged it into her throat. Blood gushed out in a mass of red over her dress down to the floor as she collapsed. Her breath wheezed for a second before it stopped altogether.

Butler wiped blood from his face. It had sprayed out from the wound, splattering him and objects close by. He knelt to confirm what he already knew. She was dead. He lifted his head as the sound of sobs became audible from the other room.

Isaac Payne dropped the poker. He stared at the dead woman on the floor before heading back to the sick room. "May they both rest in peace."

Butler stared after him, worried about Hannah and wondering what to do next.

Caleb spoke. "I'll get a blanket to wrap her up in. This family didn't do much for her, but we can provide her with a decent burial."

Butler rose to his feet. "I'll help you with that."

Chapter Thirty-One

Butler stood nervously at the front of the church. His new suit itched the back of his neck, but Hancock had insisted that he look proper for his own wedding. He sat in the nearby pews, watching Butler sweat with a faintly amused expression on his face. Next to him sat Franklin, who had arranged for the ceremony to take place at Christ Church.

The size of the place intimidated him, but he would have married Hannah anywhere. Butler had been relieved when she had finally agreed to take his hand, although he hadn't missed the wariness in her eyes. He had taken care to meet with an attorney recommended by Franklin to make it clear that Hannah's business was her own and he would not take any money from it. He also made sure that what worldly possessions he had would come to her should his life end abruptly.

His breath caught when he saw her escorted by her father down the aisle. Her simple ivory gown highlighted her fair skin and lustrous dark hair. Faith had told him she would take care of Hannah, and she had.

Hannah's hair was gently piled on top of her head while curls cascaded down the back. Butler wondered if he could persuade her to wear it like that more often. As they arrived at the altar, he could see her hands shaking. They were cold as he took them in his own. A rush of tenderness washed over him as he realized she was as frightened as he was.

The service was brief, and although he repeated everything he was asked, he could not remember afterwards what he had said. His heart had beat in his ears so loudly he could barely hear a thing. When Hannah's eyes met his, he stopped breathing for a few brief seconds until dizziness warned him to

263

inhale.

Above them, an enormous crystal chandelier sparkled as light from the enormous windows before them lit the room from the bright sun overhead. He slipped a ring on her hand that he had purchased the day before from another associate of Franklin. Butler glanced over at him. The man had seemed positively gleeful when informed of the upcoming nuptials. He happily made most of the arrangements in conjunction with Hancock. It seemed a relief to them to have something to focus upon besides the declaration that had been printed and sent out for distribution to state assemblies, conventions, committees of safety, and commanding officers of the Continental troops a few days earlier.

Hancock had allowed Butler to read a copy. Seeing Hancock's name on it, he commented. "You know, at some point, the British will see this document and come after you."

Hancock nodded. "They already know where I stand. Neither I nor my family will be safe until this conflict is over." He poured Butler a drink. "To The United States of America,"

Butler raised his glass and drank, enjoying the rare taste of fine wine. "May we both live long enough to see that happen."

"Indeed." Hancock drank deeply. "I long to go home and see my wife. Boston has suffered much for the cause of liberty."

Butler nodded. He was aware that it had only been a few short months since the British had been driven from the city. The scars still remained.

Butler walked out of the church with Hannah on his arm. He started to hand her up into the carriage but was stopped by her father. Isaac Payne looked over at him.

"I will help her this time, but I expect you to be there for her ever after."

"Yes sir," Butler replied. He prayed he would be able to keep that promise.

They headed to Franklin's home, where his daughter was hosting a wedding supper. He looked over at his wife. He had never intended to marry again after his beloved Jean had died. The idea of loving someone seemed too painful to contemplate.

Hannah seemed lost in her thoughts as well. She had never said it directly, but he knew her previous marriage had not been the stuff of dreams. He hoped that together they could find some happiness together.

"Where will you go next?" She asked. Her gaze was directed out the window.

Jeremy drew in his breath. "I don't know," he admitted. "I still have to submit my report to Washington. He's busy in New York. It could be some time before he calls me again."

Hannah nodded. "Does that mean you will be staying here?"

Butler inhaled. "I would like that."

She glanced over at him. "I asked Abner if he could arrange for a larger bed to be moved into my room."

He shot her a startled glance. He wasn't sure what to say. Finally, he stammered, "My thanks." He saw a small smile curve into her cheek.

The ring he had placed on her finger glinted as a stray band of light caught it. It was a simple thought but entwined with the promise of eternity. It was a daunting prospect at best. Butler had never lied to her about the life he lived. She had never asked him to give it up.

There were deep shadows under her eyes. It was little wonder. In the space of a week, they had buried her mother and her half-sister as well.

Faith and Hannah had stubbornly insisted on preparing both bodies for burial. He would have been happy to have found a place to get rid of Lisette Fournier's gruesome corpse. The image of her slitting her own throat still haunted his dreams. He saw no need to honor her with a funeral.

The Paynes thought differently. Hannah's father told him, "She was a product of many mistakes. Patience wanted her home. She's home now, and no one will need to worry about her ever again."

Butler shook his head. He saw her more as a rabid dog that needed to be put down, but he was not going to argue with a grieving family. Butler stood between Faith and Hannah as their mother was laid to rest. Earlier that day, he had helped Caleb and Isaac dig another grave nearby. Fournier had not come. He had left with his daughter not long after Butler had informed him of his wife's demise. The man had taken the news quietly, although he was clearly shaken.

"She is gone," He said.

Butler nodded, sparing him the grisly details.

"Will they bury her?"

"Yes, I believe they will."

"Put a few flowers on her grave, mon amie." Fournier sighed. "I must flee with my child before the militia comes after me for her crimes." With that, he walked away. Butler had no idea where he planned to go.

The horses stopped, and Butler rose to help her down.

"Who will take Faith back to Virginia?" Hannah wondered aloud.

"Your father," Butler replied. "Caleb and the others thought he could use a little time away, and Faith could use the help."

He looked up at her, lost in eyes as deep and blue as the evening sea. "I would like to stay here while I can."

A smile curved her face. "I would like that as well." Hand in hand, they walked into the house where their friends and family awaited. Butler took a deep breath, wishing he could hold on to the joy that filled his soul at this moment. He knew there would be dark days ahead, but now he had something to hold onto, a dream that gave him hope for a future he had never thought to have.

A Note from the Author

Sometimes, it is necessary to alter the facts slightly to allow for better flow of a story. While I believe in accuracy, I also acknowledge that travel in the 18th century can make interactions between characters challenging. The breakdown of the relationship between Benjamin Franklin and his son William was a terrible consequence of their opposing views regarding the independence of the American Colonies. Since this story concerns Benjamin Franklin, I also wanted to include William's voice, which required a slight altering of facts. As far as I know, the younger Franklin was never taken to a farm outside Camden but was taken from his home in Perth Amboy, NJ, to harsh imprisonment in Connecticut, which was too far away for Jeremy Butler to go question him in a reasonable amount of time. I apologize for any confusion this may have caused those whose expertise in history exceeds mine.

Acknowledgements

No one writes in a vacuum, particularly if the subject is history. I am grateful for the assistance of the John D. Rockefeller Library in Williamsburg, VA, as well family and friends who generously read drafts and made comments about the manuscript.

About the Author

Julie Bates enjoys reading and writing in a variety of genres. After spending a few years writing freelance articles, her first novel, *Cry of the Innocent*, premiered in June 2021, followed by *A Taste of Betrayal* in 2022. The eight-book series follows the timeline of the American Revolutionary War. In addition, she has blogged for Killer Nashville and the educational website Read.Learn.Write. She is a member of Sisters in Crime, Triangle Sisters in Crime, Mystery Writers of America, Southeastern Mystery Writers of America (SEMWA), and The Historical Novel Society. When not busy plotting her next story, she enjoys working in her garden, doing crafts and spending time with her husband and son, as well as a number of dogs and cats who have shown up on her doorstep and never left.

SOCIAL MEDIA HANDLES:
  Twitter: @JulieLBates03
  Facebook: Julie L. Bates, author
  Instagram; juliebates72

AUTHOR WEBSITE:

https://juliebates.weebly.com/

Also by Julie Bates

Cry of the Innocent

A Taste of Betrayal

Writers Crushing Covid, short story collection

Printed in the USA
CPSIA information can be obtained
at www.ICGtesting.com
JSHW021921101123
51573JS00004B/131